WASHOE COUNTY LIBRARY
3 1235 01318 4051
D0122047

# THE GHOSTS *of* MORNING

*Berkley Prime Crime Books by Richard Barre*

THE INNOCENTS
THE GHOSTS OF MORNING

*Coming in December 1998*
BEARING SECRETS

# THE GHOSTS *of* MORNING

RICHARD BARRE

BERKLEY PRIME CRIME, NEW YORK

WASHOE COUNTY LIBRARY
RENO, NEVADA

*The Ghosts of Morning* is a work of fiction. Names, places, characters, and incidents are products of the author's imagination. Any resemblance to actual events or to persons living or dead is purely coincidental.

"Everything I Own"
Words and music by David Gates
© 1972 COLGEMS-EMI MUSIC INC.
All Rights Reserved. International Copyright secured. Used by permission.

THE GHOSTS OF MORNING

A Berkley Prime Crime Book
Published by The Berkley Publishing Group,
a member of Penguin Putnam Inc.,
200 Madison Avenue, New York, NY 10016
The Penguin Putnam Inc. World Wide Web site address is
http://www.penguinputnam.com

Copyright © 1998 by Richard Barre

Book design by Bonni Leon-Berman

All rights reserved. This book, or parts thereof, may not be reproduced in any form without permission.

First Edition: June 1998

Library of Congress Cataloging-in-Publication Data

Barre, Richard.
The ghosts of morning / Richard Barre. — 1st ed.
p. cm.
ISBN 0-425-16300-8
I. Title.
PS3552.A773253G48 1998
813'.54—dc21 97-34963
CIP

Printed in the United States of America

10 9 8 7 6 5 4 3 2 1

To Dick Dwan

I would give anything . . .

## ACKNOWLEDGMENTS

Susan—words cannot express . . .

Many thanks to Sergeant Ron Burgess, Huntington Beach Police Department; Special Agent Gayle Jacobs, Federal Bureau of Investigation; Detective Paul Bishop, Los Angeles Police Department; and private investigators Jim Rochester and Don Clotworthy for their help. Thanks also to Shelly Lowenkopf for his counsel; Richard Danson for his surfing panache; Daniel Parker and Roger Caldwell for the Todos Santos revelations; Pierre Bouquet for his gritty first-hand knowledge of telescopes; Frank Harris for his film and sound expositions; Don Katich, Brian McCague, Jonas Marquez, Orlando Rivera, Melissa Voyagis, Patty and Dana Driskel, Jim and Gay Richmond, and Brian and Kim Jordan for their input; Ruth, Mary, and June for their usual superb effort; my editor, Gail Fortune, and my agent, Philip Spitzer, for their faith; the Santa Barbara Public Library (and all libraries) for being there; and the friends, relatives, readers, and bookstore folk who gave support and encouragement.

And I would give everything I own
Just to have you back again
Just to touch you once again

—DAVID GATES

# HUNTINGTON BEACH, CALIFORNIA, 1966

**surreal,** *that was how he'd play it—Dutch angles and following shots, the close-ups pinched tight—that sort of offness that went with the territory. The scene begged for it: boxy tract house, pseudo-Spanish with a hot-mop-and-tarpaper roof; geraniums around the foundation; dated-looking streetlights in a neighborhood well back from the water and the stores, the only hint of beach a salt-laced drippy fog that in a few hours would greet early risers like a slap with a wet towel.*

*Normal except for the spinning cop-car lights that bathed it in strobes of red and yellow. The surreal part.*

*Lannie Crowell snapped the snaps on his fleece-lined aviator vest, flipped up its collar against the dampness. Checking the settings on his old Bell & Howell one more time, he fired off a master shot, knowing he'd have to bump it two stops to even get it, overcome the inadequate glow from his jury-rigged sun-gun. Save it in the soup—always the way at KTVB, the news director there not above using Sterno if there was a chance it might develop film. Real five-cent station in a big-buck business.*

*No problem, Mom-o, Lannie thought, stay arid. Insert shots coming up.*

*He was early—earlier than he'd hit one before—and the crime scene hadn't been roped off yet, though a couple of cops were behaving in their usual officious way, shoving some wide-eyed neighbors around. Luckily they hadn't taken stock of him yet, and he was close enough to see fine. Especially when one of them pulled off the covering for a look. Through the lens, the girl, Carmen Marquez from his police scanner listenings, looked to be about eighteen, not much younger than him. A pretty thing with dark hair and smeared red lipstick, jeans and white Keds. High-school jacket over a white shirt; head at an odd angle where she lay on the cracked cement walk.*

*Knife handle sticking out of her chest.*

*Lannie took a steadying breath, tried to keep the camera still. Don't blow it now: light touch on the button, sixteen-millimeter film humping through the aperture at twenty-four frames a second, other hand fumbling with the pawnshop Uher tape recorder slung over his shoulder—positioning the microphone to advantage, ambient sound the in thing these days. How you told the real stringers from the wannabes.*

*"Jesus, Crowell, can't you think of anything better to do at four in the morning? Damn ghoul."*

*He'd seen the cop before at other scenes, a pompous fat white guy in a nylon jacket—Richard Blakley on the tag over his left pocket. Writing something now on a sheet of paper attached to a clipboard.*

*"And step back."*

*"Whatever you say, Officer Blakley. Any suspects at this time?"*

*"No comment."*

*"Somebody she knew?"*

*"For the last time, back off."*

*"Yes sir."*

*Lannie moved back, focused in again—all pro, cool under fire. Whatever happened here, the cops had their jobs, he had his. And being known to them pleased him. It meant he was on his way—KNBC caliber, sky the limit then. National news, traveling with the president or somebody, on-the-road features, room service—make Mom-o whirl around like a tornado in her little box. The one he brought out occasionally to impress girls, knowing she was right there as they did it. Those that stuck around, anyhow.*

*"Just serving the public's right to know," he added.*

*"Right to know, my ass—and kill that damn light." Blakley head-gestured to a man and woman standing quietly off to the side with a boy about thirteen. "That's the family," he said in a lowered voice. "They came home and found her. How'd you like it?" He walked away, disgusted.*

*What served for press relations these days, Lannie thought. No respect for a man's chosen profession. He regarded the three people, breaths further fogging the night air, expressions frozen in shock. Small was his first thought—small father, small mother, small boy—diminutive Hispanics dressed in light cotton windbreakers. Pale-looking small people huddled in the fragile light. He edged over in that direction, smiled sympathetically. Tried to look simpatico.*

"Siento mucho su pérdida, señor y señora. *Lannie Crowell, KTVB, hoping you'll let my viewers know what happened—what you're feeling." He said it quietly so the cops wouldn't hear, call him on what he actually was, a freelancer with no real business asking questions of anybody, let alone acting as an official KTVB news guy. But in this trade you made your own breaks, picked stuff up and went. If you didn't, somebody else damn well would.*

*For a moment the trio just stared at him, his eye to the camera lens, the shouldered Uher picking up sound on its quarter-inch tape. Like he was from another planet. Then the father spoke—slowly as if it were an effort—heavily accented, fighting for control: "Look at what he did to her, that Van Zant boy," the father said. "He murdered my baby—a poor little Mexican girl.* Hijo de puta *thinks he can do anything because of his money. You tell your viewers that."*

*An irate-looking neighbor started over, Lannie could sense it with his other eye, kept open and scanning like all the good ones did. Still he kept the B&H grinding, seeing the father put an arm around his lost-looking wife, the two of them turn away in tears as the boy glared at him, all protective rage and confusion.*

*"You happy now, spook?" the big cop Blakley said. "I sure hope so. Now take a hike."*

*Lannie was backing up, lowering the camera, wondering where he'd heard the name Van Zant before, when the sun-gun picked it up. A brief glint in the wet grass beside the walk. Quickly he shut off the light and the camera, lowered it, and knelt, pretending to fuss with the mount. Reaching a hand sideways, he took the thing in, the metal cold on his skin.*

*Why he did it wasn't clear to him exactly, maybe it was the word spoken by the girl's father: money. A sense of something. Of possibility. At any rate, it wasn't until he was in his old V-Dub Kombi, revving away from the house, that he risked a look.*

*It was a medical bracelet, one of those things that had the red caduceus on one side and the information on the other, in case there was an accident and you were unable to tell the medics you had a condition—diabetes or something—so their treatment wouldn't kill you. Phone number they could call to find out who you were, your doctor or close relative.*

*Somebody who might pay to get it back.*

*Lannie tried to see what it said on it, but the streetlight was uneven and his dash lights had burned out a summer ago, some short in the system.*

*Thinking he'd check it out later, he pitched it in the ashtray and goosed the Kombi, hoping to beat the morning crew to the developer, see what kind of shots he had. Maybe use them to land a permanent job or something. Make Mom-o proud.*

# 1
## WAIPIO VALLEY, ISLAND OF HAWAII, PRESENT

**they** were out there, all right—the Night Marchers, ghosts that stalked the valley floor on their way back to the netherworld through the secret doorway down by the beach. He'd seen them before and knew they must have seen him, but they didn't bother him. One ghost to another, so to speak.

Still, it was nothing he took for granted.

Roy Voelker knocked back a slug of dark rum, picked at a mosquito-bite scab, the fucker still itching like crazy, probably half-infected. Like himself, he thought. Rain dripped off the big mango out behind his shack, made hollow sounds on the rusting tin and curled plywood. Light from the hissing Coleman bounced a gleam off the plastic bags that served as interior decor, his Purple Heart tacked to a stud, the .45 ammo looking like little warheads as he loaded them into the clips.

The evening air gave off damp smells: earth and outhouse, sweet decay from the compost Voelker applied to the taro patch revived while claiming the abandoned shack as his own. There hadn't been even a front door on the one-room ruin then, but he'd made one. Palm fronds tacked over a frame of two-by-fours scrounged up on the road to Honokaa; the plastic bags out of a topside Dumpster.

Home sweet home.

Luckily it never got cold enough to be a problem. Like the winters in Lansing, his other life long filed away, this old dead letter at a post office. Quite the opposite: As in Nam, here the problem was growing mold—jungle rot. And right now the air felt like it: close and dank in the hooch, the inside of a car at the drive-in with the windows rolled up. Humidity putting a wet shine on his skin.

Outside the rain was finally letting up, steady drip tailing off into free-form rhythms, a grumble of retreating thunder.

Voelker took a last swig, wiped ninety-proof from his beard, and stuck the cheap cigar back in his mouth, his right eye squinting against the smoke. He eased a clip into the .45, worked the slide and the safety, wiped excess gun oil on his T-shirt and fatigue pants. Keep it oiled or kiss it off: Echo Company drill—his own admonishment still loud in his ears.

Ex-Marine First Sergeant Roy Voelker stepped out into the clearing.

It was still light enough to see, the clouds breaking up now, and Voelker set about checking the perimeter, the monofilament trip line strung with corned-beef-hash and refried-bean cans. Following the line as it dipped under croton and pandanus, wild ginger and thimbleberry. Wiggling it occasionally for the reassuring sound it gave—old habits, permanently imprinted. Like the spitting glare from a phosphorus shell.

Not that he slept much anyway. But just knowing the line was on duty helped. Peace of mind of a sort.

Voelker smiled at the thought. Fat fucking chance; hell, not even the VA medication helped anymore. All that seemed to work was the smoke he grew and the ever-increasing slugs of cheap booze, now over half his disability check. Not an encouraging scenario. Unless you took into consideration what he had riding: all the booze and dope he'd ever want before long. The check in the mail, so to speak.

Finished with the line, Voelker brought out dry wood from the shack and made a fire in the ring of stones. Light from the flames flickered around the now dim clearing, casting shadows on the shack and the jungle foliage behind, ghosts passing by like flotsam around a rock. Kamehameha kills, most likely, their heads bashed in by the big man's war clubs—regulars out here for two hundred years.

He saluted them with rum, opened another fifth.

Ten klicks down the valley, a few lights came on as the darkness deepened. Not much there, he knew, several houses, some beach campers. Outsiders—more than enough to suit him; hell, blowing up the damn one-lane in'd be fine by him.

Voelker reached in, pulled out a burnt twig. Letting it cool, he lined the char under his eyes, smeared his forehead and cheeks; felt it coming on. Felt *them* out there—small men in NVA uniforms just beyond the light. He thumbed the safety off, pointed the .45 at the jungle, and fired. A phantom went down and he spun and fired again; one reaching the perimeter jerked back into the blackness. More rounds and more imaginary targets blown away. Reload and fire, firing until the slide locked open—the targets all down now, gone in a mad minute of blue haze and near-erotic release.

All but one.

It was as though a shadow had materialized, emerged against the green, shifting and undulating now in the breeze that had sprung up. It stood there as Voelker blinked, the empty gun at his side.

"Hey, Top, how's it hanging? Nice wire, by the way."

Voelker felt his throat constrict, fingers of ice on his sac. The figure with the blackened face held a K-Bar lightly, its eight-inch stainless-steel blade catching the firelight. Without seeming to move, the apparition came closer.

"Not too chatty, huh? Funny, that's not what I heard."

From someplace far off, Voelker heard the rum bottle drop from his hand. "Stay back, goddamnit. I'm warning—"

"They can kill you but they can't eat you—remember that one? Quang Tri, I think it was." Closer now.

"Get away from me. You're not real."

It shook its head. "Guess that makes two major fuckups in the same month, Top. I look like some ghost to you?"

Everything in Roy Voelker screamed *get out of there—survive—* but he couldn't. His legs were bad-dream-leaden. He was vaguely aware of hard eyes, black pullover and pants, and the feeling he'd just been hit by lightning—even though the storm had left the valley.

# 2

as it turned out, the guy who'd snaked his wave, then made a big issue of it when Wil Hardesty protested the drop-in, was all mouth. Even so, they'd almost gotten into it on the beach, the guy coming on as if *he'd* been wronged, freaking locals thinking they owned the world, on and on until Wil left the argument to the younger dudes who'd picked up on it, shouts and curses and testosterone rising all around until a gem set arrived that had everybody scrambling back out for position.

Everybody but him.

Since the trouble with Lisa, all of it was an effort, just getting through the day most days. Let alone tilt at what the Rincon was becoming—regular zoo when the big winter swells made it the prize of California surf spots. Perfect right point break that sometimes let you rip down the entire length, wind raising spray off the lip like the smoke from a prairie fire.

Still, even the occasional forays into Hollister Ranch—gated turf with no lineups and often jacking breaks, courtesy of a property-owner friend—lately were leaving him deflated. As though he had a slow leak in his thirty-year passion for the sport, flaccidity now where tumescence had once reigned undisputed.

Hard to remember a time when he hadn't surfed. First at The Wedge, this skinny squirt who had to be fished out gasping and up-chucking, but who'd left his heart out there and soon was eclipsing his dawn-patrol pals with wild rides under the Newport Beach pier. There'd been seconds and thirds at Huntington then, La Jolla and Santa Cruz, the setup to turn pro and run the circuit before he'd pulled the plug, realizing it was somebody else's ambition. That it was he and the water—nobody else. Juice surging in there like a private tide in his veins, tremolo chord on a surf guitar.

Until now. Until the divorce.

Since he was close by, Wil made a Viennese run to the Coffee Grinder, couple of scones and a loaf of herb bread for later, then hit the road for home. Past the Rincon, around the two-mile sweep of coastline that led to Mussel Shoals and Ventura, left across the northbound traffic heading for Santa Barbara's red-tiled coziness, and into La Conchita.

Oil roughnecks had lived here in the twenties, rumrunners in the thirties, drug smugglers, surfers, and retirees since then, La Conchita now about four hundred souls. Plus California's only banana plantation, its Javas, Brazilians, and Ladyfingers ripening in blue plastic bags encasing the green clusters. And that sweet curve of beach just beyond the highway. Worth the price alone.

But La Conchita lay just under a coastal bluff that nearly ate it a season ago—as it was, devouring an unlucky line of homes when rains turned the substrata into wet soap. For days, national media and locals maintained a twenty-four-hour vigil, flooding the area at night with a cold eerie illumination.

This time, the bluff held.

Warning tape and wire fencing still marked affected structures; mud lingered in berms and piles. Residents backed cars into their driveways, quick getaway in case of further slippage. Sandbags and legal wrangle over the cleanup were further legacy.

Life in a geologic hazard area.

Wil parked his '66 Bonneville, repainted now with some of Holly Pfeiffer's expense money—Holly of the urban terrorists and the secrets from hell; woman-child Holly; pang-in-the-heart Holly. He retrieved the Southern Cross—his longboard—from the port he'd cut in the back seat, and stowed it. Climbed the stairs to the kitchen, started the Viennese going; thought how little he even thought about the mud anymore. Partly because his house was closer to the beach, out of range unless the slide decided next time to stop at the islands. But more because he'd been flattened by another force.

Lisa's little tsunami.

The divorce left him a long swim back to the surface and serious doubts about making the payments on the house. He'd refinanced, needing the equity just to take up the slack. But reality lay as close and hungry as the unstable mass up the street, and the investigations business was sporadic: accident reconstructions, occasional insurance work, some under-the-table stuff, legacy of the garbage he used to take in after Dev's dying. Devin Kyle Hardesty, child of water and to water returned—eight years now, the time like thin gauze. As for the work, lucky to get it these days.

But it wasn't enough. Even though Lisa had given him the house minus her share of the equity, her accounting practice still expanding. She'd taken next to nothing. Clean break, she called it, fresh start—hoping her spin would infuse him. They still spoke, Lisa helping him sort out the finances she'd handled for the two of them. Adjunct of her work now.

Politeness was the operative mode. But it was more a scab over the wound, masking the torn root holes still bleeding inside. Sometimes they'd see each other in Santa Barbara, awkward at first then more routine. They'd smile, have dinner when more came up than they could handle by phone. Each time he swore it would be the last, her almond eyes and black hair cut short since the split searing holes in his carefully applied exterior—delaminating it, making him want her back. Knowing it wasn't going to happen.

Typical conversation—him: "How're your folks, the orchid business, your new place, accounting." Her: "Fine, thanks—the house okay? Surfing? Your work?" Scripted stuff, like the football coach who wrote out his first plays from scrimmage. Nothing from either of them about who you're seeing, Devin memories, what's it like without me—anything of real importance. Just ice skating: smiles without warmth, nonengagement. Bullshit he'd seen so many of their friends perfect.

The big empty.

He'd been out once—twice if you counted Claire from the gym, where he signed up for an off-peak-hours membership. Forcing himself out there as much as anything. The other had been a disaster, all self-conscious talk and gestures, edgy glances. Perfunctory sex he finally called off, as much to her relief as his.

*Some life, Hardesty. Possibilities galore.*

Feeling the need for something in which to lose himself, he settled on building a telescope—a big astrological scope like the one his father constructed when Wil was in grade school. Looking at the faraway stars and planets, he and his father became close: visited Griffith Observatory, charted the heavens by season. Created something that still resonated.

So he read up, scrounged a five-foot piece of ten-inch cardboard tubing, a pair of eight-inch glass portholes, and started in. First task was fashioning the primary mirror. Which meant grinding one porthole against the other, using wax to fix the increasingly fine grit to the grinder as the headphones torqued out Beach Boys and Beethoven, Sheryl Crow and Branford Marsalis, Roy Orbison—CDs impulse-bought or borrowed from friends.

Poor man's therapy.

Five months later, after getting the glass to the required convex mirror shape, he had it aluminized. He secured the mirror, set the focal length, fastened an eyepiece purchased from an enthusiasts' journal. Finally he took the monster up to the top of Camino Cielo—renewed an old acquaintance with the stars in Orion's belt, saw the rings of Jupiter, peered into the Milky Way. Remembered the way it was before his mother veered drunkenly into a busload of El Toro recruits in 1967, taking the telescope man with her.

After two trips, he stowed the scope in the basement.

Then there were the well-meaning invitations that finally stopped coming: western-dance classes, adult ed, fixer-uppers, fun-runs, organized mixers—parallel universes as remote feeling as the craters on the moon.

The gym was an exception. At least something positive came from that, the chance to work off some of the flab accrued from his post-split torpors. And nonthreatening human contact—hi's and hellos from the morning workouters who simply vanished into another dimension after ten A.M.

Day-tight compartments. Damage control.

And then the call.

It was late, after eleven, and he was getting ready for bed, last scan of the horizon with the living-room scope, quick look at the news. He let it ring, heard his own voice say, "Leave a message, I'll phone you back." Giving him a chance to work up to responding, avoid those wanting to get too close.

Hesitation: the caller thinking it over, a salesman deciding to call back when the occupant might pick up, set the hook before the fish had a chance to wriggle off. Wrong time, though. Salespeople invariably called at dinner.

Finally a deep breath, a female voice, heavy and deliberate—drugged if he had to guess, maybe plastered. "I was hoping this is the Wil Hardesty who knew my son, Denny." Pause: "Denny Van Zant? I'll call back when someone's—"

Wil had the receiver up by then, little echos reverberating. "Maeve?" All he could say.

"Wil? It's good to hear your voice."

He'd never have recognized her if she hadn't said the name, so different was the voice. Foggy and uncertain, a 45 played at 33. Not the Maeve Van Zant he remembered: quick and vivacious, a slim blond woman seemingly just off a fashion runway, never a hair out of place.

Denny's mom. Denny Van Zant.

Lord.

Trying to recall how many years now: fifteen since the military funeral at Westwood, the long lines of black limousines and white crosses. Twenty-eight or thirty beyond that.

"How are you, Maeve? It's been too long."

"So it has," she said with sadness—or maybe it was the filter it was coming through. "Wil, I can't talk right now, but I need to see you. I'd heard that you . . . looked into things for people. Something we could keep between us." Pause. "You always were like family. You know that, don't you?"

"Sure, Maeve. You still living down in Newport?"

"Oh my, not for years. We're in Malibu now." She gave him the address, 114 Ocean View Terrace.

He asked for directions, wrote them down.

"How's Mr. Van Zant?"

"He's fine." Not much there in her tone. "Wil, I hate to trouble you, but can you make it tomorrow afternoon? That way we can take our time. Catch up a little."

"How's two? And it's no trouble, Maeve."

"Two o'clock, then. I'm glad."

"Me, too," he said, finally giving in to where his thoughts had spun off. "How's Trina?" he asked. "Still married to the—" But by then Maeve Van Zant had hung up and he was left holding the receiver and looking out at distant lights.

# 3

**tuesday** morning dawned clear, a mid-January high-pressure ridge still holding off storms that wheeled across the northern part of California. Wil left the house and eased down the drainage tunnel to the beach, clambered down the rocks to the sand. He did an easy run toward the shoals, then a hard one as far as the water would allow up toward the Rincon. Getting his breath, he watched the fat waves break, the swells pumping in from Hawaii and beyond—four-footers it looked like from here, seven to eight on the face. A lineup had formed already at the breaks. Traffic signals if it got much busier.

Without islands like those off the Rincon, the winter-born swells would arrive unimpeded. Maverick's up near Half Moon Bay would be seeing some big-wave action, and Todos Santos off Ensenada, the poor man's Waimea. Fact was, a dedicated crazy could surf the same sets at all three spots: Waimea Bay, Maverick's, then Todos, the huge swells moving like a steadily advancing army.

These places lured a different breed. Hard-core types who lived to launch themselves off the blue walls—monsters with forty-foot drops that made the most accomplished surfers remember they'd forgotten to take out the trash. Surf this—hoping your timing was precise enough to not lose it, free-fall down the face like a stone being skipped. Then carve a flat-out bottom turn ahead of the avalanche; maybe catch a tube ride if the lip held and you were lucky. And if you weren't, all you had to do was survive the turned-on Kenmore that was the impact zone, while subsequent waves bore in—as you fought the rip or tried to paddle back out.

Which meant about one percent of all surfers.

Hellmen they were called, and their code of ethics was as unforgiving as the ocean; the margins out there were just too thin for the usual bullshit. Break a rule, drop in on their wave, cut them off, and they'd as soon rip the skegs out of your board with their bare hands as shout you out of the water.

Denny Van Zant had been like that. An assured, good-looking rich kid, he'd been in Wil's sophomore class at Newport Harbor High. Wil had seen him hanging around the campus hotshots, guys with their own cars. Which put him well clear of Wil's league, bicycle-to-school-go-to-work-after, the social hierarchy crystallizing early. Denny had also been surfing longer—as Wil found out when he wiped out one afternoon near the Huntington Beach pier and took Denny down with him. He remembered it almost verbatim.

"the *hell you think you're doing?" The boy is dripping wet. Spitting out his anger.*

*"My fault," Wil says, getting his wind back. "You all right?"*

*"Where'd you learn to surf?" He has sun-bleached blond hair that he jerks back off his forehead, white zinc-oxide cream across his nose, a near-mature build that shows the effects of muscling a board. His fair skin is*

*tanned, but mottled by sunspots and pink emerging from peel across the shoulders. Blue eyes fight the glare. Like Wil, he looks not much different than the hundreds of blond surfer-boy clones on the beach this summer. Still, he has a presence about him.*

*"Didn't see you," Wil says. "I'm sorry."*

*"Yeah? You're gonna be a lot sorrier."*

*In shallow water now, this moving confrontation. Out of the corner of his eye, Wil is conscious of a very pretty girl in a two-piece, watching them from up on the beach. "Denny, come on—he didn't mean it," she calls, but he waves her off.*

*Some other boys materialize. "Goddamn grommet," one says. "Kick his butt, Den."*

*"Bingo."*

*"It was an accident."*

*"Accident, hell. You stole my wave."*

*Adrenaline time, one push over the line: "Your wave. And how's that—your old man buy it for you?" It's a cheap shot, and when the punch comes, he isn't surprised. Just at its quickness.*

*But as the boy swings, retreating wash erodes the sand from under him, dropping him to his knees in the calf-deep water. He's up in an instant. But by then Wil has his board raised, and when the charge comes, he thumps it with both hands against the boy's head. Momentarily stunned, the boy sits heavily; an incoming wave rolls him several feet up the beach. When he faces Wil, his forehead sports a red welt.*

*"Think you're hot shit about now, don't you?"*

*"No," Wil says. "But I figure I could learn from you."*

*"Drop that board and we'll find out."*

*"I'm serious, I've been watching you. How do you turn like that against a wave?"*

*The boy eyes him, skeptical; seeing nothing much happening, the others wander off in disgust. "What? Do a cutback?"*

*"That what it's called?"*

*"How long you been surfing?"*

*"A few weeks. Mostly on my own." Wil catches the boy's girlfriend get up and start down toward them.*

*"Could be worse," the boy says. "You're too high, for one thing. And your stance is wrong." He demonstrates.*

*But Wil's eyes are fixed on the girl. She has long, thick chestnut hair with a touch of gold, white teeth, blue eyes, a look that goes right through him. And that bathing suit. Twirling a pair of sunglasses, she assumes a casual stance beside her boyfriend.*

*"You mentioned my father," the boy says, taking no note of her. "You know me or something?"*

*"Seen you around school. Look, about what I said . . ."*

*"Yeah, well. It's not that far off." He extends a wet hand. "I'm Denny Van Zant."*

*"Wil Hardesty." He shakes it, feeling warm palm, the sandy grit between them.*

*"You for real about improving?"*

*Wil nods.*

*Denny Van Zant blows water off his lips, runs a hand through his wet hair. "Well, it won't get done up here. You coming?"*

*"This should be interesting," the girl says, her eyes meeting Wil's. Appraising him before putting on her shades.*

*Sixteen years old and two-thirds hormones, Wil feels his breath catch as though he's caught a runaway board in the gut. About all he can do is hope the tan hides his rising color.*

*"Hey, Mojo," Denny Van Zant says. "You gonna surf with me or leer at my sister."*

over time, he caught up, at least in terms of style. But Denny possessed a reservoir of energy Wil could only wonder at, an abandon that sometimes got him into trouble when venturing into the hot areas like Windansea, Trestles, Malibu, Rincon. One time at Malibu, after one too many locals had taken off on them, Denny called a guy out and they'd headed for the beach to settle it. So had the guy's pals, who proceeded to kick the crap out of them and break Denny's nose.

Wil remembered Denny grinning all the way home, talking about what his dad was going to say, the blood and crushed cartilage like some kind of offering, Kordell Van Zant never big on his son's chosen sport. Maeve was the one at the competitions they entered, so maybe it figured. But Wil never heard the result. Kordell had been away on business apparently, the nose reset and healing when he got back, the blood long washed away.

One of a hundred Denny stories.

Like the Easter Wil's parents let him off work to catch the big ones moving in on Todos Santos, Denny's ears always up for heavy surf. Hollow and pumping, these were beyond anything they'd experienced, thirty-foot faces bolstered by the offshore Santa Anas. Wil remembered regarding them with awe through a fog of Mexican beer they'd scored in Ensenada and brought ashore from the fishing boat that ran them out to the island. For the better part of the morning they just looked at the waves, the reef, each other.

"Damn, where is everybody?" Denny asked at one point. "You ever seen a break this empty?"

Wil chugged Tecate. "Maybe they know something we don't."

"Like what?"

"Like where to hide."

"Hey, live fast, die young. We gonna do this or what?"

They paddled out, took positions outside, one eye on the horizon. Denny led off, a trial run down the face, well ahead of the curl. Then back up the wave and out, head thrown back, howling like a banshee.

*"Andale, muchacho—go, go!"*

Wil did, timed one wrong, pulled back and caught another, a well-behaved giant that let him show off before cutting out, get his confidence up. And afterward, wide-grinning Denny, the sun, the lighthouse, Baja, the feeling of outlaw freedom, life in general. He could see Denny smiling nonstop, too—is this living, or what?

For a while it was.

Flushed with the beer and impatient, Wil jumped the lead wave in an incoming set. But what had looked irresistible turned mean suddenly as the section ahead sagged and collapsed. There was a moment of absolute clarity, a blotting out of all sound, and then tons of water unloaded on him. Tumbling, helpless, Wil felt as if he'd never come up. And when he did, it was like surfacing in a wash cycle as the rest of the set bore down, his board nowhere in sight.

The second wave hit. Bigger than the first, scouring him along the bottom, his lungs burning, strength ebbing. A notch from panic, Wil burst up through thick foam, saw rocks ahead, a looming wall forming. Third wave—and out beyond it, a line of killers waiting their turn.

*God, oh God . . .*

Somebody yelling his name then: Denny thrusting hard into the break, extending his board, the cold waxed surface something Wil could feel to this day, just as another wave arrived. Somehow they held on, somehow were able to bolt the zone, barely wide of the next thunderclap.

For a long time they just lay on the beach. It had been close and they knew it—despite their teenage bravado afterward in the lee of the lighthouse. Using the excuse of Wil's broken board, which washed up in pieces, they called it off and headed north, vowing to come back when the waves were even bigger. Salvaging what Tecate they didn't drink by pretending to be sick at the border. Saying little on the way home.

Then there was Trina.

She'd been fourteen when Wil first laid eyes on her, wondering, as things progressed, what somebody like Katrina Van Zant saw in him. The rebel rich girl hooking up with a middle-class kid not yet grown into his lanky frame. Her parents were connected, regulars in the *Register* society pages. Not strapped exactly, *his* mother and father had put every cent into the small beach restaurant they were trying to make work.

Aware of the gap, her parents were cool at first, Trina appearing to delight in their unease. But as they got to know him they warmed somewhat, at least Maeve did, inviting him for dinner a few times—mostly for her daughter's benefit, he always thought—stiff, edgy affairs with Trina not acting like herself. Occasionally she had him pick her up at her house, a big, beachfront double-lot on Lido Isle with its own dock and cabin cruiser.

Kordell Van Zant he saw largely in passing, a tan, handsome, heavyset man with a booming voice, who asked pointed questions, his wife petite and impeccable looking compared to Wil's mother, like a decoration brought out on special occasions. Still, he liked Maeve Van Zant, and believed she liked him.

Dark-haired Eric—a year younger than Denny, one older than Trina—he never really got to know, a bright inward kid who played woodwinds or something in the school band and who they'd pick up occasionally from doctor appointments or music lessons. More like he wasn't there. Like Kordell wasn't, always busy with his chain of credit dental offices, three a week opening throughout

Southern California. Sometimes Wil would hear him in radio commercials, see his face on billboards and in newspaper ads.

Then there was the photograph in his den—Kordell with football helmet thrust skyward after USC upset Rose Bowl–favorite Tennessee in '39. Dutch Van Zant, the trophies called him, the Rock of Gibraltar. Second-team All-American. Heady stuff for a too-light end named Hardesty whose prospects for college depended on earning the money himself—that or the remote possibility of a scholarship. Whenever he was in the house, he'd find a way to visit the den-shrine, feeling the man almost as a physical presence, though Wil never actually saw him there.

Away from the house, Wil and Trina would walk the island, take the ferry, spend his off days at the beach, scope out the big homes from a rented Sunfish. Pick out one they liked and pretend. Sometimes they'd meet for meals they split the cost of, get jazzed by Dick Dale and the Deltones in the maxed-out Rendezvous Ballroom, end up hot and bothered at the drive-ins.

Occasionally she'd show up while he was working, bus tables or answer the phone when it got busy. And one night, when he was off duty and his parents weren't, she came home with him—about as far from her place as you could get—to the tract house in Costa Mesa. He'd put "Moon River" and "Dream Lover" and "Since I Fell for You" on the Magnavox and they'd danced, nipped wine from a jug in the refrigerator, then done it in the single bed in his room. It hadn't been great, fumbles and hearing phantom cars in the drive, but it had given them a new status. The irony was it hadn't brought them any closer. More the feeling of reaching a plateau, their only step forward to back off.

That was spring of '66.

Just before Carmen Marquez was murdered.

Just before Denny went to Nam.

Wil watched a flight of pelicans veer out toward Anacapa Island, sandpipers following a retreating wave, then hotfooting it back as another rolled in. Despite the divorce, thoughts of Trina Van Zant seemed intrusive after so many years with Lisa. Uneasy feelings of guilt and curiosity—like peeking through somebody else's keyhole.

A pair of black Labs bounded in the shallows, and he picked up a stick and heaved it farther out. Both splashed after it, one outmaneuvering the other to race it back to their new playmate. He tossed again and the pattern was repeated—life for a moment defined by the act of throwing and retrieving. Nothing more complex than that.

Remembering the time, then, and where he had to be in a couple of hours, he threw the dogs a last one and walked back toward the house.

# 4

Wil left La Conchita at noon, time enough to take the slow lane to Las Posas, cut off the freeway, pick up the coast road at Point Mugu. Too early yet for the wild mustard that yellowed them in spring, the hills nonetheless showed rain-prompted grasses and a dusting of early ceanothus brought about by the warm weather. Not much else, though. Southern California chaparral yielded subtle hues. Like the days and seasons, tapestries in monochrome.

Past the cutoff, fields of dark earth awaited the planting of row crops; at Point Mugu, the sycamores looked naked without their leaves. Trancas, Zuma Beach, Point Dume came and went, then the big houses began appearing, raw new palazzos on the hills, walled and gated ones on the ocean side. Pepperdine University appeared left and then the long slide into Malibu, its Colony Drive legendary among film stars, real-estate agents, nouveaux riches.

Early for his appointment, Wil turned into the shopping center, filled the Bonneville at the gas station, then drove around, just looking. Limited beach access aside, it seemed vastly different from the days when he and Denny would drive up in Denny's old Jeep, face off the local hotshots, tool around trying to look cool. The big deals up from Newport.

Two blondes in oversize tops, ball caps, and sheepskin boots walked by while a Grand Cherokee with gold detailing and mag wheels sized them up, young guys with virgin-looking surfboards in the roof rack. Wil pumped the clutch and nudged the Bonneville's gas pedal, smiling at the throb it brought—a block later wondering where the hell *that* came from. Hearing Lisa say, *Yeah, right*. Imagining the grin it would bring if she were along.

If. If a lot of things.

Rechecking Maeve's directions, he backtracked to Malibu Canyon Road, took one of the spurs, and after a bit found it. At first glance the place looked like some kind of museum or institutional retreat: notched white slabs at the end of a long slope of lawn flanked by a four-bay garage nearly as big as the house. Offset concrete rectangles formed a walkway down to green-copper doors, a stylized sunburst on each. Palms and two polished granite figures softened the effect—somewhat. At the end of the walk, a footbridge led across a small moat to the doors.

Three stories, he guessed, or a generous two.

Wil lifted a doughnut-shaped metal knocker, dropped it too hard against the striker, heard the sound reverberate inside. A pretty young woman in a uniform answered, wisps of black hair falling softly from a bun. Complexion the color of strong latte.

"Sorry about the noise," Wil said. "It slipped."

"It does that for everyone," she said with a trace of accent. "We're used to it."

Salvadoran, he thought, Costa Rican—somewhere down there. "At least it's democratic."

A smile. "You'd be Mr. Hardesty?"

"A little early. Not a problem, I hope."

"No, of course not, Mrs. Van Zant is expecting you. I'm Celeste. Please come in."

He did—into vast space and brightness, stunning view through floor-to-ceiling glass across an ultramodern landscape of metals and woods, soft whites and hard planes. Windowed lofts poked out from upstairs, abstracts from the broadest walls, sculptures from low pedestals. A blue-and-yellow Calder-like mobile hung suspended between the living and dining areas.

Following the girl, Wil did a slow turnaround, then gave up.

She was smiling again, sympathizing perhaps. "Mrs. Van Zant is out by the pool. She wanted me to tell you she's having Chardonnay."

"Coffee if you have some, thanks."

"Decaf or regular?"

"Regular's fine. This way out?"

"Through the sliding glass. I'll have your coffee in a minute."

He turned back. "Pepperdine?"

"Language major from Honduras—how did you know?"

"Just a guess. I'd love to do that well in Spanish."

Her eyes lit momentarily, then she moved off into the interior of the house.

Standing on the deck, he took in the long sweep of coastline—Santa Monica Bay extending left to Palos Verdes, Malibu below, Point Dume right—then heard a voice:

"Wil? I'm down here."

He descended a concrete ramp to flagstones, native plantings, a black-bottomed lap pool. Set back from the edge, an umbrella shaded a bamboo-design wrought-iron table, wine bottle cooling in a ceramic sleeve. And Maeve Van Zant, holding a stemmed glass.

She was thin, almost totally gray now, and pale. Lines stood out around her mouth and eyes, a dull twinkle emanating from them. At least some vestige of the old Maeve, he thought, waving. Then he noticed the oxygen tank, the vinyl tubing, the blanket on her lap.

She didn't even try to get up.

He smiled, took her hand and kissed her cheek, caught the alcohol on her breath. And something else under it: cigarette smoke.

"Hello, Maeve. It's great to see you."

"Let me look," she said in a voice that sounded like it came from down deep. "My God. Young Wil . . ."

He laughed, took a chair, and sat down. "Once upon a time."

"Take off your coat, for heaven's sake. I'm the only one who gets chilled around here."

He did, draping it over the back of a chair. Loosened his special-occasion tie.

"You look good. Fit." She had on a multicolored cotton sweater with bumps in the pattern, bright silk scarf at her throat.

"You, too, Maeve."

"Well, that gets the BS out of the way. Did Celeste offer you wine?"

"I'm having coffee, thanks. Some house."

"Isn't it, though—Kordell had it built when we were entertaining regularly. Just your basic house in the country." She smiled, but it didn't reflect in her tone.

Celeste brought out a tray with a carafe, cream and sugar, and a mug, poured his coffee, and left. He added cream, returned Maeve's wineglass toast, noting the little broken veins in her face, the soft focus in her look. How thin she really was.

Putting the glass down, she said, "I was trying to recall how long it's been."

"Eighty-one, I think. The cemetery at Westwood."

"I wasn't conscious of much then."

He sipped his coffee. "Has to be 1967 before that. Denny was home on leave that spring. I remember how sharp he looked. Regular marine-corps poster boy."

Her face lit up. "We had a party. I got a rum cake with his name on it." She gazed off, staring, then caught herself, inhaled oxygen. "Never mind me, I drift sometimes. Wil, I never got a chance to tell you how sorry I was about your folks."

"Long time, Maeve. But thanks."

"I just hope they didn't suffer. . . ." Her gaze slackened again, but she fought it this time.

"No, I don't think so."

"God, I hate suffering."

"How's the family doing?" he asked to change the subject. "Everybody okay?"

"Eric has his life, he's always been a loner. I can only assume his blood sugar's still under control. Kordell's healthy as a horse if you don't count hypertension. He lives downtown now." She gave a little shrug. "Rare to see either of them."

"I'm sorry, Maeve. Their loss."

"You're sweet. Did you know that Kordell's listed on the stock exchange?" She took a long pull on her wine, poured herself more.

"The dental clinics?"

"My no, they were sold a long time ago. He's a regular medical conglomerate now—owns an HMO and a medical supply company with a pharmaceuticals division. A research lab and clinic. Eric runs some of it, but Kordell's the big boss. They'll carry him out on his shield one day."

"Eric—not the quiet, shy kid who wanted to be a virtuoso?"

Her smile was knowing. "It has been a while, hasn't it? The only music Eric hears these days is the sound of money. Kordell started him in the business right after Denny . . . went away." Her hands twisted in her lap. "God, I'd love a cigarette right now."

"Smoking's probably not a good idea around that oxygen tank."

"Exciting, though, right?" She laughed, which started the coughing, shallow at first then deep hacks that skewed the oxygen tube. As they subsided she repositioned the nose piece and hit it for a few breaths, wet rumbles coming from her chest.

"Emphysema," she said, swallowing hard, following it with wine. "What they tell me, anyway."

"Mean stuff."

She shrugged. "The wine helps. Pretty soon it'll be morphine. Lovely prospect, drowning in your own phlegm."

An angel-hair layer of high clouds was forming, softening the light and shadows on the deck; Wil let a moment slide by. "You hear anything from Trina?"

"I wondered when you were going to ask. Frankly, I'm surprised you didn't run into her."

"Trina was here?"

"She lives here. When number three went up in flames, she needed someplace to go." She formed a little half smile. "Now I know why we got such a big house. And what about you—married?"

Wil sipped coffee. "Recently divorced."

"Kids?"

*Devin surfing Picketline, his board an early birthday present—carrying him into the rusting and jagged oil-pier supports that gave the spot its name. Another image: the wind taking his son's ashes from the back of a boat.*

"No," he said. Easier than explaining it.

"Trina has two—a boy fourteen and a girl twelve. They're with number two, although she gets to visit them now and then." She saw the question coming and intercepted it. "Get her to tell it. That's not why I asked you here."

"Okay," he said. "Why did you?"

She smoothed the blanket, took some wine. "Condition one is that none of the family know. Not Kordell, not Eric, not Trina. Nobody. Are we agreed on that?"

"That's what I do, Maeve. Confidential investigations."

"I know, I checked up on you. You're struggling."

He was about to counter when she raised a hand. "I'm too blunt for my own good lately—I apologize. Who isn't struggling?" She gathered herself, reached beneath the blanket, took out a manila folder, and handed it to him.

He drew out three brief notes, the writing labored, the paper wrinkled. In order, he read:

> *Mrs. Van Zant, Your son is alive. He is not dead. I seen him. He is OK and I know where. Stand by and tell no one about this. I'll be in touch. A friend.*

Then:

> *Mrs. Van Zant, If you want to see your son again, collect $30,000 and wait for instructions. This is a legitimate business deal. It was not him they sent home in that box. A friend.*

Finally:

> *Mrs. Van Zant, Send $30,000 in unmarked hundreds by January 23rd to P.O. Box 709, Hilo, Hawaii 96721. If you tell cops, FBI, anyone—you lose. This is my last note and your only chance. A friend.*

Maeve watched him as he read, one knuckle pressed against her lips. "Well?" she said as he finished.

"When did these arrive?"

"The last one came a week ago. Five-day intervals before that."

"Police?"

"Lord, no—you saw what it says."

"You haven't sent any money, have you?"

"No. I agonized, then decided to call you."

"Does Kordell know about it?"

"No. Besides . . ."

"Besides what?"

She fussed with the blanket, took a hit of oxygen. "Dutch would think I was crazy. That someone who knew about Denny was taking advantage."

"And you don't?"

"Look at me," she said with heat. "Who knows how much time I've got? Thirty thousand I have—it's nothing when there's even a remote chance to see my son again. Can you understand that?"

*Razor-cut images of Devin; seventeen he'd have been this year.* Wil shook it off. "Of course."

"Well then . . ."

"If you're asking my advice, extortion scams like this happen all the time. Ask the FBI, MIA groups, the State Department. These vultures prey on—"

"Damnit, don't you think I know that? There's risk—I accept that. Any mother would."

"His remains were identified, Maeve. You must have seen the reports."

"Fifteen years—that's light-years in terms of technology. What if they were mistaken or sloppy, that Denny is alive. Who are *they* anyway? Faceless fools who sent him there in the first place. I should believe *them*? Maybe he's sick or can't remember who he is—who we are. What then? Why are you fighting me on this?"

"I'm not," Wil said as calmly as he could. "I just don't want to see you hurt. Look, I've seen people get their hopes up, then have to live with it when it explodes in their faces. People kill themselves over—" He caught himself. "I care about you, you're like family. Just don't ask me to add to your pain."

"Then you won't help me with this?" Tears began to well.

"He's dead. We've all hurt like hell and said our good-byes, and we'll never forget him, but he's dead. Spend it on your grandkids."

"*Them* . . ." She straightened in the chair, wiped her eyes. "I'll give you seven thousand plus expenses to deliver the money, see it gets there safe. That's all you have to do." She waited.

He said nothing.

"Please. Parents will never admit it, but there's always a favorite."

"I wouldn't know, Maeve."

She took some wine and swallowed slowly, as though cleansing her mouth for the words. "Denny was adopted. We wanted children and it wasn't working, so we found a young mother willing to give up her baby."

Wil sat with it a moment. "Denny never said—"

"That's because he didn't know. Nobody did. Then, wonder of wonders, along came Eric and Trina." Her eyes slid out of frame, came back. "You have to remember, that was a different time, people felt differently about adoption. We felt it best for no one to know. Even now."

"You were afraid she might try to contact him?"

"In a way, I suppose, but she never did." Her look was so beseeching, he had to glance away. "Don't you see? He came to me when I was desperate. Now I can be there for him. Won't you do this? If the money's isn't—"

"Forget the money. It's not a money thing." *Seven thousand dol-*

*lars: heat deferred on the house, breathing room—any number of things. Shit.*

"What is it, then?"

Wil was silent.

"He's my son. He's your friend."

*Present tense.* He looked away from her, leaned forward, hands pressed together. Looking out past the deck, the pool, the land, he saw himself, pulled shot-up and drowning from a far-off river as VC gunners raised geysers around him and the friend who jumped in after him.

"Two things," he said finally. "One, I do this because it's Denny—no fee, just expenses. Two, we do it my way. Check it out, use my discretion before I hand over any thirty thousand. That's the deal."

"I don't understand why. If I'm prepared to risk it, why aren't you?"

"That's the deal, Maeve. Or find somebody else."

> Wil—*Sorry to be so secretive. Can you meet at Gladstone's after you're finished with Mother? I'm there now. It's important.*
> *Trina*

Wil folded the note Celeste handed him on his way out, started the car, let it wind down to idle while his pulse did the same. The last he'd heard from Trina Van Zant was the invitation to her first wedding—an Irvine Ranch scion she'd known about three months. They'd been married at Disneyland, her choice—white-carriage treatment, Mickey and Minnie in attendance, no expense spared. Fantasyland. Wil remembered seeing the newspaper account of it through a haze of hundred-proof bourbon fumes. The next day he'd applied to UCLA.

As for the others, he had no idea. But he guessed no Fantasyland for numbers two and three.

He tracked Malibu Canyon to the intersection with Pacific Coast Highway, let a red-green-red cycle while he fought indecision, then turned left. What the hell, it would be good to see her after so many years, see what she'd turned into. A reunion, nothing more, *Wil and Trina* moldering away in the same mental file drawer as high school and growing up.

The thing with Maeve he was even less sure about, though she'd agreed to his terms and cut him an advance. Along with the $30,000 in a leather attaché beside him on the seat, safety-deposit-bound until he left for Hawaii. She'd also given him photocopies of the notes. He glanced at the attaché, wondering who *A Friend* was, at the kind of subhuman who'd send an ill woman's heart into arrhythmia for money. Someone he desired a great deal to meet.

And yet, strange things happened in war, survival stories amid the horrors, people somehow passing through the meat grinders with angels on their shoulders.

Wil caught himself drifting over the line, heard an angry horn, swerved back into his own lane. Back to February 1968: Hue—the first days of Tet—Denny staggering and falling in an attempt to shoulder another marine to safety. His squad driven from that section of the city; no trace of him when the battalion finally reclaimed the shattered streets. Thirteen years later, Denny's remains among those discovered in one of the mass graves outside the city.

According to the Pentagon, there'd been a dog tag, a match on the teeth from a section of jaw. Their take on it: Denny had only been wounded, a prisoner when the rest of his company fell back and were engaged by NVA blocking forces. In the three weeks until the Allies retook the city, foot by foot, house by house, Denny most likely was interrogated, then murdered—executed with the thousands of civilians, civil servants, ARVN military, police, and religious leaders caught up in the Communist offensive. Arms wired, they'd been shot, bludgeoned to death, buried alive.

Revolutionary justice in action.

Wil recalled hearing about it at Coast Guard Training Base, Alameda, his first duty assignment after officer candidate school. *Missing, presumed dead: Marine Corporal Dennison James Van Zant, Newport Beach, California*. Cold black letters on a dead white page, the rush of Denny memories spurring a Black Jack weekend and a Monday request: Vietnam duty for Lieutenant JG Sean Wilson Hardesty. Stunned initially, Lisa'd been anguished, accusatory, finally accepting. Like a person dealing with the discovery of cancer in a loved one.

Months later on a pass, Wil caught a hop to Hue, had been awed by the devastation. Near the spot where Denny fell, someone had painted, KILL 'EM ALL. LET GOD SORT IT OUT. Talking with a marine who'd been through it, he tried to picture the firefights and constant rain, the incoming artillery, rockets, napalm runs, strafings. Din and fatigue, shock and madness. One wire-service photo had it nailed: a helmeted survivor, his face like stone, eyes locked in a thousand-yard stare.

Wil said his good-byes then. But the final piece was laid in place in 1981: Denny's burial at Los Angeles National Cemetery in accordance with Bronze Star honors, posthumous. The family minus Trina leaving the limo, the casket on its stand, the low drizzly afternoon. Taps sounding in the gloom.

Seeing it again in his mind, Wil nearly missed the Gladstone's parking lot. Pulling in, he rolled down the window, let cool air wash over him, sat there a moment. Wondered that after all the years, it still felt like yesterday.

After the valet took his keys, a hostess led him to a booth where

Trina Van Zant nursed a gin and tonic. She smiled as the hostess left.

"Wil . . . God, it's been a long time."

"Hello, Trina."

She seemed smaller than he remembered, and she'd lightened her hair, swept back now. Or maybe it was just him. Certainly the blue eyes were there, the fine features. But whatever he'd been expecting, a few miles went with the territory: forehead and neck lines, several converging not unattractively at her eyes. Silver with some patina. She wore a brushed denim shirt with embroidered cartoon characters, light-colored slacks.

She extended her hands, and as she did he noted the diamond rings, tennis bracelet on one wrist, plain gold barrel on the other. The palms that gripped his were small, firm, humid—odd feeling to him, not remembering shaking hands with her before.

"Thanks for coming," she said after withdrawing them.

He slid into the wooden booth, set the attaché down beside him. "I was wondering if I'd see you. A little nervous, maybe."

"Me, too," she said. "I just didn't want it to be there. In that house."

They spent a moment smiling, regarding each other.

"You look good," she said.

"Pretty fair yourself."

"You want a drink?"

"Food sounds better. You had lunch yet?"

"No, too wound up." She drank the last of her G&T, waved to the waitress. "The clams are good here."

"Done." Wil added it to Trina's drink order and the waitress moved off to put it up.

"Nice time to be here," she said, looking around at the few diners, the ocean beyond the tinted window. "Waiting for you made me think of your folks' old place. You been back there?"

"Once, a long time ago," he said.

"It's a T-shirt shop now. Packed all the time."

"More power to 'em."

"How's your wife—Lisa, right?"

"She's fine, we're divorced. Coming up on a year."

She shook her head. "The pits, isn't it? Never seems to get easier, though God knows I've had enough practice. Did Mother tell you?"

"Yeah."

She took a little breath. "How did that go."

"We had a very nice visit."

"She's dying, you know. Lung cancer. Telling people emphysema helps her deal with it."

"I'm very sorry, Trina. If there's anything I can do—"

"Actually, there is."

"Name it."

She hesitated. "Maybe not."

"What? Tell me."

"No, I don't think so."

"All right."

She fiddled with her napkin. "I'd like you to keep me informed."

"What?"

The waitress came by with her drink and set it down. Outside the window, a pelican dove, surfaced, flew off in the direction of Point Dume.

"About what she wants you to do. Pay the money."

"What money is that?"

"Come on—'A Friend.' That money." She saw his look. "What can I say? I live there, I snoop."

"Your father know?"

"My father lives in a penthouse above his world headquarters or whatever with the cunt of the month. It's hard to say."

Wil watched her down most of the drink. "What about Eric?"

"Who knows? The human spreadsheet—my allowance minder, no less. You believe that?"

"And where does he live?"

"Off Coldwater somewhere. Who cares?"

The clams arrived and he started forking them out of the shell, dipping them in broth and melted butter. Trina finished her drink, crunched the ice, watched him eat.

"Those go well with Sauvignon Blanc." She waved at the waitress, ordered a glass for him, another G&T for her.

"No wine for me, thanks," he said to the waitress.

"Lighten up, it's on me," Trina said.

"Thanks, I don't drink anymore."

She shrugged as the waitress eased away. "Since when?" Sounding betrayed, or at least let down.

"Since a lot of days taken one at a time."

Her drink came; at first she ignored it. Finally she said, "Oh, hell," and chugged some. "Sounds pretty dull to me."

"I have stopped dancing with lamps."

She wiped her mouth, checked for lipstick on the napkin. "So you'll let me in on what you find out?"

"No."

She stared at him.

"Your mother's my client, Trina."

"Exactly my point. *My* mother. Look, I'll pay you to keep me informed. How's that?"

"Sorry. Until I hear it from her, I owe her the confidence."

"I see." Definite drop in temperature.

"Your mom said you have a boy and a girl."

"Change the subject, huh? Little Trina."

"Seemed like a plan. What are their names?"

"Michael and Laurie."

"They live nearby?"

She sighed heavily. "They live in Brentwood with their father. Do you think it's possible that Denny could be alive?"

He took a bite of bread dipped in clam juice.

"Wil?"

"You want the truth?"

"Of course I want the truth."

"Then no, I don't." He saw her face fall and felt for her, but there it was. "There's too much stacked against it."

"But you're going there anyway, aren't you? Make your rate and the hell with us. The hell with him." She gulped her drink.

Watching her, Wil wondered how many she'd had before he arrived, but he said nothing. She did, however.

"I thought somebody who'd gone over there and been wounded might have more sympathy for what we're going through." She paused; took a breath and touched his hand. Leaned toward him.

"Look, I appreciate your loyalty," she said in a confidential tone. "But it's very important for me to know what's going on. Nobody will know. Have some faith, will you?"

Anyone else, he would have smiled; as it was, he just shook his head.

"How about it?" she threw in. "For old times' sake."

"Very old."

"He's my brother. You have no right—"

"I'm sorry, Trina. It was good seeing you, but I have to get back." He waved for the check. Turning back to her, he got what was left of her drink full in the face.

Shock of watery gin up his nose, dripping off his hair and eyebrows, ice cubes in his lap. Stares from around the room.

"You always were a buttoned-up pain in the ass," she said loudly, sliding out of the booth. "Thank God we never got married."

He followed her home, first handing the waitress enough to cover the check, then screeching a left onto PCH as the attaché slid off and thumped on the floor. Honking at her whenever she began to drift from her lane; ignoring her flipping him off. Finally she made it into the driveway and bumped her green Jaguar up on the lawn as he did a U-turn and started back down Malibu Canyon, not wanting to see her lurch her way up to the sunburst doors.

As he drove he rolled down the Bonnie's windows to let the air dry his damp hair, finally rolling it up again when it got cool, the temperature having dropped since he'd entered the restaurant. Good-bye high pressure: The high clouds were starting to clump together now, the sky a faux finish of whites and blues, violets and grays. Rain before morning, he guessed. Mud watch in force tonight.

For a while he listened to a jazz program out of L.A., a taped Herbie Hancock gig. But the smell of gin and lime hovered like a mist that wouldn't clear. Finally he gave up and turned it off, ran the day back and forth in his mind: dying Maeve, spoiled drunk Trina—nights alone in a hard-edged house on a hill with a lot of stark art and old ghosts for company. Until a thought about people in glass houses slipped in, making the irony of his own situation reverberate like the shock wave from an old mortar round.

# 5

**late-afternoon** light threw their shapes ahead as they walked, the boy's hand on the girl's shoulder, fine sand kicking up from bare feet. Most everyone had left Zuma Beach by then or was hiking in the opposite direction, the final pit stop and a sandy trip home. Fighting the glare in the rearview. Visor time if you were heading west.

Despite the clouds building up now, it had been some day. Bright, clear, warm—the mountains close and showing new green from the last little storm they'd had, the boy knowing it probably wouldn't hold from the looks of that sky, but saving the best for last.

He drew the girl in as they walked, no words necessary after last night and this morning. Melody, her name was; nice sound to it. Econ major at Northridge, but not the usual airhead, serious about her work. God, he was tired of airheads. This one was fun, liked doing things on a whim. Spontaneous.

Like a dip in the ocean in January.

He shifted the boogie board under his other arm and looked at her, kissed her as she raised her face to him. "Penny?" he said. "You're sure about this?"

"I'm sure."

"Good thing one of us is."

"What—you never heard of the Polar Bears Club? Besides, we've got the blanket. Who cares after that?"

She thumped him with the duffel, but smiled and they kissed again, stopping briefly to give it some heat, tease each other a little. Then they were around the point, behind some good-sized rocks, the parking lot out of sight now, nobody else around. Getting their towels out of the duffel, spreading them out, the boy shedding his shirt, dropping his jeans, cinching up the cord on his trunks. Melody watching him hit the water with the boogie board.

After a few runs, hotdogging it for her, he let a wave slide him up the beach. "It's rad," he yelled to her. "Not cold at all."

"Yeah, right," she called back.

"Come on—before it gets dark. I'll keep you warm."

"I bet you will," she said. She unbuttoned her shorts and kicked them off, raised the sweatshirt over her head, paused for effect, then dropped her bikini top and walked toward him boldly, enjoying the look on his face. Shrieking when the foam curled over her toes.

Despite her okay face, she had a good body: breasts that barely bounced, trim little waist, ass right out of a surf-mag ad with the model walking away in her tiny thong. Starting to make him hard just watching her. He tossed the lightweight board back up on the beach, hoping she couldn't see his goose bumps from there. "You get used to it," he said. "Come on."

She did. Sputtering, yipping, rolling, diving—gradually adjusting to the water surging around them, breaking in on the point. For a while they swam, then held each other out where they could bob and kiss, watch the first car lights beginning to show up on PCH.

They were treading water, enjoying the pinkening clouds, him ready to suggest they do the blanket thing, when she said, "My God, you're freezing."

"Yeah? Who says?"

"Your leg—Mr. Macho."

Hadn't touched her there and said so. She looked at him, trying to see in the fading light if he was serious. Like *come on, don't fool around.*

"Honest," he said, smiling. "Feel this."

She was reaching for it, smirking like *oh yeah*, when her eyes went wide to a spot beside him in the dark water, made him look. Even in the twilight he could see it taking shape now. Rising.

The thing floating slowly to the surface was white-whale white and horribly bloated, a pale dumpling in a roiling broth. It had a head but no discernible features, gray hair undulating in the wash of current, legs like grotesque versions of the long white balloons pier barkers twisted into whimsical shapes for the kids. It broke the surface lazily and rolled, one tattooed arm and distended hand reaching out for Melody as she screamed and screamed and the swells heaved in on Point Dume.

# 6

Wil slept badly, the rain making him toss and turn and dream of bullets raking across the *Point Marlow*. Blowing him off into the muddy water. Then it was Denny caught in a rip somewhere and yelling out to him, Lisa warning him and Devin to be careful on Dev's last day—water demons he finally banished with three cups of strong Viennese and the inanity of morning television.

Timing a break in the weather, he went for an early walk to inspect the hillside, found his neighbors had the same idea, and cut it short, not in the mood to socialize. He showered, fixed oatmeal, and ate it; by then the travel company was open: Hilo via Honolulu leaving Friday two P.M. from LAX. Next he phoned Lisa and caught her on her way out the door, asked if she could have dinner with him.

"Thanks, but I have something planned," she said. "Anything that can't wait until tomorrow?"

"No, just talk. Thursday's fine. Seven o'clock, Paradise?"

"That works." She hesitated. "Uh-oh, Thursday's no good either, Brandon's softball game. How about lunch Friday?"

"Can't. I'm going out of town."

"Wil, is something up? You sound like it."

"One way to find out."

"Don't play games."

"You mean like baseball?"

A sigh. "All right, you win. Just don't be late like last time." She hung up.

The stupid little flush of victory lasted about two seconds, all it warranted. *Don't play games*—she was right, of course. Still, he wanted to see her. Screw Brandon.

The thought of it made him want another shower.

Once or twice during the divorce—even a couple of times after—they'd slept together; immediate but temporary comfort, Lisa's therapist going nuts when she learned about it. So they'd taken pains to avoid the occasions that led up, and that had worked. But the dissolution had never been about sex, Lisa was the first to admit, and there were times . . .

He put the thought aside, busied himself thinking about what Hawaii held. Not much, he guessed, *A Friend* most likely some crackpot with enough knowledge of the Van Zants to try for the brass ring; someone who'd been at the service, an opportunistic journalist maybe. After all, it was not as if Kordell's empire was any big secret: The family's charitable involvements in Southern California causes still were grist for the society pages, its business activities a favorite target of disgruntled editors. Especially in the independent rags.

*It was not him they sent home.*

Who knew what, and from what source?

Maeve was right in that military reports were often sloppy or mishandled, like any giant organization's. But Denny's remains cast a long shadow. No, this would be a few days in the sun, catch a wave or two after shutting down the scam. A thought nagged him, however: fifteen years since the memorial service, why the delay in coming forward? Why now?

*A Friend* would tell him, that he guaranteed.

Wil was getting set to hit the gym when he heard tentative footsteps on the stairs. He put down his nylon workout bag and stepped out on the porch—where Trina Van Zant stood looking up at him.

Her expression was sheepish. "I wasn't sure this was it. It's not very well marked."

"Who you looking for?"

"Some guy named Hardesty. Seen him around?" She was wearing jeans, boots, a belted suede coat over a bone cotton sweater, her hair moving lightly in the breeze off the ocean.

"Depends."

"On what?"

"On whether you have a drink in your hand."

She shook her head, leaned against the railing. "God, I'm so ashamed. I just seem to have a knack. Can you ever forgive me?"

He looked closely at her eyes and winced. "Better come in out of the light before you bleed to death. There's coffee, if you'll just drink it. Milk?"

"Please—and sugar." She trooped up the steps into the kitchen, looked around. "What a quaint little place," she said, catching herself. "Shit. I didn't mean—"

"Relax." Wil handed her a mug, to which she added milk and three spoons of sugar.

"Breakfast," she said, blowing on the coffee and downing some.

"Nice training table. You like oatmeal?"

"What's that?"

"How about cornflakes?"

"You twisted my arm."

He took her jacket, watched as she poured the rest of the sugar on the cornflakes and dug in.

"Don't feed you much at home, I guess."

"I prefer eating out."

Wil poured himself half a cup as she finished her second bowl, rinsed the dish out, put it in the wood drainer.

"Not bad wrist action for a girl who probably doesn't get much practice," he said.

"Be nice to me. I came to apologize."

"Accepted—providing you don't drink on an empty stomach anymore. At least not around me."

"I'm really sorry. I don't know what got into me." She drew in a breath, released it. "Maybe seeing what I'd missed."

He had to smile.

"What . . . ?"

"It's okay, Trina," he said lightly. "You can stop with the act."

He didn't expect her to start crying, and she didn't exactly, just welled up, spilled over, and looked miserable, one fist pressed against her lips. He handed her a paper napkin and she wiped her eyes, looked up at the ceiling, out the window, back at him. He started to say something, but she waved him off.

"What a damn mess I've made of things. My kids, the lunkheads I've wound up with." She sniffed. "Just a total god-damn zoo."

"That bad, huh?"

"You have no idea."

"Try me."

"I never even came to his funeral. My own brother."

"I know."

"And you know why? Because I was using—cocaine, speed, you name it. I just couldn't be there, not the way I was."

"Kind of hard on yourself, aren't you?"

"I needed somebody to kick me in the butt, and I'd isolated myself from people who'd do it. That make any sense?"

"Yes, as a matter of fact."

"Nobody put that shit in my system," she went on. "I even whored for fixes while I was married—I was high at my kid's baptism. How's that for Mom of the Year?"

He could see she was starting to lose it, the fragile wrap that held her together. "You get any sleep last night?"

"I don't sleep."

"Tell you what," he said, checking his watch. "I'm going to get in a workout while you nap. Then we'll talk." He thought he was going to get an argument, but she followed him into the bedroom, lay down, accepted the quilt he put over her. Asleep by the time he turned back from the door. Thinking about her all the way to the gym.

Not many people were there, and he was able to go at it uninterrupted—bench and incline presses, cable flys, hard biceps sets with descending weights—muscles trembling with the exertion, and his hair dripping sweat. Twenty minutes of StairMaster, twenty of stationary bike, then shower, letting the water cascade down his face, wondering at the fate that had put Trina Van Zant back in his life. Claire beamed a smile from the counter as he left, then he was outside, the air cooling his heat, clouds formed up again and threatening.

He was home by five-thirty, Trina still curled up and breathing deeply. He made himself a sandwich, settled into a book called *North Shore Chronicles*, about big-wave surfing on Oahu. About guys whose instincts to survive had gotten somehow cross-wired, their circuits happily corroded by salt water. Guys like Denny. As he was reading she appeared at the door, blinking her eyes.

"My God, it's dark outside," she said groggily. "What time is it?"

He put down his reading glasses, stretched, checked his watch. "After six."

"I never sleep like that. I'm sorry."

"Don't be. It's good having you here."

"Quiet, anyway." She yawned. "Any more of that coffee?"

He got up from the chair, put some on as she watched.

"Funny seeing you in glasses," she said, digging around in her purse, holding up a pair. "Who'd have thought?"

Sleep had cleared the red from her eyes, and she had a rosy look. The streaked hair had relaxed, wisping down around her face, making her look younger. There were little similarities to Maeve, as well—speech inflections, the tilt of her head, the way her hands moved when she talked—things he hadn't noticed at the restaurant. He handed her the mug she'd used before.

"Whatever happened to us?" he asked after she'd set it down.

She looked at him. "I don't know—time?"

"I mean us, the couple most likely to get coupled."

She sipped again. "You know what's really odd in this? Thinking about Denny being our age."

"He's not, Trina, and be careful here. It's too easy to get hurt. I told your mom as much."

Wistful smile. "I always figured he'd come walking in someday, just 'Hey, what's for lunch.' I suppose that's one reason I couldn't face the memorial service. Like that was it—over and done." She regarded the steam rising in her mug. "What's it like for you after being married to one person all that time?"

He let some beats go by before answering. "Like waking up in somebody else's life, I suppose."

"My trouble is I keep waking up in my own."

"So do something about it."

"Actually, that's why I came here." She paused, obviously building to it. "Wil, I didn't just come to apologize. I want to retain you."

"Haven't we been through this?"

"No. It's not what you think."

"What then?"

She moved to the window, looked out on the sweep of beach, the lit oil rigs farther out on the horizon—leftover Christmas trees. Drizzle spun in the outdoor floods. "I want you to find out who murdered Carmen."

Wil said nothing, just looked at her. Surprised and yet somehow not.

"Don't give me that look," she said. "Carmen Marquez."

Not that it didn't come back: the Van Zant name smeared all over the papers, Denny hauled in for questioning twice, never quite charged, but the only real suspect—last to see his pretty, dark-haired girlfriend alive. Wealthy family–poor family, the class-envy card played early and often. Finally Denny hustled off into the Marines, leaving Newport Beach under a cloud of accusation and recrimination, local activists black-and-white certain of yet another white-brown standard. Intimating that justice might instead be a pajama-clad yellow man with an AK-47.

"Suddenly, from out of nowhere—"

"I'm serious."

"After thirty years?"

"That's just it. He didn't do it."

"I don't mean that. What's troubling is the way you're referring to him," Wil said. "As if he's alive."

"No I'm not. This is just something I can do, wash the stain away. It's there, you know, still—every time the media dredges up these old cases, 'unsolved this and that.' It's always Denny Van Zant, the rich kid who got away with it."

"Assuming I could even get anywhere now, you couldn't have done this fifteen years ago?"

"Not the way I was."

"Is it because of the notes?"

"It's because without me, he wouldn't have gone to Vietnam in the first place."

"Interesting theory."

"Will you please just *listen*."

*She is seventeen to his nineteen, full of new feelings since finding the carbons in her mother's drawer. Adoption papers, a boy they will call Dennison James Van Zant. He is adopted—not bound by flesh and blood but by happenstance, the news at first taking her breath away. Then, suddenly, emotions she has suppressed or channeled into his best friend are like the steam finding its way out of a pressure cooker. Thoughts and feelings beyond her powers to put them back in any inert form.*

*It starts innocently enough, late-night beers and commiseration while sitting in his Jeep at Bolsa Chica, moon shimmer parting the ocean like a great silver causeway. His need to talk is as strong as hers—Carmen is pregnant; they've had a fight, a bad one, her nails rending the skin on his neck when he suggests not that they break up, but that she consider an abortion. Underestimating her Hispanic upbringing.*

*They have always confided about the economic similarity of their chosen relationships and Trina comforts him now, wondering whether to tell him about his being adopted. She decides to wait, and she brings out a fifth of vodka a classmate bought her. Fearing the park patrols, he suggests a place he knows—the beach cottage of a friend's divorced parents, where he's been a few times with Carmen. They pick up Collins and ice along the way, talk and drink, drink and talk. And gradually, as the fifth disappears, she's seeing him as if in a dream.*

*As he talks she rubs his neck and shoulders to dispel the tension—massaging then undressing, probing spots she has learned about from being with Wil. At first he resists, but the alcohol has done its job on him, too, and he is no less randy than she. Then her top is off and she is on him, kissing and using her tongue, caught up in the idea, the newfound freedom brought on by a simple piece of paper. She feels his sweat form and mingle with her own, the heat cauterize his wounds and burn her curiosity down to fine gray ash.*

*The next day, with police cars and neighbors filling the street outside their Lido Isle house, he is taken in for questioning in the murder of Carmen Marquez. Hours pass while she is in torment, but Denny sticks to his story: He's been out driving after a fight with Carmen—driving alone. She is safe but he is suspect. And now she is hooked into a world that gives her no peace from the cold guilt that grips her heart, the feeling of cement in her limbs. She sleeps and eats little, spurns gestures of commiseration from Wil. That Denny opts to enter the service is scant relief, and the agony of his disappearance overseas gradually succumbs to an increasing torrent of chemicals that mercifully blunts her ability to feel much of anything.*

*That is, until* A Friend.

*And seeing* him *again.*

Wil sat numbly, watching her talk to the window, arms folded over her chest. Drizzle had become rain now, deepening the dripping sounds, the soft patter on the roof. It was as if the air had been sucked from the room, leaving a vacuum that made it hard to speak or hear, for the heart to beat normally.

"I guess that covers what happened to us."

She turned from the window. "I don't mean to be insensitive, Wil, but this isn't about us, it's about clearing Den. Not much, but it's all I can give him. Can you see that?"

"Better than I could before you told me."

Her eyes searched his face. "Didn't you ever wonder about Carmen, the business you were in?"

"Maybe."

"What happened to that?"

No answer that wouldn't sound lame to her.

"Forget it, that's my guilt talking. I should go." She looked around for her coat.

"Sometimes life is more about just crawling out of the pit," he said slowly. "Maybe I've been there is what I mean."

Hope spread. "Then you'll try?"

He rubbed his eyes. "I don't know. After Hawaii, possibly. Provided . . ."

"What?"

"That you won't get your hopes up."

"That's all?"

"No. We keep things separate. No cross-pollination, no arm-twisting. You get what you've hired me for, your mother gets what I promised her. Agreed?"

"Yes."

He watched her start over to him, then stop awkwardly.

"Wil, I'm truly sorry about what happened. I jumped the

tracks and kept right on plowing over people, you especially. But for what it's worth, nobody's even come close."

He regarded her, his antenna out for the plastic phrase, the user's facile attempt at manipulation—not sensing it here. Perhaps not wanting to.

"It's a long time ago, Tree."

"Nobody's called me that in a while, either."

"What I'm saying is, sometimes it's best to jettison the baggage."

She found her coat and put it on. "Always easier said, isn't it?"

# 7

**paradise café's** outdoor lights twinkled invitingly from the patio, but Lisa felt chilled, so they sat inside, a corner table just ahead of the evening rush that filled the place now with buzz and restaurant noise. Since she was pressed for time, they ordered right away, salmon for her, chicken for him. Her blouse had a dangly jeweled pin that caught the light as she moved her hands. Tojio Shigeno's only daughter, her almond eyes taking in the room, then coming back to his. Boring right through him, as usual.

"Hawaii," she was saying now after small talk about the house, her upcoming tax season, what he was up to. "Sounds like fun."

"If you call checking out an extortion scam fun."

"You want me to water the plants?"

"Not necessary, but thanks. I should be back in town by Wednesday."

The bar girl set their drinks down; Lisa smiled her thanks. "Anybody I know, or can you say?"

He drank some of his cranberry and soda, crunched the ice. "Involves an old friend, someone you never met. Denny Van Zant."

She thought a moment. "Van Zant—his sister was your high-school flame. Katrina, right?"

Wil nodded. "Not bad."

"*She* hired you?"

"Her mom did. But she's involved—or wants to be."

Lisa raised her eyebrows. "Good luck."

"Not exactly ideal," he admitted. "But they're like family, and—"

"With side benefits."

"Come on, Leese."

"Just kidding." She sipped her white Zinfandel. Their salads and garlic bread came, and they started in.

"How's she looking—Katrina, that is?"

Despite himself, he felt heat rising up his neck.

"Never mind," she said. "It's none of my business."

"She looks all right. Little on the fragile side maybe."

"Another wounded bird."

"Don't start."

"Life goes on, is what I meant."

"Whatever you say. I didn't come to argue."

"Maybe if we'd—"

"Uh-uh." Knowing where she was headed, part of *that* legacy. "Maybe if you hadn't cast off the lines, remember? Given up on us."

"*Ménage à trois* is more like it—you, me, and the birds you brought home. Just took me a while to realize it."

"Twenty-four years?"

"No, not—"

The waitress set down their entrées and moved off. A lady at the next table feigned disinterest, but her eyes were focused on middle distance, her head at a slight tilt. Wil moderated his voice. "Look, I'm sure that stuff plays well in certain circles, but I was there, remember?"

"Funny thing about that."

"Can we try to get out of here in one piece?"

"Great. Pass the bread."

They ate in silence, glancing at each other now and then, shying from sustained eye contact until a flushed, fit-looking man in a red-and-white baseball shirt approached the table.

"Shit," Lisa said under her breath.

His hair was blond, a shade lighter than Wil's under a turned-around baseball cap; at just over six feet, he was about an inch shorter. His hard-rubber cleats clicked lightly on the floor. He smiled, thrust out a hand.

"Brandon Smith—Smith's Automotive," he said, pointing to the lettering on his shirt. "You're Lisa's *ex*."

That's how it sounded to him anyway; he shook the offered hand, hard and callused and lit with exertion. Mid-thirties, he guessed. Not that Lisa didn't look ten years younger.

"And *you're* Lisa's young man."

"Brandon's a client," Lisa said in a voice that sounded like someone else's.

Wil smiled. "And so much more."

Smith's grin broadened; he put his hand on Lisa's shoulder, bent down, and kissed her cheek.

"She's something, isn't she? How you doin', hon?" He pulled out a chair and straddled it.

"Terrific," Lisa said tightly. "How was the game?"

"They forfeited—not enough players or something. So we hit around a few times and I came over here." He waved to the waitress, called her by name, ordered an Anchor Steam, then said, "Oops, is that okay?" Looking first at Lisa, then at Wil.

"Sorry, man, I forgot you're struggling. Lisa clued me in."

"It's all right," Wil said. "Struggle builds character in some people."

Brandon Smith knocked back half his ale, exhaled loudly. "Not only that, it must be hard keeping a small business afloat these days without the right accountant." He winked at Lisa.

Her smile was stillborn.

"So—how is everything?" the waitress said brightly. Seeing their faces, she quickly slipped over to water the next table. On the other side of them, the eavesdropper had lost all interest in her dinner companions and was leaning back in her chair.

"Tell me," Brandon Smith said. "Is the life of a private dick all it's cracked up to be?"

"Brandon, please."

"Pretty much," Wil said evenly. "Nonstop action, women in distress, big bucks. Yeah, and guns, too. I mention them?"

"I don't believe this," Lisa said.

Brandon Smith looked hesitant, then sideways, then winked. "Oh, I get it," he said. "A joke."

"Not to the last guy I shot," Wil said, deadpan.

There was a crash as the woman who'd been eavesdropping lost her balance and hit the floor, taking the tablecloth down with her in a clattering heap of china, flatware, and glass. For a moment everything in the room stopped as though someone had pulled a plug.

Lisa put a hand to her eyes and sat there like a Rodin bronze; Brandon Smith sat frozen as well. Wil rose from his chair and helped the woman up, brushing salad greens and french fries off her clothes.

"My fault," he said. "Should have said something, I guess. We're in a play together."

# 8

**lannie crowell** watched Eric Van Zant welcome the L.A. County sheriff's detective and the VA investigator into his office, saw their looks go immediately to the impressive view of Los Angeles. For a second they watched a jumbo jet take off from LAX and bank left over the ocean.

"Some view," the sheriff's detective, Knowlan, said. "You get much work done up here?"

It *was* a spectacular day, Lannie allowed—storm blown out, great puffy clouds throwing their shadows against the mountains. L.A. looking cleaned up enough to take to church.

Eric Van Zant buttoned his navy blazer, made his usual attempt at a smile. "Having to meet the company payroll keeps things in focus."

"I'm sure it does," Knowlan said. "Gentlemen, Audrey Lyle, Veterans Affairs."

The woman nodded pleasantly, scanned the decor. She was about five-six, with relaxed hair something like Whitney Houston's. Mid-thirties it looked like and not unattractive. Smiles, then Eric saying, "My associate, Orland Crowell."

Lannie gave them a nod and a flash of recently whitened teeth, a business card for one each of theirs. At Eric's gesture, they took seats at the round conference table, the padded leather squeaking luxuriously as if pleased to accommodate them. Lannie adjusted the gabardine of his charcoal Armani pants, the power tie that always got the glances.

"I'm sure you know why we're here," Knowlan said. His bald head shone in the soft gleam from the trac lighting.

"Dr. McCaron called me from the clinic," Eric said. "He said you'd found Billy Dulay."

"Excuse me, but I just got in from out of town," Lannie said. "Is Billy all right?"

"Not exactly," Audrey Lyle said. "Near as we can tell, he'd been in the water about five days. He bobbed up at Point Dume, scared the bejesus out of some kids."

"Damn." Lannie shook his head, looked grim.

"We were hoping you might have something to add to Dr. McCaron's statement," Knowlan said.

Eric pondered. "Only that he'd been in Korea and suffered from advanced-stage post-traumatic stress disorder. One of our more troubled patients."

"McCaron indicated he'd wandered away before," Lyle said.

Eric turned to Lannie.

"That's right—unfortunately," Lannie said, picking up his cue. "Dr. McCaron was hired to tighten things up. To my knowledge, this is the first incident since."

"If I may, let me add something," Eric said. "While we do our best, these are deeply troubled patients with long histories of instability. They can be ingenious sometimes."

"They get out, you mean," Knowlan said.

"Of any hospital short of a prison, which we are not." Eric leaned back in his chair, drawing a little sigh from the leather. "Most of our clients are treated as outpatients."

"But not Mr. Dulay, I take it."

"No. Not with his history of self-destructive behavior."

"Any idea how he ended up in the ocean?" Lyle asked, looking at Lannie.

"None. Have you?"

The investigators looked at each other. "Not so far," Knowlan said. "No friends we know of, his relatives all dead. No one seems to have seen him."

Lyle pulled a notebook from her bag. "Dr. McCaron indicates he might have slipped away during the four A.M. shift change. Is that possible?" She looked at Eric now.

"I'll defer to the doctor on that. But I will say, we have specific procedures to prevent those things from happening. If he disappeared, it would be in spite of them—and our best efforts, of course."

Lannie eased into the break. "The ones like Billy are clever. While they appear catatonic, actually they're looking for weaknesses to exploit. All of a sudden you realize they're not there."

Lyle flipped pages. "And that's what happened before with Mr. Dulay?"

"Yes."

"The report said he ran out onto Pacific Coast Highway waving his arms. Imagining enemies chasing him."

Lannie nodded. "It's a miracle he wasn't killed then."

For a moment there was silence, then Eric said, "Well, if there's nothing else?" He started to rise.

"Would you have any reason to believe this was not a suicide, Mr. Van Zant?" Knowlan again.

Eric settled back. "Good Lord, no."

"Mr. Crowell?" Lyle asked.

"Nope."

"No threats, menacing visitors, things he might have felt he had to escape from?"

Eric rose now. "Among this group, suicide is a sad fact of life. Much as we may do, if someone truly wants to die, it's almost impossible to prevent. Now, if there's nothing else—"

"Six such deaths in the last two years, Mr. Van Zant. Would you consider that number high?"

"I'm not sure what you're implying, Ms. Lyle."

"Nothing that isn't public knowledge."

"Statistics can be deceptive," Eric came back smoothly. "I suggest you look at our record since we first acquired the clinic. I'm sure you'll find it more than competitive."

Lyle and Knowlan nodded, stood up. "Thanks for your time, gentlemen," Knowlan said. "By the way, it's not every executive who'd be so in touch with one of his divisions."

"The clinic's very special to me," Eric said carefully. "My first job was bleaching sheets for my father just after he'd acquired it. I still maintain an office there."

"How is ol' Dutch?" Knowlan asked. "Still the Rock of Gibraltar?"

Eric's face relaxed. "Always," he said. "In addition to everything else he does, he takes particular pride now in beating me at golf."

"Well deserved, I'm sure—his leisure, I mean. Tell him hello from Gene Knowlan, will you? He took care of my teeth once after a street creep bashed 'em in. Long time ago."

"I'm sure he'll remember, Detective. He remembers everything."

"You ever loan out those chairs?" Lyle said, smiling at Lannie as they left.

lannie pulled the plastic bag containing Billy Dulay's things out of the drawer and spread them on the tabletop. Ratty leather wallet with some forgotten receipts you couldn't read anymore, Benzedrine inhaler, two chewed-up lottery tickets, Timex on a pocket chain—no inscription on the back—pair of 2.25-strength drugstore glasses, a half-consumed roll of antacids, his laminated ID card, $12.27 in bills and change.

No sign of the file-drawer key.

Eric Van Zant looked disgusted. "You've searched the clinic?"

"What do you think?" Lannie snapped back. "If it was there, I'd have it."

"Of course," Eric said. "You being so thorough and all. Mind if I ask how it's even an issue?"

"How the hell would I know?"

"I don't even like to think this, but could anyone else there have it?"

"Hey, I don't see why not. You got a staff you chose yourself and a ward full of crazies. Pick one."

Eric said nothing.

"It's missing is all, a coincidence." Dropping the sarcasm in favor of a more professional approach; after all he was wearing a tie. "Besides, all the locks have been changed."

"After the fact, we hope."

"I don't know what more I can do, Eric. The files are in place and nobody's breathing down your neck. What's that tell you?"

Eric was pacing now, back and forth between desk and table, his lips a tight line, furrows above the Oliver Peoples–style horn-rims like something made by a tractor. Good candidate for a stroke, Lannie thought, Eric's lifestyle devoid of exercise from what he could tell, the guy a monk when it came to anything but business.

"Not much, I'd say," Lannie added.

"You ever hear of photocopies?"

Lannie expelled breath. "None of the meters on the machines have shown unusual activity, and that's a fair amount of stuff."

"So he took the files out and had them copied to put us off. Tell me it didn't happen."

Nothing. What could he say?

Eric stopped pacing, sat back down, idly spun Billy Dulay's inhaler on the polished surface. "It's why they were here today, I can feel it. They're toying with us."

*Jesus*. "Enough with the paranoia, all right? Go out and get laid or something. I'll even fix you up."

"Do you mind a personal question, Lannie? Why are you still on the payroll? If it was up to me, you'd be out of here as fast as I could cut the paper."

Lannie's hand reached over and gripped Eric's shirt, pulled him close, surprise on the man's face and a flit of fear—the whole idea: *put* some fear there. "Look, it's my job to clean up after you if that's what the old man says. But don't tell me what I already know, all right? Now, I'm tired and pissed and I haven't worked out in days. You dig?"

Eric swung his eyes away; he nodded and Lannie let go, watched him smooth his Ivy League shirt with the buttons on the collar, crest on the pocket looking like a cross between a bombsight and a bird dropping. Not quite his dad's six-foot-three, Eric was big enough and smart in a lot of ways, but he sure as hell wasn't the old man. Nothing the old man didn't know well enough, no mystery there. Soap opera maybe, but no mystery.

"All right," Lannie said. "I'm telling you there's nothing to trace to us even if they suspect something. Which they don't."

"How do you know that?"

"Trust me, I know cops. As much cop ass as I've had to kiss, it's a wonder my lips aren't white."

He smiled at the thought, pulling Eric into it—at least as much as Eric was capable of. "That's better," he said. "Now, you want to hear about the trip? I got some great footage. Waterfalls all over the place. Couple of naked wahinis even."

"Not particularly."

"You should get out more. See the world."

"Never mind that. The guy over there—what did he know?"

"Nothing."

Eric spun Billy Dulay's watch now, the movement making a scrabbling noise on the tabletop.

"He needed money and hit on the idea from an old article or something," Lannie said. "Quit worrying."

"He won't make trouble?"

"Not since I talked to him."

Eric started on Billy's glasses. "You have to go back."

Lannie reached over and pinned them to the table. "What are you talking about?"

"Something's come up."

"You gotta be shittin' me—I just got off the damn plane. Look at me, I'm one big wrinkle."

"Mother hired a private investigator, an old friend of my brother's. I saw the check stub and dragged it out of Celeste. She cashed it for her—thirty thousand in hundreds. Evidently the guy sent Mother notes, too. Either that or somebody he knows did."

"This friend—you didn't try to buy him off?"

"There wasn't time, he'd already left." He reached back on the desk, pulled an envelope from under the blotter. "His name's here and an old picture of him—best I could come up with. The note said the twenty-third, same deal as before. Your ticket's at the airport."

"This is the Twilight Zone," Lannie said. "I'm trapped in a damn instant replay." His head was beginning to throb where it always did behind his ear, the spur of hard cartilage. "Doesn't anybody keep secrets anymore?"

kordell van zant had his eye on the ball, was tensing into his backswing, when the PA caught him: phone call, pick it up in the clubhouse. He left his stance, shook his head; as he did, white hair came loose, which he swept back impatiently with a gloved hand. Beyond him, fairway one doglegged out to the left, the foursome ahead just now approaching the green.

"Typical," he groused to the others. "Go ahead and start. I'll catch up."

"Screw that," one of the regulars said. "We'll never hear the end of it." There was agreement from the others, laughs. "Next thing, he'll want two strokes for it."

"What I like about you guys, you're so trusting," Kordell said, bagging the War Bird, his visualizing driving the ball over the dogleg straight at the pin and on in one up in smoke. He'd told them not to call him here. Somebody was going to wish they hadn't.

Kordell clacked up the asphalt apron and the clubhouse ramp, his golf spikes becoming muted across indoor-outdoor carpeting to the counter, where an assistant manager was ringing up something for a pinched-looking woman in knickers and a tam-o'-shanter.

"Call for me?"

"Line two, Mr. Van Zant. My office, if you like."

Kordell entered, picked up the receiver, punched the flashing button, said, "Whoever this is, it better be good."

"The sheriff's people were here about Billy Dulay."

Kordell eased the door shut, expelled a breath. "Who?"

"The one we had to—"

"You know, Eric, I think I know where I went wrong with you. Next to marrying your mother, I mean."

"What do you want me to do?"

"For one thing, try acting like the president of a Fortune 500 company and handle it. I've got people waiting."

"Do nothing, then. . . ."

"Is something called for?"

"No, but you wanted me to—"

"Do your job and leave me alone. Have you any idea who I'm playing with? How important they are to what's coming up?"

"Hardesty got away from us."

"I see."

"It was too late to intercept him. He left this morning."

Kordell pulled his tan neck, thinking that it was probably time one of the plastic boys tightened things up down there. And Eric—Lord, it was like having too many leaks in the dike and not enough fingers. "We'll have a serious conversation with our old friend later. Anything else?"

"Lannie's on it."

Kordell thought a moment.

"Dad?"

"It's Kordell or sir, remember? How did his trip go?"

"He said it was a scam. Nothing to it."

"That's what he said?"

"That's what he said."

Kordell let a hint of approval creep into his voice. "Good. Maybe there's hope for this yet. Now, what about the key?"

"It hasn't turned up."

"Eric?"

"Yes sir?"

"Look harder." Kordell hung up and let his eyes drift out onto green grass meticulously trimmed and maintained, an island of order in a sea of chaos—what appealed most to him about the game. Things put right. Variants under control. Still, when he rejoined the threesome and took a vicious cut at the waiting Titleist, his fat divot and sky-high loft brought a tactful silence from the others used to seeing him snap a golf club in two like an offending twig.

**lannie** passed through airport security and sat down to wait for his flight. The window looked out on the fat jets coming and going, people bound for who knows where and back, the terminal's restless energy always good for observing the human drama. Mind's-eye stuff—like being part of people's families without the bullshit and the pain.

Finally he grew tired of the little partings and reunions and settled into his needlepoint, a complex royal-family design with petit point and continental stitches. In his opinion, Brits always did the best ones. But the French weren't bad either, the Gobelin like working on real tapestries. Made his bedroom with the chairs and pillows and hangings he'd done feel like a castle where he was Lannie the Great, women hanging off his thighs, his sword poised like in the Frank what's-his-name illustrations. Respect in all the faces. Not like here, where doing needlepoint drew the looks, the fag eyes and redneck grins. Stares from people who figured he probably ate raw meat with those fingers.

Not that anybody ever challenged him, big as Kordell's steroids had made him. But it was always accompanied by a sense of melancholy—as if he were from another time and couldn't get back.

Lannie wrestled with a particularly hard section, eighteen stitches to the inch, almost photographic when you held the pattern out at arm's length—giving it a rest finally, his fingers throbbing. Why he hadn't told Eric about the guy over there being dead he didn't know, the sucker carved up like a turkey out back of his pathetic little hovel, a hermit crab living better than that one.

Maybe it was his sense of opportunity knocking, like that long-ago night in Huntington Beach. Vibes or whatever. Still, he'd learned to trust it—sixth sense, his mother used to call it, window to the other side. Until he'd sent her there, of course.

Not that he was minimizing the savagery of what befell the guy—he wasn't, wondering now what you had to do to piss somebody off that bad. Hell, even the most depressing crime scenes he used to shoot with the old Bell & Howell hadn't prepared him for that one. Nice and ripe about now, he guessed, jungle humidity and heat having the final say in the matter.

Lannie Crowell heard his call to board, stuffed his needlepoint back in its pouch, and headed for the gate, thinking there were some real animals out there.

# 9

Wil watched the rainbow form and fade as the rain lessened then stopped and the sky got lighter, opening finally to folds of blue-gray and pearl. Far out on the bay a patch of sun rode the slate ocean, the horizon as sharply defined as if cut with a box knife. Ten minutes later the sun was out in earnest, white light splashing off the vintage buildings and streets of downtown Hilo, steam rising to complete the cycle and dry the pavement, the cracked sidewalks, the pastel storefronts overhung by wide eaves.

Wil stretched his legs across the rental car's front seat, ran the power window down, relished the breeze. Everything had a soft feel to it here, even the air—as though it were a warm stream and you were the rock it flowed around.

In the day and a half before drop date, he'd gotten to know Hilo, a time-warp town without the pretensions of the more popular—and sunnier—Kona side of the Big Island. Here, the influence of a hundred and thirty inches of rainfall was everywhere: in the absence of tourist hordes, the clouds draping Moana Kea, the cascades tumbling down black-lava beds to the bay where sugar transports once ruled. Orchids grew wild on the weathered stone walls and fishponds, in the giant aerial-rooted banyan trees.

Like the one dominating his park.

He was directly across an open block of stepped lawn from the three-story Federal Building that housed the post office; binocular distance from the bank of courtyard mailboxes and number 709. Feeding the parking meter another quarter, he strolled over to a bench under the banyan, glad to be free of the smoke-smelling rental.

He picked a dry spot, sat down, opened the paperback Raymond Chandler he'd brought along for company: *The Long Goodbye*, something he'd meant for years to reread. After a few familiar paragraphs he raised an eye to the boxes again. Nothing, no activity. Single-purpose drop, he surmised, no one in the extortion game dense enough to get his regular mail there. And yet . . .

He straightened as a young Hawaiian woman stopped at a box beyond his target. Long straight black hair, cocoa skin, dark eyes with an Eastern influence, red floral dress. Despite his attempts to abort, little pangs of Lisa started in, the way she looked at that age. He followed her progress past the flowering trees in front, down the block and around the corner, felt an emptiness when she disappeared from view.

Stakeouts were the hardest, nothing happening for too long except twisted thoughts, cold coffee, and cramped positions, brutal on your back. Hard to keep the edge. He read for a bit, then returned to the car, found a radio station playing Hawaiian, the harmonies sweetly engaging, like a trip back to the era of hand-tinted postcards, lei greeters, flushed excited faces streaming off ocean liners onto bannered docks. Time passed, eleven o'clock, noon, one P.M.—crackers and cheese, a bag of smoked almonds, bottled tea;

mail drop-offs and pickups, some of them near 709, most not. The usual stream of stamp buyers and package people lining up at the counter and gone.

At one-twenty a man in a yellow-and-green island shirt and khaki shorts sauntered in and Wil just knew. It was almost humorous, the furtive glances, the edging toward the 600–800 section. Backing off, returning as though magnet-drawn to 709—amble-in to key-turn taking a good fifteen minutes.

Amateur—had to be, he thought, pegging the man as late forties, skin leathered by prolonged sun. His eyes were hidden behind military-style sunglasses, graying hair pulled back in a ponytail. Wiry build, six-one maybe.

He waited until the man was bent over the box, fishing out the envelope Wil had stuffed with money-sized paper and timed to arrive in today's drop. Good to see it actually had. Looking around briefly, the man tucked the envelope into the small of his back, let the patterned shirt conceal it.

Wil scanned him with the glasses, saw a face that said alcohol and old acne, sun patches on his forehead. No way to tell about the eyes. Without looking back at the way he'd entered, the man turned abruptly and left by the side corridor.

Wil had his fingers on the door handle when the man reemerged, crossed Kinoole Street to a beat-up silver wagon—through the glasses a rusting Subaru. He watched the car shake as the man cranked it over several times. Finally it caught, blew dark smoke, and came toward him, south up the one-way—past him now. Wil backed the rental out and hung a left, opened about a block between them, the Subaru in no apparent hurry.

About six blocks down, the wagon made a left toward the bay, just making the light on Kilauea. Wil was timing a break, getting set to jump it, when the man suddenly pulled over. He got out, rummaged for coins, put two in the meter, shook a cigarette from a pocket pack, and lit up. Rubbing the small of his back where the envelope was, he crossed the street and entered a bar.

Wil circled, parked where he could see escape routes if the man opened the envelope and ran. He debated the wisdom of entering the bar, chose staying put. Five minutes became twenty, forty. He watched the clouds thicken, a shower dance and blow past, the pavement sending up steam again as the man emerged. He blinked, remembered his sunglasses, crossed to the wagon, looked around, pulled out the envelope, tapped it. Finally he put it back under his shirt and got in the Subaru. Wil could hear the car's door screech and bang shut.

So far, so good.

He had a final slug of the tea as the wagon left the space. Timing it so he made the light just before it changed, he followed the Subaru left along the waterfront, north along the bay. Sun was encouraging colors in the water now, deep indigo farther out, green approaching the shore, here and there flecked with white where it surged over the breakwater.

Slacking his pace to give the Subaru some distance, Wil eased past feather-duster palms, grim-looking tsunami horns, across the Wailuku River with its pole fishermen standing like human statuary, and into the pursuit.

**Iannie** watched them from his rented four-wheel-drive Tracker and smiled; not that this guy Hardesty was inept, he wasn't—but the other guy . . . Jeez, where'd they drum him up? Like something out of central casting. Fact was, watching them this way gave him something of a control rush, like he was the director of photography in an action film. The hot tail sequence: wide shot, cut to medium; close up of the faces reacting, some off-angle car inserts. Shadows flashing across the windshield, wheel shots to indicate speed.

Eat my dust, Sven Nykvist.

Locating Hardesty had been no big deal, bored night clerks ready enough to help; waiting at the hotel when the guy had come out in the morning. Not having been to bed was no problem either—he'd dozed on the red-eye, and there were always Kordell's little fixer-uppers. He put one in his mouth now, let it dissolve under his tongue, felt the surge. Point, set to Crowell. And applause.

Now, as they headed up the ocean road past trees with splashy orange-red blossoms and greenery vibrating with sunlight, stepped waterfalls, and the land beyond rising toward Mauna Kea showing its tip of snow, Lannie let himself relax a little, imagine himself as one of Kamehameha's boys, busting heads and taking big-breasted wives.

**about** an hour later the Subaru left route 19 for 240, cruised through a cluster of raised homes with metal roofs, into the town of Honokaa, where it stopped in front of a place advertising beer and cocktails. The driver stretched and entered. Once again Wil pulled into a space where he could observe, debated again about going in, decided to let it lie. Half an hour later the man came out, pausing at the door to yell something back inside, then headed for the Subaru, grinning and shaking his head.

Some blocks down, the wagon swerved across oncoming traffic and up the hill. Wil followed from well back, watched it turn onto progressively smaller streets until it hit a dirt one, braking in the driveway of a rain-streaked house with a rusted roof, broken lattice around the foundation. Wood porch almost obscured by growth.

The air was cool now, as if someone had drained it of warmth and light. As he slowed, a few drops of rain splatted the rental's windshield.

Wil parked beside a barrier of head-high crotons and shut off the ignition. He drew his .45 from under his rain pullover, eased a round into the chamber, set the safety. Cocked and locked. He stuck the gun in the half umbrella he'd brought along and strode toward the house. Past the Subaru and its bumper sticker: HOW'S MY DRIVING? 1-800-EAT-SHIT.

He knocked; it went unanswered. Banty fowl foraged in the yard. A Lab with a white muzzle raised its head from under a rabbit hutch, then lay back in disinterest.

He knocked again.

"Who is it?"

"Water man. Need to ask you about a bill."

"Clear out, buddy, it's paid."

"Not what it says here. I'll have to shut it off unless you settle up."

Long pause.

"Believe me, I'd rather not," Wil said.

"Then don't."

"Come on, gimme a break. Just doin' my job."

No response.

"Okay. But don't say you didn't have fair warning."

A cheap dead bolt was snapped back from inside, the handle turned, the door began opening. "*Goddamn it—*"

Wil shouldered hard through the aperture, throwing the man off balance onto his ass. He shut the door, lost the umbrella, aimed the .45 at the man's pale eyes, de-sunglassed now.

He thumbed off the safety. "Good news. I was lying."

The room was stale in the way of old kitchen motel units: heavy waft of dead cigarettes and bacon grease. Newspapers covered a tired couch; ground-in dirt held together a ropy throw rug. On a dining table marred with burns, the manila envelope sat next to a bottle of Seagram's 7 and a half-full glass.

The man was already casting glances at a baseball bat beside hiking boots caked with reddish mud.

"I'd advise against it," Wil said.

"Who the hell are you?"

"Relax and I'll tell you."

"Get the fuck out of my house."

"Or what? You'll jam my gun with dust balls?"

"The badges around here don't like thugs much," the man said. "Big native guys. Temperamental fuckers."

"That so? Wonder how they'd feel about mail fraud, conspiracy, extortion—cheating a Vietnam mom out of 30K? There must be a vet or two on the force, wouldn't you say?"

"The hell you know about Vietnam?"

"Trust me on that one."

The man ran a hand over his mouth; watery eyes jittered in the gray light. Rain now thrummed the metal roof and a breeze moved in the trees. Still, it was close inside, sweat beading the man's forehead.

"I don't know who you are, but I'd consider a finder's fee or something. Damn generous, considering you ain't done shit for it."

Wil could smell the two bar stops on his breath. "Name's Hardesty, private license from California. The Van Zants are old friends. Now, who are you?"

The sound of the rain intensified.

"Don't compound your mistakes here," Wil said. "My easygoing manner fools people."

The man eyed him up and down; he smiled sourly, showing stained teeth. "Look, friend, whatever you think you can do to me, I seen before in spades. Now I'm going to get up and sit over there and drink my whiskey, and you can bugger off if you don't like it." He got up slowly, moved to one of the dining-table chairs.

Wil waited until the man had taken a gulp of the Seagrams. Spotting a layer of opened mail on the drainboard, he went there: three flyers addressed to occupant, a utility bill, something from Veterans Affairs for Sergeant Charles Laird, United States Army.

A cockroach scuttled along the baseboard and under the refrigerator. Wil dropped the envelope on the table.

"That you, Sergeant?"

"No comment."

"Pension check, I'd wager. The VA know you're moonlighting?"

The eyes lit up. "Fuck you—the check's an insult considering how it was earned." Then the fire was gone, leaving them merely hollow. "Look, you know shit. Why don't you just get out of here and leave me be?"

"Why haven't you opened the one from Hilo?"

Without looking at it, he said, "Maybe I'm not the curious type."

Wil reached over, tore it open, and shook out the paper stuffing, his note reading *Stay cool and wait to be contacted. You're still in the game.* The man watched it flutter across the table, his expression blank.

"Here's how it plays," Wil said. "My client has agreed to buy the information about her son. It's not my way, but it's hers and I'll respect it—under the condition we agreed on." He pulled out a similar envelope from the pullover's front pocket, held it up, laid it on the table.

"Open it," he said.

Charles Laird undid the prongs, opened the flap, fingered a wrapped stack of new hundreds. He slipped out the remaining five stacks and wet his lips. He looked up.

"That's enough good faith," Wil said. "Put them back and slide it over."

Laird did. "What's the condition?"

Wil put the envelope back in his pocket. "Simple. Prove to me you know Denny Van Zant is alive and how, that you're not the pain-inflicting con job I think you are. Otherwise, I'm going to knock the crap out of you."

"Big talk."

"It's your call."

Laird scratched two-day stubble. "That's it? No strings?"

"Nope." Wil could feel his heart racing at the man's insouciance, a glimmer of something undreamed of. He reset the safety, holstered the gun. "After all, what's a friend for? Right, Charles?"

# 10

**they** drove in relative silence, the Subaru leaking heated air into the passenger compartment, the driver's door whistling from a sprung seal, a trade-off of sorts. Wil cracked his window. The rain had stopped now, but the tires still hissed on the pavement. They wound north, past trim homes with hibiscus hedges, shacky places farther out with dead trucks in front, then stands of ironwood, their gray-green needles more related to the steel clouds than the bright green sugarcane waving in weedy, abandoned fields. Off to the right, the Hamakua coast brooded under a graphite sky.

"Why Hilo?" Wil said finally.

Charles Laird ran a hand over his hair. "Figured I could pick up anyone behind me, and I wanted to leave enough room to get lost. So much for that."

Wil let a moment pass. "Where were you in-country?"

Laird kept his sunglasses fixed on the road. "You ever hear of Dak To? Hill eight-seven-five? Among other swell places."

Wil segued to 1967, late fall, the carnage legendary, even for Nam. "Army airborne, right?"

A nod. "I was cherry, man, eighteen fucking years old. First day we lose our captain and top, then it really turns to shit. Mortars like monsoon rain. I was a medic, but I'd never seen gore like that. Every time we tried to evacuate the wounded, the gooks'd pick off the slick. Nothing we could do, our guys buying it right there on the ground, this shitty red clay. So they call up an air strike, and what do these jokers do but walk a fiver in on the wounded. Our own damn bomb. Welcome to Vee-et-nam."

Wil said nothing.

"Damn, I still lift curtains on that one—the mortar plops and the screaming. Roasting 'em later in their holes."

"Hard to let go of."

"Some other life, maybe. You?"

"Coast Guard—XO on an eighty-two-footer during Market Time. Three rounds in a river ambush. At least I lived."

"Relative term, that." Laird shook out a Marlboro, lit it with a chrome lighter, the smoke finding the crack in the door. They passed another group of houses, a store, and some people on horseback. "Some fucking waste," he said. "Every goddamn bit of it."

"Long time to keep it on replay."

Charles Laird said nothing.

"What about the guy we're going to see?"

"What about him?"

"What's his story?"

Laird slowed for a stream of runoff. "Typical bush vet. He ain't left the valley in years. Hilo's foreign-held to him."

"Where'd you meet him?"

"The Waipio, where we're going—it's like Nam, but peaceful.

Chance to let the ghosts out of the closet once in a while, nobody down there to hear you talk to your dead."

"But he heard?"

Laird nodded. "The man still patrols, happened to be around one day when I was. We got close. I'll cash his checks for him, take stuff down, booze and prescriptions. He lives way back in there, gathers fruit and avocados, freshwater prawns. Not a bad life, actually."

"Anybody else down there?"

"Used to be a town, but a tidal wave took it out. Now it's just some families, few smoke growers farther in. Pretty inaccessible. Nobody messes with this guy, though."

"Who is he?"

He inhaled a drag, let it out. "Ex-marine top sergeant. I'll let him give you his name. Dude's not one to get on the wrong side of."

"And he's the one who recognized Denny?"

"Yeah."

"How?"

Laird downshifted to cross a one-lane bridge, hesitated. "Saw him where the river lets out, there's a spot where the natives go to surf. Said he knew him from Hue. He'll tell you."

Wil felt a chill, but overrode it. "Long time ago."

"Fuck time, those faces are burned in there. Don't tell me you don't see 'em."

"And money can have a remarkable effect on the memory."

"Hey, this guy saw your friend go down, call for help as they had to pull back. If he says he saw him, he saw him."

"I'll let you in on something, Charles, if you don't know already. My friend's bones were sent home in a hatbox. Even with the benefit of the doubt, I think you and your friend see things down there."

"Maybe that's because there's things to be seen."

Wil looked out the window. "How do you fit into this?"

"Told you, I walk point for him—figured what the hell, a few bucks for not much work. More a favor, though, one grunt to another. We drink, shoot guns at bushes, run off demons. Real therapeutic. You should try it sometime."

"Sounds uplifting, all right."

"And you sound like those VA dildos," he said. "Just get the hell away from the reminders and it'll pass—got it all figured out. Well, fuck them and you, too, pal. You ain't got a clue." His eyes seemed like torches set back in a cave, face chiseled from the stone around it.

**laird** slowed to a stop at the Waipio overlook, shifted the Subaru's four-wheel-drive into low range, then eased toward a narrow opening showing a black-diamond warning sign. Weather had thinned the parking lot to a couple of cars whose occupants stood at the rail, gaping. Wil got his first view as Laird started down the near-vertical one-lane.

The valley that spread out a thousand feet below toward a strip of gray-sand beach was about a mile wide, gradually tightening back toward even higher cliffs. Lush green covered the floor and the opposite-facing walls, which were strung with occasional ribbons of silver. At the point where the land dropped into the ocean, a more substantial waterfall plumed down to meet the surf. Tall trees, their deeper green marked contrast to the cleared areas, delineated a stream snaking through the flat. Here and there a tin roof showed.

Laird slowed through a hairpin turn. "Some'n else, huh?"

"Regular Garden of Eden."

"I meant the road."

"What happens if you meet somebody coming up."

Laird grinned. "Pull over and hope for the best."

"Over where?"

"There's places."

"What's over the far ridge?"

"Another valley—even more remote. Hike there, you bring a cell phone."

Wil squinted down at where the stream entered the bay, saw wave action, too high up to tell how good, nobody out there now.

"Is that where your man saw him?"

Laird twisted the wheel through a hard left and back around a pothole. "If he says so. What's your history with this guy?"

Wil pictured Denny slashing through the beachbreak, cutting out with a careless flip of wet hair. "We were tight before he left for overseas—high school and Jaycees. The closest I'll get to a brother."

"Yeah, I had some like that. Always wound up with their guts in my hands. You learn from it—don't get close."

"You lived, they didn't, Charles. Start a new chapter."

Laird eyed a flushed woman hiker trudging uphill. "Right. You thought about what you'll say to your buddy when you see him?"

"One step at a time, thanks."

"Whatever—just have the money ready. This ain't no reunion."

The wagon swerved around a fallen rock, and Wil took in sheer drop, the tops of trees. "Get us there, Charles. That's all I ask."

Ten minutes later the road hit bottom. Laird released the compound drive, increased his speed on the pocked gravel surface, passing trees with fist-sized fruit hanging, guava bushes he pointed out, spindly *hala*, with the leaves that made good mats, tree ferns taller than he was. The air was warm and still—perfumey, like a strand of blossoms around the neck. Soft light filtered through the clouds hovering above the rim.

"How far back does it go?" Wil asked.

"Six, seven miles. Way back in there's ancient *heiau* sites, burial grounds, old foundations—shit like that. Some wild pigs."

"*Heiau* . . ."

"Means 'temple.' See those concrete steps? That was a church before the wave came. School, houses, the whole shot—gone. Just like that."

Wil tried to imagine that much water a mile inland and couldn't. Later they passed a 4X4 going the other way, Laird slowing to talk pidgin with the occupants, Hawaiians in tank tops hauling out bags of cut taro. They crossed the stream then, the Subaru sliding until it bit into the opposite bank and pulled off the road. Laird reached into the back seat, found a cop-style long-barreled flashlight under a pile of limp clothes.

"Not a good place to be in the dark," he said. He got out, banged the door shut and relieved himself in the bushes, started up a thin trail. "Time to walk."

"How long?" Wil said to the man's back after doing the same.

"Don't be in such a lather. You'll bug the gods."

"The gods . . ."

"Royal blood used to live down here, Kamehameha for a time. Spilled a lot at the *heiaus*. Those gods."

"Ah."

"I shit you not, the place is haunted. Ask anybody—the Night Marchers'll steal your soul if you look at 'em."

"It's my client's money I'm concerned about."

"Typical *haole* attitude. Save my breath."

They walked for a while without talking. Stream and bird sounds were loud in the quiet; plants competed for sun under spreading trees showing new leaf. Yellow lichen grew along the branches.

"Some waterfall," Wil said, looking left.

"That's Hiilawe—used to have a twin, but the state appropriated its water. Fucking government." He stopped a moment, cocked his head.

"What?" Wil finally asked.

"Seem to you like somebody's following us?"

"No."

"I ain't much in a car, as we've seen, but out here . . . Coulda sworn I saw someone."

Wil felt a prickle, vowed to pay closer attention, ignore his throbbing feet.

Laird shrugged. "*Pakalolo* patrol probably."

"*Pakalolo* . . ."

"Cash crop—the machete and M-16 crowd. Me and the top are cool with 'em. No sweat."

Laird led them away from the stream, across an open patch with taro growing, through a forest along the base of the cliffs, then the stream again, old lava formations, pools fed by small stepped rushes. Wil checked his watch: four-thirty—another hour or so of light left. Almost to the head of the valley, signs of inhabitance well behind them now.

They made for a descending ridge, around it, toward a small shack with jungle and a big mango tree behind it. About a hundred yards from the shack, Laird put his fingers to his mouth and whistled.

"Gotta be careful how you approach. Around here, anyway." He whistled again after getting no response.

Nothing. Birds and wind.

"Strange. He knew I'd be coming today." Laird scoped a slow

circle, spit in the grass. "Well, hell," he said. "Happiness is a cold LZ, right?"

"Depends on how cold," Wil said, not liking it much.

"Just have the money ready."

Wil trailed him toward the shack, a moldering pile of plywood and black plastic, rusting metal and dirt-caked sheets of fiberglass. Off to the side a blackened fire ring. No signs of life.

Fifty feet from the door, they caught wind of it. No doubt.

"Shit," Laird said. "*Shit, shit, shit.*" He ran for the door, yanked it open, and went inside, tacked-up palm fronds bumping shut on a rusted spring. Seconds later he burst outside, face drained of color.

"Inside's trashed," he said. "Check the back."

But Wil had already started that way—eyes watering, the smell of death like an assault, not long in finding the source.

The thing that had once been a man in camouflage pants and threadbare tee now dangled by its feet from a branch of the mango. Flies and other insects created a black, crawling shroud along the wound, the spilled entrails. Where the scalp had been, exposed bone showed under its own carpet of buzzing flies. Dark strings ran from nose and mouth, the knuckled ends of the curled fingers.

Wil pressed his handkerchief to his face. He was conscious of the buzzing, of Charles Laird retching.

"That him?" he finally asked.

Laird nodded from one knee, threw up again.

Wil forced himself to look at the body. Hard to tell what the decomposition rate would be here, but he guessed accelerated; three, four days seemed a reasonable estimate. He turned away, focused on Laird.

"You have any idea who did this?"

"Fuck you," Laird said, still looking at the ground.

"Give me a name, Charles. What's his name?"

*"Go fuck yourself."*

"Come on, this is no time for it."

But Laird was heaving again. Wil left him and went inside. The shack was dim and smelled of body odor, rotting fruit, and marijuana. Supplies and personal effects were strewn over a smashed wood cupboard and table; a cardboard trunk lay empty on the floor—save for a snap box that looked like one that Wil had stashed at home. He opened it. Folded tightly within the curve of the lid was a letter, noting the award of a Purple Heart to Sergeant Roy Voelker, United States Army, March 10, 1969.

Then he saw it—nailed to a roof support in the corner, the effect in the fading light one of melancholy, as though the medal represented the high point in a doomed life.

"Hey," Laird yelled from outside. "I wanta talk."

Wil broke his thought, called back, "All right—hang on a second."

Choosing his footing, he eased through the chaos, pushed open the thatch door, and stepped down.

Just as Laird rose up alongside.

The blow came from two o'clock. Sensing it, Wil was able to twist left, take the heavy long-barreled flash on his forearm, which went instantly numb. Laird's next blow banged hard off his ribs, doubling him over and leaving him wide open to the looping swing that arced down across the back of his head.

**he** couldn't have been out long, because when he came to it was still light, though fading, and Laird was kicking him in the leg. Actually there were two Charles Lairds and his head screamed when he tried to move it, so he didn't.

Laird grinned down at him. In one hand he held the envelope with Maeve Van Zant's $30,000; in the other, Wil's .45.

"Funny how things work out, ain't it?" He raised the gun slightly and squeezed the trigger.

Earth erupted next to Wil's face. He felt the heat of muzzle gas, the sting of burned powder, the explosion seeming to tunnel right through his eardrums into the center of his brain. He managed to raise his right arm over his eyes.

"Put a fucking gun in *my* face. How's it feel now?" Laird kicked him again, yanked Wil's arm away from his head.

This time there was only one image.

"You get to see it coming." Laird straightened up, aimed at a spot between Wil's eyes. "This one's for Roy."

The end of the barrel grew as big as a well casing, Laird's teeth into a Cheshire-cat leer. Wil's breath caught in his throat.

"Not worth it," he croaked.

"Yeah it is. See you in hell, Ho Chi Minh."

Then an odd thing happened. There was a gunshot, but Wil felt nothing from it, no impact or loss of consciousness. Charles Laird, however, coughed as though getting sick again, righted himself, looked surprised. After that, the left side of his head bloomed red and disappeared.

Wil was still trying to grasp what happened when Laird landed heavily across his legs. In the silence that followed, he felt hot and distant; with effort, he determined Laird had been shot and that he was unable to rise. Not that it was an immediate priority. His head hurt and his left arm throbbed as the feeling returned, and it seemed as if from another plane of existence that the male face looked down at him.

It was black, with chiseled features and an almost Egyptian look to the eyes. White sweatband over a shaved head, short-trimmed

Vandyke beard, a diamond stud—Wil was also trying to imprint sleeveless T-shirt, biceps like bowling balls, cargo shorts over muscular thighs when the face spoke.

"Son of a gun. Things sure go to shit fast, don't they?" He brought the muzzle of a revolver up, scratched a place under the sweatband. A square-faced watch stood out on his wrist.

Difficult from this angle to tell how tall he was; not overly, Wil guessed. But he was losing it now, fading in and out as the man lifted Charles Laird off him as though he were weightless.

"Hope for your sake this joker don't have the virus," he said, regarding Wil's blood-spattered face. He was holding the envelope now.

"Think my arm's broken," Wil said thickly.

"I wouldn't be surprised. How's the head?"

"Still there."

"Kind of underestimated him, wouldn't you say?"

"Um. I know you?"

"Nope, but don't worry. I'll see this gets where it belongs."

There was a crinkle of paper—the last thing Wil remembered as the man's face spun away down a retreating tunnel that flared suddenly like the film burning in a projector before fading to black.

# 11

*the three guys are bigger than they are—twenty pounds a man maybe—and older by a good five years. Early twenties, somewhere in there.*

*"Where you two assholes from?" the tall one says. He has a buzz cut, wide shoulders, lean muscular stomach over blue-and-white surf jams.*

*"Wherever you're from," Denny says, trying to move by him. "I'm the guy next door."*

*"You're the wiseass I remember, all right. Warned you once, this beach is locals only," the one with the lifeguard trunks and peeling shoulders says. "You don't seem to get that."*

*"Some gotta learn it the hard way," the tall one adds.*

*Wil watches the stocky one with the surf knots on his insteps edge in behind Denny. "Come on, Den. We don't need this."*

*The tall one puts a hand out, shoves him back a step. "I'm talking here, boy. You deaf?" The tips of his fingers leave white marks on Wil's sunburn.*

*"We're not looking for trouble," Wil says.*

*"But you found it." Lifeguard Trunks.*

*The stocky one snickers.*

*Denny half turns so he can take in the one behind him. "My friend's a lot more polite than I am, jerkoff. Don't push your luck."*

*It's all bravado, of course, the odds seriously stacked against them. They've seen the three before, intimidating other surfers into abandoning Trestles.*

*"Jerkoff," the tall one echos. "Whoa—these dudes are bad news. Better let 'em pass."*

*The other two look at him, grudgingly move to the side of the trail with practiced expressions of dismay. It's obvious what's coming, but the way out is single file. A gauntlet.*

*Denny looks at Wil. "Go. Get out of here."*

*"Not this time," Wil answers. "Age before beauty."*

*"Three months? You're shittin' me."*

*"I rest my case."*

*There is a look between them he will always remember, then Denny says, "Ah, the hell with it," and lashes out at the tall one, the blow catching him just below the temple.*

*Tall Boy jerks, staggers forward a step, drops to his knees. Meanwhile Wil has grabbed a handful of sand, which he throws in Lifeguard Trunk's face; Lifeguard screams—just before Wil stiff-arms him off his feet. Wil then turns on Stocky, who backpedals, wide-eyed.*

*"Hey, hey," he says. "We're done here. Gone."*

*"Don't forget your friend," Denny says. He kicks a dazed Tall Boy down the trail.*

*"Fuck you." Lifeguard Trunks is backing away now and blinking, eyes watering badly, the area around them rubbed red. "You bozos are dead meat."*

*"Not today," Wil says, slapping palms with Denny. "Not ever."*

*They pick up their gear and start up the trail.*

*Wrong move.*

*Denny catches the throwing motion and yells, "Look out," but it's too late. The rock that leaves Stocky's hand on a hard flat trajectory ricochets off Wil's skull under his right ear, and the next thing he knows, Denny is kneeling by him, saying, "Damn, it's really bleeding. You able to walk? Come on, Mojo, talk to me."*

"he's coming around, Detective. Give us a minute, please."

Wil was conscious of female voice, sound of footsteps, smell of institutional food and air-conditioning. He blinked open to peach walls, IV setup, TV on a wall mount, thin blinds.

Left arm the size of his calf.

He went to scratch the insect crawling in his hair, felt the tug of a strap.

"I'm sorry, Mr. Hardesty, but we felt it necessary. You were compromising the stitches." She was youngish and concerned looking; trim in her pastel uniform. MS. KEPANI on her name tag. She released the restraint, and he touched a line of knots stiff as a vegetable brush.

"What about the arm?" he asked in what sounded like a dated recording of his voice.

"Doctor will brief you in the morning." She fiddled with his IV line, checked the bag.

"Any chance you might give me a hint?"

"Well, I suppose it can't hurt." She saw his look.

"Puns R Us, Ms. Kepani?"

"No need to be flip," she said. "Your arm is badly bruised, as are your ribs. Doctor will show you the X-rays."

Wil let out a breath.

"You've lost some blood as well. Now—would you care for a walk to the bathroom?"

"I thought you'd never ask."

"Very well."

"There you go again."

Ms. Kepani smiled slightly. She reached down, unhooked the IV, assisted him to his feet.

The room spun. She waited with him for it to pass.

"Doctor said to get you up and moving, Mr. Hardesty, so let's do it."

"Easy for him to say."

When Wil emerged from the bathroom, there was a Hawaiian man dressed in casual pants and reverse-pattern shirt sitting in a chair he'd pulled forward. Leaning on his elbows.

"Don't get up," Wil said.

The man straightened. "Pretty full of it for a guy who's been in and out for seven hours."

"Probably the medication," Ms. Kepani said, helping him back into bed and fixing the sheets. She used a button to raise the bed, then handed him the adjuster.

He ran it up higher. "You two carry on. I'll pretend I'm not here."

"You almost weren't," the man said as Ms. Kepani left the room. "The Waipio can be an unforgiving place."

He was about forty, dark eyes and brown skin, a mustache showing threads of gray. Perhaps twenty pounds he didn't need on a six-foot frame, but his look was anything but soft.

"So can certain people."

"Tell me. Last week a family of five gets shot and burned up back in there. Drug wars. Now this garbage."

"I'm afraid you have me at a disadvantage," Wil said.

"David Ohana, Hawaii police. Homicide."

"Mind telling me where I am?"

"Hilo. The upcoast cops figured we'd be getting together, so they had you sent here. You weren't very coherent till now."

Things spun and twisted, vague recollections of rain and night sounds, pain that brought him in and out of fevered consciousness; dawn light and voices arguing, a nightmare portage—by hand at first, then a vehicle of some sort. "Who found me?"

"Honokaa station got a call there were bodies back in there, better hurry if they wanted the one left alive."

"Any idea who made the call?"

"No make on that, but it sounded far off. Got some lost people down there who like it that way." He ran a thumbnail over his mustache. "But enough about us. You talk now."

Without naming Maeve Van Zant, Wil ran through the reason he was there: finding Laird, then Voelker, the attack on him. Losing the money to whoever had shot Laird.

"The black guy—tell me about him."

"Never seen him before."

"How'd he know what you were carrying."

"I was pretty out of it. I suppose he had time to check the envelope."

"Just your basic opportunist."

"I didn't say that."

"Uh-huh. And he's the one who shot Laird?"

"Right."

"Not you."

"You check the wounds?"

"As we speak. You have references?"

Wil gave him Mo Epstein and a superior-court judge he knew

up in Santa Barbara County; Ohana wrote them down, put the notebook in his pocket.

"We'll get your statement in the morning. The ME should be finished by then. Meantime I've got a man outside the door."

"That to keep me in or somebody else out?"

Ohana stood, eased a kink out of his shoulder. "Both. Laird was harmless—collected his checks, belonged to the local veterans' groups, wound up in the drunk tank about twice a year. Your basic shadow. Voelker's another story. Couple years ago our guys ran him out of the valley for baiting a drunk then making sashimi out of him. Self-defense, of course. Word was he was tight with the dopers. Those guys got a long arm in this area."

"But not much hard time."

Ohana's expression hardened. "You notice the cane fields around here—the way they look? Sugar's dead, as in tax funds to shut these cowboys down. As it is, we have to beg, borrow, and steal."

He opened the door, looked back. "Remember it if you're tempted to go back down there and look for your friend. That's assuming you slide on this."

The door hissed shut behind him.

**the** pain in his arm awakened him several times before midnight, when he finally gave up and buzzed Ms. Kepani for a painkiller. But the dose was light, and about four A.M. he was awakened by a rushing sound. Through a muddle of sleep and medication, he homed in, finally made it as waterfall, a local landmark immediately downriver from his hospital room.

He ran the bed up to look out the window.

Waxing moon lit the gorge where the falls cascaded, creating stipples of light and shadow with the trees. It also lit the parking lot, and the figure of a man. He was leaning against a car, his back positioned against the source of light. His arms were crossed; shadow covered his face. Even so, Wil could make out whitish hair and the glow of a cigarette.

He was looking up toward the room.

For a long time Wil returned the man's gaze, hoping to make out a distinguishing feature, something to commit to memory. But aside from the motion of smoking, the man didn't move, and the next thing he knew, Wil was opening his eyes to torn clouds turning pink, empty lot where the figure and the car had been.

shortly after the doctor told him he had a deep bruise but no fracture, keep the arm wrapped and slung for a week, go easy on the ribs, that they were holding him one more night for observation, David Ohana returned with a tape recorder and took his statement.

"Anything yet from the medical examiner?" Wil asked.

"They're shorthanded—the word now is late afternoon. Good you don't have anything pressing."

"Just a life."

"Lucky at that." Ohana rose to go, had his hand on the knob. "Later."

"Last night," Wil said. "Did you have a guy in the parking lot—very light-colored hair?"

Ohana looked at him curiously. "Why?"

"Thought I saw somebody, is all. Seemed to be looking up here."

"You remember what he looked like?"

"Nothing beyond that I'd swear to."

"This one carry a flashlight, too?"

"Touché, Detective."

"Take care of that head, Mr. Hardesty. All sorts of things can slip through the cracks."

Wil watched him leave, heard him say something to the cop in the hall. The rest of the day he spent without the refuge of sleep—doctor's orders. His arm still throbbed, nurses bugged him for samples, and CNN was nothing but politics. Good news came in the form of Ohana's call to let him know he was cleared for release, that his story matched enough of what they'd pieced together from the responding officers, crime-scene photos and analysis, the autopsies of Laird and Voelker.

"We can reach you at the California address and phone number?"

"Yes," Wil said. "What happened to Voelker?"

"Some doubt in your mind?"

"Just wondering. Sometimes it's a cover."

"For what?"

Wil glanced out his window. Pink oleanders formed a hedge near the emergency-room entrance; yellow trumpet flowers tumbled over a lava-rock wall. Two little girls looking like strawberries in their red muumuus danced across the street with their mother.

"I don't know," he said.

"Well, not in this case. The guy was butchered and left to die holding on to his insides."

"Any idea by whom?"

"Somebody who wanted to learn something would be my guess. Or maybe to send a message. We'll find out."

"I'm sure you will."

"Haven't had a change of heart, have you?"

"You'd rather I make something up?" He heard Ohana muffle the phone, then he was back on.

"Mr. Hardesty, I have to leave for Kona, so I won't see you again. Are we clear on that?"

"Clear."

"I sincerely hope so. The officer will take you by the station to pick up your things. He'll drop you at the airport."

"I appreciate it."

"Just so there's no misunderstanding, I voted against releasing you. Aloha, now, you hear?"

David Ohana hung up the phone.

Later Wil went for a walk around the hospital. Most of the dizziness was gone and his arm felt better, the prospect of home energizing him. He made some calls: the airline to arrange his flights, Lisa to tell her what happened, her concern evident at first, then a shortness in her tone—as if she'd heard it all before and wasn't going to let it get to her this time. Still, making him promise to call when he got home. He reached Maeve, reported the basics: no Denny confirmation, just hearsay; his underestimating Charles Laird, the money stolen—

"I don't care about the money," she said. "What about you?"

"I'll be back about six tomorrow, your time."

"Are you sure you're okay?"

"They like to be certain, is all." He paused for an orderly to announce dinner in a few minutes. "Wish I had better news, Maeve. I know what it meant."

"Nothing's changed your mind, then—about Denny?"

"I'm sorry."

Long sigh. "I'll have Lannie pick you up at the airport."

"Who?"

"Lannie Crowell. He works for Kordell and Eric, but he owes me a favor."

"My car's in one of the lots."

"He'll find somebody to drive it back."

"It's really not necessary."

"Don't argue with me. It's what he does, okay?"

"Sure, okay."

"You've kept track of the hospital and doctor bills?"

"Yeah. Maeve, do me a favor, will you? Tell Trina I'm all right?"

There was a pause. "Wil, of all the mistakes she's ever made—"

"I know. I'll be in touch." He hung up, feeling spent.

Dinner was an ordeal he endured, his mind on Ohana's remarks instead. The detective was right—he could easily have been set up or killed by elements beholden to the marijuana interests, Voelker and Laird in good with them. Fragments of that night came back—small sharp pieces that defied overall definition, no matter how hard he concentrated. He tried reading his Chandler, retrieved from the rental, but the type was small and his eyes were tired; after a late appearance by Nurse Kepani, he turned off the lamp, lowered the bed. Following momentary restlessness, he slept, untroubled by the dreams of the last two nights.

Until the phone rang.

Groggy, he checked the face on the room alarm; picked up the receiver. "Yeah . . ."

No one spoke into white noise.

He let a moment go by. "Hello . . ."

Nothing. There was an odd feeling in his stomach, a tightness. "You got a wrong number. I'm hanging up now."

"Wait a minute. . . ." The voice was low, graveled—as though forced through distressed vocal cords. Hard to tell with the connection the way it was. Like cellophane being crinkled.

"It's four in the morning. Tell me why."

Fade up, the caller walking or something interfering.

"That's it. Don't call this number again."

"Open your ears," the voice said. "Voelker's favorite thing was wiring prisoners up to the field phones and turning the crank on 'em. His next favorite was writing the home folks, telling them he needed money to conceal their son's involvement in civilian massacres. The list goes on."

"Payment in full, is that it?"

"Go home."

"Who is this?"

Static swirled and diminished. "Nobody you'd know. Nobody at all." The caller broke the connection.

Following an impulse, Wil raised up, widened the blinds, looked out in time to see red taillights leave the parking lot and whip a left toward the ocean.

# 12

**diamond head** from the air and the white-lace triangles of waves breaking on Waikiki Beach were the lone highlights of his flight home. At least they caught a tailwind and made it in just over four hours. By that time his arm hurt and his head ached from the blow and the stitches and trying to fit things together in a realm where nothing came close to fitting.

All he knew was that he'd added significantly to the manual on coming up short—taken by surprise and nearly killed, robbed of money he was supposed to shepherd. Failed totally at shedding light on whether Denny, why Denny, if Denny. Stellar job all around. And who was watching his room that night, the same man who'd called? Why the call, anyway? Why not just let him slip away and be gone? Obviously he was no threat to anybody, he didn't know shit.

Or did he?

Then there was whatever it was about the voice he couldn't put his finger on. Good metaphor for the trip, he thought as the plane landed. Nothing like not knowing what you didn't know.

Waiting until the parade of aisle jammers had cleared somewhat, he nonetheless bumped his arm retrieving his carry-on from the overhead, swore too loudly for a grandmotherly type who gave him a caustic look, then tweaked his ribs when the carry-on tipped as he wheeled it down the passageway.

*Great day. Nice fucking life.*

Shaking his head, he watched two attractive flight attendants—*nice sex life, too*—hurry off down the terminal together. Directly past the thick-bodied black man who'd shot Charles Laird and lifted Maeve Van Zant's money as he lay helpless on the ground.

The man raised his head as they made eye contact. "Well, look who's here," he said. As he smiled his Egyptian-looking eyes became slits.

Wil just stood there.

"Lannie Crowell," the man said. "At your service."

It was odd seeing him at eye level, or almost. He was about five-ten to Wil's six-two, but far wider and bodybuilder-cut. He wore a sleeveless sweatshirt and baggy pants, black-and-white cross trainers. His ears were small and flat, the right-side diamond stud more prominent than Wil recalled. He was speculating on where to land the first punch when he remembered his cast.

"I know," Lannie Crowell said. "Can't decide whether to thank me or cuss me." He picked up the carry-on as if it were a toy. "I do have that effect on people at times. Hey, man, you comin' . . . ?"

**the** parking structure was bathed in off-pink light, its glow adding an unreal element to the rows of packed-in vehicles. The air had an edge, a chill dampness worlds apart from Hawaii's warm caress. Be easy to get used to that, Wil thought as they approached a limousine that had parked across two spots.

Lannie Crowell went to a white Trans Am parked next to the limo, turned a key in the tail, hoisted in Wil's bag, and shut the lid. He then went to the limo, tapped on and opened a rear door as a jumbo jet thundered over.

"Your welcoming committee," he said, cocking his head toward the interior.

Wil bent to enter the limo, caught the outline of chauffeur up front behind soundproof glass, faces older but remembered as he stepped in and took a seat opposite them. The interior smelled of leather, cigar smoke, and whiskey. The door shut behind him.

"I can offer you Scotch," Kordell Van Zant said without preamble, gesturing at the bottle of Glenfiddich on the small foldout table. Two glasses on it were half full, a third sat empty. "Bourbon, if you prefer." He had on a Harris-tweed sport coat over white polo shirt, charcoal slacks. His face was tanned but not relaxed.

"No thanks," Wil said. He looked at the younger man in tie and navy blazer. Mid-forties, roundish face, undistinguished features. Slightly pudgy, if he had to sum it up, with a hint of mean in the eyes. Like the kid in biology class who got off on dissecting live things, a chance to take it out on something weaker. "Hello, Eric. Long time."

Eric Van Zant nodded at him. "Hardesty . . ."

"Lannie said you'd been injured," Kordell said, regarding the sling.

"Something like that."

"Touch and go is how he put it."

"Describes his part, all right. The go, especially."

"Then you're not aware it was Lannie who called the police?"

"No, I wasn't," Wil said. *And there goes that theory.*

"He's quite good in emergencies," Kordell went on. "It's a talent." He swirled the Scotch, savored it, sipped. "The bottom line is you're back safely."

"And here with you—wondering why."

Hard eyes took him in; Kordell said, "I'm curious. Have you ever considered the possibility a smart mouth isn't the brightest idea sometimes?"

"Once or twice."

Eric leaned forward. "What did you find out from the man who picked up the money."

Wil just looked at him.

"Client privilege might apply in other circumstances, Hardesty. But we're not only family, we're in a position to be of value. Inquiries Lannie made indicated that might not be unwelcome."

*Inquiries . . . son of a bitch.* "That Lannie gets around, doesn't he?"

"We could even arrange for the thirty thousand he brought back to wind up in your account."

"Very subtle, Eric. You'd probably be good with a baton."

"We can also be . . . adversarial."

"The world is full of adversaries," Wil said. "You still play the oboe?"

Eric Van Zant's eyes bored into his and he swallowed. "Clarinet," he said softly. "I played the clarinet."

"I stand corrected."

For a moment no one spoke.

"Hardesty, based on your history with us, I find your attitude not only distressing but surprising," Kordell said finally. "Be that as it may, how do you justify fueling a terminally ill woman's hopes to feather your own nest?"

"You know that's not true."

"Perhaps. But some people I know in law enforcement might not agree. Whether you've crossed a line inadvertently or intentionally will be up to them." He drained his whiskey. "Assuming you maintain your position, of course."

"Sounds serious."

"Then you're getting my drift."

"What I'm getting is bullshit," Wil said, suddenly aware that this absurd conversation was more words than he'd ever exchanged with Kordell Van Zant.

"Exactly right," Kordell said. "It's trouble none of us needs."

Another jet flew over, the sound muffled this time by the closed windows, the cush padding. Wil shifted on the seat, felt Hawaii.

"Well, that's it for me," he said, reaching for the door handle. "No need to see me out."

Eric leaned over and grabbed his arm. "My brother is dead and buried. What possible good can—"

"I don't think you want to do that," Wil said. "With the kind of day I've had, this could be a real turning point."

Eric Van Zant glared, but released his grip.

Kordell said, "This isn't nineteen sixty-five, Hardesty, and you're not welcome in our lives. If you try contacting my wife again—a sick delusional woman who's never come to grips with her son's loss—you'll regret it. I'll see to that personally."

"Funny," Wil said as he opened the door and edged out. "I recall when you were Dutch Van Zant, the Rock of Gibraltar. All-American. You ever think about those days?"

lannie crowell exited the parking structure and headed for the kiosk. He handed the man his ticket and the money, then turned left into the traffic, little tire chirps as he shifted up, the Trans Am's big engine growling powerfully.

Fine mist began to form on the windshield.

"Where to?"

"Lot C," Wil said. "You know where that is?"

"Oh yeah." He punched up a CD and Martha and the Vandellas started in on "Nowhere to Run." "You'll tell the old lady that taking your car was your idea?"

"I'll tell her."

"You're sure about it?"

"I'm sure."

"All right, then. Ain't gonna argue with not driving all the way to La Cucaracha." He pulled up at a red light blooming in the mist, tapped the wheel in time to the music.

"La Conchita," Wil said. "Means 'little shell' in Spanish."

"Whatever."

The light turned green. Lannie charged smoothly off the line.

Wil said, "Long way from a sixty-six Bonneville."

Lannie threw him a glance. "You got a Wide Trac? I always fancied that year. Plenty of power."

"Just don't look too close at the fit."

"Gotta keep your eye on what matters, let the rest go." Lannie Crowell's head and shoulders began to roll in sync with "Dancin' in the Streets." "Love the old stuff, don't you?"

"Yeah. How long you worked for Van Zant?"

"Damn—forever, it seems like. Nineteen sixty-six. How'd that go with Eric and the old man?"

"You should know. Just a couple of fun-loving guys."

Crowell looked at him, then he hit the pulse switch and the wiper blade swept across the window. He smoothed his beard. "So. You gonna thank me for saving your life?"

"Sure. Thanks for saving my life—shithead."

He grinned. "Don't mention it."

"I'll say this, you're not bad with a gun. That part of the job?"

"Job's whatever they say it is, man. What working for somebody means."

"Which explains why you left me out there like that."

"I had things to do. Business."

"Yeah. The money."

"Hey, nothing personal—okay?" Sounding put-upon as he swung around a pickup turning left. As though the conversation had also turned without his permission.

"Kordell mentioned you'd called it in."

The wiper pulsed again; Lannie hesitated. "More or less."

"What's that mean?"

"Hey, no phone, big hurry—I figured you were resourceful, and I was right. Truth is, I told this guy, and he said he knew somebody with a cell phone who'd do it."

Wil felt a little tingle move around the base of his scalp. "What guy?"

"The guy out there walking around, white hair and a scar for a face. Some weirdo is all. Count your blessings, man."

The tingle became prickles. "What'd he look like?"

Lannie shrugged.

"It could be important."

"Why?"

"Because he might have been the one who took out the first guy, Voelker. Like this Hawaii detective thinks I did."

"Damn cops. Okay, it's like I told you—tore up, like maybe he'd been in a wreck or something. Hey, you seen *Braveheart* yet? There's a movie for you. Fucking unreal sound and camera work."

Wil let the Bonneville warm up before taking off, Lannie Crowell now a pair of taillights leaving the lot. He stretched as best he could, ate trail mix from a stash in the glove box, then dialed up a station playing jazz. Coltrane, from the sound of it.

Question was, who was the white-haired guy Lannie talked about? Fair chance it was the same man who'd been outside his hospital window the first night, and the cell phone fit for his four A.M. room caller.

Somebody after Voelker for an old wrong? Plenty of those, apparently.

Friend of Denny's from Nam? File that one.

Denny? *Right. With ID'd remains and a grave in West L.A.*

Who then? Worth pursuing? Nope—that was Ohana's job; buzz off, that message loud and clear. Let alone the welcoming committee's. Hard to blame Kordell and Eric, he allowed—nothing he hadn't expressed in person to Maeve, just more forcefully delivered. Tough to gauge the measure of the threat, though, or who might act on it if he persisted. Kordell most likely; he had the resources, the connections. With Eric he could only speculate—he seemed a watch-your-back kind of threat, where Kordell appeared more the revving-bulldozer-at-the-front-door.

Moot point, of course.

He calmed the idle, slipped the Bonnie into gear, eased toward the exit, fumbling with his good arm for his wallet at the gate. Driving one-handed was awkward, but he settled in on the northbound 405. He was feeling renewed from the trail mix and the brisk air coming in the vents when he made a decision to wrap it up tonight. Save another trip down.

Wil swung off the 405 at the 10, cruised through Santa Monica, and emerged on Pacific Coast Highway. Twenty minutes later he was turning up Malibu Canyon, then Ocean View Terrace, when he saw the flashing lights.

About where the Van Zant house was.

He approached slowly—no doubt now: sheriff cruisers, ambulance, county coroner's van. The cruisers still had their bars going, the effect jarring against the white slab walls of the house, the set-in walkway, the palm trees and lawn sculpture.

Wil drew in so as not to block the van. As he crossed the grass toward the house, a chill starting in, a deputy came forward.

"You are?"

"Friend of the family, Wil Hardesty. I have business with Mrs. Van Zant."

"That won't be possible," the deputy said.

The chill spread. "Why not?"

"Mrs. Van Zant is dead. We're asking that unless it's urgent, visitors contact the family tomorrow."

Ice cracking; cold drop into black water. "Can you tell me what happened?"

"Sir, I'm going to have to ask—"

"Wil—" Trina Van Zant was coming up the walk, her face haggard and drained in the light. She noticed the deputy. "It's all right, he's a friend. Thank you."

"Yes, ma'am." The cop cast a hard look at Wil, went back to his perimeter.

"You're hurt," she said, touching the sling.

"I'm fine, Tree." He saw her red eyes. "Just take it slow."

She took his good arm, pulled him along. "She's gone, Wil. I can't believe I'm saying it." At the front door to the house she stopped, as though reluctant to enter, put a handkerchief to her mouth, shook her head slowly.

"What happened?" he asked.

"I don't know. She was fine this morning—better than she's been in days." Her voice wavered, steadied. "After lunch, I went out. When I came back, Celeste said she'd gone in for a nap. After three hours we got concerned because that was long for her. The door was locked. I got scared and called 911."

Wil guided her to a bench by the moat.

"She took pills—there were a lot of prescription bottles. She must have been saving them."

"Tree, I'm so sorry."

"Will you please tell me it's a dream? Tell me it's a damn dream."

Wil put his arm around her as the tears came. Another deputy stepped outside, spotted her, came over. "I'm sorry, ma'am," he said. "Would you be able to verify your mother's handwriting now?"

Trina wiped her eyes. "Yes, of course." She took Wil's arm and they followed the deputy inside, Wil waiting at the bottom of the stairs as she went up. Within minutes she was back down, looking unfocused.

"What a fucking family," she said to no one in particular. "She might be alive if we'd been there for her once in a while."

"Excuse me," the deputy said. "We've reached Mr. Van Zant and your brother. They're on their way."

If she reacted at all, Wil missed it. "Why don't we go out by the pool, Tree?"

The deputy looked at him. "Sir, your name, please?"

Wil told him and they walked outside—around and around the deck, while she let out a litany of sorrow and guilt, Wil lighting cigarette after cigarette for her, punctuation for the self-flagellation. Like a storm, it blew itself out then, and they sat at the table where he'd first talked with Maeve, Malibu's lights forming a pulse of color at the bottom of the hill.

"She left a note?" he asked finally.

Trina nodded; Wil waited but there was no elaboration.

"I really should go," he said. "If Eric and your dad—"

"No. Please."

He told her about the airport.

*"I don't care. I want you to stay."*

"All right. We'll wait in my car. But I leave when they get here."

As they walked toward it Trina said, "She mentioned you—something about it not being your fault. That she'd find him on the other side."

He was conscious of their breath in the cruiser's light. "At least she's free of it. Some blessing in that."

"Maybe Denny is, too," she said.

"What are you talking about?"

"The note. She says she was the one who stabbed Carmen Marquez."

# 13

**the** check for $12,000 arrived Friday. Wil put it aside, read the handwritten card:

> *Thanks for trying—hope this covers it.*
>
> *P.S. Don't feel bad, dying's no way to live. When you're in the tunnel and the train's coming, you can either tremble or head for the light. I'll take the light. Maeve*

As he did things around the house he recalled when he was young and shy and smitten with Trina: Maeve's sense of humor and charm; the way she included him without hesitation. Drawing him out at dinner, making him feel what he had to say was important, glad that he was Denny's friend, and enjoying the dance he was in with her daughter.

Grace. That was the word for it.

He tried phoning the house, got a recording that they weren't taking calls just now, and left no message. Then he remembered the hour: *shit.* He showered and dressed in loose clothing—khakis and a denim overshirt—the process taking twice as long as normal, but the arm somewhat improved. Cursing time and his inability to adjust to it, he drove to the Coffee Grinder, where Lisa already had a sidewalk table, lidded paper cups in front of her.

"Sorry I'm late."

She kissed his cheek lightly, withdrew to look at his arm. "How is it?"

"Turning some pretty snappy colors."

"How long do you have to wear the sling?" She had on a plain silk top that set off her hair and eyes, a navy skirt. Pearls he'd given her one birthday.

"Up to me, the doc said. Couple more days." He touched the back of his head. "Luckily the stitches are self-dissolving."

She bit her lip.

"Hey—it's worse than it looks. Honest."

She forced a smile. "Hardest head in the business, right? Until somebody—"

"It's not your problem anymore, Leese. Remember?"

"No." Her eyes left his face, regarded the mountains. "I was sorry to hear about Maeve."

"Yeah, same here." He sipped coffee through the hole in the lid, spilled some, wiped it up with a napkin. "How's Brandon? Still smoking them in?"

"How would you like it if people categorized you only by your surfing?"

"I can think of worse things. My investigative talents, for example."

"I'm not sure I—"

"It's nothing very complicated. I got careless, didn't see it coming. Specialty of mine lately."

She said nothing, just made circles with her cup on the tabletop. Across the street a man and woman held on to a toddler trying to walk, his intent face turned up to theirs.

"Sorry," he said. "No point in digging *that* up."

"No," she said. "I was just thinking that you aren't the only one."

"What's that mean?"

She let out a breath. "This little problem with the IRS I didn't catch. Bev's appealed, but our client's threatening to sue."

"I'm sorry, Leese. Serious money?"

"Serious enough if it goes against us. Fifty thousand dollars."

"Whew. There anything I can do?"

"Nothing I can think of."

"Brandon any help?"

"Why would you ask that?"

The father picked up the toddler, who squealed as he was gathered in. "Supportive is more along the lines of what I meant," he said.

"Yes. Well, he sort of is. . . ." Her gaze broke off. "The truth is we haven't spoken in a while. He's been really busy with work."

Wil shook his head. "Life can be a real kick in the pants, can't it?"

**thursday** he was able to reach Trina and found out Maeve had requested cremation with a scattering of ashes, a memorial service afterward at the house. Three o'clock, she told him. Please come.

"You think that's a good idea, given how your father feels?"

"Fuck him. Eric, too, if it's not what they want."

"Have they said anything about the note?"

"You mean about Carmen? Not a word."

"What do you think?"

"You knew her—how can you even ask that?"

"Did she say why in the note?"

"What difference does it make? It's not true."

Wil said nothing.

"All right—she says she went to see Carmen about her ruining Denny's life. Carmen got mad and attacked her, Mom defended herself with a kitchen knife. She never came forward because she was scared." Trina paused for breath. "There—and if you believe that, don't bother coming." She hung up the phone.

For a long time Wil considered calling back, but at the eleventh hour he slipped on a sport coat over the sling arrangement and headed for the Van Zant house. It took him a little over fifty minutes.

Celeste let him in. After commiserating, she told him everyone was outside, an area by the pool where he could see heads gathered. Uniformed catering staff came and went with the urgency of last-minute details.

Wil eased out through the glass doors. On both sides of the deck, tables were heaped with food, white-coated servers standing by; to his right a woman bartender silently arranged glassware, bottles, limes, napkins. Bunched white ribbons adorned the cypress trees leading down to where someone was addressing the group.

Wil joined them, nodded to the older couple he stood beside—like the rest, handsomely turned out and self-assured. He looked for Trina, saw her up front listening to a cleric emote about the kind of person Maeve Van Zant was in life. A number of guests then stepped forward in sequence to echo the sentiments and relate personal anecdotes.

Wil looked around, saw Lannie Crowell in a double-breasted suit nod to him, go back to listening. Eric Van Zant glanced his way, leaned over to whisper something to Kordell, who looked over his shoulder and glared, then said something back to Eric. After a moment Eric left his position and came over, his face tight with distaste.

"You have your nerve, Hardesty. You also seem to have a hearing problem."

The older couple pretended not to notice.

"Did you hear what I said?" Eric added.

Wil met his look. "Try and remember where you are, Eric. I came because I thought a great deal of your mother."

"*Did* you?"

"Yes."

"And yet you drove her to this."

Curiosity overcame the couple; they stared openly. Wil noticed Trina among others turn and glance back, Kordell gesture to Lannie. He could smell the alcohol on Eric's breath.

"I didn't hear you say that, Eric. This time."

"Am I supposed to care?"

"Considering the circumstances might be a better idea."

"And I want you the hell out of here. Now."

"I'm sure you do." Wil saw Lannie moving over; even the person speaking had paused to listen.

*"I invited him,"* Trina said to Eric as she came up. "He's a friend and a guest. Go make money or something."

Eric turned and open-handed her across the face.

Everyone stared now, all pretense at ceremony gone. Trina raised a hand to her cheek, her eyes wide. Kordell seemed rooted. Breeze ruffled the pool's surface, the white camellia blossoms set adrift on it.

Wil saw Lannie moving through the crowd just as Eric did. A wicked light came into Eric's eyes, and he lunged.

It was so drunkenly obvious that Wil had time to brush it off, protect his arm by spinning away, while Eric's momentum carried him into a woman poolside in a wide-brimmed hat. For a moment they teetered on the edge, mismatched and reluctant partners clawing at each other for balance, the woman shrieking as they lost it.

The splash darkened the clothes of bystanders in the front row.

There was a collective gasp and a rush forward, men reaching out to give them a hand as Wil felt an iron grip on his right biceps.

"Chill out, Wide Trac, you don't want this. Time to go play where you're welcome."

**wonderful** day he'd had so far—couple of meaningless errands, some paperwork, wheel-spinning on either side of a what-the-hell nap. After a refrigerator-cleaning dinner, he'd propped himself up on pillows, the TV on low, some old movie he'd remoted to but still had no idea about. He flipped again, hit a British soccer match; again to yet another legal expert putting his spin on the trial of the century. Then an infomercial about the world's best mop. Fill in the blank. Finally Wil turned it off, picked up his Chandler, turned on a reading lamp.

Outside, the breeze had risen, nandina bushes tapping the siding like someone wanting in; surf whumped the beach, the waves walling up in the offshore wind. Tomorrow should be a fair day to venture out, lose the sling, and wash away the residue from yesterday: Eric and the woman soaked and sputtering, Trina and Kordell going at it, crowd sounding like angry bees as Lannie escorted him up the steps and through the house to the front doors.

"Don't think I'd plan a house call anytime soon," he'd said as Wil crossed the moat. "Eric's a lightweight, but he's mean—liable to sic *me* on you. Stay out of trouble now, you hear?"

"Swell job you have, Lannie."

"Hey, gotta be good at something," he said, shutting the doors.

Bizarre came to mind: a family with every advantage that could think of nothing better than to war with itself. And yet he harbored no illusions about families, especially those with money. Not after bumping up against Holly Pfeiffer's relatives a year or so ago: betrayal, threats, abduction, abandonment. Murder. The ties that bind.

The phone rang. He checked his watch, old habit: eleven-fifteen P.M.

"You were right," Trina said before he could speak. "I was wrong."

"Frankly I don't think right and wrong had much to do with it."

"Oh?"

"More like manipulating a situation," he said. "Using someone to stick it to other people."

"You can't think that I—"

"Don't bother, I'll live with it and so will you. Just don't expect me to buy in next time."

"You're full of wisdom tonight."

"That was my last hurrah. Good night."

He put the phone down and turned off the light, was beginning to spiral down into sleep when he heard the knock. He put his robe on over his shorts and went to the door. Opened it and saw her.

"My God, where were you, in the driveway?"

"Gas station," Trina said. "May I come in."

"I'm not sure that's a good idea."

"Then it must be. Look, I was trying to apologize. At least let me do it inside."

He moved aside to let her pass, conscious of her fragrance as she did. Something with orange and—

"I'm sober, I want you to know that. In spite of everything."

"Congratulations."

"Don't be a bastard."

"Too late. How's the war zone?"

"Same as before. Watch yourself with that bunch."

"Thanks."

"Look, I'm sorry about what happened," she said. "It's true I wanted you there for more than one reason. I'm not proud of that. I just didn't think it would get so out of control." She looked for reaction, went on.

"I couldn't stay there—in that monstrosity. I hope you understand, but if you don't . . ." Her shoulders slumped. "I'll be going."

He looked at her, saw vulnerable, exhausted, sincere. Or was it him? "You want some decaf?"

"Only if you're having some."

He scooped some into a filter, set the Braun going as she took off her suede coat. She had on jeans with a silver conch belt, white blouse, blue-and-green scarf. She rubbed her eyes, walked to the window, stood there as the coffee dripped.

"You ever walk on the beach when the moon's full?"

"Not much lately." He poured it into mugs. "Milk and sugar, right?"

"Thanks." She took hers, sipped some. "So you don't get out much?"

He let the steam from his warm his face. "The divorce is pretty recent."

"A year, you said."

"And counting."

"The story of my life." She shook her head, set her mug aside. "Whatever happened to those two dumb kids slow-dancing to 'Moon River'?"

"I thought we'd covered that."

Her eyes betrayed her. "Look, I'm not saying we don't drive the bus. But can't you at least allow the roads are laid by somebody else?"

"Who the hell am I to allow anything, Trina?"

She came and stood before him, looked into his face as though in search of something. After a moment she leaned into him, put her hands around his waist, head against his chest.

He could feel his heart beating as he held her, felt her hands go inside the robe. He bent and kissed her, felt it come back harder and coffee-flavored, her tongue moving over his teeth, himself growing as she pulled him to her. Her conscious of it, playing to it.

He led her to the bedroom, watched as she got out of her clothes, gently stripped him of his while the wind outside gusted off the bluffs and moaned around the windows.

Her breasts were beyond what he remembered: womanly now, the tan lines around them and her sex beckoning, charged. As they molded together, kissed and heated themselves to boiling, as he finally entered her, it was as though thirty years had melted away and he was heading up PCH with the top down and the radio blasting, Trina Van Zant was the hottest thing on the beach, and a giant wave was sweeping him up and over the edge for a long torrid ride down the break.

he fixed breakfast, oven-baked eggs and sourdough toast with black cherry jam. They talked about old times, made love again more slowly, showered, then sat out on the deck to let the sun dry her hair, the wind gone with the bright morning.

"So what's next?" she asked after a bit.

"Huntington Beach."

"Something I said?"

Wil thought about Maeve's check and her suicide note, the Waipio and what happened there. About Denny. "Figure I owe some people," he said.

"Then you don't believe she did it?"

"Her challenging Carmen Marquez's pedigree and not mine? No, I don't believe she did it."

"Then why?"

"Put yourself in her place, seeing a chance to take it with her. All the pain and blame. What would you do?"

She thought about that, shook her head. "I suppose. You have any ideas about who really did?"

"Not yet."

She looked out to sea, Anacapa Island showing its tip, Santa Cruz its canyon-etched profile. "It's beautiful here," she said, and after a moment: "So how was it? Compared to 1966, I mean."

He smiled. "Either we've gotten better, or what's left of my memory fell out of my ear last night."

She watched a flight of pelicans V up toward the Rincon. "Better than with Lisa?"

He looked at her. "Come on, Tree. What is that?"

"I'm only asking."

"Why stop there? Three husbands is stiff competition, too, pardon the pun."

"Sorry. Just my insecurities vomiting up."

He took her hand. "You being insecure is beyond belief. You have to be aware of that."

"And you didn't answer my question."

The phone rang. He went inside, got it in the bedroom: Lisa, asking him if she could come over to get some things.

"How's tomorrow sound?"

"What's wrong with this afternoon?"

"Not a good time, Leese."

She was quiet. "Somebody's there. . . ."

"Uh-huh."

"Don't tell me, let me guess. Trina Van Zant?"

"So—has Brandon been heard from yet?"

"Don't be like that." There was a pause. "No, he hasn't. Not yet."

"She needed some comforting," he said. "That's all."

"Interesting interpretation, but you don't have to justify it to me." She hung up.

Justify—is *that* what he was attempting? *Get a damned grip*. As he replaced the receiver, Trina said from behind him, "No need to answer my question, Wil. You just did."

"Tree . . . wait a second."

"No, don't, I can find my way out. And thanks so much for the comforting."

He heard her Jaguar start, turned from the window, saw a flash of color under the bed. In a second he had the scarf and was racing out the door, halfway down the stairs, waving it, when she spotted him and braked. He opened the passenger door, held it out to her.

"Didn't want you *having* to come back," he said.

Her eyes stayed fixed on the steering wheel. "I wouldn't have. But thanks."

He bent to touch her; she shied away and raced the engine. "Sorry," she said, "I need to be somewhere."

He nodded, pulled back; as he did he saw something on the seat, reached down, and touched it. But the streak was dry and set dark and his fingers came away clean.

"About the only thing I haven't screwed up today."

She leaned over to see what he meant, brushed it with her hand. "So I still like hot-fudge sundaes and spill them. Sue me."

He kissed her cheek, and this time she didn't turn away. But neither did she return it. He backed out, shut the door, watched her lever it into gear. As she turned to watch behind her, her eyes swept his face briefly. Then she was gone in a peel of tires on gravel.

**lannie crowell** cursed the bleeder he'd hit with the syringe, the Kleenex soaked almost entirely red. But it was slowing now, and he was able to unpeel a bandage and slap it over the puncture, hoping none of this new batch had leaked back out the muscle.

*Better living through chemistry.*

For a minute he was tempted to do it again, even picked up the vial before changing his mind. Easy does it, he told himself, gotta be careful, cutting-edge shit; better too little than too much. Look at Billy Dulay and the others. Still, this batch had passed with flying colors according to Kordell. None of the usual hot-flashing and that bullshit.

*Here comes something and it feels so good.*

He stood in front of the mirror, gave it some power moves, flexes and squeezes to ridge up the muscles. Yeah, that was it—that's the way you do it. He held one until the veins began to pop, spiderwebbing now on his chest, pectorals shredding, the ridge between them nearly swallowing his chain. Abs forming into the six-pack configuration, delts and lats flaring, traps webbing at the base of his neck.

*Yo, Mom-o—how 'bout that little boy now?*

He gave it a couple more angles, critical glances and nods, his tomorrow-morning workout already taking shape in his mind when the phone rang.

Lannie crossed the oak floor, took it before his answering machine kicked in. "Yeah . . ."

No one answered, but he could hear breathing, a sound like smoke being inhaled and expelled.

"Hey, sugar, that you?" he asked.

Nothing.

"Come on, baby. Too late to be playing games."

Still nothing. A thought crossed his mind.

"Wide Trac?" Wild guess, but what the hell, that guy Hardesty might still be ticked off, getting the boot that way at that damn disaster of a memorial service.

"Okay, that's it," Lannie said. "Time to stroke your bone on somebody else's dime."

He was lowering the receiver when he thought he heard somebody say his name. "*Sleep well, Lannie,*" something like that. He raised it again, but there was nothing this time but dial tone.

the man with the white hair and the scarred face replaced the cell phone in its holder. He smiled. Much as he was capable of.

Savor each step, he told himself, let it play out according to plan. Slowly—like fire creeping through a ville. He took a deep drag on the cigarette, let the smoke curl around his face, then crushed the butt in the car's ashtray.

By the glow of the visor light, he thumbed another name into the palmtop's keyboard, shook his head as it came up. Bloodless technology in the service of blood sport. Fucking amazing.

He reached for the phone.

## 14

**before** leaving for Huntington Beach, Wil called *The Orange County Register*, determined that editions dating back as far as 1963 were kept in the periodicals section of the Santa Ana Public Library. After a dreary two-hour drive through Wednesday-morning traffic, the air like mud soup, Wil got off the 405 and headed inland toward the Civic Center and a spot in the parking garage.

Downstairs, a librarian set him up with microfilm and a viewer, not long before he found first mention of it. As though it were July 1966 again and he'd just picked up the paper in front of Terrance and Esther Hardesty's Costa Mesa tract house:

LOCAL GIRL MURDERED

*Stabbed Teen Dies on Front Lawn*

Huntington Beach. *A seventeen-year-old resident of this community was found stabbed to death by her family returning early from a weekend trip to Mexico. Huntington Beach Police investigators speculated that*

*Carmen Alva Marquez, of 347 Huerta, was stabbed inside the house, then staggered outside in search of help that never came. . . .*

Wil recalled his reaction: *My God. Carmen? Dead? Can't be . . . not our Carmen . . .*

He set to it and read, the story brief and on the inside of the local section. By next edition, however, Carmen had made the inside of the first section, complete with photograph. Wil touched the black-and-white newsprint, marveling at how young and pretty she'd been, things taken for granted then in his ardor for Trina.

She could have been a model. A young Rita Moreno.

BOYFRIEND DETAINED IN MURDER

*Newport Youth in Custody*

Huntington Beach. *A suspect has been detained in the murder of Carmen Alva Marquez, the local girl found dead early Sunday by her family. Dennison James Van Zant, 18, of Newport Beach, is being held for questioning. According to police investigator Mark Campanelli, Van Zant was the last to see the Marquez girl alive, having left her house around one* A.M. *in the aftermath of a quarrel. The body was discovered at four* A.M. *by her family. Sandor Marquez, father of the girl, was adamant police have the right person in custody. . . .*

Once the connection to wealth and power came to light, reporters had a field day: first names, front pages, lurid innuendo. He remembered the feeling of helplessness—Denny in custody, Carmen dead. Then:

AUTOPSY SHOWS CARMEN PREGNANT

*Finding Indicates Double Murder*

Huntington Beach. *In a tale rivaling popular fiction, the question looms large: Did Dennison James Van Zant, handsome scion of the Newport*

*Beach Van Zants, stab then turn his back on girlfriend Carmen Alva Marquez, leaving her to die alone? Or, as he contends, was she alive when he stormed off following their late-night altercation. That is the question police and most of this seaside community are asking. But enter now an even darker side to the tragedy. Carmen was pregnant. Two, it turns out, have died in front of the modest neighborhood home. Leaving Sandor and Guadalupe Marquez to cry out for justice. . . .*

He remembered another paper's twist, the tabloid-style headline permanently imprinted in his mind. The sickening feeling of seeing:

"MARRY ME," CARMEN BEGS VAN ZANT BOY
*"For Baby's Sake," Is Murdered Girl's Plea*

On and on until Denny was released—not enough to charge him, but more than enough to outrage Hispanic activists, their perception of his guilt like the spreading stain from an ink bottle. The court of public opinion. So that when he was inducted into the Marines a day later, the community, indeed the county, heaved a collective sigh—as though an impacted tooth had been removed. Following a last spasm of vitriol in Letters to the Editor, the incident became yesterday's news to all but a few.

Wil remembered their parting: awkward male posturing and teenage optimism, discomfiture underlying their upbeat see-you-laters and give-'em-hells. The catch in his throat as Denny roared away in the Jeep, dust lifting into the late-afternoon sun—feeling its diminishing warmth in the concrete as he sat there on the steps, fighting the burning in his eyes.

He shook himself free, phoned the Huntington Beach Police Department, double-checking the appointment he'd made for that afternoon. Good he'd checked, they told him, his contact there had been called away. Tomorrow would be better.

Wil set up a one o'clock and told them he'd call to confirm, had lunch at a deli, thought about what to do with the time. He retrieved the Bonneville, dropped down Harbor Boulevard into Costa Mesa, and cruised his old house, now a peeling rental with a sign in front and pickups on the lawn, and the family restaurant—as Trina had said, a T-shirt shop. It was like coming back to a movie after going out for popcorn: things had gone on without you—players. Even though the memories of what happened hung around like heat phantoms on a desert highway.

Close as he was to it, he took the bridge over to Lido and the old Van Zant house. Structurally it was unchanged, the big two-story already side to side on the narrow lot—living and dining rooms facing the water, bedrooms over the garage doors. But the color scheme was different and some plantings. Either that or . . .

There it was, the feeling of being watched. He turned in a leisurely arc, not wanting to spook whoever it might be, but saw no one. After a bit he let his eyes drift back to the house, where the windows reflected only afternoon sun. So much time, and yet . . .

Tires crunched; a woman on a fat-tired bike, grocery bag in the basket, parked and entered a house two doors down, a neighborhood-watch plaque prominent on the siding. Wil saw curtains part around her face in an upstairs window, a phone in her hand.

He got back in the car, crossed the bridge, picked up PCH. Heading toward Huntington Beach, he wondered about all of it, how fast life could change—a perverse hand suddenly rearranging the chessboard. *Here, deal with that.* He looked left at the surf breaking, pictured Denny out there, that full-tilt style of his.

Roadwork had narrowed the lanes down to two. Suddenly Wil saw the flash of a white Jeep two cars back in his rearview and felt a stab at the heart. The Jeep had swung around to pass, swerving back just ahead of the oncoming traffic.

"den, *goddamnit, back off." The rush of air into the topless white Jeep drowns Wil out, and he yells it louder.*

*Denny just smiles, points to the after-market speedo: a hundred mph coaxed out of the big Chrysler V-8 he's spent the last two months installing—the summer of Wil's Southern Cross odyssey into surfboard making. This is the payoff: inaugural flight, the oversize tires whining like runaway dynamos.*

*They're barreling back from Joshua Tree, just them. Desert diorama on either side, intense blue sky, arrow-straight two-lane stretching out as though it goes on forever. Their sleeping-bag covers flap like tissue paper behind the bucket seats; Wil's T-shirt feels as though it's being ripped off him, and his eyes are watering behind his sunglasses. There's a look on his friend's face, something he hasn't seen before.*

*A hundred five.*

*Hundred ten . . .*

*"Gonna get us killed," Wil hollers, even though there's a surge of elation at their sheer reckless abandon. A thought flashes: the gas pedal and the brakes—Trina's description of her brother and him.*

*Denny looks at his friend. "What? You want to live forever?"*

*It's a semi-joke, macho posturing at best, but it comes at a time when Denny's hands grip the wheel too casually, the front end in need of alignment or something. Because suddenly the vibrating Jeep starts to drift, as though feeling a call of its own. Denny's smirk fades. His eyes snap back to business, but now he overcompensates and the Jeep begins slewing back and forth across the empty lanes, Denny braking frantically and Wil holding on for dear life as the wheels on either side abandon the ground with each lean before slamming back down.*

Jesus, Mary, and Joseph . . .

*"Don't roll it," Wil screams. "Let it go."*

*Denny somehow hears and the Jeep plunges out into the desert. The uneven terrain snaps their heads forward, their butts off the seats until, in a spray of gravel and locked-up wheels, they come to rest against a yucca, Denny thrown clear and Wil's bloodless hands virtually riveted to the dash handle.*

*Bruised, his tongue lacerated from the bouncing, breathless and spitting red, Wil staggers over to where Denny has landed in a clump of creosote bush and hears wild laughter. As Denny extricates himself his grin seems to split his dirt-streaked face.*

"God*damn. Tell me you don't live for moments like that.*"

A break came and the white Jeep swung out again and went for it—the space ahead of Wil, three car lengths with room for two. It whipped by the two cars behind like they were standing still, then pulled even, daring the Bonneville to slow, clearly not enough room to beat the truck coming head-on unless it did. As Wil touched the brake the Jeep shot ahead, angled in as the truck driver laid on his horn, the sound like an opposing train blowing past on parallel tracks.

Wil caught a glimpse of lone driver looking straight ahead, and then the Jeep was passing again, heading into the sun. Lost to the glare.

He took a deep breath, felt the adrenaline rush peak and an uneasy feeling with no logical basis whatever. Reaching for the radio, he dialed up an easy-listening station, tried to wind down with it, though it took several miles, and he almost missed his turn.

Relying on memory, he cut into Huntington Beach and, with surprising ease, found himself in Carmen Marquez's old neighborhood. The vacant lots had filled in, trees were fuller, and the streetlights looked more efficient. That was about it for change, houses included. Two- and three-bedroom boxes with one-car driveways and stressed lawns, they had a sense of resiliency about them—like shirts passed down—threadbare and ill-fitting now, but still functional.

He stopped across from a familiar-looking one, approached a Hispanic man about his age screwing a fan sprinkler onto the end of a hose. Onions were frying somewhere; several doors down, two little girls in bright bows played Frisbee with a dog.

"Excuse me," he said to the man. "Have you lived here long?"

The man just looked at him.

"Hoping you might have known the Marquez family. They owned this place at one time."

"When was that?"

"Mid-sixties."

The man shook his head. "Why you want to know?"

"Old friends," Wil said. "Any idea where they might have gone?"

"Nope." He gestured to a boy about four standing with one hand on the faucet beside the steps. "You can turn it on now," he said to him.

Water erupted from the sprinkler head.

*"Menos, menos . . ."*

The boy turned it off.

*"Poquito mas . . ."*

Gradually the boy bracketed the flow until he got an okay sign.

"He's learning," the man said, directing the spray onto a bed of purple-and-red flowers.

"I know the feeling," Wil said. He grinned at the boy. *"Tu hace bien trabajo."*

The boy's eyes widened; he looked at his dad.

"Well . . . Aren't you going to say thanks?"

The boy chirped the word, then ran into the house as though being chased.

"Some hombre you got there," Wil said. He was halfway to the curb when the man called out.

"The green one over there, he's been here forever. Try him."

Wil waved, crossed the street, and pressed the bell at the green house. There was no answer; two more rings yielded nothing. As he was leaving, the man called out, "Try later. Sometimes he goes out drinking."

"Any idea where?"

The man shook his head, moved the spray off the flowers. "Dude's kind of a loner."

"Thanks," Wil said. As he pulled away from the curb the boy ran out and locked onto his father's leg. Wil could see him tracking the Bonneville down the street as the arcs of bright water swept across the grass.

Wil turned off PCH up Malibu Canyon, away from the pre-sunset sun that had been in his eyes since he made the decision to see Trina, not leave it the way they'd left it. As he pulled in he could see her Jag in the garage, an older red Tercel with Celeste in it backing out. Turning around and heading toward him.

She rolled the window down and smiled.

"How you doing?" he said, returning it.

"Better now the day's over." Celeste brushed back hair that had fallen.

"One of those."

"Eric was here. Talking about selling the house, dividing up Mrs. Van Zant's things." Concern evident in her tone.

"No sweat. What do you want to bet one of her friends is just dying to employ you?"

"I'm not worried about that so much, she wrote me a nice letter. It's the effect he has on Mrs. Bannister."

"Who?"

"Trina."

Wil realized he hadn't known Trina's married name and felt odd. "Is she all right?"

"I think she is, but he's such a bully. She was working in the garden when I left. Should I announce you?"

"I'll do it, Celeste—thanks." Wil watched her drive out, then headed for the sunburst doors, banged the knocker twice before Trina answered. Faded denim and red baseball cap, muddy garden gloves, smudge of dirt on her forehead.

"Hi," he said. "You okay?"

"Why wouldn't I be?"

"Celeste said Eric had been by."

She relaxed a little. "Right. I thought you meant something else. Come in."

He stepped inside. "I did actually. I came to apologize."

"Not necessary." She turned, walked back toward the glass wall and the deck beyond. "No more sling?"

He shut the door and followed her out onto the deck. "No, and yes, it is necessary. I'm sorry. I only wish I could have the words back. Wherever they came from."

She began troweling potting soil into a clay urn with strawberry plants coming out the top and sides. "Forget it. Just do me a favor and don't con me into something else, okay?"

"I don't remember conning anybody, Tree."

She put down the trowel, shook dirt off the gloves. "No? Then it's probably just me doing my best to mess things up. Either way, who needs the pain, right?"

"Would you rather I left?"

She took a deep breath, looked at the ocean and the setting sun, gold light bathing the slope and the pier and the town below. "No," she said softly. "But I don't want to hurt anymore, and if there's a way, I'll find it."

"Nobody owns the franchise."

Her eyes were liquid. "Have you ever gotten so dug in that even when you know you're wrong it makes no difference?" She shook her head, removed her gloves, tossed the cap down with them. "Pretty apparent where my kids get it."

"Listen, you're talking to the world's expert—never met a problem he didn't slide over and make room for. Imagine living with that. Ask Lisa sometime when you have a few hours."

"Is that what happened?"

"To Lisa and me? Partly, I guess. But then questions are more my forte than answers. Which reminds me: Can I buy you dinner?"

She wiped her eyes. "No. But you can let me fix something here."

They ate sandwiches from leftovers and a tired green salad at one corner of the big dining table overlooking Malibu and Pacific Palisades. Pale stars and a half-moon showing, Venus bright in the west. She told him things about her husbands and kids—holding them when they were young, things they'd done together in her drug-free moments. Growing close to Maeve again only to lose her; deflecting the topic of Eric and her father when he brought them up.

He told her how his Coast Guard work had led to what he did now—what he liked about it: the making of things right, however small. Finally about the surfing accident that took Dev—his role in it, the ache of losing a son never-ending, but his guilt at least lessening with time and the inevitable accommodation. Peace of a sort.

She toyed with her fork. "You ever think peace of a sort is all we're destined to get?"

"I don't believe that."

"And any day now there'll be proof."

"How'd a nice girl like you get to be so cynical?"

"One too many hot-fudge sundaes."

They smiled at that and he reached over, ran a finger up her forearm, warm from an afternoon of sun. Her fingers came to rest on his as he went over seeing the microfilm of Carmen's murder, the rush of memories it brought—this separate reality into which you could dip your hand, like a pool lined with coins. Only when you reached for one, it was just slightly out of line.

"I have an appointment tomorrow with the Huntington Beach PD," he said. "They agreed to let me see the old files."

"Any thoughts?"

"Yeah. They're not dumb and this was high-profile. It's also cold as ice. Be a mistake to get your hopes up."

"You don't have to disclaim for me."

"I'm just laying it out. Better to know going in."

"Right—you're right, of course." She leaned her head on her hand. "I was just wondering. . . ."

"What?"

"About the kind of man he'd have been, with all he had going for him."

Wil said nothing.

"Guess we'll never know," she added softly.

"If you're back to seeing yourself in it, don't. Nothing you did made it happen."

"This from you?"

He smiled. "Forgot to mention I give better advice than I take."

She leaned over and kissed him, after which they cleared the table and loaded the dishwasher in a kitchen about as big as his house: stainless-steel sinks, wood islands with cutting boards, high-tech cooking surfaces, trac and indirect lighting, marble countertops, fresh flower arrangement in a glass vase, every appliance known to man. As he was toweling off the countertops the phone rang.

"Probably Eric about the will. All I need right now."

"Don't answer it."

But she was already going for the wall phone. "You don't know him. He'll just keep calling."

Watching her move—hair shining, nose sunburned, and the denim shirt making her seem about seventeen—was like being back at the Lido house, thinking she might disappear if he took his eyes off her. It made him feel good.

"Enough for one day, Eric." She glanced at Wil. "Eric . . . ?"

Wil walked over.

"*Say something. . . .*"

He took the receiver and replaced it, hung on to her hand. It was cold now and small feeling. "It's okay," he said.

"Someone was there, Wil. I could feel it."

"Probably just a wrong number."

"*Bullshit. I could feel it.*"

He looked at her, read her face. "It's not the first time, is it?"

She shook her head.

He picked up the receiver, listened, left it off the hook. "When?"

"Three times in the last two days."

He decided to say nothing about Hawaii—too farfetched, whatever *it* was. "Know anybody it might be?"

"No." She rubbed at goose bumps. "I'm getting the weirdest feeling. Will you stay here tonight? Hold me?"

"Sure." He held her then, giving her a smile he felt less than he showed; walked around with her as she dead-bolted the doors, checked everything out, went upstairs. While she was in the bathroom he kicked off his loafers, eased out of the shoulder rig, stacked the pillows on her big bed, and lay against up them. In a bit she came out in a cotton flannel nightgown and lay down next to him.

She touched the wrapping on his arm. "Does it still hurt?"

"Not really."

She reached down, drew the spread around them. "Thanks for staying."

"Can't say I wasn't hoping you'd ask."

In a short time her breathing evened off into a smooth deep rhythm. He was also aware how good her hair smelled. Distilled sunshine, warming him. Warming . . .

Suddenly he was awake, the dream having something to do with not being able to remove his hands from a Ouija board, the messages increasingly hellish, the senders legless faceless men he'd seen at the field hospital in Nam where they'd first sent him to stabilize his wounds.

Easy, he thought, just a dream. Deep grounding breaths. Check the time. Late—three o'clock by his Indiglo watch.

Trina had rolled away from him and lay curled up, making little sleep sounds. Moon showed in the far window; he slid out and moved a chair over to sit down, let it pass. Pale light bathed the deck, the pool, the hillside. An owl flapped past, dove at something up the slope. Cloud wisps glowed silver.

He padded to the bathroom and used it quietly, came back to the chair, sat awhile, then slipped down the hall to the overlook above the living area. Paused a moment there. Saw movement.

At least he thought he did.

Refocusing, he strained to dissect the shadows, but they revealed nothing. He crept back to the bedroom, checked to see that Trina was still asleep, got the .45 from his shoulder rig, and eased back into the hall. Pausing at the vantage point, thinking now he'd most likely imagined it, he nonetheless descended—one stair near the bottom creaking slightly under his weight.

He found himself on the tile leading to the kitchen, aware of the cold surface through his stockinged feet; aware also of the glow coming from the den down the hallway to his left. Gun in the ready position, he moved toward it, saw the small battery lamp on the desktop, several open drawers. He stepped through and scanned hurriedly. Heard a door open in the direction of the kitchen.

The jarring shatter of glass.

Racing out, he stopped short at the kitchen entrance, the sound's full impact apparent in the shards of broken vase reflecting the faint light coming in through the open door. Chill air met him and chaos, flowers strewn like fallen soldiers among the minefield.

# 15

**kordell van zant** looked out at the spread of lights jittering up from West L.A. and Hollywood, strolled to the window across the penthouse, and took in airport, South Bay, downtown. On and on it rolled, filling the horizon. An encompassing creature that withdrew vampirelike at the onset of dawn.

Not long until the blue neon VAN ZANT sign two floors below him on twenty shut off, the eastern sky already starting to pale.

He sipped coffee from his old dental-clinics mug, which for some reason had called to him this morning. It felt good in his hand—solid, comforting. Like being up at four-thirty, behind his desk and in control at five-thirty. Everyday patterns long ago adopted and ingrained like an implanted chromosome.

He liked the thought—sculpting yourself through force of will, making things happen rather than letting them, the norm for most people. The years were like that, he thought, molten present challenging you to shape it before it hardened into twisted past that could just as easily become your legacy if you let it.

Speaking of which, what was done was done now. Let it go. Still it was hard not to look back and see Maeve.

He let himself into his mirrored workout room, slipped out of his terry wraparound, tried to focus on the six-foot three-inch, 220-pound frame that used to pass for a good-sized offensive lineman. These days, six-three–two-twenty might get him a tryout at strong safety, outside linebacker if his burst to the passer was under 2.5. These days, 290-pound defensive linemen caught and dragged down 4.5 speedburners.

Not that he hadn't had a hand in that.

Both hands more like it—up to the elbows.

And here they came, the strobelike images of Maeve again: awkward photos in a family album, unexpected in light of things long left behind. Bumps in the road. He banished them by sighting in on the task ahead: fifteen minutes of exercise bike, fifteen on the treadmill, then StairMaster; quick shower and done. Ready for the daily check of the divisions, adjustments to his schedule, first scan of the NYSE, opening bids on Van Zant Inc., the VZAN listing still bringing the same little charge as the day it first hit the big board.

He mounted the bike, started pedaling, pictured his afternoon. Impromptu was the idea—staged, of course—trade reporters arriving breathless just as he finished up at Riviera Country Club and his thousand-a-hole match, some golf-crazed Asian investors the mark, a ground-floor opportunity he'd agree to discuss after letting them hang fire for twenty-four hours. The buzz, reporter-fed by his answers to their questions: Kordec-Z, the first radically different, side-effect-free antidepressant, Van Zant the sole proprietary developer. Nice ring to it, the market potential explosive.

Rocket fuel in its effect on the stock price.

A punch of the wall-TV remote brought up CNN, a probe they were doing on crime in Russia. Some fucked country after seventy-plus years of Communist rule, he thought, watching it unfold. Everybody standing around with his finger in his ear wondering what to do next, nobody knowing borscht from belt-tightening. No wonder the crooks were winning—couple of years, maybe three, before it blew. He made a mental note to put someone on it: tricky, certainly, but a potential gold mine—ex-commies just begging to be Van Zant distributors. Little pyramids waiting to happen.

The door opened and Claudia or Cindy or whatever her name was poked her head in. One bare shoulder and a perfect breast showing.

"Honey, I can't sleep," she said, finishing with a little pout.

"So get up," Kordell answered.

She lowered her eyes to half-mast. "Bet I can make something else get up."

He ignored her, the corruption of the Soviet justice system holding his interest now. A little money in the right place . . .

She stepped into the room, naked except for tiny pink panties. Her image suddenly became an infinity of mirrored Cindys.

"Well . . ."

Despite himself, his eyes dropped to her body, saw Maeve at twenty-two. As if she'd suddenly materialized and stepped between them. "Put some clothes on," he said.

"*Duuutch* . . ."

"Then get out."

She smiled crookedly, trying to decide whether he was serious, trying to get the joke if he wasn't. She was like that.

"You hard-of-hearing or something?"

"Papa Bear's sure grumpy this morning."

"I'll have your clothes sent over, and you can pick up your money later. Payables—fourth floor."

Her face looked as if he'd just run over her dog. "Dutch, please. I didn't mean anything. . . ."

"That's precisely it, Cindy. You don't mean anything."

"My name's not Cindy, it's Christine—and you don't have to be rude. It's not my fault your wife killed herself."

"What did you say?" He stopped pedaling.

She took a deep breath, crossed her arms across her breasts. "I'm not, like, dumb, the way you've been to me since she died—cold and everything. I'm a good person."

Kordell hit the mute button so there'd be no mistaking his words. "What'll you be when I throw you off the building?" he said.

It took three hours by the time they were finished, Wil and Trina giving statements, hers more along the lines of what an intruder could be after; no idea, she kept telling the deputies, her nerves barely in check. By seven-thirty, they'd finished lifting whatever prints they'd found and the last of the paperwork. Telling her someone would be calling later from Burglary and to please be around.

"You okay?" Wil said as he was about to leave for Huntington Beach.

She nodded.

"I'll be back tonight. If not, I'll phone."

"Don't say that."

"These guys rarely come back after getting run off. Keep the doors locked. See if Celeste can stick around."

She sighed, resigned. "You think it was the caller?"

Wil bent to pick up a shard of glass from under the dishwasher. "Whoever it was, he knew what he was doing. Either that or he hadn't gotten very far when I surprised him." He threw the glass in with the rest of the trash. "How well do you know what's here?"

"What kind of question is that?"

"Might check to see if anything was planted." Her look said it all. "It's just a thought. Bye."

He held her, felt the tightness in her back and shoulders, rubbed them, kissed her. Then he was starting the Bonneville and heading down the hill, turning left at the light, cutting inland at the 10, south on the San Diego, plenty to occupy his thoughts. Why and who? What fit and what didn't? What the break-in had to do with last night's call.

A little over an hour later he left the freeway and cut off at Main Street, cruised past the Huntington Beach Civic Center and down to the ocean. There was time before his appointment, so he had a late breakfast amid newish stores, hyper-looking architecture, designy colors—glaringly out of sync with the bulk of it: wood-and-stone bungalows, weathered old two-stories, plaster apartments with bright doors and window moldings. Oleanders, geraniums, hibiscus bushes. Pier jutting out from the base of Main . . .

*The waves are small, two-to-three-footers favoring a style like Denny's: athletic, hard-charging, risky—determined to make something out of not much. It's early yet, but he's the clear leader after the first heat, his distinctive cutbacks bringing hoots from the beach gallery and the crowds lining Huntington Beach Pier.*

*From the get-go, Wil tries a different tack. More consistent, trying for length of ride and calmer turns, substance and control his only chance against his friend and rival, the juke wizard.*

*That day, at least, they leave the pack behind, conditions and wave forms proving opportune. Still, Denny enjoys a substantial lead going into the final heat. They set up outside, waiting. . . .*

*"Third wave, all you," Denny calls. "Money time, Mojo."*

*"Fat chance," Wil says, knowing full well where the five-foot photo-op check is going and it isn't his way, winner take all the setup: bye-bye motorcycle he'd had his eye on, the guy having to sell cheap because of military induction.*

*"Don't hand me that fatalist crap," Denny says. "Things happen."*

*Wil ponders his options as the wave approaches, decides to try a backdoor move that might net a tube ride and gain some points for at least a charge at it. He times the wave and starts his run—then catches a swirl of movement in the corner of his eye, familiar surfboard and rider.*

Goddamnit . . .

*Wil completes his run knowing Denny's drop-in will draw the interference flag and it does, the lead now sliced in half. As Wil watches and fumes from inside the break, Denny grabs a lesser wave and goes aggressive where a conservative ride will easily ensure him the $1,500 prize money.*

*Halfway into a real crowd pleaser, Denny derails and wipes out to groans, and it's over. Wil takes it on points.*

*Denny's grin coming out fades at the look on Wil's face. Still, he says, "Some run, Mojo. Way to go." He extends a hand that slowly lowers when Wil's isn't offered.*

*"Things happen, huh? The hell you think you're doing?"*

*Denny stops short. "Being a good sport. What's it look like?" He flips his wet hair back, runs a hand over his face.*

*Wil's eyes bore in. "The last thing I expected from you. Pal."*

*The spectators begin to notice something's wrong; they fall silent, as do the sponsor reps preparing to award the mocked-up check. Banners around the stand pop in the sudden quiet. People on the pier lean over to ask those on the beach what's going on.*

*"What's that supposed to mean?" Denny says.*

*But his expression betrays him.*

*"Everybody with eyes knows you threw it, Den, and if they didn't they do now. How do you think that makes me feel?"*

*"I don't know," Denny blusters. "You tell me."*

*Wil's rage erupts in a sudden violent shove that sends Denny backward, where he lands splay-legged and red-faced. Hands gripping sand.*

*"Hell of a way to treat a friend," he says.*

*"Friend?" Wil spits the word as if it's a curse. "Better find somebody who'll explain the meaning. You don't have a clue." He turns toward the platform where the sponsors stand openmouthed. "Give it to charity," he shouts. "At least they deserve it."*

Wil grinned at the recollection, the stir it created on the circuit, their reconciliation after Denny's clumsy but sincere attempts at apology: *Hey, I blow it, I really blow it—friends again?* something like that. Onward and upward when you're eighteen, he thought, paying his bill. Still twenty minutes till his appointment.

He found a pay phone, got Lisa at work. "How's it going—the IRS thing?"

She asked him to hold while she got it in her office; a minute later she was back on. "The hearing's Friday. We've done all we could. At least our lawyer thinks so."

"He any good?"

"He's ex-IRS. We hope so." Wil heard her muffle an aside to someone, then: "Listen, I have to go. My one o'clock's early."

"Good luck, then."

Pause. "Wil, I'm sorry if I made you uncomfortable the other day. I was way out of line."

"I'll live. And remember, those IRS guys have bigger fish to fry than you."

"Right," she said. "And thanks."

The Police Building was one of several situated around a

stepped-down area flanked by pines and jacarandas. Still thinking about the call, Wil asked at the front desk for Sergeant Buckhalter, his contact, detective in charge of Crimes Against Persons. Buckhalter met him on the second floor, examined his license, joined him in a conference room. White shirt and tie, clip-on holster, graying hair over tan features, a tennis player's build.

"Sorry about yesterday," he said, explaining he'd been in obstetrics, watching his third daughter arrive.

Wil congratulated him.

"Life's great counterbalance," he came back. "Okay, you mentioned an unsolved." He checked his notes. "The Marquez girl."

"July, sixty-six," Wil said. He explained his interest in broad terms.

Buckhalter wrote on his pad, said, "Wait here." He left, came back several minutes later with a black vinyl binder three inches thick, and set it on the conference table.

Hand on the binder, he said, "If I haven't said so, Mr. Hardesty, this works both ways. We're happy to help, but we expect reciprocity if you come up with something useful. Plus everything that's there stays there. Are we understood?"

"Understood."

Buckhalter took his hand back. "Give it to Paula outside when you're finished, or you can find me in my office." He made a point of leaving the door open, Paula glancing his way once then down at her desktop.

Wil opened the binder, checked the contents page: crime-scene log, crime and death reports, follow-ups, victim information, coroner's report, suspect information, SIU findings, evidence—yellow and white sheets representing hundreds of hours of investigative work.

Crime-scene photos: He looked, saw Carmen sprawled in front

of the Huerta Street house, knife handle protruding from her chest, face drained of color. He shook his head at the vital person she'd been, the grainy ugliness of her death; willing himself dispassionate, he went on. Polaroids showed a youthful, T-shirted Denny: ID bar askew, face showing exhaustion, defiance, fear, confusion. *Suspect D. J. Van Zant* in marker pen on the back.

Merely the beginning.

Much later, tapped out on lifeless facts, Wil returned the file, asked if they stored evidence from that old a crime. Paula buzzed Buckhalter; the sigh was audible. "Have him come back in an hour," he said through the box.

Wil found a Starbucks, cooled his heels, came back in an hour. In another ten minutes Buckhalter entered with three grocery-sized paper bags. Opening the first, he brought out several items of bloody clothing—shirt, jacket, jeans, bra, panties—the blood brown and fissured after this long. The second bag held the knife, its crosshatched handle showing why fingerprints had been a washout; jewelry Carmen had been wearing that night; her blood-spattered Keds and blue-framed glasses; Denny's ring on a gold chain. And letters—poignant expressions of love and lust, imaginings about a future that looked all but certain.

*Keep going.*

The last bag contained pieces of bloodstained carpet, a sample of clean carpet, blood vials marked *Suspect Van Zant* and *Victim Marquez*. Wil finished making notes, asked indulgence in two more questions, starting in before Buckhalter could decline.

"First, are any of the investigating team still around?"

Buckhalter dropped half glasses in place and turned a page. "Mark Campanelli's funeral was two years ago. Phil Sawtelle retired around eighty-five and moved to someplace in Wisconsin."

He buzzed out to the desk, asked Paula to check for an address on Sawtelle. "What else?"

Wil flipped to the photo section, pulled out a glassine sleeve. Among the dozen or so crime-scene shots inside it, one framed the house, the drive and walk, Carmen's body—and something else, edge of frame.

"Am I wrong or is that the tail end of a news camera?" Wil asked, pointing.

Buckhalter bent closer. "Probably some TV stringer getting the bum's rush."

"Any idea where the film would be now?"

"Not here—probably at the station he worked for." He ran a hand over his forehead. "Look, I don't mean to be rude, but this one's been in our craw for thirty years. We had this Van Zant kid dead to rights, and all of a sudden he's walking away. I understand you have a job to do, Mr. Hardesty, but so have I." He began repacking the evidence bags; as he did, Paula buzzed in that Sawtelle's mailings had been canceled, no new address.

"I appreciate all the help," Wil said, closing his notebook and getting to his feet. "Your new arrival have a name yet?"

The detective's face relaxed. "Melissa Ann. Eight pounds four."

"Nice going."

"Thanks," Buckhalter said. "Not much without family are we?"

# 16

**four o'clock:** From his car phone, Wil spent the next half hour dialing TV stations, connecting finally with the only news department that "might still have" coverage files on the Marquez case—iffy, but he could make an appointment if he wanted, the production assistant due back at five. He left a message on her voice mail, decided then to take a flyer on her being in when he got there, Brea about an hour away, depending on traffic.

Something, anyway.

En route, he redialed, caught the production assistant in this time, explained what he was looking for. She said she'd check archives, see what they had, that it sounded improbable but kind of interesting; come around to the rear if he got there after five. She sounded young.

Following her directions, he found Brea among smallish rolling hills dotted with oak, sycamore, and pepper trees; horses here and there, a countrified version of the endless tracts he'd been driving through. More turns and a longer stretch and he was circling up a two-lane road toward a leveled-off spot, long building marked KTVB in raised letters. He parked, knocked at the glass door around back, was greeted by a woman he put at about mid-thirties—bone jeans, green blouse, brown hair that settled nicely around her face.

"You're the one who called?"

"Hardesty, yes." As she looked him over he pulled a business card from his shirt pocket, handed it to her.

"Private investigator—my, my." She led him down a narrow corridor to a tight little office: bulletin boards full of tacked-up things, commercial-grade video equipment, computer setup on a metal desk, a sign on it that read, KARI THAYER, PRODUCTION ASSISTANT. Armless chair she gestured him to.

She saw him looking at the sign. "Means sooner or later everything winds up in my lap." She leaned forward. "I did some checking—this case you're interested in was hot stuff. There anything in this for me?"

Wil smiled, liking her directness. Still, he downplayed his explanation. A bit here, a bit there; nothing about his connection to it.

"Okay, time out," she said after he'd finished. "With two raises in nine years, I'm looking around. I admit that. You need my help because I'm it here, nobody else will bother. How about agreeing to an exclusive, if and when a certain substance hits the fan."

"Happy thought, Ms. Thayer, but it's way premature. I don't even know what I'm looking for yet."

"Yet," she repeated.

"You always this hard-nosed?"

She removed a note from one of the boards, crumpled and round-filed it. "With a thirteen-year-old son, a cheapshit ex-husband, and a degree in journalism, what would you do?"

most stories that old weren't around anymore, the problem one of too much stuff and too little space to put it. But with a story that big and local, the old film would have been transferred to videotape when the station switched to that format. Even so, stories much past the mid-eighties were history.

Unless you knew where to look.

"My boss was cut loose last year," Kari Thayer was telling him as she turned on the light in a small space jammed with racks and boxes. "Twenty years' experience, but I came cheap. God, I love the nineties."

"What's in here?" he asked.

"Our big chance."

"I wish you'd stop saying that."

"Just kidding. I have to get ready for broadcast now, but I'll check back." She wheeled in a cart full of equipment, found a wall outlet, plugged in the cord running from a bar of plugs on the cart. "Have a ball," she said on her way out.

Forty minutes later he found a couple of old stories about the 1971 Sylmar Earthquake, nothing earlier. He was about to give up when he came across a box labeled MARQUEZ MURDER in with some other two-inch spools. Which eliminated the three-quarter-inch cart player.

He found her in the studio, a high-ceilinged, polished-concrete expanse where a made-up anchor sat listening to a surly kid in headset and network bomber jacket complain about something. She was patching power cords into a rolling floor camera.

"Kind of a bad time right now," she said, casting a nervous eye at the kid. "You find anything?"

"I don't know." Wil held up the video box.

"Of course, it would be two-inch." Not looking back, she hurried him down a corridor to a smaller room with a glass panel in the door. In seconds she'd threaded the tape in one of the machines, turned on the monitor, pressed the PLAY button.

"I can't promise anything. This thing's on its last legs it's so old."

"What do I do?"

"Cross your fingers," she said on her way out. "Hit OFF if it starts chewing up the tape."

The machine groaned as it turned the spools, but the picture came up all right—on-location segments mostly, reporters commenting on unfolding developments. Denny being led in for questioning, shots of the Van Zant house, interviews with classmates Wil vaguely recalled, detectives updating the media, Kordell and Maeve looking haggard, the Marquez house much the same as yesterday.

A seven-inch black-and-white universe.

Then the shots he'd been waiting for: initial crime-scene coverage, night footage clearly the work of another photographer. Amateur looking and grainy, it was like an experimental noir film, close-ups and angles that distracted rather than compelled. Still, it had an honesty that matched the grim looks of the detectives, the wrenching expressions of the Marquez family as they responded to questions. Silent mouthings overdubbed by the commentary.

Wil stopped, reversed the tape, pushed PLAY: impossible to lip-read, given the state of the film. He tried several more times, then gave up and went back to the studio, found it dark, the set and cameras left in place for late news.

Kari Thayer was in her office. "I was just coming to find you," she said. "How'd it go?"

Wil told her about the film, asked what might have become of other footage from the first night, particularly if there'd been sound recorded.

She thought about it. "If the quality was that different, it was probably done by a freelancer. You come across any old film cans?"

"Nope."

"Quarter-inch sound tape?" She spread her hands to indicate the size of the box.

"Wouldn't they be in with the video stuff?"

"Probably not. If it wasn't used, it either wasn't good enough or the sound bites were off."

"Meaning?"

"Preempted because of what was said."

"What about outtakes?"

"Same with them." She swept hair off her face. "This new evidence you're looking for?"

"At this point you kind of go where it takes you. Listen, I appreciate your trouble, Ms. Thayer—"

"Kari."

"Kari. Thanks. Can I interest you in a quick pizza or something?"

"Nice idea, but I'm stuck here till sign-off. On the other hand, nobody'd stop you from having one sent up." She opened a drawer, handed him a take-out menu and the phone. "The Canadian-bacon-and-pineapple's killer."

After he'd ordered, he made a credit-card call, telling Trina he'd be in late, don't wait up. Hurry, she said, Celeste can only stay until midnight. Okay, he told her, just finishing up.

"Wife or girlfriend," Kari asked afterward.

"Very old friend."

"Serious?"

"Serious as it gets these days."

She looked at him. "Hot damn, I just had an off-the-wall thought. One last possibility."

the twenty-four-hour storage unit was tucked into a grouping of commercial buildings down the hill. Wil pulled in, scoped out the number matching the key Kari Thayer had given him, and tried the lock. It opened a Sheetrocked eight-by-twelve-foot windowless room, packed to the ceiling with dust-covered boxes and vented by louvered metal inserts. Light from a single low-watt bulb.

Two hours later he'd gone through about half of it: records, files, outdated forms; boxes of videotapes—old shows, station-sponsored community events, news coverage. Remains awaiting disposition, an invisible carryover on somebody's annual spreadsheet. Dust layered everything like a cheap effect; it got on his clothes, into his nose and lungs, swirled around the light until he had to take frequent breaks just to let it settle.

Midnight came and went, then one A.M., the night air at least cooling him during the breaks. At one-thirty, he heard the car phone, ran to pick up.

"Wil, where are you?"

"Stuck, Tree. Nothing to do but keep going." He explained where he was, the necessary vagueness of what he was doing, his explanation sounding lame even to him. "Are you okay?"

"Why wouldn't I be? Celeste takes off, you don't show, and every shadow's a bad guy. That's about it."

Wil heard a long swallow, glass on glass. "How's booze going to help?"

"Great, you getting righteous on me—that's all I need." She took a deep breath. "Wil, I'm scared."

"I know. Didn't the cops send a car by?"

"They said they'd do what they could. Pretty reassuring, huh?"

There was a click and a buzz, and it seemed to Wil as if the dust had followed him out to the car, making it hard to breathe there as well. He was heading back when an older-model Jetta turned into the lot and parked next to him.

Kari Thayer cut the lights and the engine and got out. "Doing any good?"

"Not in some circles. You get the station squared away?"

"Finally. Anything juicy turn up here?"

"Yeah, the history of TV. How come you're not home in bed?"

"I thought you could use another pair of hands. There's always hope, right?"

"Sure," he said. "Why not?"

It took another hour and a half for them to come up with it, a battered unmarked box within a larger one labeled ELEMENTS, KBTV NEWS, what seemed like the fiftieth of its kind. Taped to the film can rubber-banded to the quarter-inch tape box was a strip of yellowed masking tape with the notation: *Marquez Crime Scene 7/7/66/4:30 A.M./Nonstop Productions.*

Kari slid the bands off, peeled off film. "Sixteen-millimeter, non-sound," she said, appraising it. "The pieces of white tape indicate scenes removed that would correspond to those you saw on the video."

"There a way to view this at the station?"

"Nice try. Your best bet's a used-equipment store or a film-studies class. You'll need to splice those edits."

"What about the sound tape?"

"Just find a reel-to-reel. We have one, but it means coming back. It was down the last time I looked."

"And if I borrowed these?"

"Borrowed what?" she said.

He smiled at that, touched. "Might be taking a big chance. You know that, don't you?"

"Big deal. Problem with me is I haven't taken enough chances."

"Thanks, then."

"You're welcome."

They turned off the light and locked the door; as they were walking toward the cars she said, "It's not much, but I've got a spare bed and bath you'd be welcome to."

It was hugely tempting, the way he felt—bone weary, filthy from the dust, the pizza doing flip-flops. He checked his watch, saw almost four A.M.

"It's no trouble," she added. "Brian's at his dad's this week."

"That's really considerate, Kari, but I have to go. I'm way late as it is."

She nodded slowly, accepted the hand he offered. "You'll find the freeway that way, second signal. A block up, there's an all-nighter with fairly decent coffee." She smiled thinly. "Good luck. There's always hope, right?"

the man with the white hair and the scars on his face eased toward the house. He paused a moment to see if there was movement other than the television flickering through the upstairs window he knew to be her bedroom, then eased through a break in the outside lights.

He'd watched the security company roll up yesterday afternoon in their little van, walk the property with much pointing and nodding, make notes in their notebooks.

Made him want to laugh.

It wouldn't matter—nothing they could do that he hadn't seen before. Hardly more trouble than turning the key in a lock. Just the way he was doing now.

Seconds later he was at the foot of the stairs, satchel in hand and listening for his prey as a big cat might, every sense tuned to it. Picturing what was to come.

He found himself wishing he had more time.

Quietly he withdrew the cell phone and thumbed in a familiar number, heard it ring above him. Then he started up the stairs.

# 17

wil swallowed the last of his restaurant coffee, saw other drivers hoisting mugs and such as they drove, their eyes zoning out ahead of them. Even at four-thirty in the morning, the westbound lanes were nearly full, downtown workers getting a jump on the hour-plus commutes, truckers heading for their morning drops, car pools with the usual backseat zombies and sack-outs.

Living the dream.

He set the empty cup aside, fingered the tape box and film can on the seat beside him, the whole thing with Carmen Marquez and Denny feeling like some amorphous mass twisting and changing shape each time he looked at it.

*Marquez Crime Scene 7/7/66/4:30 A.M.*

*Nonstop Productions.*

Funny how certain he'd been about his friend's innocence back then, knowing him as he did. Close as brothers ever would be. But over the years something had crept in—Vietnam and the business he was in notwithstanding. The suspicion, reinforced daily, that people were capable of anything given the right circumstances. Just check the news.

Certainly the facts pled guilty: the fight with Carmen, scratches on Denny to prove it; a pregnant, short-fused girlfriend, Denny by all counts the last to see her alive.

Maybe the press actually had it right for once. And yet he refused to believe that—even now, not deep down; bleeding headlines and class hatred didn't make it so. Even the cops, straight-lining to their typical how-it-seems-is-the-way-it-is conclusions had no lock on the truth. Not that they weren't correct often enough.

Tire thump returned him to his own lane.

Then there was the Hawaii thing; the guy outside the hospital who'd called his room, known about Voelker in Nam. Same one who'd harassed Trina and broken into the house? Or was it somebody else, someone he didn't even dare hope about? And if by some twisted miracle it was Denny, why the subterfuge?

*There's always hope:* Kari Thayer.

He made a mental note to poke into some military records, try to flesh out the picture. This dancing with bones was getting tedious.

As he approached East L.A., traffic heavied, dropped in speed as the 60 crossed the 5. Then he was out of it, up and running toward the ocean, the sky paling in the rearview—blush of pink, hint of sun, then first blaze of light. He rolled down the window to get a preview of the day, punched up an all-news station, and in twenty minutes had enough dreck to last the week. At six-fifteen, he tried the house to let Trina know he'd be there in under half an hour, two rings so he wouldn't wake her completely in case she'd been able to fall asleep.

But the phone was busy.

It was busy all the way there, one explanation Trina taking it off the hook in case the caller had bothered her again. Another that she simply was talking with someone. Or a number of people.

This early?

Fighting unease, he angled in so Celeste could get around him when she showed up for work, then noticed her red Tercel through the open garage bay. Off at midnight, in by six? He got out, walked to the bay, and stepped inside, waited for his eyes to adjust.

Felt rather than saw the shape beyond the cars.

He found the light switch, flipped it on.

Celeste had not gone home; nor had she arrived early. She was hanging upside down from one of the beams, her face black from settled blood, torso covered with burn marks, a strip of the same wide silver tape that bound her wrists and ankles taped across her mouth. From the look of it, she'd been dead for hours.

*Son of a bitch.*

Wil rasped in deep breaths, told himself Trina was either alive or she wasn't. Don't make it worse by giving a killer the edge.

He drew the .45, armed it. Stepping outside into sunshine and birdsong, he edged around back, eased himself in with the key Trina'd given him, aware of his own sharp smell, his rapid pulse and breathing. Standing in the foyer, he listened for long seconds, heard nothing, saw a phone extension, and raised the receiver.

No tone.

He did a fast scan of the downstairs, found nothing, and headed up, gun sweeping for targets as he went. Upper landing: all quiet. Every room but hers: nothing out of place thus far. Outside her door now, heart pounding: He dropped to one knee, listened, twisted the knob, and shoved inward.

Still nothing . . . nothing . . .

He saw the bathroom door closed, heard the light sound of water behind it. Same drill, desperately fighting the urge to kick it in. Easing it open instead.

It was a big bathroom and not much light, but he spotted her immediately. Water trickled from the spa's gold fixtures, and as it did, Trina's face hovered just above the rising surface, every muscle taut and straining to keep herself from drowning.

Before Wil shouldered the gun, cut the cords binding her, pulled her out and the tape off, her eyes revealing glints of things best forgotten, he saw the words scrawled on her forehead in bloodred lipstick:

*I'm this close.*

"He showed me Polaroids of what he'd done to her," Trina was saying, the horror still lurking in her voice like a half-skinned animal. Recounting it again after the sheriff's people had taken their statements, danced with the details in seeming slow motion, dusted the lipstick holder and the bedroom-bathroom for prints Wil knew wouldn't exist, left finally after the van bearing Celeste had eased away.

"What kind of *person* would do that?"

He shook his head I-don't-know. But they're out there, he wanted to say—the cross-wireds and the short-outs. Lovers of their work.

They were sitting outside under the big umbrella, Trina on one of the lounges, Wil figuring the bright day and sunlit pool, the view might act as distractions. But it was as if a chain-saw movie played ceaselessly behind her eyes, and he couldn't reach the switch. She fumbled in her bag for more pills, knocked them back with the vodka she'd poured after the last detective, the one in charge named Ethridge, closed the doors behind him.

"I'd doubt they're finished yet," Wil said. "Maybe you should throttle back."

"Maybe you should mind your own business—it didn't happen to you. You weren't here, remember?"

"I remember."

She looked at her hands as though they belonged to someone else.

He gave it a minute, until she'd settled back against the upright. "Okay if I ask you something?"

She nodded.

"When they questioned you about the writing, what did you say?"

"What do you mean, what did I say?"

"I mean any detail could be important."

She took a breath. "He told me it was a message for Denny. That he'd tried to get where Denny was out of Celeste first, then me. Celeste didn't tell him anything, so he killed her."

Wil said nothing, just looked at her.

"What . . . ?"

"That's it?"

"Of course, that's it. What do you think?"

"I think it's the wrong time to hold back, Tree."

"I don't believe this. The son of a bitch nearly killed me. Don't you think I'd have told him something if I knew?"

"Did he say why he thought Denny was alive?"

"No, and I didn't ask. He's crazy. Wil, why are you *doing* this?"

"Because 'I'm this close' means no more phantom calls or break-ins. It's like he's under pressure to make something happen."

"For God's sake, what?"

Spinning cherry thoughts that wouldn't land. "I don't know."

She drained her vodka, stared at the horizon; light flared from the pool and splashed little moving reflections on the umbrella's underside.

*Get it together*. A thought flashed: "Denny must have sent stuff back from overseas. Did you or your mom save any of it?"

She pondered, but he could see the booze and pills were making it increasingly difficult to focus. "Mail or photos, souvenirs—like that."

"Hold on, I'm trying to think," she said with annoyance. "Three households, I have no idea where the letters are he sent me. Mom must have something." Measured words, on the verge of slurring.

"Any idea where she'd have kept them?"

He waited as she yawned, tilted her head back, closed her eyes.

"Tree?"

"Feels good." She sighed. "*So goood . . .*"

Wil went inside, got a blanket and pillow, arranged them and the umbrella so it shaded her. Then he went to work on the house.

He spent an hour going through Maeve's room, strangely untouched, as though no one in the family had dealt with her passing. Odd nothing turning up, he thought, prime turf to find mementos from a treasured son. But nothing, not a letter. He broadened the search to storage closets, built-in wood cabinets with doors, upright files, and open shelves. Even the den yielded nothing.

Two hours down.

Moving to the storage side of the garage, he checked some cartons he'd seen before, then a metal cabinet backed up and bolted to the far wall. Locked. Resisting the impulse to use a crowbar, he ran a hand over the sides, the bottom, the dusty top, and found what he was hoping would be there—keys on a twisted piece of wire. The lazy man's security system.

Large boxes inside. Then a smaller, unmarked one behind some others—as though exiled from the house, he thought, opening it.

Part of its contents were effects the Marines would have sent home, others were pure whim: pens and watches, swizzle sticks from GI watering holes, painted mugs, air-force-style sunglasses, a dragon-embroidered silk jacket, disk of hard-caked surfboard wax, photos of a trim, into-it-looking Denny—some with Vietnamese bar girls, others while doing laundry or cleaning his weapons. One with him in shorts, holding a beat-up surfboard while a promising break formed up beyond white sand.

*Damnit.*

He found a stack of letters and opened them carefully, absorbed the words in the warm, still garage, dust from the cartons spinning in the shafts of light and the pungent smell of oil and rubber evocative of another time in his life. He found the same complaints about heat and humidity, insects and monsoons, boredom and savagery *he* used to write home about; the usual proscribed vagueness concerning places and operations. Surfing was unreal, the young girls and kids friendly, the countryside breathtaking and undeserving of war, the enemy cunning and hard to engage.

Echo Company's chain of command drew fire. The old man—a just-promoted major named Kuykendall—was "BC" to the grunts, aka "Body Count"; the XO, a spit-and-polish type, was "Candy Bowers." A second lieutenant named Neves showed up as a guy you could talk to, get loaded with. Most NCOs—Korean War vets and new-blood lifers—weren't that sharp, but knew their shit in the field. Standard stuff, fatigue and resentment harder to disguise in some letters than in others.

Wil took note of the names.

Then there was the artificial cheeriness about time passing and not to worry, more danger crossing PCH on a Sunday. Hoping the money he'd sent Carmen's family hadn't been returned. That his father might have mentioned being proud of him.

Laird's words reverberated: *some fucking waste*, no argument from Wil. He was putting the letters back in the envelope when a black-and-white photo he'd missed fell out. Three men, their expressions pre-action serious: Denny, a soldier he didn't recognize, and one he did after studying the face. Out of habit, he flipped it over, saw:

*Me, John, and Roy. Phu Bai. 1967.*

Same handwriting as the letters.

The John he didn't recognize, but the Roy was unmistakable: Voelker—right-side-up, thirty years younger, and alive.

Wil slipped the photo into his shirt pocket, closed up the storage cabinet, and stepped out into the sunshine.

## 18

**eric van zant** watched the man with the scarred face and the white hair enter his outer office, scrutinize the Remington bronzes, the paintings, the two-way mirror, smile slightly into it, then look away. He slid the Jasper Johns lithograph back into place across the mirror and buzzed the receptionist.

"Send him in," he told her. "Then take the rest of the day."

As she was thanking him he cut her off, put on his suit coat, stood behind his big desk. Not quite right. He moved to the floor-to-ceiling window overlooking Santa Monica and the ocean. That was it, arms folded, facing the view. The vision thing. Man among men.

The door hissed shut; Eric was able to pick up his visitor's reflection momentarily in the window. He let a few beats go by before turning to face him.

Not there.

As Eric's eyes swept the room his high-backed desk chair swung around to face him. Irritation flamed on his neck, lit his ears: The man's hands were resting on the arms as if they belonged there, one leg at ease over the other. Relaxed looking: olive gabardine suit, blue shirt, batik tie. Even the scars looked at home.

In *his* chair.

"Good to meet you finally," the man said in an odd dry voice, the smile there, but no move to shake hands. "I believe you know who I am."

Late forties to early sixties, Eric guessed, somewhere in that bracket; hard to date him with that hair. Tall and lean and tightly coiled. That was it—a snake in a business getup.

"That depends," Eric said, unfazed by his observation.

"John Pomphrey, Euphrates Limited." British? No, more like Australian; by his tone, no offense taken at Eric's abruptness. "We've been crypto-networking back and forth; that is, my group has. Are we safe talking here?"

"We own the damn building," Eric replied.

"Not exactly material for certain ears, would you say?"

Like the guy who did those shrimp-on-the-barby ads, the same inflections. "It's clean. I'll vouch for security."

"Your future." The man shrugged. He drew out a computer disk. "Everything's here. Also delineated is what happens after your—after Kordell Van Zant's removal from power. The disk is coded against intrusion. Save for the one we have, it's the only copy. Is that understood?"

No percentage in answering a patronizing question like that, so he ignored it, savoring instead the little flush at the words *removal from power*. As though he'd taken niacin. "You'll appreciate why I want to view it now."

The man spread long, slim fingers—*be my guest*, as if to say.

Eric went to his desk, waited for the man to vacate his chair; for a second he thought he wasn't going to, but then Pomphrey rose and moved to the window. Eric sat down, feeling no warmth from the man's residual presence. He popped the disk in, entered the code, waited while the data came up on his laptop.

"This amount is different than we discussed," he said.

"You're referring to your compensation."

"It's almost double. Is that a mistake?"

"Perhaps in some minds. Not in ours."

The heat had reached Eric Van Zant's scalp now; he ran a hand across it, felt dampness. "And this changes nothing in the arrangement? My overall place in things?"

"See for yourself."

Eric scrolled farther, his velocity and comprehension the product of Southern California's first speed-reading clinic. Second nature by now.

"As you see," Pomphrey said from the window, "Euphrates has certain expectations for the firm. We believe in expressing our gratitude to the person or persons who realize them."

"And if for some reason they don't?"

The Aussie slipped into a guest chair, his smile noncommittal. "Why think that way? In addition to your staples, our people are impressed with your personal experiments into growth hormones and chemical behavior modification. Given our Asian distribution channels, we see only upside."

"I assume you've read the entire report."

Pomphrey adjusted his tie. "The vet deaths? We're not worried about that. It's the big picture that concerns us."

"You haven't answered my question."

Dark eyes zeroed in. "All right. In the event expectations are not met, we recalculate. In our business, many things are factored in, not just profits."

"Respectability, you mean."

The smile froze. "Not a word I'd have chosen, so let's be clear. We're used to returns sizably above your own. Certain methods we employ permit this. As chief executive officer, you'll participate in the rewards. It's all there."

And it was. Putting a damper on his initial annoyance, Eric ejected the disk, pocketed it, leaned back from the computer. Time for a little demonstration of leadership himself.

"Tell me . . . John. What is your position within the triad?"

"I don't remember using that term."

"I did."

"Euphrates is a legitimate—"

"It's a facade for an international drug cartel. Who do you think you're dealing with?"

John Pomphrey folded his fingers. "We believe a business either evolves or it dies. As we're now involved in luxury automobiles and high-technology items acquired for offshore customers—in addition to our bread and butter—we prefer the term 'group.' Tell me if that doesn't sit well with you."

Eric was aware of his sweat beginning to cool.

Hearing no comeback, Pomphrey went on: "My current role is to facilitate, that's all you need to know. I will add, the improvement in your situation was at my suggestion."

This was not going at all as he'd planned, Eric thought. The son of a bitch was preempting him. Just like the old man did.

"I sense confusion here," Pomphrey said. "Why is that?"

Eric took a breath, tried to regain his momentum. "Facilitate," he said caustically. "The spic girl's dead, my sister is almost killed, the police are involved. By whose order, for Christ's sake? If that's what you call planning, this may not be a good match."

Now he was rolling; cut this pompous ass off at the knees.

John Pomphrey rose from the chair, returned to the window.

"Such an amazing view," he said. "All those people down there running around. You ever think about that, Eric?"

"Is there a point to this? I'm very busy."

"There is for the wise businessman. Come over here, and I'll demonstrate."

From where he was, Pomphrey's eyes seemed lidless, unblinking; Eric felt a tremor of something resembling fear. Which made him doubly determined not to show it. He stood and went to the window. And suddenly he was aware of only floor-to-ceiling glass between him and a twenty-story drop.

"Look down there. Long way to fall, wouldn't you agree?"

"Which proves what?"

Pomphrey lightly placed a hand at the base of Eric's neck. "What separates you from them is the risk you're willing to take. Otherwise we wouldn't be talking. Agreed?"

"So?"

"So when all that's between you and a drop like that is this fragile"—he tapped the tinted thermal pane with his free hand, his fingernails making a thin brittle sound—"it's wise not to start throwing bricks. Do you get my point now?"

The sweat was back—hands, back, brow, all over. He figured it was best to nod, so he did.

Pomphrey's voice lowered, lost its salesmanship. "Hear me, sport. We play for keeps. Big risk, big reward—for all involved. But when this much is at stake, impediments become ex-impediments."

Eric's mouth was far too dry to risk speaking.

"Present company excepted, of course. But need I remind you of one that remains?"

This was getting out of hand; he tried leaning back from the window, but Pomphrey held firm. Seemingly without effort.

"Hello, Eric . . ."

"No," Eric said finally—all he could muster.

"Good. But since we're new to one another, I'm going to validate your question with an answer. Timing is everything in this. The maid was an object lesson to your sister. Your sister was an object lesson to your brother. Your brother—whom we have no choice but to assume is alive, even if he isn't—is a threat to you." He released his grip, smoothed Eric's shirt.

"There. See how easy it is when you keep your wits?"

Eric nodded. He even managed to keep what churned inside him hidden until the Aussie had left by the VIP elevator. Seconds after the door hissed shut, however, Eric was slamming up the toilet seat in his private washroom and bending over the bowl.

**lannie crowell** shook hands with the hotel's managing director, a balding, intense man with a European accent right out of a flavored-coffees ad. PR seemed to be his function, sending Lannie off with the real operatives. Following the resident manager now, plus the director of security and head of engineering, Lannie could smell the lingering scent of the managing director's fop cologne. He was tempted to go wash his hands, but resisted the urge. Instead he strolled the premises, getting the full treatment, how glad they were Van Zant Inc. had selected the Azure Bay for its annual shareholders meeting. Sure it would be a mutually profitable association.

On and on.

Already there was a buzz about Kordell's forthcoming announcement, business weeklies and trade journals fanning the speculation. Bits of chum to trigger a feeding frenzy.

Lannie was aware of the openmouthed looks from guests unused to a physique like his. Let alone a down-dressed brother commanding such deference from three impeccably suited white guys. "So," he said as they cruised plush carpet that must have cost a good eighty bucks a yard. "The Oceana Room. Tell me about it."

Kordell had made the selection twelve months ago, of course. But Lannie figured what the hell, no harm in milking the deference angle, only half listening to the pitch as they approached polished wood doors the head of engineering hastened to pull open for him.

Chandeliers and paneling, round tables with white cloths, massive video screen, no windows to distract: The room *was* good. Now Lannie went to work, questions about emergency exits and guest-check procedures, security systems in place, screening of employees, advance list of who'd work the function. Questions about the computerized a/v stuff he couldn't resist asking.

They were inspecting kitchen access when his cell phone went off, Lannie saying to the trio, "We about done here?" after he'd answered it, heard who it was. Shaking hands in turn and watching them leave him to the Oceana Room and Kordell Van Zant.

"Yes sir, I'm alone now," he said into the flip part. Feeling sheepish at the vibes the empty room was giving him, remembering that scene in *The Shining*—Jack Nicholson cracking up, seeing things in this big haunted snowbound resort hotel. Spooky as hell.

And cut: ". . . trouble at the house," Kordell was saying—on the road, from the sounds of traffic in the background. "Some soon-to-be-dead SOB murdered that little Mexican maid and nearly drowned my daughter."

"Jesus," Lannie said. "She okay?"

"Self-sedated as usual, but all right. I need you to get up there."

After thirty years Lannie still marveled at the man's control; somebody nearly killed *his* kid, he'd have been climbing the walls. By the tone of his voice, all in a day's work for Kordell Van Zant.

"Hardesty's up there with her," he added.

"Wide Trac? What's he doing there?"

"I want him out of the picture, Lannie. Is that understood?"

"Sure. How badly?"

"Just get it done."

"Right. Shame about the Latina. Who do they think did it?"

"Some psycho—no idea beyond that. Sounds like he was after information about my son."

"About Eric?"

"No, Lannie, not Eric." There was a pause, a sounding of horns, then Kordell was back on, an edge to his voice. "Is there anything you might have left out about Hawaii? About Denny or that man Voelker?"

Recalling the guy hanging there in the tree, Lannie felt a lurch and righted it—thirty years of trust gone if it came out he lied, why he did still bouncing around in his head.

"Nothing that comes to mind."

"But Voelker admitted it was a scam when you saw him?"

*Braided nylon rope creaking, black flies laying eggs in the man's entrails.* "That's what he told me."

"Nothing else?"

"No, sir."

"Well, try and recall something. And while you're at it watch Eric's back for me, starting now. You never know."

"Yes, sir. And the thing with Hardesty? Don't give it another thought."

Lannie clicked off in response to Kordell's breaking the connection. Putting the phone back in its holder, he was aware of a piped-in Carpenters instrumental oozing from the ceiling speakers, whisper of conditioned air, tightness in his jaw, hot wetness on his palms.

Wil handed Trina her double-strength, added milk to his own. She had the look of someone just emerging from sleep—defocused eyes, blank stare, slack puffy face. Navy sweatshirt over jeans. He waited, checked the wall clock: almost two.

Halfway through it, she said dully, "I can't stay here."

"I know some private security people. They can be here tonight."

"No—I'd still feel him everywhere."

"Do you have someplace you can go?"

She shook her head, stared into her mug.

"What about your exes?"

"The only one who'd have me is number two, and I won't expose my kids to this."

He was about to say something when she met his eyes.

"Period," she said. "End of discussion."

"All right. How about friends?"

"That might work if I had some."

"Still the poor little rich girl."

"Don't make fun, Wil, I'm not up to it. And hand me that decanter, will you?"

"I don't think so," he said. "You want to hit the reef, go for it. But don't ask me to open the cocks for you."

She tried a hard glare that dissolved and broke off, got up and came back with the decanter, slopped vodka into her coffee, and raised the mug. Turned away, blinking. "*God,*" she said, lowering it. "It smells like turpentine."

"Probably have a similar effect on the pills you took."

"Can't you just be my friend?" She pushed the mug and the decanter away, looked tired and sick, and his heart went out to her.

"I am, Tree. It's just that I've seen the same shuck before—too many times in the mirror."

"So what do I do?"

"*We* do, remember? I forgot you're nearsighted as well."

She hesitated. Then her face softened and she put a hand on his—a light touch that set something off inside him.

"What about Celeste?" she asked.

"The police are notifying her relatives."

"I want to do something. *What*, I don't know, but something."

"There's time," he said. "But about now, what about your dad's place? Or Eric's?"

"We'd kill each other in twenty-four hours, most likely less. I'm not kidding."

Half a minute passed, in muted clicks from the battery-driven wall clock; finally he said, "There's always my place. It's not much, but you're welcome to it."

"Too far."

"Yeah? Too far from what?"

Her eyes left his face. Clutching her sweatshirt, she rocked back and forth on the kitchen stool. "I told you, I can't be alone right now. How about if we just drive?"

**lannie** waited for the connection to go through, a feeling he knew how this conversation was going to go.

Kordell picked up. "We secure up there?"

"Not exactly, boss."

"Meaning what?"

"Meaning everything's locked up tight, but they're not here."

"Maybe they're down talking to the police, or shopping. Any number of things."

"Not from the note in the mailbox." Lannie flipped up the folded paper, read him the part about requesting a hold on delivery until further notice.

"Shit," Kordell Van Zant said. *"Son of a bitch."*

Lannie watched a woman neighbor look up from her pruning as though she'd heard the profanity clear over there. He waved and she turned away with a suspicious look before going back inside.

"I can see her car in the garage," he said. "But his Pontiac's gone."

"All right," Kordell said at length, a forced calm Lannie knew well. "Nothing's changed. You'll just have to work harder."

"Sir?"

"At finding them. Get in the game, for Christ's sake."

Lannie gripped the phone tighter as he walked. "I'll check out this La-something-or-other place where he lives. Maybe they've gone there."

"Waste of time, Lannie, there's nothing they can do from there. Think why she hired him in the first place."

"Right."

"And what's at stake—for everyone. Do you get my meaning?"

"I get your meaning."

"Then why are we still talking?"

"With all due respect, sir, is there a chance you might be wrong about this guy? Maybe if you offered him money . . ."

"I'm not wrong, Lannie."

"I thought he was an old friend."

"Why am I not getting through to you? I want her back and this guy on the sidelines. However you have to do it."

"What about the other dude? The one that hurt her?"

"Him definitely, but first things first—nobody fucks with my family. You of all people should know that."

# 19

"this is like going back in time," Trina said as they parked across from the old Marquez place. Four-thirty after their trip down through Sunday traffic, the bright day had retreated into a standoff with the coming twilight. Kids on bikes, noisy swallows darting through the cooling light and shadow, zipped over the raised sidewalks and worn asphalt of Huerta Street.

She raised an arm to show him goose bumps. "Don't you feel it?"

Wil nodded, not wanting to minimize her feelings. But having been here once already, the truth was he'd been thinking more that Sunday meant nobody'd be open or around to play Kari Thayer's sound tape, sync up the crime-scene edits. Nobody at the license bureaus to check into Nonstop Productions. Longshots, but something—like the neighbor who hadn't been home. Two days and forever ago.

"Stay warm," he said, getting out of the Bonneville. "I'll wave if he's inside."

The door to the neighbor's house was under an overhang that

prevented rain from reaching a line of distressed-looking bushes. It was further concealed by a black screen and crosshatched aluminum bars. He knocked, rang the bell. Knocked again. Rang and knocked.

Nothing.

A peek through sun-faded drape backing showed an unlit living room, threadbare sectional and recliner, folded-out newspaper over one arm. Wil shook his head toward the car, motioned he was going across the street, saw her put a hand to her mouth as he approached the old Marquez place.

The main door was open; drifting through the screen, kitchen noises, the aroma of roast, small-sounding footsteps in response to the bell. Then the boy stood looking up at him with wide dark eyes. Wil smiled, was about to say something when the boy giggled and ran back the way he'd come.

"*Mama—vengate.*"

But it was his father who came to the door.

"From a couple days ago," Wil said.

"Sure," the man said. "Any luck across the street?"

"No. And I was wondering if you'd seen him, what his name was—that is, if you don't mind."

The boy materialized behind his father; reflexively, the father's hand dropped to the boy's head.

"Avenal. Joe Avenal. He drives an old Caddy."

"You've seen him?"

"Just after you left."

"But you have no idea where he goes?"

"I didn't—until Estéban and I tried a new place for ice cream last night. You know the neighborhood at all?"

"Some," Wil said.

"Turn right at the next street, follow it to the stoplight, keep going till you hit Golden West. Art's Bar. And if I know this guy, which I don't really, he's probably there now." He held a thumb and little finger out, cocking it back and forth. "Get it?"

Wil nodded. Late-afternoon light fading outside pick-your-poison bars, one name blurring into another; neon curlicues humming above dead-fly windowsills. Straight shots and cold beers, the numbing slide into night. A very long night, as it turned out.

"Thanks. I appreciate it."

"What's this about anyway? The guy in trouble?"

"No. Just some questions I had about a thing that happened a long time ago." He smiled at Estéban, said, *"Hasta luego, hombre,"* and left to laughter that carried him down the walk, all the way across the street.

**art's bar** anchored one wing of a low-end cinderblock mini-mall. Airborne grit had worked itself into the textured yellow front, the stark rectangular sign, the markings dogs had made around a headless faucet. Visible inside the glass door was an L-shape buffer of paneling covered with printed announcements. Next to the Bonneville, the only other vehicles at that end of the lot were a blue Ford pickup and an early-model Seville, black with oxidized patches on the hood.

As Wil shut off the engine Trina reached for her door handle.

"Not a good idea," he said. "Two people are more intimidating than one. Plus we have no idea who we're dealing with."

"But I want to come in."

"I'll try not to be too long."

"You're afraid I'll drink."

"I'm afraid of spooking this guy and not getting a second chance. Cut me some slack here, okay?"

"Sorry. I'm not feeling very well."

"Hang in, kid. You're the designated backup."

He squeezed her arm, drew a smile, felt her eyes follow him as he opened the glass door and eased around the divider—into dim light and "American Pie" finishing up on the juke, a middle-aged black man shelving liquor bottles. The other occupants were a denim-clad couple at one of the tables and a heavyset mid-fifties type leaning on his elbows, a half-full draft and a dish of bar mix in front of him on the counter.

The faces regarded him briefly, then swung back. "Drift Away" came up, the Dobie Gray version.

Wil ordered club soda, change in quarters for a five. He went over to the box and, after deliberating, fed it the quarters, punching up a dozen Top 40 hits from an all-seventies retro playlist.

As he came back the barkeep gave him a nod. "Every bit helps."

"Nothing like the good stuff, is there?" He half emptied his drink.

"Got that right," the barkeep said. "You from around here."

"Used to be. Back when most of it wasn't here. Just a sleepy little beach town."

The heavyset man finished his beer, tapped the counter. As the keep was pouring him a fresh one, he said without looking over, "Great place to live then."

Wil just nodded.

"When were you here?"

He caught the man's eyes in the mirror. "Sixties, mid to late. I went to school just down the road. You?"

"Born here and never left. Makes me wonder sometimes—motherfuckers shoot your ass off now, you say some'n they don't like. Hell, even if you do."

Wil speculated on how long he'd been drinking; from the slur, long enough. Broach or schmooze? Play to the guy, he decided, see what came of it.

"Not much of an improvement, is it?"

"That's the understatement of the year."

The barkeep poured out a pair of Black Russians and took them over to the denim table, then went back to replenishing condiments at the far end of the bar.

"Trouble is, nobody gives a damn anymore," the man said. "Too busy or some'n—kids running wild in the street, nobody saying no. Didn't used to be like that."

"Bad, Bad Leroy Brown" began playing, the man humming along with the opening. "Now, there's a song. Imagine how big Jim Croce would have been."

Wil nodded. "Our loss."

The man extended a hand across two stools. "Joe Avenal," he said.

"Wil Hardesty." He shook the hand.

"Music's an example. Try finding something decent these days."

"Forget it."

"Nothing like this stuff. *Damn.*"

For a moment they just listened to the song bridge and cycle, Croce and the backups wail on the chorus. Wil waved at the bartender, nodded as he moved to get the refills.

"*Prosit,*" Joe Avenal said as the keep set glasses down. He lifted his, took quick swigs. "Man after my own heart."

"*Prosit.*"

"So. What do you do?"

"I fix things for people," Wil said. "Some of this, a little of that. Not much money, but I like it. You?"

"Railroad worker, or used to be before de-reg. Got a class-action suit filed, but I'll probably be dead before the lawyers turn loose of it."

"The bad guys always find a way to skate."

"No argument from me."

On the box, Stealers Wheel slid into "Stuck in the Middle with You." Avenal tossed off his beer, nodded at the selection, tapped out the rhythm on the counter. Wil waved for refills, laid a twenty on the counter, let some time pass.

"Speaking of headlines," he said, "you remember that murder? Right around the time I left. Rich kid did his pregnant girlfriend and got off." In the mirror, he watched the party mood slide from Joe Avenal's face.

"Rule one," Wil added. "Have the bread, you make your own rules."

Avenal's eyes went to his beer.

Wil said, "You around here for that circus?"

"Yeah, you could say that."

"Should have lynched the punk, you want my opinion. So what happens? He walks, just like that. I mean look at the—"

"Maybe you shouldn't believe everything you hear."

"Mockingbird" came up, Avenal brightening enough to pound some out with the Taylors. He waved at the keep. "Mind if I get something to chase this with? Beer tastes stale after a while."

"Your call," Wil said.

Avenal ordered a straight shot and the keep put it down. Whiskey fumes swirled around Wil's face—a feather boa laced with razor blades. He eased the shot over.

"What's that mean, I shouldn't believe everything I hear?"

"About that kid. I mean maybe he didn't do it."

"And you lived here—followed that thing like I did?" Incredulity bordering on derision. "Sorry if I act surprised."

Avenal knocked back half the shot, poured the rest in with his beer. He looked at the denims, moony now, their heads nearly joined, glanced at the barkeep busy washing glasses. He pointed to his eyes. "You see these?"

Wil nodded, saw also starburst veins, strawberry nose, stroke-in-the-making flush.

"I seen that kid leave her house, the one you're talking about. Saw the one later, too."

"The hell you say." Conspiratorial.

"I'm tellin' you, that girl was alive when the one kid left. There she is, big as life, lookin' out the window. Shootin' daggers at him."

"No way."

"Whaddaya think, I'm makin' it up? Twenty-one years old I was, livin' at home. *Across the fuckin' street.*"

"You lived—"

"Told you I seen it. You believe me now?"

Wil nodded grudgingly, new respect. "So what about this later one? Young, old, boy, girl—what?"

Avenal drank, wiped his mouth. "Didn't get a make on 'em, just a look-see. See, I was gettin' down with some 'ludes and shit in my room, and after that I kind of nod out. Next thing I know, there's cop cars all over the place. Scared the hell outta me, I'll—"

"You tell the police any of this?"

"After doin' drugs in my own house? My old man woulda killed me if he'd known, regular TV preacher without the TV. I was already on probation for selling weed. Deal was, I could live at home if I went straight."

"So you said nothing."

"Right then, anyway. But it got to be too much, the fuck-over this kid was gettin' in the press. So I went and told 'em what I seen." He finished his beer and chaser.

"And?" Wil about ready to tear it out of him.

"This one cop, he listens for a while. Then he calls me a junkie, unreliable, and if I bother him again, my parole's history. Next thing I know, the kid's out and in the service or something."

"That's it?"

Avenal shrugged. "Figured it was the old man's money got him off, but this time it was okay, see? What could I add? I'd tried, right?"

Wil said nothing.

"You do see that?"

"Yeah, I see it."

"More'n likely he's retired by now, this fat pension comin' in." He made wet zigzags with the shot glass. "Woulda been me if I'd been smart."

Wil looked at nothing, saw a serious-eyed man-child, M-16 in hand, looking back at him from another world. After a bit he noticed the couple had left, Joe Avenal's glass had stopped moving, Trina peering at him from behind the divider, *how much longer?* written on her face.

He stood up, tossed another twenty on the remaining bills. "What the hell, Joe, live it up," he said. "Friend of mine's paying."

He was nearly to the door when the juke started in on "Time in a Bottle."

**they** ate fish-and-chips at a diner on the pier, not tasting much beyond the first few bites. After speculation by Trina about Joe Avenal's story getting the case reopened, Wil talking her down with what it took to *get* a case reopened—let alone on the testimony of a Joe Avenal—the night wound down to them watching a restless surge roll up on the beach. Sunday strollers, their numbers thinned by the lateness and the coming workday, passed by their window as though reluctant to call it a weekend.

He remembered the photo in his pocket, handed it to her, watched the smile form and fade as she took in Denny, gently touched his image.

"Where did you get this?"

"The garage," he said. "Locked away in a storage cabinet with some letters and things."

She let her finger slide along the deckle edge, her eyes up to Wil's. "My father's idea of a clean break. I remember him telling Mom one night it wasn't healthy to dwell on Den, that she had to go forward. You see what I mean about him?"

"Maybe he had his reasons."

*"Oh, please."*

He reversed it so she could read the back. "Are these names familiar to you?"

"No."

"So you don't recognize the soldiers with him?"

She turned it back over, looked more closely. Blanched.

"What is it?"

"This one in the hat and sunglasses. He—"

"John."

Her eyes left the image, drifted back to it. She swallowed.

"What is it, Tree?"

"I don't—"

"It's okay. Whatever you're thinking."

"Last night . . ."

"What? The guy from last night?"

"With scars on his face, it could be. But the hat and sunglasses . . . I think so, but . . ." She shook her head. "*Damn.* Not much help, am I?"

"Better than nothing. Don't worry about it, we'll get there."

She touched Denny's face again. "He looks so perfect, doesn't he? Like he owned the world."

"Maybe he did for a while." Wil finished flat lemon-lime. "How about a walk? Get some fresh air."

She nodded, and he put the picture back in his pocket, buttoned the flap. He held the door for her and they stepped out into chill air, the likelihood of rain. As they walked she took his arm, her closeness warming him. They nibbled mints he'd bought at the register, found a bench at the end of the pier, and settled in, the surge less apparent in the deeper water, more a quiet pulse.

"Do you think this Joe Avenal actually saw Carmen's killer?"

Wil said, "I think he thinks he did, and living there puts him where he could have. Who knows how much of it's drugs and booze?"

"*Because* of what he saw, maybe?"

"Possibly."

"Why didn't the cops take it seriously?"

"The source, I imagine."

She was silent.

"Right, I don't buy it either. Just because nobody else in the neighborhood saw anything at that hour doesn't mean Avenal didn't."

"So why, then?" she said.

"I don't know. But he's definitely haunted by it."

"Not enough."

A night bird veered into the light, screeched once crossing the pier, and faded into darkness.

Wil said, "Time took care of any credibility he ever had. Besides, he thinks he did do something and nobody listened."

"He should have talked louder."

"That occurred to me once or twice."

"So what now?"

"See if we can find something to corroborate it," he said. "About all we can do."

"And if we don't?"

"We keep going. We've got the stuff from the TV station. And there's always tomorrow—the private eye's pal."

She looked up at him. "Any chance I might be a private eye's pal?"

"It's a short list." He leaned over and kissed cold nose, cold cheeks, cold lips, felt it come back, the taste of mint and chocolate, her hair as it brushed his face. He kissed her again, this time longer and harder.

"Just like 1966," she said as they came up for breath.

"Better," he said. "Mintier."

"You know what I mean."

"I think so. You want to find a cheap motel?"

"If we can't find an expensive one."

they took the first vacancy they saw, an older L-shaped place on a sidestreet up from the beach. Patched carpet over a slab floor, worn curtains over balky windows, faded colorprint of poppies over a too-hard bed. The gas heater smelled of dust when Trina worked the thermostat, and the plastic curtain leaked, so that after they'd showered, Wil had to put the spare towel down.

None of it mattered.

Pulses racing by the time they dried each other off and rolled into bed, they kissed, fondled, coupled as though there was no tomorrow and no yesterday, both running on empty, finishing in a rush what they'd started on the pier. And afterward, winding down with the fading *tick-tick-tick* of the cooling heater. Floating away to the sound of rain.

Wil woke from dead asleep to an empty bed, the bathroom light on as they'd left it. After a moment to get his bearings, he called her name, heard silence, got up and checked, his need to use the bathroom forgotten in not finding her.

Only shadows.

Trying not to heed his inner alarm, he put on his pants, found the .45 where he'd left it and the room undisturbed as far as he could tell. He checked his watch: four-twenty A.M. Parting the drapes a crack, he looked out at the last of the rain wheeling through floods at each end of the building, the lot empty save for two cars well down from their unit and the Bonneville just outside the office.

Where he saw her.

She was at the pay phone, canted slightly away from him, one arm against the wall for support. Despite the drizzle, he could see smoke rising from her cigarette. Her head was angled down, lips seeming to brush the mouthpiece as she talked.

# 20

**monday** dawned the color of unset cement, the streets of Huntington Beach still wet from last night's rain. Trina had slipped out around seven for coffee, back with capped paper cups and a good-morning kiss just as he was getting up—something he could get used to, he told himself. Last night he'd felt her come back to bed and feigned sleep, deciding to let it go. No real point, beyond the friction it would cause—her for being challenged, him not wanting to see a lie in her face. Assuming the worst, of course.

No reason for that, he rationalized. None whatever.

Still, by the time they got organized and walked to a breakfast place nearby, it was gnawing like his hunger. To the point where he had to bring it up.

The hour, of course, she told him, looking mildly surprised. Not wanting to wake him after forgetting she was supposed to check in with her mother's attorney, who had a practice in New York. It was about the settlement, nagged at her as she lay in bed, drove her to call. Much later than seven-thirty Eastern Time and she'd have missed the guy altogether.

And was there anything else on his mind?

Just how to put that restless energy to work more productively; he smiled—enjoying the wink she gave him back. Thinking how good she looked as he left to use the restaurant's pay phone. Gone was the worry of yesterday, the bags and pallid color that went with what she'd been through. She was back and it showed.

Dialing, waiting, then: "Hello."

"Hi, Leese, I forgot to call. You hear anything yet?"

"Not so far."

"It *was* Friday, though, right?"

"Yes, but that's typical. Waiting for the IRS is like waiting for the lab to tell you about a biopsy."

"So maybe no news is good news?"

"That's the bright side," she said. "Where are you?"

"Huntington Beach on business. Why?"

"A police detective called here earlier." She paused. "Have you done something?"

"Not that I know of. What did he want?"

"For me to call him if I heard from you." She spelled the name, Buckhalter, read him the phone number. "When I asked, he said it was important."

Wil said nothing. Whatever the cops were or weren't to a private license, having them after you was not one of the good things. If that's what it was.

"Wil, I'm going to sound like a broken record, but—"

"Thanks, Leese, I'll handle it. And good luck on the other thing."

Hanging up, he put in a call to Huntington Beach PD, gave his name, and asked for Buckhalter. Heard the detective was away from his desk, but they'd page him. A moment passed.

"Hardesty?" Buckhalter sounding out of breath.

"How's your girl—sleeping through the night?" Wil expected a comeback about new babies and their sleeping habits, but Buckhalter's reply was dead flat.

"Something's come up that needs clarification," he said. "When can you stop by my office."

"Clarification about what?"

"Where are you right now?" Delivered as it was, not an idle question: up-antenna time. A trace on the line, had to be. But why?

"I'm around," he said. "Tell me what's up."

"It would be much better if you came in."

*Think*—maybe put the trace to work for *him*, the cop anxious to keep him on the line. Another two and a half minutes, if he was figuring correctly.

"Tell me," he said. "How routine would it be for a cop to ignore an eyewitness? One that showed up after the fact?"

Buckhalter hesitated. "Depends on the witness. If you're talking about the Marquez thing and the witness had anything substantive to add, it would have been in the file. Who we talking about here?"

"No idea about the cop, but the witness is a guy named Joe Avenal. He lived across the street. Still does, in fact."

"Interesting you should bring up that name."

A door burst open behind him and a waitress emerged with a tray of breakfasts balanced on one hand, pot of coffee in the other; she smiled as he got out of her way. He said, "You know the guy?"

"Yeah. Total flake—combination medicine chest and liquor cabinet. So far Avenal's confessed to about eight murders and twenty rapes. Anything that draws attention."

"Come on, Buckhalter, not even a report? The cop threatening his parole if he didn't shut up about what he saw?"

"That's what *he* said, you mean."

Wil could see where this was going, how much time he had left. "So you won't talk to him—even if he maintains he saw somebody leaving the Marquez house after Denny?"

There was muffled sound, Buckhalter's hand over the mouthpiece, then he was back on. "I'd have no objection," he said. "Except Joe Avenal's not around right now."

"He's not exactly hard to find."

"No disagreement there. Somebody already did—early this morning behind Art's Bar. Had a plastic bag stuffed down his throat."

Things went suddenly quiet, narrow, hot.

"The bartender described you to a tee. So did Avenal's neighbor. Both said you had a real hard-on for the guy."

"He was alive when I left him, Buckhalter. That's the truth."

"Where were you around eleven last night?"

"Out walking."

"The bartender said you didn't look too pleased when you left. He thinks maybe you waited outside for him."

"That's a crock. Why would I?"

"Trying to clear your friend comes to mind. Nobody else was much interested in the guy."

*Think.* "You already said he was a flake."

"Yeah, but you didn't know that."

"It wasn't me."

"Shit happens," Buckhalter said. "We're not unsympathetic. Come set us straight."

Which meant leaving Trina alone, him detained, questions fired over and over like being wrapped in spiderweb; too much left to chance with the scarred man walking around. By his watch, fifteen seconds left. Ten. Five.

Wil cradled the receiver. As he walked slowly back to the table the waitress was holding a coffeepot and chatting with Trina, who gave him an impatient look when she saw him. After the waitress topped his mug and moved off, he set down money to cover the tab.

Trina searched his face. "What is it?"

"We have to leave," he said. "Now."

**prowl** cars already had found the motel—three of them, their lights off. One of the cops was talking to the manager, others came and went from inside the room.

As they watched from well back the one cop left the manager and walked to his radio.

"Good-bye Bonneville," Wil said.

"My God. What do we do?"

"You remember your Hail Marys?"

"Me?" she said incredulously. "You're not serious."

"You got a better idea, go for it."

Just short of a run, no looks back, he led her down their alley, over three more, then back toward the commercial district and a phone, Trina on the alert for more police cruisers.

"How did they—"

"They must have been looking for the car. Arenal's neighbor, probably."

"Why is this *happening*?"

He threw a quick look down a street before leading her across. "Somebody not wanting it dug up would be a fair assumption. Any idea who?"

"No," she said. "Do you?"

"Only that I was warned off by a couple of Van Zants."

"You can't honestly believe they'd—"

"This way," he said. "The shopping arcade. You save your credit cards?"

She reached a hand into her purse. "Somewhere in here."

"Good. We're about to see how far your married name takes us."

They entered the arcade, found a phone by the rest rooms, secured a cab, and reserved a car at a rental office in Newport Beach, the cabdriver smiling at the prospect of the fare once he finally showed. Wil waved a twenty at him for stepping it up—late for a wedding, he explained. Twenty-two minutes later it worked again at the rental counter, the woman readying the papers in time he'd never seen before.

That was the good news. Offsetting it: Trina Bannister's credit card—and two others she had with her—failed to clear. Without cash to cover the deposit, Wil had to use one of his, traceable to the car once the cops got around to it. Riskier, but out of options.

Still, once Newport got increasingly south of the rented Lumina, overcast giving way to partial sun and the promise of more blue sky, he felt able to breathe again, collect his thoughts. Let alone set them going on the film can and the tape box bulging the pockets of his field jacket.

usc film school—one of Kari Thayer's recommendations—seemed the most immediate possibility, three o'clock now as they cut up the 110 toward L.A. and Exposition Boulevard. Long time since he'd been on campus: couple of football games to watch O.J. run opponents—one of them UCLA—ragged just before Nam.

Wil turned off at the signs, approached the jumble of buildings rising up on the right. Parking took a while, and asking for directions, but by three-forty, they were checking an information board in one of the cinema buildings, knocking at an open office with a Chinese-looking man about twenty-five on the phone. Eyeing Trina more thoroughly than Wil as he hung up.

"Something I can help you with?" Thick glasses and black hair.

Wil explained what he needed—syncing up old sixteen-millimeter film outtakes with wild sound. He showed him the film can, the tape box and date, told him they were fighting a deadline, wondered if he knew anybody who might be interested.

"I might be, if you don't mind a wait."

"How long a wait?" Trina asked him.

He checked the watch face on the underside of his wrist. "I TA a lab from four to five-thirty, give or take a crisis. After that, I'll have access to the equipment. That work for you?"

Wil considered the lateness, his chances of hooking up with another school or TV station at this hour. He nodded.

"Good. I'm Eugene Chen. How's fifty sound?"

"For the job?" Trina said.

Chen smiled. "Not quite. Per hour. And no promises—old stuff like this is generally the pits."

"All right," Wil said. "Where do we meet?"

Chen showed them: a big room with individual stations and students talking in groups or reviewing notes. He shook hands and went inside, leaving them to wander the campus, find a food area where they ordered salads, pizza slices, a moon-sized cookie they split.

"Penny for your thoughts?" Wil asked, watching her toy with the crumbs for several minutes.

"I have to go back," she answered. Beat sounding.

"I know. I was trying to think of a good lead-in, actually."

She let out a breath. “It has nothing to do with being with you.”

“It has everything to do with that. Your name’s not on anything down there. Right now the police don’t know about you.”

“No, but *he* does. Count on it.”

“He . . .”

“Who do you think canceled the credit cards? Who’s the one person in my life I can never get away from?” She swept the crumbs off the table. “That was no foul-up back there.”

“Your father did that? Why?”

“Because he could. Just his way of letting me know who’s boss. That my little escapade is over.”

“You can’t be serious.”

“I am dead serious.”

“So why do you play on his terms?”

“Why do you think?” she said. “I have to live. You have no idea what he’s capable of—what and who he uses to get what he wants. Like me, back.”

Wil rubbed his eyes, feeling the tension and fatigue in them. “Everybody has options, Tree. He doesn’t have to be one of yours.”

“That’s easy for *you* to say,” she flared.

“Come on. You’re not some kid.”

“You don’t know what the hell you’re talking about.”

“And you’re starting to piss me off,” he said, sparking off her. “But your being on the run with me makes even less sense.”

She laughed bitterly. “As if my life did.”

“Drama aside, we both know you’ve got too much to lose.”

“That’s one way to put it.”

He let it pass. “At least let me take you.”

“No, I’ll take a cab. It’s better that way.”

“Damnit. He’ll hurt you only if you let him, Tree.”

She looked at him a long moment; whatever her thought, it went unexpressed. Then: "What are you going to do next?"

"Now that you've righted the universe?" Wishing he could take it back the second he'd said it.

*"Fuck you."*

He glanced around, saw interest among a couple of tables, and looked it off.

"Wil, I—"

"Forget it, Tree, I was out of line. Memo to client: I intend to keep at it—at least until I check the film. I'd hate to think I was going along with somebody's game plan by turning myself in."

"Then you'll let me know?"

"That's the deal."

She fumbled in her purse for cigarette money, finally took some he gave her. "Wil, I'm sorry if I'm not strong like you," she said, putting on her coat. "This is about him and me and not being sixteen anymore. Look . . . just don't make the mistake of underestimating him."

He was thinking of hitting her with, *Is that what Denny did?* something to take it further, but in the end he said nothing. He just watched her walk away.

**eugene chen** was getting it in stereo from two young women who glared alternately at him and at each other over a viewer setup. He gestured for Wil to take a seat and in another ten minutes disengaged himself and walked over.

"Don't tell me," Wil said.

"Their project's due tomorrow, and it's nowhere near ready. I'd shine it, but they're my students, and if they look bad, so do I. A teaching job here depends on it."

Wil checked his watch. "I don't mean to come between you, but where does it leave us?"

Chen looked over his shoulder, shook his head. "Three o'clock *mañana*. Earliest."

"Anybody else here able to help me?"

"With hot splices and sound sync? I doubt it—it's just a really bad time right now. Once I get rolling, it'll go fast."

Wil drummed his fingers, reflexed another look at the time: going on six, nothing much he could accomplish anywhere else. *Shit* . . .

Chen read it in his face. "Tell you what. Leave me the stuff, and if it's doable, I'll get it ready before you come. Best I can do."

Wil considered, then reached into his pockets. He handed over the film can and the tape box, explained again what it was. That he hoped to make sense of some crime-scene outtakes—the voices particularly.

Chen popped open the can, checked the white-tape splices. He did the same for the five-inch sound reel. Raised an eyebrow.

"Is there a problem?"

"Hope not."

"It'd be a first," Wil said.

"Time-consuming is all." Chen heard rising female voices behind him, added that he had to get back to the project from another planet. The way it went sometimes.

Wil asked him if there was anyplace to stay close by, heard probably not with an SC-hosted basketball tournament in full swing, the motels jammed with players and fans. Chen wrote something in his notebook, tore it out.

"I live walking distance with some people," he said. "Just tell 'em I said it's okay to use my room." He handed Wil the sheet. "I sure won't be in it tonight."

"It might come to that. Thanks."

"Just don't expect the Biltmore."

Leaving him to the students, Wil found a phone and checked his messages: not much beyond one from Buckhalter and a client questioning an invoice. He dialed information for a number he hadn't yet committed to memory: Mo Epstein's new office.

"Sheriff's Homicide, Lieutenant Epstein."

"Try and sound a little cheerier. At least you don't have clients to answer to."

"Not yet, anyway."

Budget cutbacks were Epstein's big worry these days, the specter of layoffs after threatening for years to quit the LASD. Can't live with it, can't live without it—that was Epstein, whose impolitic directness had probably killed off any chance of further promotion. Good cop, strange bird is how Wil knew him—since Nam, in fact—somebody who'd give you the shirt off his back, then tell you how much he paid for it. But in a world of acquaintances, a friend was a friend, demonstrably so in Epstein's case. And if you sought perfection, you might as well forget it.

"What's up with you?" Epstein added.

"Just one winning streak after another. You want to grab a French dip?"

"Somebody roll you for the stars in your eyes?"

"Cynic. I'm stuck downtown. Phillipe's agreeable?"

"In a heartbeat, but not tonight. I'm knee-deep in human refuse—some little gang shit who flayed a twelve-year-old with a horsewhip when she wouldn't come across for his homie. But enough about the City of Angels. Dinner's all you called about?"

"My God, you're suspicious."

"So what *are* you working on?"

Wil told him something about it: Denny Van Zant, extortion, murder.

"Van Zant," Mo said. "Where have I heard the name?"

"The old man's high-profile. Kordell. Big medical money."

"No, I mean in-house. There another guy in the picture?"

"Eric handles company ops, at least ostensibly," Wil said. "The old man's the CEO."

"Right, I got it now. It was during a sit-down with our Feeble friends—you know, to avoid stepping on each other's jockstraps? Al Vega mentioned they were keeping an eye on this guy."

"Eric Van Zant?"

"You might want to confirm it, but yeah—unless my mind is totally shot. Which could be after a full day of this bullshit."

"Hard to see Eric on anybody's list, let alone the FBI's."

"What they all say."

"So how was Vega?"

"You know he jumped a couple of rungs after the Pfeiffer thing."

*Holly Pfeiffer kidnapped; Special Agent Al Vega coming down on him, butt out or face the consequences. Finally softening his stance when Wil had it all but nailed, stepping into media range as enthusiastically as Wil retreated, up to here with all of it at that point. Post-Lisa, post-Pfeiffer, post-everything.*

Pre–Maeve Van Zant.

"You wouldn't have a number to get me past the soothing recorded message, would you?"

Wil heard him fumbling pages. "It's a good thing there's no money in what you do, or I'd be after my cut." He related it as Wil took it down, thanked him. "So. How's single life treating you."

"Never better," Wil said. "Can't think of why I stayed married so long." Too close to home; leached of humor, his sarcasm sounded merely tired and bitter—a used tea bag. About the way he felt.

"My son, listen to your Rabbi Epstein, who's been to bat himself and whiffed. Take two nymphets and call me in the morning."

"*Mazel tov*," Wil said. He hung up, fed the machine, and dialed the number, got an answering machine anyway—not surprising at seven P.M. But at least the voice was familiar: FBI Special Agent Albert Vega telling him to leave a message.

**the** house was two-story and beat-up; the bed was a torn sleeping bag on a box spring. People came and went noisily, and the place smelled like old TV dinners. But it was convenient and safe, good as he was going to get without having to pile back in the car and hunt motels, the thought like sandpaper on a raw nerve. Let alone the risk.

Besides, there was a time, he thought—after an hour of running Lannie, Eric, Kordell, Avenal, and the scarred man through his head—when fuck-it was the only sensible attitude. The complaint window is closed for the night.

Shoes off and a too soft pillow doubled under his head, he drifted. Far away . . .

*They've driven all the way to Rosarito Beach for the party. Buffeted by Jeep draft the whole way down, Denny and Wil are already flushed from the margaritas they'd fixed at home and taken along in a thermos jug they all had nipped from, Trina and Carmen included.*

*By five o'clock, when they'd pulled in, the revelers—a swelling mix of gringo surfers, hippies, youngies, and druggies, plus Mexicans of every stripe—are either in the water, dancing to rock music, toking up, or drinking keg beer around a bonfire that lofts sparks at the darkening sky like burnt offerings. Fifty going on a hundred-fifty by nightfall, when the band really shifts into high gear—"Louie Louie" the double clutch.*

*Bodies writhe in the light cast by smoking tiki torches, car headlights, the bonfire—silhouettes responding to the music and to more primitive internal rhythms. Already couples are pairing off.*

*Sweaty from dancing, Wil and Trina stumble out of the pack, hold plastic cups under the hand spigot as the girl runs foam over the top, holds her hand out for payment in lieu of shouting over the din.*

*Wil puts a five in it, gets his change, and they move off to neck in the dunes. Almost there when . . .*

*Raised voices from the fire area: "The fuck's the deal,* puta*? You gotta have our women, too?" Heavy Mexican accent followed by a voice they recognize immediately: "Get your hands off her."*

*"Oh, shit," Trina says, and they burst through a gathering circle of drinkers, potheads, and space cadets to see Denny faced off with a cholo type gripping Carmen with one hand and an evil-looking switchblade with the other.*

*Carmen's eyes are wide, her brown face pale and pleading as the knife makes deliberate arcs in front of Denny's chest. Shouts in both languages start up:* Hijo de puta, *fucking asshole, gringo* pendejo, *spic bastard. . . .*

*Gasoline spreading toward the open flames.*

*The Mexican says, "My turf,* cabrón*—she goes with me. Tonight she gets* un hombre verdadero*."*

*Shout of assent: Wil notices people leaving the band to swell the ranks, calls for blood in the voices.*

*Carmen struggles in the cholo's grasp. "No!" But it's almost lost in the shouts. "Dennnyyy . . ."*

*"Wil." Trina has his arm now.* "Do something. . . ." *Several Mexicans clench and unclench fists; one looks over at him, grips a Cuervo bottle by the neck, daring intervention. In spite of it, Wil moves forward a step.*

*Denny sees him and holds up his hand—stop in any language, my show. He reaches into his back pocket, pulls out the Jeep keys, tosses them. The meaning is clear: Get the car ready, Trina out of here before it blows. Recognizing the potential.*

*Wil takes Trina's hand, presses the keys into her palm. "Face the exit," he says into her ear. "Engine going, lights off. If there's an obstacle around—a log, something like that—drag it in behind you."*

*"I can't leave him," she says, the flames mirrored in her eyes.*

*"No choice," Wil says with heat. "Go!" He watches her sprint for the parking area, decides he's never loved her so much.*

*The band has stopped playing now, the crowd surging in waves toward the fire. Yips and shouts, bullfight loud.*

*Wil elbows his way back to the front; Denny sees him without Trina and nods—just as the cholo slings Carmen down and slashes Denny's biceps. Blood streams down his left arm, begins running off his fingertips. Carmen scrabbles across the sand to Wil, screams when she looks back at her boyfriend.*

*Wil puts his lips close to her ear, tells her to move out for the Jeep; like Trina she refuses at first, then at Wil's look, she complies, forgotten now by the crowd. Someone steps up, a gringo in a tropical shirt and a joint going.*

*"Guy with the knife's an off-duty Rurale," he asides. "I saw him beat up a kid, near kill him. If it was my friend, I'd get him the hell out of there."*

*Wil nods, but the gringo is gone, leaving only reefer smell. He yells a warning to Denny about the Rurale. Somewhere a horn sounds, and raucous laughter; soot from the tiki torches momentarily flattens in on the crowd like barbecue smoke then drifts upward again. Oddly, Wil is conscious of the thumping surf.*

*With the girls gone, Denny's full attention is on the Mexican, circling now as Denny waits. Drips from his arm pattern the sand.*

*At the crowd's urging, the cholo lunges again; Denny feints and lands a hard right the Mexican takes flush on the nose. He steps back, blood welling out—the distraction Denny's been waiting for.*

*He dodges a reverse-grip upthrust, bangs a left off the side of the cholo's temple, then another—for if the Mexican is armed, Denny is quicker. Finally he aims one at the arm holding the knife, and it drops to the sand.*

*As if to catch his breath, he backs up a step, a move the cholo takes as his opportunity to retrieve the blade; by the time he realizes his mistake, Denny's foot is a blur. The kick snaps the cholo's head back, silencing the crowd with the dropped-melon sound and ending the fight that fast. Except Denny is on him now, fist after fist driven into the blood-slick face—a piledriver rearranging flesh and gristle and bone until finally Wil is able to hook the drawn-back arm and pull him to his feet.*

*Running him through the sand and the smoke and the catcalls toward the waiting Jeep, the crowd parting grudgingly, shoving and fuck-yous growing between the fired-up Mexes and gringos, Trina gunning it until their tires burn rubber—until they're done looking for lights behind them—only then does Wil reflect on how close they've come. And the look in Denny Van Zant's eyes.*

# 21

Wil had to wait for the bathroom, but the morning shift left fairly early and he was able to shower and borrow a razor, finger-brush his teeth, feel human again after a departing student took pity on him and shared her French-press coffee. By seven-fifteen, he was on the house phone—quarter a call—to the number Mo Epstein had given him.

This early, Al Vega picked it up himself.

"Breakfast on me, your choice," Wil said after telling Vega who it was. "Chance to catch up on some things."

"Name one that would interest me," the FBI agent said neutrally.

"Eric Van Zant. Not to mention letting me congratulate you on your promotion."

There was a pause as Vega caught the drift—what goes around comes around. "Van Zant might interest me if you hustle," he said. "But no promises—and I've got meetings after ten."

Wil took down the address, retrieved the Lumina, and decided on surface streets at this hour—Hoover–Alvarado–Sixth–Witmer. He entered the restaurant just ahead of Vega.

Vega shifted a newspaper up under his arm, and they shook hands, Wil noticing a sharpness he hadn't picked up before—upscale power tie and Bally moccasins instead of the rumple he remembered, crisp white shirt. Unconcealed, however, were the same dark eyes and penetrating gaze; the same throw-me-a-curve-and-watch-what-happens-next way about him.

Wil raised his orange juice glass. "Quite *GQ*, Special-Agent-in-Charge Vega."

"Not in-charge yet, Hardesty, but the thought's nice. You still doing it the hard way?"

"What way isn't?"

"I can think of some."

Wil sipped his juice. "You offering me a job?"

"Not now, but stranger things have happened."

The waitress came and took their order. Muffins arrived wrapped in a basket; Vega nodded at a table of men across the room. Wil saw them scrutinizing him.

He said, "Would I wind up looking like them?"

"Moot point. Still, having you around might make it easier to deal with you."

"My needs don't amount to much. Besides, look how well things turned out last time."

"You keep mentioning that."

"Do I? Unsubtle me." Wil broke and buttered a muffin. "How's the family."

"Fine. Your wife?"

"We got divorced."

"I'm sorry to hear it."

"Life's full of surprises, all right. So, what about Eric Van Zant?"

The server set their breakfast down—his Spanish omelette, Vega's sausage and French toast. The dining room pulsed with a pleasant mutter and clink.

"Excuse me, but I was led to believe an exchange might be on the menu," Vega said.

"Do they teach you to talk like that or does it come naturally with a promotion?"

Vega smiled, waited. Minus details, Wil explained his association with the Van Zants, intimating that whatever Vega might be interested in, he'd be on the lookout for.

"Son of a gun," Vega said, forking in French toast. "An extra pair of eyes and ears."

"Can't have too many, right?"

"You always work both ends against the middle like this?"

"If I believed that, Vega, I wouldn't be here. But maybe you're right. Maybe this wasn't such a good idea." Now he waited.

Vega wiped his lips. "I suppose it wouldn't do me any good to ask how you knew I might be interested."

"These wild psychic hotlines. Never know what you're going to pick up."

The FBI agent sucked his teeth, drank some ice water. "Okay. Van Zant's veterans' clinic has been losing patients—six suicides in two years. Enough to raise a few eyebrows. The VA's strapped, so they asked us to look into it. We got wind of possible irregularities."

"What kind of irregularities?"

"Drug testing on patients, things like that. Eric apparently treats the clinic as his baby, so the guess is if things are going on, he either instigates or knows about it."

"What's your source?"

"You know better than that."

Wil took a final bite of omelette, got out his credit card, stood up to go. "Sounds like it's all under control. Don't take any wooden nickels."

"Sit down, Hardesty. One of the vets—who shall remain nameless—contacted us, a friend of one of the dead guys. He's convinced this one, a Korean War army clerk named Billy Dulay, got offed."

"But he has no proof."

"No."

"And . . ."

"According to him, Dulay got hold of a key and was planning to copy some documents before he washed up at Point Dume a couple of weeks ago. Our guy doesn't know what they were, but he thinks it's related."

Wil pondered. "You ever hear the old man's name mentioned? Kordell—aka Dutch?"

"No, but we're not particularly overwhelmed by the source. Some schizoid who needs drugs to keep from crawling under the couch."

"You're all heart, Vega."

"You want heart, buy a valentine."

"There you go again."

This time Vega laughed. "Everybody's a damn critic in this town—probably good or the movies'd be even worse than they are. That all you want to extort from me?"

Wil pulled out a piece of paper. "This should be a slam dunk."

Vega unfolded it, looked up. "Kind of pushing your luck, aren't you?"

"Two weeks for me, one phone call for you."

"Kuykendall, Bowers, and Neves: Who are they?"

"Marine officers who served in Vietnam with Denny Van Zant. Echo Company chain of command, circa 1968."

"What's your interest?"

The waitress topped off their coffees, asked if there was anything else, then moved off. Wil added cream to his.

"I'm trying to fill in some blanks. Figured guys he fought with would know him better than a service record. Assuming one even exists today."

"And you want me to preempt the process."

"Trust me. It has nothing to do with your case."

Vega looked at the paper again.

"It's the computer age," Wil said. "Chips do all the work, remember?"

Vega gave him a look, took the paper, and went toward the pay phones; from where he sat, Wil could see him dialing. Within minutes he was back, picking up his newspaper, pulling sunglasses from his suit coat, and putting them on.

"I've got a break around noon," he said. "Call me then. And make sure your eyes and ears are in good working order."

Wil watched him make his way toward the door.

"Take that up for you?" the waitress said, reaching for the check and looking relieved that finally the table was going to turn.

**kordell van zant** teed up a new ball and took a few practice cuts, gratifying air whips that brought visions of booming hits and slack-jawed competitors. Twenty-two stories below, out beyond the glass, traffic moved silently, people went about their businesses—among them, a murdering crazy with scars on his face and a fucking meddlesome holdover from a life Kordell could barely remember.

Christ, what next? he thought, settling into his stance: head down and slightly canted, right little finger hooked inside gloved left forefinger, weight evenly distributed. Couple of measured breaths to relax.

*Arnie at St. Andrews. Flag barely visible in the mist. American pride on the line.*

Feeling the moment, Kordell brought the club back into a coil of energy that still amazed cronies with its range of motion, then released smartly into the ball. Hip turn, whipcrack sound, classic follow-through: a money shot in anybody's language. He retrieved the ball from the netting, teed it up again.

Now, if he could just do that on the goddamn golf course.

There was a rap at the door, Lannie's head in the opening: "You wanted to see me, boss?"

Kordell rested the club on his shoulder, not wanting to release his just-positioned grip, then gave it up and put down the three-wood, one hand on the butt of the shaft.

"How's she doing, Lannie?"

"Still sleeping, last I checked. Looks like the fight's gone out of her."

"Yeah, and I'm turning pro," Kordell said, replaying the nasty scene they'd had in front of Lannie, accusations flying back and forth like ninja knives. "She hates me. For as long as I can remember, she's hated me. Whatever I do, it's personal with her. Probably because we're so goddamn much alike."

Lannie said nothing, just let him run with it.

"Parenting's a bitch, Lannie, all hard choices and fuck-yous. Do your job, see the world for what it is, act accordingly, and you're the bad guy. Always."

"She is a handful."

Kordell walked to the window, thinking they could be talking about some seventeen-year-old instead of a grown mother with her own kids. The way he used to think about Maeve sometimes. "Curl your hair, some of the stunts she's pulled," he said. "Hell, just look. She's *still* doing it."

Lannie toed the carpet.

"You don't approve, do you?"

"With my history, I'm no one to—"

"Try."

"Sir, it's not my place."

"Your place is to give it to me straight, not blow smoke up my hole." Kordell spun angrily and windmilled the club, nearly missing the net and hitting the window; ripping off his glove, he paced the room to redirect his energy.

Back to 1947, college—his biggest challenge then an assistant football coach named Buddy Warburn after this whippet-legged defensive tackle had slipped Kordell's line holds and creamed his quarterback five times. Cost USC the game. Warburn, the toughest man and only father figure he'd ever known, raking him over the coals in front of the entire team. Instilling the fear of God like some ranting Baptist while he'd made Kordell stand there in a dress and flowered hat he'd purchased at the Goodwill. So from that time on, no matter who the opponent, they never scared him as much as Buddy.

Jesus, the echos from it could still bring a sweat—which said something about how deep inside they'd lodged. Still, no matter what Buddy Warburn said or did, it was infinitely better than this war of attrition with his own family. This death of a thousand cuts.

*Deep breath. Let it go.*

Suddenly he wished he could tell Lannie what was going on, this latest tar pit. Unburden himself.

Not a good idea.

"Never mind, Lannie. I'm fine."

"Look, boss, I—"

"Onward and upward. What's happening with the arrangements?"

Lannie expelled a breath, told him about the hotel falling all over itself to cooperate, the a/v stuff alone a PR man's wet dream, Kordell listening to about half of it.

"You hang on to your Van Zant stock like I told you to?"

"Most of it," Lannie said.

"Very wise of you. As you'll see."

"The hotel was saying that shareholders are checking in already—five days early."

"People with more leisure time than brains."

Still, it showed the anticipation, Kordell thought. He retrieved the three-wood, returned it to the bag. Started unbuttoning his polo shirt. Lannie took it as shower time and made for the door; Kordell brought him up short.

"I want a firm hand on things, Lannie, no surprises. Right about now is when I get nervous."

"You?"

"Take my word for it."

Lannie's round face meant well, but his Egyptian eyes gave off skeptical. "I hope you're not nervous about this other thing."

"The drunk in Huntington Beach."

"Him, yeah."

"Two birds with one stone, you said."

"It worked, didn't it? They'll find Hardesty. The longer he stays out, the worse it is for him."

Kordell sighed. "You ever hear of Murphy's Law?"

**eric van zant** cinched up his tie, clipped it to his shirt with the company-logo tie clip, the little VZ symbol hard under his thumb. *Not long now*. He paused in front of the mirror to comb his hair where it still had a tendency to rise up.

Ice-blue eyes made contact with his from across the condo's living area: suede couch and chairs, big-framed impressionists, edgy decorator touches from his ex-fiancée's designer.

"*Have a good day, honey,*" John Pomphrey said in the kidder falsetto he used to jerk his chain. "*Hurry home.*"

Such a bad idea having the Aussie move in for the duration—the perfect safe house as he put it. Gated community, ample room, split level for privacy—regular deep cover. But it was like having James fucking Bond as a houseguest: eyes that never left his, mind filing every quirk away like a human database. Not to mention the comings and goings at all hours, the shoulder holster and night clothing, the hair now light brown from a bottle.

Reminders he was playing in an entirely different league.

Not that he'd had much to say about it; Pomphrey had simply moved in, taking it as a given that Eric's condo would be more secure than anywhere else he could think of, the why being easy. Nobody ever visited the place.

His luck.

But if that's what it took, that's what it took. Eyes on the prize, the stakes more than worth the inconvenience, nothing less than control of Van Zant Inc. More important, an end finally to his denigration. An end to HIM. The Anathema. Even so, there were times lately when Eric wondered if he wasn't trading in one form of denigration for another.

*No going back, not now.*

As he did when such thoughts occurred, Eric ran through the positive side of the ledger and felt better. Where was it written you had to *like* your partners, people with whom you shared absolutely nothing but this pieced-together Frankenstein called a company? Certainly not at Van Zant, where your superior-for-life was your father, all over you for the failure you'd become in his eyes. Eyes that made you feel as if they could melt the flesh from your bones, crack them, and extract the marrow. Dissect your soul under a microscope and find it wanting.

Forever wanting.

Past John Pomphrey reading an Asian newspaper and smoking one of his hideous Indonesian cigarettes, an expansive deck, descending chaparral, and Coldwater Canyon slid off toward a horizon made indistinct by smog. Business, Eric reminded himself—keep it impersonal, always his father's admonition. Besides, what he was doing was nothing the old bastard wouldn't engineer himself were the shoe on the other foot. And years earlier, most likely.

*Well, guess whose blood runs in these veins? DAD?*

"So," Pomphrey said, looking up again. "Are you going or are you staying?"

Eric walked over from the mirror. "I want to know something," he said.

"And what's that, my man?"

"I'm not your man."

"Touchy this morning."

With effort, Eric met the eyes. "That's neither here nor there, is it?"

Pomphrey threw up his hands, mock surrender; get used to it, Eric thought. "How close are you to locating my brother? Assuming he's even alive."

"About the same as before the asshole intervened."

"When you almost killed my sister."

"I've explained all that. Right now I've got your old man to worry about. As for your brother, he appears to be a nonfactor, wouldn't you say?"

Eric let the question hang. "How are you going to handle it?"

"What's that, Eric?"

"You know what I mean."

"Not afraid to say what you mean, are you?"

"Of course not. I just want to know how you're going to . . . remove him."

"I see." The prick cat-and-mousing him.

"Fuck you and your games," Eric blurted. "I'm entitled to know."

John Pomphrey rose. He smiled, the simple act pinching the scars into patterns you didn't want to contemplate too closely, Eric wondering how many men still walking around had done so.

"Time to grow up and play with the big boys, Eric. Say it: *How are you going to kill my father, so that I'll be the man?*"

"On second thought, I'd rather not know."

Pomphrey's eyes had filled with a strange light. He came closer. "Say it. . . ."

"I'm leaving now."

Pomphrey unsnapped the weapon in his holster, an ugly black thing—something Denny might have been proficient at, Eric's distaste thereby assured. He touched the muzzle to Eric's cheek, thumbed back the hammer.

"Say it," he said again. Softer this time.

"I hate guns. Please put that down."

"Say it or what we remove will be your head."

One step shy of panic, a tilt either way now, sweating. "And blow the deal? I doubt it."

"Whole different scenario. Kill you, deal with him."

"You're bluffing."

"In five seconds we'll see—I will, at least. One . . . two . . ."

No doubt in those eyes. None.

"Three . . ."

"All right, I'll say it."

"Four . . ."

God. The room was spinning now, the muzzle dry ice against his skin. *"How are you going to kill my father . . . so that I'll be the man?"*

Pomphrey's face showed something that looked like disappointment, then it relaxed and he withdrew the gun. "Just in time," he said. "Saved the cleaning lady a lot of grief, that's for sure."

Eric's mouth felt like a paste jar left out too long.

"To answer your question," Pomphrey added, "I haven't decided yet."

Eric fought an urge to gulp air, for once wishing he was at work. Oddly he found himself wondering what color shirt he'd wear now that the blue one was sweated through.

"Speaking of obstacles, that reminds me," Pomphrey went on—as though nearly blowing a man's head off amounted to not much. "The aborigine, your father's head of security . . ."

"Lannie Crowell," Eric managed. "What about him?"

"Where's he live?"

"He has a place out in the valley—up Topanga Canyon."

"How about something a bit more specific?"

Glad for the distraction, Eric found his electronic notebook in his briefcase, thumbed up the directory, wrote down the address. He handed the note to Pomphrey, who scrutinized, then tore it up.

"Boy's got quite a build on him. He as good as he looks under all that muscle?"

"My father seems to think so. His steroids literally made Lannie."

"I'm asking you, Eric."

"If it was up to me, he wouldn't be anywhere near this company."

"And how long has he been?"

"Thirty years this August."

"So what's the deal? Why is he?"

Launching into it, even the carefully abridged version, Eric figured he might as well plan on showering again and changing into a whole new set of clothes.

**how** *to kill the old man . . .*

Not at the hotel, that was obvious; the shareholders needed to be in a state of concern for the future of their investments, not panic, John Pomphrey thought as he dropped down Coldwater. For this to work, they had to be ready to embrace the takeover as something vital to their interests.

By now they'd already gotten wind that a white knight, a fellow shareholder and international player named Serge Hollings, was preparing a bid for the company that would make their eyes pop. Not just the usual stock run-up, but with plans to double it within a year. And that was the conservative scenario.

Pomphrey waited out the signal at Ventura Boulevard. Global was today's game—worldwide markets, distribution efficiencies, economies of scale. Van Zant, their story went, had reached a plateau, held back by its current leader; good as old Dutch was, he could take them only so far. This was the logical next step. And John Pomphrey—not to mention his employer, Euphrates Ltd., who happened to own Mr. Serge Hollings—would take it, operative word *take*. Probably before the news of Kordell Van Zant's accident had cooled in *The Wall Street Journal*; conceivably even before Mr. Serge Hollings rose days hence amid the hand-wringing to save VZAN from its inevitable plunge, the big funds and market makers jumping ship as analysts pumped out increasingly bleak reports.

Right according to plan.

Pomphrey found the turn he wanted, watched for the street highlighted in the Thomas Guide open on his seat. No, the hotel was simply part two of the master plan.

Part one was what John Pomphrey was thinking might be the solution for all concerned. The only problem was making sure a certain aborigine did not become a factor. Which explained why he eased into a parking space across the street from the gas-company service yard, idly wiped off the end of his pistol barrel where it had touched Eric Van Zant's cheek, flipped on a talk-radio station, and waited.

# 22

al vega kept him waiting ten minutes before coming on.

Thinking perhaps Eugene Chen had overestimated his time frame, Wil had returned to the USC cinema building, confirmed the exact opposite. Chen, if anything, was running later than expected.

"Your call," Chen had said, looking fried. "You want the stuff back?" Little shrug to let him know either way was cool.

Five was now the appointed hour.

Looking to fill the time before noon—and Vega—Wil made calls: first, Veterans Affairs, finally getting through to a human who told him the files on Dennison James Van Zant would be at the records storage facility, St. Louis, Missouri. Next-of-kin access only—which meant Kordell, and there went that idea. Besides, Wil had been through service files before and found little of substance and nothing between the lines.

File it under remote.

Next he tried Buckhalter, asked the person who told him the detective was in a meeting and couldn't be disturbed if anything new had surfaced on the Avenal killing. Nothing they were releasing at this time, the voice said. When she asked him who it was calling, Wil hung up.

Lisa was out when he tried her. On the positive side, Bev came on when she heard who it was and told him they'd secured at least a postponement from the IRS. Something anyway.

"You'll tell Lisa I called?"

Sure, she told him, and after a pause: "Why don't you two just cut the crap and admit you made a mistake. I don't know how your love life is, but this Brandon is not the answer. Only one who doesn't see it is her."

"Thanks, Bev," he said.

"Anytime."

He rang off. After a fast scan of a news-rack *Times*, it was noon and he tried Vega—on hold for the FBI agent his current status. Penance for the imposition, Wil assumed.

"You still there?" Vega finally asked.

"Rumor has it."

Vega snorted. "I can see why you're good at this. You have absolutely no sense of time."

A student in grunge clothes eyed him and the pay phone he was using; checked his watch and shook his head.

"Make that sense, period," Wil said. "Any luck on the names?"

"You got something to write on?"

"Kind of question is that for a pro?"

"Okay. Lieutenant Colonel William C. Kuykendall died in seventy-nine. Complications from Agent Orange, or so his widow maintains."

"Good luck to her. What about Candy Bowers?"

"Last known address for Franklin L. Bowers was someplace in Wyoming. The captain hasn't returned a query in years."

"Strike two."

"Second Lieutenant Steven D. Neves still lives in San Pedro. Cashes disability checks at a grocery store near his house."

Wil took down the address: 1844 Delmont. "What kind of disability?"

"No idea. Okay with you if I go now? There's a meeting with my name on it about to resume."

"Thanks, Vega. At least one taxpayer's grateful."

"Hey, it's a start."

As he hung up, looked around for a trash can to pitch the newspaper into, the student said, "Fuckin' ay, man, it's about time. You ever think about anybody but yourself?"

"Not sure I'd recommend it to you," Wil answered. "It's harder than it sounds."

"**What** do you mean she's gone? Tell me she's in the bathroom or doing a workout or something."

"I wish I could say that," Lannie said, fearing the explosion he was sure would come at any moment. "But I checked the whole floor and she's . . . not there."

"What about her clothes?"

"They're gone, too."

"Anybody downstairs see her go? Never mind, she'd have taken the private elevator. . . ."

Here it came, any second now, the incompetent muscle-headed son-of-a-bitch part; not really meaning it, Lannie knew, just getting it off his chest. He tried to maintain eye contact on the phone's video monitor, Kordell Van Zant looking about ready to blow, when the man surprised him. Yet again.

Taking a deep breath, he leaned forward. "Forget it, Lannie, not your fault." He reached for a cigarette and lit up, something Lannie hadn't seen him do in years—not since he'd moved out of the Malibu house for a parade of penthouse bimbos who'd finally nagged him off the habit.

"My daughter goes where she goes and always has. But at least it won't be back to Hardesty anytime soon. I did make that clear, didn't I?"

"Yes sir. Clear as day."

Kordell drew in a lungful, released it slowly at the ceiling, the cloud looking to Lannie like maybe his anger dissipating upward. Leaving who knew what behind.

"Lannie, are you familiar with that old saying about the sins of the father being visited upon the children?"

"Heard it once or twice, I suppose."

"You believe it?"

"No idea, boss. Why?"

"Because they've got it backward is why."

His thought triggered a rush of others in Lannie: coming home one day from school to find his mother smack-fucked and shacked up with the dealer he'd cut to pieces after finding Gwenie drowned in her bathtub; Mom-o's life fading as Lannie's bloodied hands bore down on her junkie throat. Two worthless lives for one priceless baby sister, the cops having to tear her body away from him when they arrived. And after it, two years in juvie, a foster home and a lot of bullshit counseling, a little camera his big escape from a fucked-up world. Reality he could create and control.

It was a moment before he could say anything. Not that it mattered: He was facing an empty screen.

**san pedro** was pretty much the town Wil remembered from undergoing his preinduction physical there in the sixties. Commercial blocks leading up from the bridged harbor and the shipyards, slate water and loading cranes, blue-collar neighborhoods, a few more prosperous ones.

Delmont Street was not among those.

Wil found the grocery store Vega had mentioned, a mom-and-pop establishment with a soft-drink name sign, the usual loungers out front. Two blocks up, he came across 1844: slant roof overhanging the porch, rosebushes, wood siding, wrought-iron bars across the old-fashioned windows.

He parked the car and approached, saw a bearded blond man shucking what looked like pea pods into a bowl. The man looked up; Wil asked for Steven Neves, already deciding too gringo and too young to be this guy. Mid or late thirties, if he had to peg him—tight jeans and rolled-up T-shirt sleeves.

He handed him a card, waited till the man looked up. "It's about a mutual friend."

"What friend is that?"

"An old one. From Vietnam."

The man looked at Wil's card again. Deciding about him.

"Dead, most likely dead," Wil added.

"That atrocious war."

"You could say that."

A shrug. "I'll see. But Steven usually naps about this time." He put down the bowl, went into the house.

Wil waited, saw a curtain part, the nap as ready-made excuse, the man back at the door.

"All right," he said. "He'll see you."

Wil climbed the steps, entered to chest-high paneling topped by wallpaper, flowers on the dining table, hardwood flooring with ramps at the door moldings. Here and there, framed figure studies—charcoal or heavy pencil. He commented on them, caught *no big deal* in the man's look.

"You do these?" he asked.

A nod. "Why?"

"They're good." Figuring he might need an ally, he extended a hand. "I'm Wil."

"Douglass."

Squeak of rubber behind him, a voice like Lee Trevino's: "Takes a lot to tear me away from the Internet, bud. I hope you're worth it."

Wil turned, saw a man about his age in a walker: gray-black hair worn long, plaid flannel shirt over an olive tee, sweatpants, leather slippers. Coarse brown skin the texture of an orange.

"Steve Neves," he said.

"Wil Hardesty. Thanks for seeing me."

The blond man ran a hand over his beard. "You need me for anything, Steven? Aquavit?"

"Thanks, hon, it's a bit early for that." He looked at Wil.

"Water if it's no trouble."

The blond man disappeared through a bead-hung door.

Neves cleared his throat. "Case you're wondering, Douglass there saved my ass a few years ago. Got me out of my wheelchair and into this gadget. In here, we show our feelings. That put you off?"

"Nope."

"Then sit and be welcome. What friend?"

Wil sat. "Denny Van Zant. I'm hoping you remember him." But it was clear that Neves had, his openness fading, the eyes going slightly to hood.

"Maybe I do, maybe I don't. Why don't you give me a reason."

Wil did—their history, Maeve's call, the extortion notes, looking into Carmen's killing. Trying to find something in what happened over there, the man the boy became.

Douglass reappeared and set down water with lime on a coaster, then went out on the porch. Neves looked at nothing as Wil drank.

"Funny how his name still has an effect on me."

"Why's that?" Wil said, setting the glass down.

"You'd have had to been there."

"Coast-Guard river patrol qualify?"

"The water sprites?" Then: "Naw, fuck that. Blood's blood and the hell with the rest." He held out a fist Wil bumped, took the return hit. "Plenty of guys come out worse. Denny, for instance."

"Were you there when he joined Echo Company?"

"Sure, right out of Pendleton—half-confused, half-hot-to-trot. Not like I was much older than him, just more experienced. Eight months in-country and counting down. To this, it turned out."

"When did it happen?"

"A month after Hue—this open spot between paddies I was aware might be mined but was so beat I couldn't give a rat's ass. Six pints of O-pos later and a crip at twenty-three, that's when I cared. Back home hearing I was a baby killer who got what he deserved, that's when I cared. Never did forgive myself. It took Douglass for that."

"How'd you get to know Denny?"

"He replaced a grunt in my squad. We hung and smoked dope, got to be friends—and not in *that* way, if you was thinking it. Just common ground, two SoCal boys a long way from home."

"What was he like over there?"

He mused so long that Wil thought about rephrasing it. Finally Neves said, "You watch old movies?"

"Sure."

"Ever see *Beau Geste* with Gary Cooper?"

Wil searched his memory, came up with Beau/Cooper sacrificing a cush life for the foreign legion, where they wouldn't ask about things like stolen family jewels; the tyrant sergeant finding out; dead legionnaires watching their duel at the besieged fort. "Somewhere along the line."

"Well, that's who Denny reminded me of—that same sense of honor, what he thought was right. Make sense?"

"Yes and no."

"He just had this . . . certitude," Neves said. "I think it related to what got him there—the whole thing with his girlfriend's murder, the toll it was taking on his family."

Wil pulled out the Denny-Roy-John photograph, handed it over.

Neves gave a rueful smile, a shake of the head: "Getting home, I couldn't wait to put it all behind me—out with the garbage. Now I wish I'd saved at least the pics."

"Did you know these guys Roy and John?"

"Oh yeah."

More there, Wil figured, so he asked.

"Roy Voelker was a sure-as-shit, son-of-a-bitch lying motherfucker. Nobody I knew had any use for him. Finally got drummed out for extortion."

*His next favorite was writing the home folks, telling them he needed money to conceal their son's involvement in civilian massacres*—Hilo: the phone voice describing Voelker. Validation.

"And John?"

"Smart, dangerous. He got plugged in when our demolitions man went down—field assignment after some bloodbath or other wiped out his own troops. Guy was Australian. Roy and him got tight—"

"And took Denny under their wing." Wil bridging off Neves's tone.

A nod. "I always figured him too smart for that, but—"

"Any chance he saw something in *them*?"

Neves shrugged. "What he really wanted was to make his old man proud, this wheeler-dealer type. All the letters Denny sends, the asshole never once writes back. To my knowledge, anyhow."

"What came of the association?"

"Bad fucking karma. John had this big China-white connection. Runners and bagmen, the whole nine yards—regular Al Capone. Voelker had an interest in anything that brought him coin."

"Denny got involved in dealing?"

"That surprise you? Hell, everybody *did* 'em—not heroin necessarily, but one thing or another. Which only made other people want to sell 'em. Make money, like Denny's old man, if you get my meaning."

Wil paused, trying to see it, not doubting Neves, but—*hell.* "How long did this go on?"

"Until the CO got wind."

"Kuykendall."

Nod. "We kept waiting for the shit to fly, but it never did. Camp was one big rumor mill."

"What are you saying? Denny cut a deal?"

"At first I thought so," Neves said. "Until I found out it was him who *went* to the CO, took responsibility for it." He shifted in the chair, trying to get comfortable. "This was after the shit John brought in killed a couple of grunts, broke Denny up pretty bad. CO let him skate, so it'd look like Denny was snitching out the others, working a deal for himself. Guaranteed unhealthy, if you were the snitch. CO figured the pressure would make Denny turn 'em to save his own hide."

"The old cop trick," Wil added to it.

"Funny thing. Kuykendall used to be a cop."

"Did Denny give up Roy and John?"

"No—even though it turned *him* into a pariah. Guys didn't like anybody cutting off their supply."

"Even though it was bad . . ."

"Hey, you were there. When did rational play a big part?"

"So what happened?"

"Hue is what happened—gettin' our asses kicked. Every available gun up front."

*Here it comes*, Wil thought. "Who saw Denny fall? You?"

"Voelker did." He acknowledged Wil's look. "Roy said they got separated, cut off. No beef there—guys screaming like you never want to hear. Whole divisions ripped apart . . ."

He drifted and for a moment Wil thought that would be it. But Neves said, "Do me a favor: There's a bottle of aquavit in the freezer. Bring me a shot glass and one for yourself."

Wil did, minus the glass for him. He watched Neves pour, toss it off and exhale, blink and wave the bottle at him.

"No thanks."

Neves poured himself another, pounded that down. "This is why I stopped hanging out with the vets."

"Say the word and I'm gone, Steven."

"Thought you wanted the skinny on your friend."

"I do, but not this way."

Neves tossed the bottle back to him. "Thanks for the thought, but I gave up suicide benders. Finally got more to lose than I'm willing to give up."

**black** smoke scrawled up from one of the container ships; breakout sun angled in to illuminate a plant in the window: three-fifteen by Wil's watch. Interspersed had been a dip in by Douglass to announce he was going out shopping. Seeing the flush on Neves's face, he'd shot a look that said *back off* before he left.

"So," Wil said, intending to. "Denny and Voelker?"

"That's right," Neves answered. "John What's-His-Face, too."

"I don't understand."

"John was the wounded man Denny was trying to help when he got hit."

Resounding *clunk*. "The same guy Denny was possibly turning?"

"You got it."

"And Roy Voelker is telling you all this?"

"Right. Said he'd been driven the hell out of there, lucky to make it back. Nothing he could do."

"I see."

Neves half smiled. "You mean, did I have a fair idea Voelker'd shot 'em both to cover his ass on the drug thing? Left 'em for dead?"

"Something like that."

Neves shifted positions again, grimaced as something hurt. "Damn straight I did, for what that was worth. Fair ideas bought you jackshit over there."

Wil said nothing.

"Look, I don't know what kind of war you had, but mine was about learning what you're capable of."

*Open your ears*, the voice says. *Voelker's favorite thing was wiring prisoners up to the field phones and turning the crank on 'em.* Neves had to have known.

"Or what you're not," Wil said.

"Whatever. Four weeks later I had a whole new set of problems."

Wil tried the scenario on for size: treason and murder, Denny shot by his own countryman. Years later Voelker getting his—not from someone bent on extracting information, as he'd originally thought, but on revenge.

Maybe.

"You see anything to the extortion notes?" he said. "Denny making it out?"

Neves looked out the window. "No. But then I wouldn't trust the military to ID a street sign, let alone human remains. I seen 'em in action."

"What about John?"

Neves shrugged. "Shit's been known to float. That kind, anyway."

*Nobody you'd know. Nobody at all.*

Wil checked his watch, his five o'clock with Chen history if he didn't head out ASAP. He thanked Neves, remembered he still didn't know John's last name, and asked. Thinking he knew already what the pale rider was capable of.

Neves pondered, shaking his head finally. "Been trying to recall it the whole time and haven't. I'll see if my boy Candy does."

Something clicked. "Candy—not Franklin Bowers in Wyoming?"

"Idaho now, for what it's worth." The slight smile broke back. "We stay in touch, some of us from Echo that made it home. Think I'm bad—that sucker *never* leaves *his* computer. You got a phone where I can reach you?"

# 23

Iannie crawled along with the late-afternoon traffic, barely conscious of the exhaust sting in his eyes, the hint of rain in the piled-up clouds. He was looking forward to getting home to his weights, busting a bead with some serious iron before it got crazy with the meetings, the twenty-hour days that would leave him torpid and spent. First Kordell announcing his new antidepressant, Kordec-Z, at the gathering for trade and consumer press; then the reception for bankers and the like; then the shareholders meeting, older types seeing dollar signs on everything but the corporate toilet paper, the ones already there keeping the hotel staff hopping, clubs and bars jamming till all hours.

Made you wonder how they behaved at home.

He eased the Trans Am over a lane, anticipated his little rituals: warming the vial, filling the syringe, rubbing his skin with alcohol. The building tingle when the cells were falling into line, all on the same page and ready to burn. That was the beauty of Kordell's other magic formula. The hit-and-run *now* of it.

Try that with the FDA: Man'd be a hundred before they started using it on mice even, bureaucrat jaws dropping as they checked the quantum-leap rates of growth, the unmicelike feats of strength. Lab-coated dunces who in general had no idea of the progress possible when you weren't a slave to politics, and especially to cost.

What were a few lives, after all? Men whose existence was similar to a candle's glowing tip after the flame had been extinguished. Lives you could pinch out now and make mean something or watch sputter and die of their own lack of heat.

He thought about the last one, Billy Dulay, who might have sailed through fine except for a bad habit of looking into everything. *Getting* into it, too. Still, that one had turned out all right, he had to admit, Eric having no clue, just his paranoia—justified, it turned out. Lannie owing Billy Dulay quite a lot, it turned out. Something Eric would discover if he tried to pull any shit, post-Kordell.

Lannie left the freeway for Topanga Canyon Boulevard, saw Billy Dulay pleading, him telling the little guy to relax, there'd be no pain, just a gradual relaxing. Plenty of guys with cancer would kill for an exit like that, but Billy not listening—struggling and kind of keening. Lannie trying to convey no sense in fighting it, going out like that all charged up and negative. Restless, unhappy spirits were the result, according to an article he'd read on the subject. Shades who got stuck between worlds—neither here nor there. Just fretful and powerless and upset.

Thinking about it made the back of Lannie's neck prickle.

The Plymouth cutting him off and his honking at it returned him to more practical matters. Like how he planned to pump Kordell's big moment with a gift of his own. Something he was going to dust off after nearly thirty years—give or take a couple at the beginning when he'd felt the need to shake it out from under his cuff, make sure Kordell got a glimpse. And the point: Don't fuck with me.

Even then it was more gesture than threat.

After that, he'd simply stashed it away—a memento of sorts till now, Lannie still full of Kordell's letting his hair down earlier, letting him in: man-to-man, like he was a confidant or an equal or something.

He'd never had a father in his life, not remotely, but he figured it had to feel something like that. And as far as now instead of the actual anniversary in July, it just seemed more important to find the right occasion than adhere blindly to a date on the calendar that each year fell on a different day anyway.

His thoughts jump-cut: back to the day after the night, 1966. Being ushered into Kordell's office, showing him what he'd picked up and where—young and scared and about to break the law a second time in twenty-four hours. Big time. Still, feeling his way through at full speed, nothing to lose. His amazement at the man's reaction, Kordell calmly sizing *him* up and *counter*offering. Knowing then he was in the presence of greatness—a man so focused that even with his own problems he could see inside a skinny, on-the-make black kid putting up a front that could crumble at any second, but somehow hadn't.

It was like coming home and this time finding Mom-o drying Gwenie off after her bath. Both smiling up at him. Everything okay.

Lannie spotted the small S&L, chosen because it maintained the late hours he often needed—now in particular, figuring this was like a rainy day, one of those. Fact was, a couple of drops already were spotting his windshield. Obviously a good omen.

Whistling, thinking of ways he might present it to Kordell—privately, of course—and the look on the old man's face, he eased into the S&L's modest parking lot.

**once** he got his bearings at the store and restaurant, the narrow lane was easy enough to find, and well down it toward the creek, a cinderblock house with plate glass under the roofline to admit light and look modern. Nobody around one of the major charms of the place.

All of which suited the man in the gas-company uniform and truck just fine.

He parked nearby, pulling the truck in under a tree that concealed it better than he'd hoped. Still, he made a show for anyone who might be watching—not that anyone was visible. But he was by nature deliberate, which explained a good many things, not the least of which why he was still around when most of his cohorts were dead.

He broke out his tools, and for a moment listened to the creek, surprisingly audible down the steep ravine. He strode to the house, circled it, found the back door, and approached confidently—standard procedure, no doubt. Regular company man, he thought wryly, thinking of the chuckle it would bring some Thai businessmen he knew.

In practiced seconds he was inside the house, taking in the living area that had been turned into a workout room. Chrome free weights in black iron racks, slide-on plates racked in others; several benches, some with incline feature, each with its own weight bar; military-press machine and one for leg squats; cable pull-downs and a hang bar for pull-ups. Treadmill and StairMaster for cardio.

Serious shit, John Pomphrey allowed—not to mention serious money. Before checking the rest of the house, neat as a pin and modest, except for some pistols in a wood cabinet, elaborate needlepoint on the walls, and a few cameras, Pomphrey pretty well had settled on the focus of Lannie Crowell's life. After a quick peek out onto the deck, shadows having crossed it and sliding into the ravine now, he returned to the weight room, a plan forming as he sat running his hand over the grip finish on one of the bars.

despite heavy traffic, Wil got back to USC just before five, the trip from San Pedro filled with Denny thoughts: Denny hungry to make the Rock of Gibraltar proud of him; Denny caught between John, Roy Voelker, and Kuykendall; Denny cut off with the very soldiers who must have heard he was going to—or had already—ratted them out, hard labor or worse in store for drug profiteers who poisoned their own.

All at nineteen.

Then the firestorm: bullets downing first John, then Denny; Voelker checking hurriedly for signs of life before pulling out, his problems behind him for the time being. Back to safety, freedom, his scams. And finally, the Waipio. Put together from what Neves said, it made sense.

But who then killed Voelker?

John? *Denny?*

Dead men both, according to facts and odds, best-guess scenarios. But if Celeste's killer—and nearly Trina's—was the same as Voelker's, and John and Denny both somehow miraculously *had* lived, each had a burning reason to gut the man who'd left them to the mercies of the Communist interrogation squads.

Denny: bone fragments, piece of jaw, his dog tags.

*Reality check.*

John. John who?

*Without a name, nobody—yet.*

Wil found a parking place eventually, and Eugene Chen, looking tired and working on a beer. Feet up on the desk.

"We still on?"

Chen let his feet down, swiveled toward him. "Been ready since three, believe it or not." He emptied the beer bottle, pitched it. "God, this job. Sometimes I feel more like a referee than a TA."

"Thanks again for the digs."

"No problem. And the wait gave me a chance to see what we're dealing with. Splice it up."

Wil followed him to a smaller room with a screen and projector set up on a metal cart. The film was on the feeder reel—minus the white tape.

"Actually, it went fairly fast." Chen dimmed the lights, turned the power on the projector, the fan whirring to life. "You know who shot this stuff?"

"Somebody called Nonstop Productions," Wil said, the name reminding him to check county and city license bureaus for that year if anything panned out, most likely scenario the info long since purged. Municipal-court records were another possibility assuming a small-claims filing against Nonstop—iffy at best.

"Freelancer in the mid-sixties," he added. "Ring any bells."

"Nope, and I'm not surprised. Real amateur—made the stuff I was looking at last night seem like Haskell Wexler shot it."

"How about the sound?"

"No slate, no way to sync it up except hit and miss. At fifty an hour, I thought I'd better check."

"Can it be done?"

"Easier to run the film first. You see a spot where you want sound, I'll mark it. Then we'll play the tape, isolate the cut, try to slip and slide. If we need to get real precise, I'll make a mag stripe."

"A what?"

"Never mind. Just watch."

Chen levered the projector into gear; after black leader, the images came up—night shots, grainy but arresting: the crime scene as noir.

Wil leaned forward. The footage was similar to what he'd seen at KTVB, but he could see why these were outtakes: light flashes, blown focus, run-ons that went nowhere. Little of consequence or content.

Now and again, the photographer would lose track and not stop filming—home-movie style—as if he was distracted by something. In one series, a cop approached to say something confrontational; Wil had Chen mark it, and they went on. Another series had Sandor Marquez, flanked by wife Guadalupe and son Matteo—strange how the names came back with the faces—responding directly into the lens.

Mark it again.

Without the scenes already lifted for the TV story, the film went by fast: marginal stuff that did more to set the tone than add much. They were almost to the end when Wil asked Chen to repeat a shot, the photographer backing out of a close-up, becoming distracted by something and letting the camera drop. Presumably toward the distraction.

For a moment the camera settled, picked out something, then cut away to another vignette as the photographer realized what he was doing, wasting film. Still, it was almost clandestine the way it suddenly left the object.

"Any idea what that is?" Wil asked.

"Something reflective. That blur before the cut looked like a hand."

"We see it again?"

They did, Wil going micro on it.

"Hard to tell," he said to Chen. "Can we freeze it."

"Best to transfer it to video, go frame by frame. If you want, I'll do that while you're checking sound."

Wil nodded and Chen rewound the film, put the spool back in the can, then showed him how to run the sound tape.

"It spliced up to about ten minutes worth," he said. "FORWARD, PLAY, STOP, REWIND. Good luck."

"Why's that?"

"Guy obviously went to the same school for sound as film."

With Chen gone, Wil turned to the tape recorder, wondering if it all wasn't an extension of the same drill, the eighty-plus percent that always seemed to accompany inching toward the light of day.

He pushed PLAY, heard a young male voice trying for calm and detached, not quite getting it: "*Arrival time, four-fourteen A.M. Scene is 347 Heurta Street, Huntington Beach. Victim's name is Marquez, Carmen, about eighteen—dead from a knife wound, handle of which may be seen. Wild sound follows.*" There was a pause, then: "*This tape is the property of Nonstop Productions, Anaheim, California. Unauthorized use is prohibited.*" As much afterthought as disclaimer.

Wil stopped the tape and made note of it, Anaheim at least something to pursue if further listening warranted.

He resumed, fascinated by the time-machine ambience—the sound somehow more real than the images. Police radio, the comments indecipherable; neighbors, he assumed, also indecipherable; vehicles arriving and doors thudding, footsteps, voices now, some indistinguishable, others—

Bolt upright, hit stop, then REW; after several spoolings, he pushed play again.

"*Jesus,*" a voice said out of the sounds—then somebody's name. "*Can't you think of anything better to do at four in the morning? Damn ghoul.*"

It was the scene he'd noted, the police officer confronting the camera—flat and thin, but the clearest voice thus far. He ran it back and forth across the head, prickles starting when he was willing to admit it sounded like *"Crowell."*

The more he played it, the surer he was. Come on, he thought, cold water time, the coincidence way beyond . . . And yet there it was: *"Crowell."* Over and over until he thought he might be wearing out the tape.

So what—plenty of other Crowells around, just look in the book. He made a mental note to do that. Besides, there was no first name.

Get it together.

He tore a corner off his notepad, slid it into the spool, pushed play again, the paper catching in the tape, going round and round like a little flag. He took a deep breath, concentrated on the sounds at hand; not far until:

*"And step back."*

*"Whatever you say, Officer Blakley. Any suspects at this time?"*

*"No comment."*

*"Somebody she knew?"*

*"For the last time, back off."*

*"Yes sir."*

Wil pushed STOP. Blakley was a name he remembered from the reports—scene control or something. He noted the name, went ahead. As did the confrontation:

*"Just serving the public's right to know."*

*"Right to know, my ass—and kill that damn light."* Pause. *"That's the family. They came home and found her. How'd you like it?"*

This time Wil let it run, knowing from the film what was coming next: Sandor Marquez looking into the bright light, blinking as the man behind it approached him.

"Siento mucho su pérdida, señor y señora. *Lannie Crowell,*

*KTVB, hoping you'll let my viewers know what happened—what you're feeling."*

As if suddenly he was there, the light in *his* eyes; not conscious now of the back-and-forth, only what came up each time: *Lannie Crowell . . . Lannie Crowell . . . Lannie Crowell . . .*

He willed himself to finish, from far away heard Sandor respond: *"Look at what he did to her, that Van Zant boy. He murdered my baby—a poor little Mexican girl.* Hijo de puta *thinks he can do anything because of his money. You tell your viewers that."*

Now he knew why the clip hadn't been included in the TV story; named accusations and profanities, even untranslated ones, were more than enough to get it squashed back then.

There was a pause, then last tag—Blakley's voice, offscreen from when Wil had run the film through: *"You happy now, spook? I sure hope so. Now take a hike."*

*Spook*—Blakley's racial prejudice nailing it down.

*Lannie Crowell.* Shape at least to the light.

Deep in the crime scene, thoughts forking like the lightning in a clash of fronts, Wil didn't hear Eugene Chen return.

"What's with the face?" he said beerily. "Looks like you've heard a ghost."

**they** finished up in the video room, having spooled through what was left of the sound tape. No more voices, no further Blakley revelations, Wil telling Chen he'd found what he needed, precise sync unnecessary. When they entered, he saw a black-and-white image frozen on the video monitor.

"There it is," Chen said with enthusiasm. "Last frame before the cut."

Wil said nothing, just let the image register fully, afraid he might be jumping to conclusions, wanting to hear it from another pair of eyes.

"Well?" Chen said.

"You got an idea what it is?"

"Don't you? Look—here, here, and here—above the hand reaching for it. Gotta be a bracelet, right?"

"Maybe."

"Maybe, my ass. That's the chain, that's the medal part." He paused, his impatience barely in check. "Come on, you see the twined snakes? Gotta be one of those emergency things you wear to save your life when you got a medical problem."

Wil sat alone in the office while Chen made an out-of-beer run preparatory to totaling up his bill. Payable upon presentation—in cash, Chen had made clear; no plastic, no checks.

Actually, he was glad for the time to think.

So do it, he told himself, not wanting to let the suddenness after so much of nothing color his reactions. *Lannie Crowell:* Tomorrow he'd attempt a check on Nonstop with business registrations. Just to make certain.

And yet he knew. Having spent time with them, in various stages of dress and undress, he knew Denny never had worn a bracelet like it, nor Trina, nor Carmen. He'd have noticed one on Lannie, too, he figured, the possibility it might have been *his* bracelet he'd dropped and was retrieving. The chance that after thirty years the condition prompting it was no longer a problem.

But it didn't feel right, feelings counting for something in this. Lannie, by his own admission, had started work for Kordell in 1966. July, possibly? Around the time Denny entered the military?

Reminder: Call personnel tomorrow and see if he could coax a date out of them.

And if it *was* July, what then? Lannie used the bracelet to blackmail Van Zant? To what gain? Usually blackmail involved money, the vampire sucking the victim's blood until either it flew away full or sucked too hard. Usually blackmail was messy and filled with animosity.

Usually . . .

Roll-the-dice hypothesis: Could Kordell have turned things around on the kid while giving Lannie what he thought he wanted, whatever that was? You didn't become a Kordell without the moxie: file under possible. But *whose bracelet?* chafed. Recollections: Kordell wih hypertension, Eric with blood-sugar problems—Maeve's words—medical-bracelet candidates both, from what he understood. So which would have ordered a replacement bracelet July/August 1966? Phone time tomorrow—assuming the company was still going.

Chen entered with a six-pack in one hand, a piece of paper in the other. He offered Wil a beer, shrugged at the no-thanks, presented the paper.

"So what's the damage?" Wil asked without unfolding it.

"Two forty. Can't do better than that."

Wondering whether Chen was referring to Wil or himself, Wil peeled off campus-ATM twenties, feeling the pinch as they left his hand. Nagging him to get in touch with Trina about expenses.

Chen put the cash in his pocket. "You're welcome," he said.

Lost in thought, Wil already was moving toward the door. "Sorry. I appreciate it.

"Whoa, almost forgot." Chen rummaged on the desk, found pinkish slips under the six-pack. "Phone messages. While I was playing referee." He handed them over.

Damp from condensation, the first was from Trina—one-forty P.M.—call her at a number that was unfamiliar looking. The second was from Steven Neves—four forty-five. It read: *Candy remembered—it's Pomphrey. Said to tell you if the fucker ain't dead, do us all a favor.*

**trina** stepped over a piece of unpoliced crime tape; caught by the breeze, it was slowly fluttering its way down the hillside. With the day all but gone and threatening clouds further lowering visibility, she figured now was as good a time as any to see without being seen—either by neighbors or . . .

She tried not to think about that one.

Instead she focused on the house—beyond its stones and slabs and angles, beyond the impressive facade—to its heart. What it represented. Deriving courage from the thought, she let herself in the side door.

After a moment for her eyes to adjust, she was able to comfortably decipher familiar shapes and spaces, objets d'art. Still, she was careful to stay well back from the windows. She was sure the house was empty or else she'd never have gone back inside. With this much time gone, all the cop comings and goings—perhaps even surveillance, though she'd spotted none—the man with the scars was unlikely to be anywhere nearby.

Unlikely . . .

Taking no chances, she went to the kitchen, took a butcher knife from the rack and felt its heft, held it out at the shadows. At HIM. *Not this time, you murdering fuck,* she thought. After a couple of minutes, and with visualization techniques learned from her numerous brushes with therapy, she was able to take the knife room-to-room-to-room with growing confidence. Until more or less satisfied no one else was there.

*Stay centered.*

Returning to her room, she stuffed some clothing and effects into a duffel bag from her closet and carried the bag downstairs, eyes scanning continually for movement in the darkness now forming like black pools in the caverns of the house. So far so good.

She slipped out the same side entrance. Taking her time to avoid open spots, she made the garage and let the door beside the far bay ease shut behind her, found and deactivated the wall timer controlling the outside spots. On time and in time: She'd remembered correctly.

Lacking windows, the garage was much darker, and she turned on her small pocket flash, by its beam rummaged until she found the cabinet Wil had described—being careful, of course, to avoid looking at the spot where Celeste's body had hung. She recalled the Polaroids the man had shown her, fought new shivers.

*Keep going.*

She tipped over a nearby tool case, shoved it against the cabinet's doorless side, stepped up, felt for the key, and there it was. Right on top where Wil said he'd replaced it. Inserting the key in the lock, she opened the doors, checked each box until she found the one with Denny's letters to Maeve, the personal effects he'd sent her—Trina, like her grieving mother, never knowing it was right under their noses all this time.

Precisely where a loving husband and father had stashed it.

She imagined him locking the door, smiling in that smugly self-satisfied way of his. One more problem handled, Maeve's maudlin lack of discipline nipped in the bud. Heart surgery, Kordell Van Zant style.

She shook off the thought, toted the box outside. Pausing to sling the duffel over her shoulder, she made her way back down to the dirt access road below the property and the Jaguar, reinstated along with her gas and credit cards. After she'd agreed to stop this "willful madness" with Hardesty.

It had been like a scene from a bad soap: Daddy dearest standing before the full-length windows, looking out on all he surveyed. The master in high dudgeon. Dealing with her as he would an independent-minded subject. In truth, that was all she and Eric and Den and her mother had ever been, even though she was dead now and free of him, thank God.

*Subjects to rule.*

Trina tossed in the duffel, hoisted the box into the backseat beside it. Opening the Jag's trunk, she removed the four heavy canisters and wrestled each back to the house, stopping several times to get her breath. Finally it was done and she was inside again, removing the tops of first one canister, then the second and the third, sloshing the contents around where she thought they would do the most good. Saving the last for the liquid trail she backed out a safe distance.

Chest heaving, she stood a moment, taking in the lights of Malibu, hints of wild-something-or-other in the damp air, the sweep of coastline. A few drops of rain had started to fall, the mountains behind her buried now in cloud. Too little too late, she thought, reaching into her pocket for the throwaway lighter purchased along with the canisters.

There was a *whump* as the gas ignited and raced in a flaming river for the target, larger *whumps* as individual rooms, then stairwell and upstairs became fully involved. From out near the pool, she heard the sound of windows blowing out, a roar of release; things screeching and groaning, buckling and collapsing. Sirens from far down the hill.

She pictured Maeve Van Zant smiling.

Her, too, she realized, glancing in the rearview mirror as she drove away, the fire showing yellow red and leaping high above the house. Twisting and dancing in obscene tribute to the archdemon who'd built it. And for the first time she wished her mother hadn't removed his things from the house.

# 24

Lannie never saw the man with the gun.

No reason to suspect he was inside the house, waiting to emerge after Lannie'd shot up and was starting to pound out some serious reps. First he knew was during flat bench, 365 pressed above his chest—in the zone, a nice warm pump already starting in his pecs.

"You don't worry about not having a spotter?" The voice lightly accented and coming from out of sight behind him.

Lannie settled the bar in the rack, blew out a breath, hacked off that he hadn't seen it coming. But from where? Had to be the laundry room off the garage, the only place he hadn't checked.

*Goddamnit.*

"Hands on the bar, please, eyes straight ahead." A chromed revolver with a very long barrel tapped the steel, Lannie feeling it through his hands, the gun about a .40 from the looks of the bore. Big mo-fo. Things not looking too good right now.

"That's right."

The more he considered his position, the madder at himself he got—maybe not so bad, he figured, release a little steam and buy some time. "Where's your damn sense?" he said angrily. "You fucking don't do that when somebody's lifting. Thing can be dangerous."

"Lot of weight, all right. What's your best?"

"Yeah, like you're really here to discuss that." If only he could get a good look at the guy. He heard the scrape of chair legs, squeak of leather seat cushion.

"Can't fool you, Lannie," the accent said, Australian if he had to guess, that hard nasal twang. Like somebody'd messed with his adenoids. "Actually, I came here to kill you."

The revolver going to full cock. Pausing to let *that* sink in.

Lannie felt the sweat coming now, but damned if he was going to come unglued. Think yoga. *Think.*

"I hear wheels turning, Lannie. Waste of time and testosterone. See, I'm better at this—every phase—than you are on your best day. Think been there, done that. Am I getting through?"

Lannie said nothing, beginning to wonder. After all, he was there in his house, wasn't he?

"Earth to Lannie . . ."

"What do you want from me?"

"How many reps can you do with the setup you got there?"

Lannie felt a chill on his burn, a flutter down deep.

"Eight—maybe ten. Depends."

"How about if your life were at stake? Fewer than ten, I blow your brains out, go have a beer." Beer coming out like *beah.*

In spite of the position he was in, he almost laughed. "Spare me the handjob, Jack. If it's money—"

He felt something squirt onto his bare chest, glimpsed the syringe it came from, heard: "Made a little cocktail from your stash—

the ones I recognized, at least. These things can be tricky in combination, you know that? *Dangerous.*"

Mimicking his line about it. "Bullshit, that stuff's—"

"Trust me. I've been studying what the old man's been doing in his little labs. Cousins of Kordec-Z. You've been a lucky boy so far."

Gravity was cooling off Lannie's forearms, the blood leaving them, his hands still gripped above his eyes.

"But then so has Kordell," the man added. "So far."

"What you know about Kordec-Z?"

"Why, everything. What it cost to make—in money *and* bodies—what it's supposed to do for the company, this week's big announcement. What's going to happen instead."

The man walked around so Lannie could see him from where he was lying on the bench. The hair didn't compute at first, less white than he remembered from the Waipio. But the scars did. And the way he held an imaginary cell phone to his ear.

"Remember me?" he asked, with a little smile.

## "eight . . ."

*Deep breath, hold it, now . . . push.*

"Nine . . ."

*Mind is everything . . . let's go.*

"Nine and a half . . ."

*God!* Lannie let out a bellow he hadn't known was in him and clanged the bar into the rack.

"Not much for form on that last one," the man with the scars said. "But we'll count it. This time."

Lannie's breath came in ragged gasps; stars jittered around the periphery of his vision. He dropped his arms straight out from his chest, like a man on a cross.

The gun muzzle came to rest in his scalp. "Ah-ah, back on the bar, please. There's still Plan A."

Lannie couldn't answer.

"This is L.A. People *get* murdered here during home break-ins. You think the cops are going to care?"

"*Fuck you.*" Pathetic sounding even to him.

Something chrome was dangled across the bar above his eyes: a pair of handcuffs. Followed by another.

"The left, please, then to the bar."

"You gotta be kidding."

He felt as much as heard the hammer cocked back. "Guess that's it, then, sport. Try not to splatter too much."

Lannie did as directed.

"Now slide your left hand over and do the right. . . . That's it."

Lannie felt the gun leave his head, heard a plate slide onto first one end then the other.

"Might as well make it a challenge, don't you think?"

"Who the fuck *are* you?"

"Call me John. Eric does now."

"That's what this is about? Little Eric getting his jollies?"

"Don't worry about him. Eric's right on schedule."

"On schedule for what?"

"What's coming his way. And something surely is."

"This being a part of it."

"This? This is just the beginning—a little side thing I have in mind. Now up. And this time keep it up."

Lannie raised the bar, in seconds feeling the sweat begin to pour off him, his arms holding but starting to tremble.

"There's some things I want to know, Lan. Things only you have the answers to."

"*Go fuck yourself.*"

"This stuff you're using: I know where Kordell makes it, where it's stored in TJ, how you bring it across—Eric's been real good about that. What I need to know from you is, what's it feel like? What are its properties? How much is enough? What would too much be?"

*"Fuck Eric. And how the hell would I know that?"*

"Because you're a guinea pig with vocal cords and half a head on his shoulders. Right what I need."

Lannie said nothing. Let *him* talk, maybe figure an angle.

"The world is waiting, Lan, big bucks in its grubby little fingers. It wants to know, therefore I do. Now."

Lannie heaved, clanged the barbell back in the rack. No reaction yet—so far, so good, maybe a way out of this yet. Cooperative but assertive: Bargain a little, lose the cuffs, lock his palms around old John's temples, and crush his head as he would a melon, the seeds going every which way, pulp out his ears. The big revolver might be a problem, but hey—anything was possible

"Sure, Lan. Rest a second."

Lannie heard things rolling in a box then. Mom-o's curlers, it sounded like, on those nights when she was clean and sober enough to *do* her hair—funny how it came back to him after so many years. Like she'd beamed it there or something. But he knew it was his vials and syringes, not much mistaking the sound or what the Aussie said next.

"We're talking personal best here."

**after** a number of tries, Wil finally reached Trina at nine A.M. from his Santa Monica hotel. Home had sounded infinitely better after finishing with Eugene Chen, but not going there was safer, given Buckhalter's people probably had a watch on the house. Besides, he'd only have to come back again. Earlier in the morning, he'd gone for a walk on the beach to try to sort things out. Make full color out of old black-and-white.

*Lannie Crowell, KTVB, hoping you'll let my viewers know what happened—what you're feeling.* Freelancer Crowell passing himself off as a reporter, the least of his transgressions the way it looked. Add evidence tampering, obstruction of justice, conspiracy, and most likely blackmail, you had not a bad day's work.

Wil pictured the dark-skinned hand again, the instant of reaching for the bracelet, an act triggered by what? Brass-ring dreams? Hearing Sandor Marquez spit out the golden name Van Zant? Seeing the thing as a way out? Or had it been sheer impulse: worry about it later, no thought given to the risk, what the ramifications might be? Then or now—wondering if even Lannie would recall.

Questions spun, numbered balls that refused to drop: *what, who, how, why.* Until both the carousel and the pier's new Ferris wheel movements seemed appropriate to his own thoughts.

Before leaving Chen's office, he'd been able to extend his luck to reaching a Santa Barbara expatriate named Howie McEwan, whose butt he'd once pulled out of a wringer involving an ex-girlfriend's erotic tendencies, some missing credit cards, and Howie's employability. Now laboring in the Los Angeles Hall of Records, Howie was in position to tap both superior- and muni-court arrest histories—things Wil could do himself with enough time. But the clinker once again was the wait—several days that could mean something with John Pomphrey out there.

Ergo, no contest: weekend surf lessons at the Rincon and a place to stay the price—Howie's yearning for Santa Barbara working for *him*. He'd agreed to have something on Lannie Crowell—if it existed—by early afternoon.

As for Trina, she sounded in a fog, having trouble at first even recognizing his voice.

"You all right? Did I wake you?"

"Not really. Wil, I . . ."

"You called me, remember? It's been a little hard connecting." Curious about the cause of the fog—booze, pills, drugs? Hell, get off it: her life, after all. Abundantly clear from the other night.

"Wil, I called because I need to see you."

"Where are you?"

"Some motel—I don't mean here. Wil, I did something. . . ."

He felt a little trip, the pin on a grenade. "What, Tree?"

"Later . . . I'll tell you later."

"When and where?"

"I don't . . . can't . . ."

"Come on, talk to me."

"Wil, please . . ."

He took a breath. Easy—someplace easy: "How about the beach?"

"No. It's too public."

"What have you done, Tree?"

Long pause, then: "That meditative garden. Off Sunset near PCH. You know the one?"

Lake, flowers, quiet: just off the thoroughfare and a thousand miles away. "Yeah. What time?"

"Time?"

"Right. It's nine o'clock now."

"Eleven," she said finally. "Wil? Do you think you . . . think it could ever be the way it was again? With you and me?"

Hard to think of it as anything but classic backslide manipulation. Yet something in her tone sent him back to where "Moon

River" played on a tinny bedroom stereo and two kids clung to each other, not wanting it to end. Ever.

Dial tone brought him back.

Fighting self-pity but not very hard, he finished dressing and went out to get coffee. Sun played tag with the breaking clouds, and a breeze off the ocean accompanied him to the three-block promenade mall, then back again to his room.

French roast kicking in, whitecaps on the bay and deli bagels with cream cheese making him feel better, he put in another call, this time to Mo Epstein—sheriff's department homicide bureau having jurisdiction via Malibu on Celeste's murder. Possible suspect: John Pomphrey, Australian demolitions specialist on temporary assignment to American forces, 1967–68. He went on to explain the specifics: Pomphrey missing in action at Hue, presumed dead; the photo in among Denny's things; Trina's thought it could be him without scars.

In a way he was glad it was only voice mail, Epstein generally in a bind regarding the longshots he drummed up, this being a beaut. In fact, mere mention of the term *PI* was almost guaranteed to set LASD teeth on edge, brass ones in particular. But the case was hot and Epstein was inclined to take him seriously because of their history; telling Wil he'd help where he could, despite regs against nonofficial use. Databases talking to databases—what they were there for, Mo maintained. Give the bad guys fits.

Not that he held out much hope.

Ten o'clock: He dialed Van Zant Inc., got a receptionist, then a secretary who told him Mr. Van Zant would be in high demand the next few days—in and out. Smarter to try him the following week when things had calmed from the annual meeting, this being an important time for the company and Mr. Van Zant in particular. Despite it, he left a message: Hardesty wanting to talk ASAP and alone about a bracelet with links to a close associate; pick a time and place.

Good luck, she told him.

At ten-thirty he checked out, drove PCH to Sunset, turned right, and almost missed the unobtrusive sign. Pulling into the near-empty lot, he caught sight of Trina's Jag. Early.

He left the rental and made his way along the trail—bushes and trees showing new leaf, winter florals, vines coming into bud. At one end of the lake, a houseboat sat in repose; on his left, the windmill/chapel stood out against a notch in the hills. He kept walking: past the square-arched memorial, religious statuary, benches tucked in among the foliage.

It was on one of these that he saw her: elbows on her knees, head down. Smoke from the cigarette she held curled around hair that looked marginally combed, falling forward like streaked brown water on either side of an imprecise part.

She looked up, tried to smile at his approach, but it stuck partway, slipped into vacant. He held her briefly, neither of them saying anything until they broke and sat down.

"Thanks for coming," she said finally.

"You're welcome, but aren't we a little beyond that?"

"Wil, you need to know something up front." She took breaths, as though prepping for a long dive underwater. "I burned it last night. At least it was burning when I left. Fire trucks were coming up the hill."

Boom, just like that: With difficulty he let it filter through him, figuring calm for the most good. "The Malibu house," he said.

She nodded, refused to meet his eyes. "I used gasoline."

"Jesus, Trina."

Tears started. He waited them out, watched her swipe at them with her hand.

"Guess you showed *him*, all right."

More breaths, trying to regain her composure. "Please—try and understand. Just for once, I wanted to hurt him back. The way he'd hurt her."

"So you torched it." He looked out at the lake: Ducks poked around in the reeds and lily pads; farther out, an aeration sprinkler threw water high in the air, catching the light.

"Tree, I wish I could offer something insightful and forgiving, like I feel your pain or something. Like you hadn't had advantages most people only dream about."

"There's a price for all that."

"There's a price for everything. That's how it works."

The tears started again.

"Cry over a plant, why don't you. It might appreciate it more."

"Wil, please, I . . ."

He stared at the water. "If I recall, you made a choice the other night. *Him*. For better or worse."

"Don't you dare put it like that. What was I supposed to do?"

"How about live with it? It happens every day."

She rubbed a spot on the back of her hand.

"Look, what the hell do you want from me?" he said. And so much for calm, retreating in his wake like a swan run down by a hydroplane.

"Help, advice, friendship—I don't know. . . ."

"You ever think of calling him to apologize?"

"I'd die first."

"I see. How about turning yourself in?"

"You're a fine one to talk. No, I didn't mean—"

"Sad, isn't it?" he said, not looking at her. "Us. This. What it's come down to."

She ground her cigarette out, began twisting the bands on her right ring finger. "You want to know something? I used to daydream about you proposing to me—what being married would be like. Last night when I couldn't sleep, what bothered me most was what you'd think of me. That's what I really regret."

She reached a hand out, caught his and held it to her damp cheek as two kids and a parent strolled by, tried not to stare. In a minute they were lost from view.

"Let's get out of here," she said urgently. "Go far away—Tahiti or someplace." Not waiting for him to reply: "Start over. There must be something I'd be good at, and there's always work for you."

He looked at her, tried to read her face.

"Now—this minute," she added. "What do you say?"

Sincere came through. For a moment he let it take him: the simplicity of it, the newness; her wide eyes, the lethargy in them replaced now by flashes of light.

Then the wave retreated, leaving cold wet sand.

"It's not hearts and flowers in a notebook anymore, Tree. No matter how much we wish it was."

"Yeah? What's here that's so goddamned important? It's going to hell anyway—why not just let it?"

He shook his head. "That's exactly why I can't. Mr. Responsible, remember?"

The flashes died, but she met his eyes anyway. "Of course. It was a dumb idea. Just me getting carried away."

"Not dumb, Tree—never dumb. Let's clean this up first, think it through. Seriously, if it's what you want."

Her smile was barely that. "Sure. Look, I've kept you long enough. I really should go."

"Not before you hear some things." He told her about the film, the tape, the bracelet, his theory—product of last night and the morning beach walk: her father turning Lannie's attempt at blackmail to his advantage; keeping Lannie close with money and a position—a stake in it. He went through his visit with Steven Neves, what he'd found out about Denny, about John Pomphrey. The three of them in the photograph.

She looked out over the lake. "God, it's even worse than I imagined."

"At least I'm getting somewhere."

"And you think whoever wore the bracelet killed Carmen?"

"Works for me. Do you recall who in your family it might have belonged to?"

"Not Den, that's for sure."

"What I figured."

"Both Daddy and Eric had them at one time. I don't think Eric does anymore."

Wil thought about that: next step was contacting the medical-emergency-alert companies; maybe enlist Buckhalter, if he'd listen. He mentioned it.

"Don't hold your breath," she said. "Daddy was giving money to the police down there as recently as when he moved out. I saw canceled checks once on his desk."

"We need to talk to him."

"Right. After what I did to his house."

"We'll figure something out," he said.

"What about Eric?"

"Your father before Eric, I think."

"You said he wasn't in."

"The message I left will interest him. Meantime, do you know where Lannie lives?"

She nodded, and he didn't know if it was the way her hair moved or the carousel and the Ferris wheel grinding to a halt, his thoughts going linear again—what the feeling was. But it was there.

**Lannie** hadn't reported in yet. Not unusual for him, the receptionist stated dryly; often he was gone for days at a time, his position as security chief a mobile one. Thinking he'd try for a date of hire, Wil asked and was referred to an underling in human resources who confirmed the information was confidential. Later for that, he thought, some ruse bound to work.

He tried the home number Trina had listed, got Lannie's machine, and left no message. Calls to the lab and veterans' clinic went nowhere as well, no one had seen him. He tried corporate again: nothing yet from Kordell. Standard for this week, the secretary reminded Wil in I-told-you-so tones.

Probably sifting through the remains of his Malibu house, Wil figured: likely talking to arson people, naming possible suspects. Like a disgruntled, on-the-run private investigator named Hardesty. He shook his head, just hearing that one unfold.

At one, he reached his hall-of-records source, Howie McEwan.

"Okay," Howie came on. "I checked superior for felonies, municipal for misdemeanors. Double session, I'd say."

"Since when have you made it through a morning with me, let alone a full day?"

"Since this new surf-fitness routine I'm into. You got a pencil?"

"Poised."

"Not much need," he said. "Crowell's clean as a whistle, except for some traffic beef *beaucoup* years ago. Report had him listed as Nonstop Productions then—piled into a guy at an intersection who swore he was loaded. Got settled out of court. *Nada* since then."

*Bingo on Nonstop*, Wil thought. "What year?"

"February, sixty-six."

"Good, Howie, thanks."

"One other thing. There was a juvie flag in the jacket."

"Sealed record? What for? I wonder."

"Two days surf city and the house for a night alone?"

"Jesus, take the deed while you're at it. What'd you do, break the seal?"

"Thirty-five years, you'd crack and peel, too—I just helped a little. Seems our man Orland Crowell had a checkered youth: several classmate beefs, one with a teacher. Then a very large one. You listening?"

"Don't oversell, Howie."

"Right. Turns out he killed his mother, then nearly cut her head off. At thirteen, no less. Special circumstances, the fact she was a junkie, got him a foster home, probation, the usual. Just goes to show you."

"What's that?"

"Brother was ahead of his time in more ways than one. Surf's up, dude." Howie clicked off.

Wil parked the rental Lumina on a quiet side street, and they headed out in the Jag: PCH to Topanga Canyon Boulevard, Trina riding shotgun so she could concentrate on finding Lannie's place. From her look as they turned off, she seemed relieved not to be going near Malibu, Wil trying to figure out some mitigating spin on the fire and coming up with zero. Just the inevitable deferred.

Inland, the air grew warmer and vegetation thickened, canyon walls and bare-limbed sycamores rising from the creekbeds, the road going switchback. Wildflowers laced the turnouts and the fringes; little enclaves came and went, the roofs of mixed-bag houses. Past a grouping of these, she put him on alert, trying to recall the turnoff from some long-ago obligatory open house, during which she'd gotten blasted with husband number two, making it home in their Porsche 928 in coaster-ride fashion.

"There, on the right," she said finally.

Wil followed her point, eased the Jag onto a single-lane path that curved past scrub oaks and low growth, by asphalt driveways leading down to tile roofs, until finally a bend appeared, and around it Lannie's white Trans Am. He pulled up behind it and stopped.

The house beyond it was basic Valley, lifted up and plunked down in a canyon setting: no lawn, no sprinklers, no flowers, no trimmed hedges. Just a eucalyptus, couple of stunted pines, and some ceanothus, a certain hideaway character. Wood deck extended out over the slope leading down to the creek.

Wil felt the hood of the Trans Am. Cold. He approached the front door, pressed the bell, waited; knocked and knocked again, this time louder. The air smelled of creek. Insect hum droned like a high-tension power line.

Not liking it, he gestured to Trina watching, then eased around back, hoping for a look in from deckside. He heard water running now, the sound coming from a greenbelt of willows and cattail. Planks creaked as he stepped onto the deck: blackened hibachi on the railing, weathered lounges here and there. Shading his eyes against reflection off the glass, he looked inside to a small but neat kitchen. Pots, pans, and utensils hung from a rack over the stove, a ricepaper globe over the light fixture. In the adjacent dining room, a samurai sword hung on the room's paneled wall.

Teak, it looked like, the cabinets as well. But it was the doorway that led into a living area beyond that held his attention. From the chrome-and-black vinyl equipment, it was more gym than living room. Which would explain the bare leg and cross-trainered foot.

For a moment Wil thought Lannie might be resting from an intense bench routine, but his tap on the glass brought no reaction. Leg and foot did not move.

He tried the glass doors: shut tight, a length of pipe in the slider. Scanning for other windows, he saw a small one with glass louvers behind a pop-out screen he was able to dislodge with his pocketknife. Sliding out the louvers, he eased himself into a bathroom, all indigo tile and more wood.

Kitchen and dining room, the door with the leg.

Lannie Crowell lay on the flat bench, hands still gripping the bar, as if struggling to lift it off his throat where it had come to rest—an inexorable avalanche. Wil did a quick calculation: over 500 pounds; saw Lannie exercising alone, pushing his luck beyond its limit and missing the rack, somehow not dumping the plates until it was too late. The bar squeezing the life out of him. Flattening and snapping his neck as his breath left.

Macho obvious. Or was it?

What seemed more so was Lannie's obvious experience with weights, surely with exercising solo. Hell, the equipment was better than at most pro gyms. At least the ones Wil had been to.

He looked closer, saw the needle tracks, and it began to come together—impaired judgment or heart failure: OD all over it. Lannie Crowell RIP.

By his doing? Or *HIS?*

He turned to searching the house, particularly the bedroom. Needlepoint on chair seats and wall tapestries reminded him of Reanne Rodriguez's guest room—of staying there after having to explain to her how he'd lost her husband to a killer named Sanchez he'd been hired to find. Couple of years and a lifetime ago. Obviously needlecraft was one of Lannie's passions, too, a work in progress beside the bed.

Next to it on the floor, between a clean-topped dresser and lamp table, were socks, boxer shorts, striped shirt, oversized khakis—abandoned in haste, or so it seemed, Lannie anxious to get to his workout after arriving home. Wil went through the pockets, found business cards in the shirt, bills in a money clip, stainless-steel pocketknife, ballpoint, lip balm, couple of credit cards in the pants.

Plus a jeweler-size manila envelope marked *West Valley Savings Bank*, no entry where the safety-deposit number went. Blanks also for the dates-of-deposit and withdrawal lines.

Just above the bulge.

The flap was only tucked into the envelope's seam, not sealed. Wil opened it, let the bracelet slide easily into his hand, thinking *has to be.* Medical-emergency insignia on the faceup side, registration and phone number on the other; base metal showing through spots in the chain and the bracelet's thin edges. Overall patina of age.

For a moment he just held it, wanting its vibe; then he slipped it back, pocketed the envelope. Wondering at the strange circularity, his taking it now from Lannie.

Which assumed a great deal, granted.

Not having called the number on the back, still a chance the thing belonged to Lannie. If that were the case, though, why not wear it? Obviously he'd had it a long time, most likely in the deposit box, the date on somebody's log at the savings bank if it came to that.

But time was now: bureau drawers, finding nothing that might relate, closets the same—guns and knives, some martial-arts devices showing up as tools of quite another talent, plus a pile of muscle mags. In one drawer he found a stash of syringes and vials with cloudy liquid in them—hits on the steroid use, especially after sniffing several and getting no odor, a characteristic. In another, he found a glass dish full of bar matches, picked up the top one, good reason why it had called to him.

*Art's Bar*, it said. *Huntington Beach.*

*Son of a bitch:* easy seeing Joe Avenal's arm twisted until he screamed, a plastic bag jammed down his throat. Simple enough for a man as strong as Lannie and a man as drunk as Avenal.

Wil went through the rest of the house, places somebody might hide something; no time for a thorough tossing. The killer—assuming there was one, robbery obviously no motive—could already have tipped the cops to the location, get two birds at once. Nothing he wanted to risk much longer.

Little turned up—his planner with largely indecipherable notes, a few skin mags and videos, multicolored condoms and flavored gels, none of which Wil chose to touch. One last shot because he was in the bedroom: Thinking it was the last place Lannie'd hide anything because of his work, and the last place you'd look because of it, he shoved a hand deep between mattress and box spring.

Reaching the middle of the bed to pull out . . . what?

He spent a moment opening the large blank-faced envelopes, found what appeared to be a file-drawer key taped to one of the manila folders inside. Thumbing through the photocopies now: enough to get a feel for the reports he was reading.

As he was putting the sheets back in the envelopes, he heard a cry from the living room and found Trina gaping down at Lannie's bloated face. Fast-swallowing as though trying to dislodge a bone from her throat. Behind the hand cupped over her mouth, her color was as off-white as the walls.

He went to her and gently eased her away, stood so it forced her to look directly into his eyes instead. Which is how he was able to see it coming. Luckily she held off until he could get her to the bathroom.

# 25

**eric** watched John Pomphrey cleaning one of his guns, the big chrome revolver looking like a damned howitzer. Finally he realized he was getting nowhere with the cost figures he was going over, having taken the afternoon off not only to catch up, but because it was becoming impossible at the office, the old man all over everything. Despite Eric's telling him time and again that his end of it—the anticipated effect of Kordec-Z on profits—was covered. Backward, forward, upside down, inside out.

Hell, why wouldn't it be? He was the one who'd tracked them.

The phone rang and activated the answering machine: another call from the old man, this time having to do with the Malibu house. As if he could give a shit, a firestorm the best thing to happen out there in years. Should have thought of it a long time ago.

"Tell me," he said to Pomphrey after Kordell's voice had clicked off. "Was that your doing?"

"Now, why would *I* burn it, Eric?"

He shook his head. "Had to be my fucking sister, then."

"I don't know," Pomphrey said, "but I'm pissed. Hell, I'd already planned to live there."

"You what?"

"I have quite fond memories of it. The upstairs especially." He spun the revolver's cylinder, clicked it back into line, tested the hammer positions. Then he started on the automatic. "Fine-looking woman, your sister. Nice ass."

"You're disgusting."

Pomphrey smiled, sighted the empty automatic in on Eric's face, watched him flinch as he snapped the trigger. "Stranger bedfellows have happened in the name of business." Keeping the gun on him, little jerks as he mock-fired it.

"I've asked you not to do that."

"Oh, yeah. Guess I forgot." He lowered the gun.

"What is it?" Eric asked. "The weapon, I mean."

"Tell me you really care."

"Look, I'm trying here. What is it?"

"All right. It's a .44 magnum with a six-inch barrel—gas operation, rotating bolt, black oxide finish. No more nine-mil for this boyo. Not after Hawaii."

"What happened there?"

"I told you before, nine-millimeter is what happened. Not enough juice."

"But you said you'd hit him."

Pomphrey smiled. "I hit him, all right. But I like to peel back the eyelids afterward, peer into the void—just me, I guess. Why? You still worried?"

"Should I be?"

"Can't think of a reason now." He fed in a clip, worked the slide, set the safety and the pistol down. "How's the meeting prep going? Not that you're going to need it."

Eric went with the new direction, glad of it. "Why do you think I'm here and not there? Two fucking days—and I'm not sure I can stand it *that* long."

"Two days till the meeting," Pomphrey corrected him. "One till kickoff, pardon the pun."

"What about Lannie?"

"There's a boy should have been more careful."

Eric swallowed, clicked the lid shut on his laptop. "How did he die?"

Pomphrey's eyes were black stones. "Like they all do, Eric."

Wondering at the ease with which he passed it off, the mere thought of what it took to kill someone as strong as Lannie, Eric stood, walked to the kitchen, and poured two shots of Canadian whiskey—what the pain in the ass had been drinking ever since he got here. A step above mouthwash as far as Eric was concerned. Nonetheless a gesture of respect. No more Lannie, Kordell alone: The thought hit him with something he hadn't felt in years—excitement. Handing Pomphrey one of the glasses, Eric tipped back the other and drank. Coughed at the heat.

"Little early for it, don't you think?"

"No, I don't, *John*. And I've come to a decision on something." Eric steadied on Pomphrey, looking at him for as long as he could before breaking off, sending his gaze out over the Valley and the layer of grunge. Anticipation ran through him like electricity. No more bullshit, just the bigs now—understanding what was expected of him, a warrior armed and ready for the fight, his true role. Just hadn't known it until now.

"I want to be there," he said, the voice and words feeling strange at first, then more comfortable as they hung there—tangible things almost. Pennants seized in bloody battle.

"Are we clear on this? I want to be there when you kill him."

For the first time Pomphrey's smile seemed real. "What a thoughtful son," he said.

Wil had Trina pull the Jag over at a closed restaurant with a pay phone outside. He fed the coin slot, dialed the number off the bracelet, got referred to another number, and as cars whizzed by on the two-lane, pretended to be an EMT with a life-or-death playing out, relaying the ID registration number—adrenaline jacked into his voice for emphasis, his Coast-Guard first-aid training coming in handy. After a bit, yelling over his shoulder at an imaginary associate, he rang off and got back in the car.

"Well?" Trina asked.

"You ready for this? It's Eric. Hypoglycemia."

Her face revealed nothing.

"Shy little Eric with the oboe or whatever it was . . ."

"The clarinet," she said tonelessly.

"Look, I want to put some miles between us and the house back there. You okay to drive?"

She nodded, started the car and put it in gear, eased up to the roadway, looked back as if to pull out. But nothing happened. She just sat there, hands gripping the wheel, eyes fixed—as if she were seeing something else entirely.

Wil took it out of gear, walked around, guided her to the passenger side, got back in. He readjusted the driver's seat, waited for a break, then hit it, half expecting law to come screaming toward them from the other direction. There was none, however, and after a straight stretch, they were around a curve and climbing a ridge, heading for bright ocean off in the distance.

*Malibu: They've driven up from Newport because the surf reports have been touting four to eight feet at the break called Outside, the best it's been anywhere this month, a so-far-crummy October. It's Wednesday, and they've pulled little brother Eric out of school with a bogus note from Maeve per Denny's promise to take him along when it heavied up—put all their dry runs and two-footers to work, Denny spare-time-attempting to make a surfer out of him.*

*Eric's eyes are wide as he paddles to keep up.*

*"Good, man," Denny calls back. "Just a little farther out. Past those rocks."*

*"No way," Eric insists. "The waves are too big out there."*

*"It's okay here, if he wants," Wil chimes in.*

*"Look, Mojo, who's leading this mission? Okay isn't good enough for my brother. Right, Eric?"*

"It's too big out there!"

*"No such thing in our book," Denny says. "Come on, you're not some chickenshit. You're a Van Zant." He paddles back, begins to move Eric's board ahead.*

*Eric continues to protest, but Denny is oblivious and soon they reach the spot. "As we were saying," he says.*

*"I want to go back," Eric says.*

*"Same here, bro, and here comes the bus. Get ready."*

*"I don't know, Den," Wil says, coming up beside him so Eric won't hear. "Don't think I'd want to be a beginner out here."*

*"Last time, Mojo, this is the way to learn. You know it and I know it. How far would you have gotten if you hadn't pushed yourself?"*

*"It's different for everybody. He's scared."*

*"No he's not," Denny counters, trying to pump his brother up, build his confidence. "That's not fear, that's anticipation. You gotta learn to read people better."*

*The set is almost on them.*

*Denny says, "Okay, Eric, it's like I told you. We give the first two a pass and grab number three, all right? Just pretend it's a two-footer at Fifteenth Street. Nothing to it."*

*But Eric is looking over his shoulder at the waves bearing down, his face as pale as the foam inside the break.*

*Swells one and two roll by, most of the lineup taking off, then number three is there, a good ten feet in height, Den yelling last-second encouragement before hitting it himself. On a hunch, Wil hangs back, sees Denny into it and ripping, Eric rising haltingly to one knee. Only to freeze and sink back down.*

*Too far forward on the board.*

*As the walled-up wave begins to spill, the board nose-dives, taking Eric with it. Wil watches the wave crash in on itself, Eric's board leap skyward and tumble back, head for the beach with no one aboard, no leash in those days to stop it.*

*No Eric, no Eric, no Eric . . .* Shit.

*Wil paddles for the spot, points the Southern Cross out, then rolls off. He's about to dive blind when five feet away Eric bursts up choking and coughing, tendrils of kelp wrapped around him. Seeming to pull him back.*

*Wil corrals his board, yells to Eric that he's coming, hang on.*

*But Eric is beyond it. Panicked, he whirls and thrashes: He's beset by serpents, giant squid, dead people determined to drag him down. Wil has seen the look before and has no desire to face a drowner's frenzy. He pushes the Southern Cross at Eric, yells for him to grab hold, then comes in from behind and thrusts him, kelp and all, up onto the surface of the board.*

*Gradually Eric calms as Wil untwines the kelp, throws it off in handfuls. As he does he looks for Denny, sees him nowhere as the next wave heaves up under them to break farther in, and Wil kicks for shore. Then they're stumbling from the water and Denny is racing up, eyes like saucers, face white under his tan.*

*"I saw the board come in. Oh my God, Eric—are you all right?"*

*Eric vomits at his feet.*

*"It's okay, it's okay. It's all my fault," Denny says in anguish, bending over him to reassert order and fairness to a world gone suddenly and incomprehensibly off its axis. "We had it going there," he says to Wil. "What the hell happened?"*

*"You had it going, he wasn't ready. The board pearled on him."*

*"Fuck that piece of shit, Eric. You got a new one coming, if I have to make it myself." The bluster is crackle thin, fresh-formed ice on a lake of remorse and fear.*

*Eric manages to lean back on his ankles. His eyes are red, face green; Medusa-tangle hair adds to the look of death warmed over. Around the beach, people are staring. One comes over to make a suggestion about what to do when you've swallowed a lot of salt water, then leaves.*

*"I screwed up bad, Eric, I am truly sorry. Tell me you're okay—please."*

*Eric's eyes pin on Denny, then break off. He hawks and spits on the sand. In a voice sounding coarse and older from retching, he says, "Get away from me. You're not my brother anymore."*

At Will Rogers State Beach, he found a spot and they pulled in. For a time they just sat, taking in its pulse: waves, seabirds, joggers, sunbathers, families. Harmless, innocuous, bright things.

Trina chugged four of Wil's aspirin from a water bottle in her purse. She shook her head. "I've never seen anything like back there."

"It's my fault. I should have warned you off."

"I didn't know what happened to you. I got scared. God, poor Lannie."

He nodded, seeing it again: the swollen face and ruined neck.

"Wil, is that—this—really what you—"

"Generally not, no."

"That is, until we came back into your life."

He tried smiling at her, to no apparent effect.

"Do you think it was an accident?"

"Lannie's dying that way? No, I don't."

"Why not?"

He shifted in the seat. "Because I know guys like him, Tree, guys who've worked out for years. Lannie knew the drill—weights, juice, what he could and couldn't handle. I'm not a big believer in coincidence."

"Why would somebody want to kill him?"

He thought a moment. "What exactly did he do for your father?"

"Lannie? I think he's listed as corporate head of security."

"So he protected him."

"Among other things," she said. "You think it has to do with that?"

"I don't know. But if I wanted a crack at The Man, I'd sure want Lannie out of the way. Wouldn't you?"

"I suppose."

Wil watched two little boys about five and seven pack sand into plastic pails, turn them upside down, admire the result, try to get their father interested, to no avail. "What puzzles me is why the bracelet like that—why now?"

She was silent; then: "Just a thought, but did you see his planner—the entry for Saturday's meeting?"

"Nothing I much remember."

" 'B to K,' it said. How about 'Bracelet to Kordell?' "

Wil shrugged. "Kind of a reach."

"Maybe not. Over the years Lannie and my father got close—not that I was around a lot, but that's the way it seemed. I know it drove Eric crazy; he despised Lannie. I mean, here's my father encouraging Lannie to invest in his company, giving him money advice. Eric told me he heard them on the phone."

"So?"

"So if what you say is true about Dad responding to the bracelet by taking him on, maybe Lannie was doing something symbolic. Thirty years together or something."

Turning it over in his mind, not rejecting it altogether. "How many years does your father have before Eric takes over?"

"He owns fifty-two percent. He'll go till they bury him."

"I wonder."

"Not sure I get your point."

Wil said, "The bracelet wasn't what kept Lannie in place, it was being good at what he did. Maybe, as you say, bonds developed between him and Kordell. But here's Eric who has no use for Lannie coming up in the rearview mirror. It's just a matter of time. Once again Lannie acts to secure his future."

She looked at him. "What?"

"The papers I found under the mattress were drug application histories—experiments, from what I could tell. I have to check out the names, but two-to-one they coincide with the vet suicides at the clinic."

"Where did he get them?"

He told her about Vega's input: suspicions of drug testing on patients; one patient, Billy Dulay, making documentation copies before disappearing, washing up dead. "My guess is, Lannie found them when he went after Dulay, which he certainly would have. Maybe even made the copies himself, recognizing what they meant. Kind of a trait of his."

"The bracelet wasn't enough?"

Wil watched the five-year-old trample the seven-year-old's sand castle, mother intervening at the howls, father still lost in his paperback.

"Think about it: What good was the bracelet after Lannie took it? All Eric had to do was swear he'd lost it somewhere—how was Lannie going to prove where without incriminating himself? Now maybe Lannie was prepared to do that figuring Kordell still would want to keep it quiet—there had to be some basis for the deal. But your father must have been aware of its real value."

"Basically it told him who killed Carmen."

"Yeah. And who didn't."

She fumbled for a cigarette, punched in the car's lighter. With difficulty, she lit up, taking the cigarette out of her mouth finally and touching it to the coil. Sucking in like Maeve taking a hit of oxygen. "Are you saying he might have put Denny up to enlisting?"

"What I think is that he saw a way out by telling Denny he had a duty to the Van Zants, then greasing a few palms to make it happen. Good-bye problem."

"Even for my father, that would be a new low."

"An adopted son he never cared about versus flesh and blood? Eliminate a scandal before it ruined him? You tell me."

For a while she just smoked and looked out the open window. Wil took her hand, felt ice; small tremors, like aftershocks from a fault deep under the skin.

She said, "You really see Eric killing Carmen?"

"Then, no. Now?" He shrugged.

"Time to ask him, maybe."

"Better to go in with something."

"Like what?"

Wil rubbed his eyes, resettled his sunglasses. "A motive is always nice. What about unrequited love?"

"Eric for Carmen? Come on. He never even had a girlfriend in high school."

"Spin it backward," Wil said. "He keeps calling, sending her letters she rips up. She doesn't tell Denny because Eric's her future brother-in-law, or so it's looking. To get him off her back, she admits she's pregnant, something she's barely told Denny about. Maybe she threatens to go to his father—or worse, Denny. So here's Eric, love to hate in two seconds. Long story short, he picks up a kitchen knife and stabs her. Crime of Passion One-A."

She noticed her cigarette had burned almost to the filter and stubbed it out, snapped the ashtray back in place. "He was seventeen, for God's sake. You remember how young that is?"

"Love and hate turn the world, Tree. On better authority than mine."

For a moment they were quiet. Out on the beach, the kids threw sand at each other, hitting mom, who gave them each a swat. "So what do we do now?" she asked.

"Keep thinking. Who benefits from something happening to your father?"

"Who else?"

"Exactly."

The family packed up and walked toward their station wagon.

"You're not going to tell me you believe *Eric* killed Lannie?"

"No," Wil said. "But Pomphrey interests me for it. He had to have made it out. Too much points to it."

"Why him, then?"

"It comes back to Eric somehow. Maybe Pomphrey's working for him."

She thought about it a moment, obviously trying, but not getting there. "Eric's no initiator, he's weak. If my father didn't protect him, the business would eat him alive."

"I doubt he sees it that way. And Pomphrey belongs to somebody." He pulled out the photograph, scanned it one more time. "Pomphrey ran bad drugs on his own people—the guy I talked to from Denny's company said so. Another said kill him if I got the chance." He put the photo back. "Which tells you something."

"Yeah. That my own brother wanted me dead."

"I don't think so," Wil said. "What would Eric have to gain? My point was, bad as it got, I don't believe Pomphrey meant to kill you, or you'd be dead. The thing I don't get is why he was so obsessed with Denny. Why he nearly killed two people to find out if they knew where he was."

As the parents were brushing sand off the two boys, the older one hit the younger with his pail. Howls started again, cut off by the closing of the car doors, the starting of the engine.

"God, I'm tired," she said. "How about getting a drink?"

"How about seeing the Rock of Gibraltar instead."

# 26

the call from Kordell hit the machine at three-twenty; it was almost five-fifteen now. Wil listened to the rest of his messages, activated from the gas-station pay phone, heard one from Lisa—nothing new on the IRS, just wanting to know how the thing with the cops worked out. One from Mo Epstein had come in just after four, saying he was leaving at five-thirty if Wil wanted to talk before Monday.

He dialed LASD headquarters, waited while they ran a page for Lieutenant Epstein, heard, "Your lucky day, Pedro, I was almost out the door."

"Sometimes it all just comes together."

"Speaking of which, did I see a Murder-Wanted-for-Questioning with your name on it? Huntington Beach comes to mind."

"No idea."

"Some advice from a friend: Take care of business before it takes care of you."

"Thanks, I'm working on it," Wil said. There was a screech of brakes from out on PCH, a blare of horn; he put a hand over his ear to block the noise.

"Your own personal love affair with the automobile?"

"Not exactly. Score something on this John Pomphrey?"

"Yeah—imagine that. Enough to wonder why an international killing machine might be hanging around the neighborhood. Interpol has a real interesting history on him, unless you know that, too. Just a feeling I'm getting."

*So Pomphrey did survive. How? What did he know about Denny?*

"Excuse me?" Mo said to Wil's thought.

"You overestimate me, Mo. I'm all ears."

It took ten minutes; hanging up, he phoned Van Zant Inc., heard Mr. Van Zant currently was at the clinic and would be until evening. Wil took down the number, called there, and was immediately put through.

"I have very little time, Hardesty," he came on with. "State your business."

Bull rush, no end-arounds—the man himself. "Bracelet links," Wil said to match.

Pause. "How can I put this? My family's unfortunate association with you has led not only to my wife's suicide, but a seven-million-dollar house up in smoke. Are you hearing me?"

"Maybe it's time you looked in the mirror."

"What's that supposed to mean?"

"You figure it out. And you're right about the time. I'm not sure you have much left."

"Is that a threat?"

"Not from me, it isn't. Despite what you may think."

"All right," Kordell Van Zant said finally. "Be at the clinic in forty minutes or I'm gone. You know where it is—off Chatauqua?"

"I'll find it."

Line buzz; Wil hung up the pay phone and got back in the car, Trina pale and looking at her hands as if somehow they still reeked of gasoline.

"He's at the clinic. Can we make it in forty minutes?"

"Probably," she said. "Did he mention the house?"

"Yeah. It's my fault."

"This is not a good idea. What if Eric's there?"

"The possibilities are endless."

*"This is not a fucking joke."*

"No," he said, turning the key. "It surely is not."

the Van Zant Clinic for Rehabilitative Medicine was tucked back in a canyon that ran from the ocean north toward Sunset and marked the line between Santa Monica and the city of Los Angeles. Up from the canyon floor on the L.A. side.

Classic SoCal Spanish, circa the twenties: stucco walls with decorative balconies, curving-tile roof, deep-set openings for windows; bars on these, Wil noted as he parked the Jag in the small front lot under sycamores. In fact, the main building appeared to have been a two-story residence, added-on wings jutting back from each end. He caught tranquil courtyard behind high walls lined with broken glass, a fountain's splash through heavy iron gates.

Inside, men wheeled cardboard boxes across Mexican tile waxed and buffed; the receptionist directed him toward a staircase. Passing a window, he could see Trina out in the car, her face grim-set after refusing to come in. Guilt, anger, hate, alienation, he thought—the Van Zant basic food groups.

He topped the stairs leading to the east wing, noted a reinforced barred door standing open, Dutch Van Zant at the far end of the hall, arms folded over a white golf shirt, navy windbreaker and slacks. Expecting him.

Nobody else around, even in the TV lounge he passed.

As he drew closer the older man eyed him as he would a disease, turned, and strode into the office behind. Wil followed into sparse: table and chairs, furniture indentations in the carpet, squares of unfaded paint on the walls, abandoned phone on the floor.

Paper shredder in one corner, its bag stuffed full.

"What happened?" Wil asked, taking one of the chairs. "Your guests forget to shut the door on their way out?"

"I've decided to close the clinic," Kordell Van Zant said, sitting down at the table between them. "It's being announced tomorrow."

"Business is that dead?"

"Not dead, more trouble than it's worth. These days, the real money's in pharmaceuticals—where I intend to concentrate."

"I was thinking one too many Billy Dulays."

There was a flicker on the tan face, gone then. "That's all you came here for? Too bad Lannie won't have the pleasure of throwing you out."

"Nice segue." Wil reached into his pocket for Eric's bracelet, landed it on the tabletop, watched for reaction, nothing showing beyond a glance—about what he expected. He steadied and launched:

"July seventh, 1966: Lannie Crowell picks this up at an early-morning murder scene he's stringing for KTVB. Even catches the event on film, though inadvertently. See, Lannie forgot the out-takes—maybe he never saw them. But I did. I also found *that*" —he nodded at the bracelet—"and called to see which of you it belonged to. Just as Lannie must have done when he heard the name Van Zant on scene. Pretty soon he's at your door looking to make a trade. The bracelet and Eric's involvement in Carmen's murder for a pile of your money. But Lannie has no idea who he's dealing with, and all of a sudden he's on the payroll, right where you can keep an eye on him, make sure he doesn't do something stupid." Wil leaned back. "Not bad for an ex–USC lineman."

Kordell Van Zant smiled at the zinger; he reached into a drawer under the table, found a package of plastic-tipped cigars, unwrapped and lit one. "You never graduated from UCLA, did you?"

"Nope."

"And now you're here with your little pocket tape recorder, hoping I'll blurt out something. I don't know why, but I gave you credit for more."

"You know what time it is?"

The older man checked his watch. "Six-forty. Why?"

"So noted. Lannie's dead, Kordell—murdered—though it was made to look like an accident." Wil took a certain satisfaction in the way the man sagged, but both sag and satisfaction were gone in seconds.

"How do I know you're telling the truth?"

"Trust me—he had five hundred pounds of barbell across his neck. I broke into his house and found him, along with the bracelet. And if I'm wearing a wire, I've just incriminated myself on tape."

Kordell set the cigar down behind him on the windowsill. He took a deep breath, looked at the ceiling, cleared his throat. "Goddamnit to hell," he said quietly. "Son of a bitch. Why Lannie? Why him?"

"Trina asked the same question—"

"The little firebug. Get to the point."

"I want to make a deal—information for information. Straight across."

"What kind of information?"

"I want to know what happened back then."

"In exchange for what?"

"In exchange for saving your life. That's why Lannie was killed. To get to you."

"Not enough. This company is bigger than me alone."

"Everything you've built, then—your legacy. Such as it is."

He retrieved the cigar, puffed it back to life. "My legacy is for others to emulate, if they can."

"Save it for the shareholders, Dutch. And you're a bad liar."

Smoke swirled around him, rose to the ceiling. "Well?" he said, after adding to it. "You're still here, aren't you? Nobody's thrown you out yet."

Wil nodded. "So we have a deal?"

"I suppose I have no choice. And I'm waiting."

*Seven come eleven.* "All right—I believe the threat has to do with Eric. It may even come from him personally."

Kordell said nothing; after what passed for emotion at the news of Lannie's death, disdain seemed familiar and welcome, back where it belonged.

"Think," Wil said. "Without Lannie running interference, Eric has a green light."

"To do what—knock me off?" He drew off the cigar, held it in, released it around his eyes. "You know something? I almost wish it were true. But my son is what often happens to men who aspire, the result of some perverse draw. You mentioned Billy Dulay. Why do you think I'm shutting down the clinic, because it's so well run? Eric may be many things, Hardesty, but strong enough to overthrow me, he is not."

Wil tossed the bracelet over, watched Kordell catch it, look at it in spite of himself. "He's killed before. And you're thinking he hasn't the balls?"

No reply.

"Trina thought Lannie dug it out to present to you—an anniversary gift or something. Pretty soft, huh?"

Kordell's focus *went* soft and inward. "It was never more than a token, even then—something I made very clear as we were bargaining."

"The press would have had fun with it, though, wouldn't they?"

"I just admired Lannie's enterprise."

"Saving Eric's tail, you mean."

"Call it what you will. Eric was only protecting me."

"From what?"

He took in more smoke. "Are you really that dense? The girl needed money for her family, and she was too proud to get it from Denny. It was business. I just wasn't careful enough."

Like a phosphorous shell bursting, white-lighting every dark crevice: "It wasn't Denny who got her pregnant, it was you. And Eric found out."

"Eric just tried to reason with her."

"He secretly loved her and she betrayed him—twice. First with his brother and then with his father. Tell me I'm wrong."

"My son is no murderer."

*"He killed Carmen Marquez. He's capable of killing you."*

*"THAT WAS AN ACCIDENT."*

"Maybe. But what followed was no accident, was it—selling Denny out."

*"Tread lightly, boy. Or it's you and me right now."* His eyes were live coals; a vein throbbed on his forehead. "Now—you want to talk threats, I'm listening. But we better be talking about more than just Eric here."

Wil expelled breath, took the threat as solid, the man in athlete's trim for his age, wide and racked with muscle across the shoulders. Fists ready to go. Patience, he thought—and pressure.

"If I'm right, Eric is hooked in with the same man who killed Celeste and almost killed Trina. His name is John Pomphrey, an annual Interpol pinup since the 1980s. I found out today he's an advance man and enforcer for a Thai drug cartel acquiring legitimate concerns—like the Mafia did in Vegas. His job is to make things happen."

"By killing me . . . ?" He looked amused.

"If they want a Van Zant Inc., who do they target? The Rock, who they know will fight? Or Eric, the weak link—a rubber stamp away from power?"

He was thinking about it, Wil could see that. "Your turn now," he said. "Pomphrey wanted information from Trina about Denny. Why? What do you know?"

"Nothing," Kordell said. "Dead and buried. End of story."

"Bullshit. You know something."

"Why would Eric want me dead when all he has to do is wait?"

"Is that what *you'd* do?"

"I'm not the issue here."

"Yes you are, that's what I'm trying to tell you," Wil said. "Put yourself in his place, seeing you determined to go on forever. You still think it's not possible?"

"People like that would tear his heart out and feed it to him—he'd see that. My son isn't dumb."

Wil banged the table in frustration. "*Fucking unbelievable*. It's one thing to be blind, another when you blind yourself. About the last thing I'd expect from you."

"I don't—"

"Then brace yourself, Dutch. It's about to be open season."

He could see it working in Kordell Van Zant's silence, in the man's expression—as if he'd eaten something that tasted bad and didn't know where to spit it out. But he did finally.

"All right," he said. "I'm asking."

"Asking what?"

"You carry a gun?"

"That depends," Wil said.

"On what—money?" Kordell snorted derisively.

"On whether I'm that inclined to use it," Wil said. "Now, let's have it on Denny."

*He has seen her a number of times in the company of his adopted son, Denny: Carmen, her name is, the Mexican girl from Huntington Beach. During dinner arranged by Maeve, he finds her irresistible, everything his wife is not: all heat and innocent seductiveness to Maeve's educated primness and icy blond reserve. Or maybe it's just him, wanting something and determined to get it.*

*He picks her up at school on a day when he knows Denny is off somewhere—Mexico, as he recalls now, the irony not lost on him. At his insistence, they stop at a restaurant where he's not known. His proposition stuns her at first; all indignation and youthful fire, she is the most desirable creature he's ever seen. Money, of course, wins the day, as it always does—money and the threat of losing Denny, his trump card. At the motel, she is tearful. But he knows something about all this and soon she is resigned, if not willing. That comes later.*

*A month passes. Two. Three.*

*She misses her period. Not only that, despite precautions, Eric has seen them together. Bad enough. But something else has happened; Carmen Marquez suddenly has become aware of her leverage, demanding her freedom from him as the price of the abortion he insists she have.*

*His creation, turning it around on him.*

*Eric confronts him, and he tells Eric she's blackmailing him, never dreaming Eric might take action. But he does, and when Carmen tells him the story, Eric covers his ears, nearly losing it right there. And when she won't let up—releasing an anger at the Van Zants, Denny included now, that has gone beyond her ability to control it—Eric does lose it, her eyes widening in astonishment at the knife he's plunged into her chest. Making little hurt sounds as he turns and flees.*

*At four-thirty* A.M., *just as the alarm is going off, Eric appears in his bedroom, separate rooms the state of things between husband and wife now, thanks to his philandering and the split that has developed ever since Eric was conceived—Maeve and Denny vs. him and Eric, or so it seems. At any rate, the boy is virtually in shock—his son, the executioner. Biological son: a distinction reinforced hours later when Denny is held for the murder and the whole thing becomes a giant sump threatening to suck in everything Kordell has worked to achieve. Let alone what he has yet to build.*

*The Crowell kid is, of course, a blessing in disguise. For without him, his flesh and blood would be disgraced and in jail that night. Lannie Crowell he knows exactly how to deal with: find out what he wants and provide it—in this case position and a lifetime of drugs, new-generation steroids he's already begun experimenting with.*

*Money is hardly even a factor—beyond the ludicrously low amount he lets Lannie determine.*

*Regarding Eric's tenuous position, he has but one option: explain the situation to Denny, make clear what he expects, contact a Marine general who's an old friend. It's done—gradually things die down, his primary objective. Life resumes. And somehow Denny's disappearance overseas and subsequent burial, though devastating to Maeve, is like closure for him.*

*Not that he doesn't try to feel something.*

*But even that fails: Denny isn't blood. And blood tells.*

*Meantime, like a baptism, he's immersed Eric in the business—flawed Eric, the rightful heir. He is hard on Eric, as he is on Trina, but life is hard. Hard is love, hard is right: Buddy Warburn, his old line coach, taught him so.*

*Hard wins. And only winning counts.*

Wil called time out, hit the head and the water cooler. When he came back, Kordell was staring out the window.

Sensing Wil's return, he went on, his back to the room:

*Time passes, Van Zant Inc. grows like Lannie on steroids—Lannie the human experiment, Eric's blueprint for later testing at the clinic. Eric has grown also, but out of balance: good with figures and detail, stunted and wanting as a leader—an accountant or CFO at any other concern, painful at times to watch.*

*Eventually, not just painful.*

*Experiments with antidepressant drugs the firm has been quietly developing and testing are mishandled. The suicides that result—PTSD cases—bring dangerous scrutiny. Particularly when it's suspected that one of the patients capable of such has fled with incriminating documents. Billy Dulay, Lannie acting to minimize Eric's lapse—on Kordell's order.*

*Then the thing with Denny and the notes. Maeve bringing in—*

"What was Lannie supposed to accomplish in Hawaii?" Wil interrupted. Pushing him.

"Exactly what he did. Nip it in the bud."

"Literally."

"Your getting hurt was unintentional. By the time I could do anything, you'd left. Maeve certainly wasn't about to tell me."

"No, I suppose not."

Kordell turned from the window, his face sculpted. "What do you know about a sickness like hers? Going on and on about him for years—hearing him at night, feeling what he felt. Like it was happening to *her*. Nothing I could do to end it."

Wil flashed on the box in the garage.

"I'll give it to her, though. She had guts."

*Guts . . . Jesus.* "Why'd you send Lannie after me and Trina?"

"What the hell would you have done given the circumstances? Just let you put a gun to my head?"

"Kill some barfly loser the cops didn't even take seriously when it happened?"

"Lannie got carried away, I admit. But he was a conspirator now. He had a stake in it." Pause. "Same as Katrina did."

"Getting away from you, you mean."

He smiled coldly. "Why do you think she was so determined to find out who killed Carmen? Why then? Why you? I've seen her in action—she could have had *you* anytime she wanted, married or not. You given any thought to that?"

Wil said nothing, something stirring in his gut. A thing buried alive that scratches its way out of the grave to look at you with burning accusing eyes, because you'd put it there. All the while telling yourself you hadn't.

"Probably sucked you in with that old shit about fucking Denny. Feeling guilty and wanting to clear his name. Sound familiar?"

*Bam, bam, bam, bam;* more doubts pounding against their hastily constructed coffins.

"Ever since her husbands cut her off, she's been after the big score. Blackmailing me or trying to because I had sense enough not to give her carte blanche. That's the real reason she hates me. And you finding out Eric did what *he* did and Lannie's connection to it gives her leverage enough to pry the gold right out of my teeth. Congratulations—you're a living extortion note."

Sweating now, his mind scanning for confirming data; getting hits only on Trina and money. From the beginning.

"Want confirmation? Why do you think she drove away just now? Because she knew that somewhere along the line, I'd cut through the crap and lay open her little scheme—tell you the truth about her for once." He smiled, his eyes becoming slits. "Have a look out the window if you don't believe it."

Wil did, stood there frozen.

"You see the goddamn Jaguar I bought her down there?"

Empty space between white lines. "*No.*"

"Ain't love grand? Join the club, Sherlock, you've been had."

# 27

john pomphrey watched the setting sun, last glow through ragged clouds reminding him as always of napalm. Hell's nebula. Raging, devouring, scarring. And afterward, being given up for dead, the Cong only too willing to trade him for whatever they could get, in this case a couple of low-level operatives. Nothings. Later, the excruciating sessions to peel off his burned dead skin; botched grafts when all else failed. Torture worse than any he'd endured in the camps.

Hell, the camps had been a picnic by comparison. Especially when his captors had learned of his white-powder and black-tar connections. Preferential treatment all the way: wine and roses, damn near. Women, of course—largely wives and daughters of the jailers who took their cuts.

Until the napalm.

He looked over at Eric, made the obvious comparison. Eric was no Denny, that was certain, and it struck him how completely different two brothers could be: Denny lean and hard, dangerous in an offhand way; Eric in the general mold of his father, but more like Jell-O not yet hardened. Unlikely ever to harden.

Chance, he supposed, himself very different from his own brothers—him the youngest—at least forty years ago his last basis for comparison. Probably all dead by now.

Fuck it. There's today and tomorrow, and that was it.

"We go tonight," he said suddenly.

Eric looked up from his laptop, its glow highlighting his round face and thinning hair, the white button-down shirt. "I thought you said tomorrow."

"Tonight, Eric. Before he's had a chance to hire himself another aborigine."

the call came while they were still figuring the probability of it: Eric wanting a private meeting to go over last-minute details for the press conference and shareholder presentations, some numbers changing unexpectedly for the better. Must-includes, the Kordec-Z projections looking even brighter due to an accounting procedure he'd come up with. Something he needed to demonstrate—tonight: ten o'clock at the penthouse.

Actually sounding enthused.

"What do you think?" Kordell asked after he'd hung up.

Wil looked at him, still hearing *why then—why you?* the knowledge he'd been had still burning like an out-of-control adolescent flush. *Join the club.* Even worse, hearing it from *him.*

"I think you have about—" He checked his watch. "Two hours."

"What if we don't go?"

"Then you've lost the edge, knowing when it's coming. Them not knowing you know."

"So what do we do?"

"Let's clarify 'we.' "

"I thought you said—"

"What about Denny?"

"Goddamnit, how many times do you have to hear it? Denny is dead."

"But Trina told you something—didn't she?"

"*No.*"

Wil powered down the last of a stale-tasting sandwich Kordell had pressed the kitchen into making. "I wonder how they'll do it?" he said. "Probably induce a stroke or a heart attack—that's what I'd do. Make it age-related. Simple enough when you have the right drug."

"Fuck yourself, Hardesty. I know people. I'll demand police protection."

"Perfect—they love this kind of stuff. Shouldn't take long to set up. Plenty of manpower these days, and so easy to explain."

Kordell turned back to the window; nervous hand through silver hair. "All right—she came to see me, what of it? Said she'd seen him alive. I told you she'd say anything."

"What did she want?"

"Money, of course."

"For what?"

"Status quo. She said she'd found out the truth from Denny. That it was Eric who killed Carmen, and I'd sent Denny away to stop the investigation. Sacrificed him, in essence, to Eric and the business—nice story for the media and the shareholders. A million a year from now on and she'd keep it under wraps."

"This was . . ."

"Three weeks ago," Kordell said. "After Maeve got the notes."

*Just before she came begging HIM.* "And you told her what?"

Kordell turned back from the window, the harsh office light

adding wrinkles, shadows, lifetimes. "I told her she was dreaming, no way in hell could she prove anything."

*The key to it all.* "Weren't you curious how she knew?"

"Why should I be? She'd tried similar things before—wild theories fed her by her mother."

"But this was right on," Wil said. "Didn't you at least wonder where she'd gotten it? Given the notes, at least."

"Whatever you're implying, I'm telling you—Lannie found no evidence of Denny when he went over there. Twice. And without proof, none of this other bullshit meant anything."

"Enter the seeker of proof. No wonder you sent Lannie after us."

Kordell rolled the dead cigar in fingers Wil felt like breaking.

"Who did you think almost killed your daughter?"

"Some nut, I figured."

Something in the tone: denial. "Jesus, that's it? After he nearly drowns her for information? *That is it?*"

The man was pacing now. "People have tried getting money out of me for years. For all I knew, this was part of her scheme, right down to the maid. And don't kid yourself—if that meant sticking it to me, she'd do it."

"And now she has," Wil said, thinking about the envelopes full of drug-experiment documentation he'd left in her car. Plenty for some eager Fed prosecutor to nail Van Zant Inc. with, even if they were copies, the originals doubtless contributing to the bulge in the shredder bag. Not even needing Carmen Marquez now, the irony of *that.*

"She has thanks to you," Kordell said.

"Right."

"*Just so that's perfectly clear.*"

He tried to put a lid on the steam rising, genuinely tried. But it was like contending with a shot valve, a watertight door without a seal, everything in him wanting to blow the smugness off that face.

"Something I'd seriously consider, if I were you," Wil said finally. "About tonight."

"What's that?"

"Start hoping to hell I'm good enough."

**they** reached the Van Zant building at nine-fifteen, traffic and signals permitting, Wil wanting to scout the penthouse, get a feel for it. After Kordell parked his big BMW 7-Series in the basement garage, they caught a delivery elevator in anticipation of possible ambush in the personal one. A floor shy of the penthouse, they left the delivery elevator and took the stairs, emerging in a hallway just down from the personal elevator and double mahogany doors.

All was quiet—normal per Kordell.

Inside included.

Outside and two floors below, the Van Zant sign blushed blue, its neon glow filtering in through floor-to-ceiling window slats. Minimum interior light, Wil told him as he adjusted rheostats accordingly: the chairman/CEO planning an early evening. Anticipating tomorrow's hectic schedule.

While Kordell attempted to settle his nerves with a drink, Wil canvassed personal office, living spaces—hard and sharply contemporary—small laboratory, marble bathroom with skylight, high-gloss master suite; guessing the layout sprang from the same designer who did the Malibu house. Liking it about as well. He looked in on the exercise room and equipment, seeing Lannie's hand in its outfitting, then checked the balcony.

Dazzling view greeted him to the south and west, a blanket of lights starting at Santa Monica Bay and extending forever. Kordell's magic kingdom. He pulled himself up the maintenance rungs on one wall, saw double-ridge copper roof descending from the concrete core housing what had to be elevator shaft and stairwell.

All clear.

He let himself down, took in the night. No stars showed and a light breeze wafted up hints of ocean, the misty feel of rain coming. Twenty-two stories below, miniature cars moved and turned, dark shapes with headlights. Windows in other high-rises reminded him of tiny television screens, dramas or comedies unfolding, depending on which you dropped in on.

All those lives being played out, he mused. Like civilians in wartime: no sense of what was about to happen up here. Who would live and who would die. If . . .

He spent a moment envisioning possible scenarios, eliminating most of them. There seemed no reason for Eric and Pomphrey to expect anything but what they expected—Kordell alone, perhaps going over notes of his own in anticipation of Eric's input. Thinking about tomorrow. Tired from a long day. Vulnerable.

Or so it would seem, Wil hoped.

He spent the next fifteen minutes discussing his plan with Kordell—let Eric commit, then take control—laying it out for him, thinking iffy at best, the man trying to focus but seemingly adrift. At ten till, there was a soft knock at the double doors, followed by: "It's me, Eric."

Kordell looked through the glass eyepiece and nodded.

"Nobody else. He's alone."

"All right," Wil said, trying to fathom the meaning. He positioned himself behind the side Kordell would open, drew the .45, nodded for Kordell to get the door.

Eric came in wearing a light gray raincoat over white shirt and khaki pants. Kordell closed the door behind him, twisted home the dead bolt as Wil brought the muzzle of the .45 up under Eric's ear.

"*Goddamnit,*" Eric said.

Fear and surprise—good. "Put down the briefcase and take off the coat. Slowly, that's it, let it fall. Now stand very still."

"Fuck you, Hardesty. What's this son of a bitch doing here?" All bluster now as Wil patted him down, told him to move away from the raincoat, which he checked to find nothing there either. Computer printouts and a laptop in the case—nothing remotely threatening.

*Great start.*

Eric turned to Kordell. "You want to explain this?"

Kordell Van Zant stepped forward and slapped his son very hard across the face, Eric recoiling from the blow. As he straightened, Kordell slapped him again, both shots sounding like branches snapping.

"*My own son,*" he said. "You make me sick."

Red bloomed on Eric's face, bright blotches that stood out against the white. His dark eyes glittered and he appeared anything but soft now. "Wonderful," he said. "Just terrific." His head jerked in Wil's direction. "What's this piece of shit been telling you?"

Kordell raised his hand as if to slap Eric again, stopped halfway and lowered his arm, spoke as if exercising great control. "I gave you everything. I gave you life—not once but twice, if you remember. And all you can think to do is betray me? Throw me out with the trash?"

"Whatever the hell you're talking about," Eric spat, "I came here to show you something, and that's what I intend to do."

*So much for the script,* Wil thought. "How about if we sit down," he said. He holstered the gun, moved them slowly toward the living room.

"That'll be the day, when you toss *me* aside," Kordell said. Stance wide, fists clenched, as if staking out a section of the room. Daring incursion. "Where's your backup—what's his name, John somebody. . . ." He looked at Wil.

"Pomphrey," Wil said.

"Pomphrey," Kordell echoed. "Man lose his nerve?"

Eric blinked, widened his eyes. "*Who?*" Almost convincing. Until his eyes slid off his father to a spot over Wil's right shoulder—where the sound came from: a shell being jacked into a shotgun chamber. All business.

"Somebody mention my name?"

Wil reflexed a hand into his coat, heard: "Hah-ah—easy does it, gun on the floor with two fingers. That's a good boy. Now step back. Nice and slow."

Gravelly; light Australian accent—what he couldn't put his finger on that night in the hospital, drugs and static the twin filters. He did as told, sized up almost his own six-two, longish hair darker than he remembered, thigh-length black coat, turtleneck and jeans, Mephisto walkers. A sheen of moisture glistened on him; scar tissue served for brows over steel-shot eyes. His hands were mottled and hairless, the fingers stumpy, as though fashioned from clay by someone inexperienced with anatomy.

The short-barreled pump wavered not a bit.

*Bathroom goddamn skylight,* Wil kicked himself. *Son of a bitch.*

"Damn details, kill you every time," Pomphrey said as though reading his mind. His foot sent Wil's .45 under the sofa. "Not much of an improvement on the aborigine, are you? Damn waste of breath trying to warn you off."

"Why did you?"

"Never hurts to anticipate trouble. Didn't know who you were, but I figured anybody that lucky to be alive might listen. Obviously not."

"I hope you burn in hell," Kordell said.

"Not before you do, you old pirate."

"What kept you?" Eric said heatedly.

Pomphrey gave a smile, or what passed for one. "Interrupt a tender father-son moment? No way," way sounding like *wye.* He one-handed the shotgun, reached into a pocket, pulled out a smaller-than-TV-size remote.

"Would you like to see how I used the time before you got here?" He pressed one of the buttons.

At electric plugs around the room, green lights came up on small disks Wil wouldn't have suspected even if he had noticed them. A similar dot glowed on the remote. Pomphrey raised it to let them see a red button.

"I push this, those suckers light up. Way hotter than the wiring fire they'll suspect." He looked at Eric. "You see now about deciding how to do it? The Malibu house inspired me. Just seemed so perfect."

The remote went back in his pocket, and he drew out a black automatic with a reinforced barrel, Wil thinking magnum from the looks of it. And likely him blamed for this fire, too.

Assuming it went according to plan.

"What do you want?" Kordell asked. "If it's money—"

"A bite when we can have the whole thing? Tell him, Eric." He laid the shotgun on a table near the couch, let the magnum settle easily between Wil and Kordell.

"About fucking time," Eric said. "When you die, *Dad,* the shareholders are going to panic. And you know why? Because thanks to you, they think I'm worthless. But guess who's finally going to win the lottery."

Kordell shook his head slowly. "Eric, when the sharks get done feeding, there won't be enough left of you to care. Open your eyes."

"Ah, but I have—*Dad*," Eric said. "Who do you think arranged this? Signed, sealed, and about to be delivered."

"A contract to these people is the same as toilet paper. Whatever you've signed, it's a death warrant."

"Exactly right. Yours."

"Stop acting like a snot-nosed kid standing up to his father. If I don't level with you, who does? If I don't push you, who does? Him?" He shot a look of pure contempt at Pomphrey before coming back to Eric. "You're my son, and I love you. Call this off before it's too late."

"Love?" Eric said incredulously. "*Love?* After forty-six fucking years, you have the gall to throw that in my face? Love for whom? I *killed* for you once, goddamn you. And all it ever was to you was *my* fuckup. *My fuckup.* Well not anymore."

Kordell let go a breath; when he spoke he sounded like a man addressing someone not in the room: "Nothing's ever enough, is it? What do you want from me?"

"It's very simple. I want you dead."

"Please," Pomphrey said. "I hate fighting."

"Before this goes any further, I've already given the cops your name," Wil said. "You really want to risk them finding bullets in us?"

The smile was more a leer. "Cops have been after me forever, and here I am. Besides, you ever seen phosphorous burn? When these things are done, if they find teeth, they'll be lucky."

"That what happened to your face?"

"I think you're about to find out."

"All of you can go to hell," Kordell said suddenly—a boxer not yet recovered from a fight-ending blow. He turned toward the rear of the penthouse. "I'm tired. I'm going to bed."

Pomphrey fired, blowing a hole the size of a baseball in the couch, the sound alone stopping Kordell in his tracks. "Maybe you'd like to hear who made my face this way, old man—and what I did to him later. Fun story, if I do say so."

"Goddamnit," Eric said, recovering from his flinch at the shot. "Get on with it."

"What story?" Wil said.

"Fuck you. It's *him* I want to hear it."

Kordell sank back against the sofa. "What does it matter? We're dead anyway."

"See, Eric? Maybe I'll make you tell it."

*"Are you going to kill them or talk all night?"*

*"Shut the fuck up."* He looked at Kordell. "You don't know it, but your boy Den and me were like this at one time." He crossed his fingers. "Then he got all righteous. Long story short, we wound up in this prison camp in Laos. Rats the size of dogs, mosquitoes like hovercraft, pus leaking out of our wounds—MI-fucking-A. We decide to wait it out—not much choice. Then it's three years after the treaty's signed and nobody seems to give a shit—nobody's government anyway. On the plus side, things have loosened up enough to plan a sprint. But we need a distraction. Fire, Denny comes up with, not bad. Only as I'm hoochy-cooing the guards with some white powder, he's torching this barrack turns out has napalm under it the bastards have stockpiled. All of a sudden everything's on fire. *I'm* on fire."

Pomphrey paused as if seeing it, shook it off.

"Needless to say, I don't make it out. But I live, and years later

I'm working for this Thai bunch, and who do I find out works for them, too, doing the same kind of waste disposal? Right you are—Den—up to here with humanity. Problem is, I can't return any favors just yet 'cause it's against house rules, and these were people you did *not* cross. Anyway, I'm patient, and finally old Den makes his mistake—refuses to do this Waipio drug family who won't fall in line." He smiled. "Now the good part: Guess who gets the contract on the family *and* on our boy?"

"You saw him?" Kordell was on his feet now.

"Not only saw him, old man, I nailed him. One night about three weeks ago. Now sit down."

He sat.

"Who killed Voelker?" Wil said into silence.

"Me—who else? SOB must have thought *all* his ghosts were coming to get him—even had a trip line out. First Denny of all people, surfing *there* of all places. Then me, looking for him." The gray eyes brightened. "Old Roy never could keep anything quiet, though—especially at the end, bleating like one of those pigs they got down there. How do you think I was able to find sonny boy in the first place? Doubt he figured I'd be on him so quick."

Kordell looked at Eric. "You threw in with a man you knew shot your brother?"

"Not my brother, and never your son, *Dad*, so take the act and shove it. Pomphrey, do your damn job."

"You in that much of a sweat to die, laddie?"

Something crossed Eric's face, a cold shadow. "Don't screw around."

"Anybody want to tell him?"

"He means it, Eric," Wil said. "What did you think?"

Eric's jaw went slack. Smiling again, Pomphrey looked around, coming back finally to Eric, still staring at him.

"Nothing personal," he said. "Just business."

"We have a deal. . . ."

"Ask your old man how it works."

*"We have a deal. . . ."*

"How about a prize for most gullible instead?"

A set look came over Eric's face, as though everything had come into focus—someone handing him a pair of glasses that brought up the fine print, the truth in nightmare black-and-white. His smile was rock fissuring under extreme pressure.

"All my life," he said, shaking his head like a man weary of foolish things. Blindingly clear in retrospect. "My whole life . . ."

"Get a grip, Eric," Wil said. "That shit's what he wants."

"So, who'd like to go first?"

*"My whole goddamn life."*

Wil saw it, even put out a hand to pull him back. But Eric was beyond him, beyond Kordell.

*"ERIC!"*

"Ah, a volunteer," Pomphrey said. He fired twice, the heavy magnum loads raising ugly blooms on Eric's shirt, flinging him backward as though off a trampoline. Splaying him brokenly across a low-backed chair.

*"NOOOOOOO!"*

Kordell threw himself onto his son, pressed the wounds as though he could stop the blood, pulled back a red hand, regarded it in horror. He gave an involuntary jerk. Then he rose, fixed murderously on Pomphrey, and started forward, his jaw working but no sound coming out.

Pomphrey smiled, raised the gun to meet him, and at that moment Wil lunged, going in low to upend the table at Pomphrey's face, dive for the shotgun as it went over. He felt two rounds buzz him as he grabbed it and rolled, heard an impact he recognized as gun meeting flesh followed by a grunt and thump of body falling before he let off all five shotgun shells at where Pomphrey had been, the noise horrendous in the hard closed space. He rolled again, this time drove the couch over, feeling magnum fire punch through the stuffing, choky shit that feathered the air white. But there was the .45 and his grip on it then, and he thumb-released the safety, snapped off two quick rounds—a general idea where his target was better than nothing, clear he'd missed with the shotgun.

Aware the rounds had opened his position to return fire, he scrambled around the opposite end of the couch, risked a look, saw gun fog and through it, Kordell rising, holding his head, lurching back toward Eric. Then movement down the dim hallway. The sound of a door sliding shut. The snick of a lock.

Wil checked that he hadn't lost his backup clips. He swept back to see Kordell cradling Eric's head, trying to press life into his dead face. Blood coming down from his own wound.

"HE'S DEAD, DUTCH, NOTHING YOU CAN DO. GET OUT BEF—"

Explosions tore through the penthouse, light brighter than he could look at. Searing heat, alarms adding to the din, the sprinkler system sputtering on but having little effect beyond creating roiling clouds of vapor. Air in the room going fast, their chances literally going up in smoke.

"GO—TAKE THE STAIRS. NOW!" Not waiting to see whether he did or didn't, Wil stumbled down the hallway toward the bathroom, the smoke here at least lighter. He stood back, put the rest of the clip—five hollowpoints—into the door and heard things blowing up inside: marble, tile, metal, glass. He kicked through it, saw the black automatic amid the chaos, blood on it and the tub where Pomphrey'd stood to reach the skylight, now dark and lidless. Standing under it, shoving in a new clip, he felt mist coming through. And the heat reaching for him.

"YOU'RE DONE, POMPHREY. GIVE IT UP."

Scramble on the roof, the sound of stumbles. Wil holstered the .45, leaped, and pulled himself through the skylight; scanning, he saw Pomphrey climbing the copper incline, halfway to the concrete core, freedom behind the door leading to the stairs.

He fired twice.

Pomphrey flattened on the copper, slid several feet down the wet surface before regaining his hold. Sprawled there, he reached into his coat and pulled out a long-barreled chrome revolver.

Smoke rose through buckled seams in the roof.

Wil yelled, "Here's a story for *you*: Guess who tried to save your ass at Hue? Denny. Now throw it down." But he knew Pomphrey wouldn't, and he ducked away from the shots, almost falling back through the skylight. When he looked again, recoil had driven the man another two feet down the incline.

"Denny's dead—chew on that," Pomphrey yelled back. Fire was chasing the smoke out of the cracks now, steam rising all along the wet copper. Like something out of Dante.

Wil pictured the whole thing going. "It's over. Lose the gun, and I'll get a line," thinking maybe he could snag a bath towel, something with some length and heft. He glanced behind him. Smoke billowed out from where he had his feet locked, the heat intensifying where he lay—reminder that the bathroom had become an inferno as well. There was no going back.

Thoughts of Denny. Of Celeste and Eric. Of Trina desperate for air. The look in those eyes.

Without aiming, Pomphrey just a shape through the smoke now anyway, he fired and kept firing until the slide locked on empty.

Three booms came back, the muzzle flashes like heat lightning, bullets sparking off the metal close by.

Followed by a frenzied scrabbling and a high-pitched scream that faded off into the night.

But by then, Wil was on his feet, straddling the roofline, slip-sliding on twisting buckling copper toward the safety of the stairwell.

he passed firemen in full gear humping up the stairs, shrugging it off when he asked if anyone else had made it out. As he descended, the roar of the fire diminished; at lobby level, he threaded his way through more fire people, loud direction giving, radio communications. Then he was outside, looking up at helicopters buzzing what looked to him like a volcano erupting from the top of the Van Zant building.

Burning debris arced into space, sputtered out, and hit the ground around him; ash rained more slowly. Drizzle cooled his scorched face.

*"Hey, you. Back behind the line. Now."*

Wil waved in the direction of the fireman pointing at him, moved toward yellow-and-black barriers, slipped between them. From here, with the increased angle, the scene was even more dramatic. The two floors below the penthouse were heavily involved now, window glass bursting into the street as each new office went up. All around him fire engines throbbed, emergency lights flashed, radios crackled, media questioned fire-department spokespeople. Around the perimeter, police directed traffic and crowds, their collective necks craned upward for a look into hell.

Sparks erupted as a floor caved in on the one below.

Wil milled around looking into each face, searching but not seeing him. Hearing snatches: . . . *no determination yet on the man who fell . . . all systems responding . . . extremely aggressive fire . . . three down with smoke inhalation. So far.*

Wil saw the paramedic vans, went over that way.

And saw him.

He was sitting on the rear bumper of one, breathing from a portable oxygen tank; blanket across his shoulders, gauze strip holding a once-white bandage to his head. When he saw Hardesty, he took the mask away, nodded as Wil came up.

For a while they just sat and watched it burn, a giant match flaring against the lowered sky, helicopter searchlights picking out details and helping direct suppression efforts. More snatches came: . . . *firemen making a stand at the eighteenth floor . . . unconfirmed survivors . . . possible other fatalities.*

"So it was Pomphrey who went off," Kordell Van Zant said at length.

Wil nodded.

"Then my son died for something. At least it's some comfort." He brushed at singed eyebrows, silver hair curled brown from the soot and heat. His face and hands showed ugly splotches beginning to blister.

Firemen raced around, all grim efficiency, some barking orders. Wil was conscious of a roaring in his ears. His own face and hands still felt the fire, and he reeked of smoke. He glanced at Kordell's bandage, the red stain there.

"He wasn't able to put much force into it," the man said, noticing. "You had most of his attention by then."

"All told, I'd say we were damned lucky."

"You're wrong. Eric gave his life so we'd have a chance."

"That's one interpretation," Wil said.

"It's the way I'm telling it. My word against yours, if necessary."

"You are some fucking piece of work, you know that?"

"Better than you have said so."

Wil spat out an acrid taste, tasted it still. "Get out, Dutch. Today. Resign or fire yourself or something, but get out. You let this happen. Even you can see what it cost."

"Quit—just like that?"

"Romans used to fall on their swords. Those who didn't were hacked to death."

"So I do, then what? Go die alone?"

"If you don't know, I don't know what to tell you. Even if I gave a shit."

A moment went by. Wil watched a fireman come to an upper window, signal something to the forces below. Kordell bent to rest his elbows on his knees, focus on his hands.

"Nobody's clean, Hardesty, nobody who plays to win," he said. "You're either hard enough or you melt when the acid gets thrown around. You know it as well as I do."

"Dutch Van Zant to the Centurians. I don't know what's worse, hearing you say it or trying to convince myself it's bullshit."

"Obviously you'd prefer a pound of my flesh."

"Why not?" Wil said. "You're where it started."

"Well, I wouldn't hold my breath."

"We'll see."

"I doubt that. My insulation is very thick, and I have very good lawyers. They're already working on Trina's arson thing."

*Trina's arson thing. Jesus.*

"Flesh and blood," Kordell said to his expression. "That's all that counts. The rest means nothing."

"You're actually proud of her, aren't you?"

"She's my daughter. She's all I have left. Leave it at that."

Wil shrugged, looked at shapes twisting in the fire; the hoses and men and equipment deployed. Kordell started to say something. Instead he cleared his throat.

"I don't see any further point to this. Beyond sending you a check, is there anything else?"

"Yeah. How about telling Buckhalter I didn't kill Joe Avenal?"

"The drunk . . ."

"He wasn't always a drunk."

"Look, they're good cops down there. They're not in my pocket, no matter what you think."

"I didn't say they were."

"Then I'll see what I can do."

Wil stood slowly, already feeling the stiffness in his joints, the knots in his muscles. Things really starting to hurt. "See you in court, Dutch. If there's any justice left."

Kordell Van Zant pulled the blanket off and straightened up, Eric's blood a dark Rorschach blackening his shirt. "Hardesty, nobody helped me on the way up and sure as hell nobody's going to grease the skids if I go. Your idea of justice interests me not a goddamn. But I'm glad you made it out. And I'm glad you were his friend."

# 28

**grilling** started in the next day at ten A.M.

First he went through it for Mo Epstein, which took about four hours, the LASD's primary interest centering on Pomphrey as the killer of Celeste and Lannie, Wil telling them everything he knew short of incriminating himself and Trina on the break-in. Then Al Vega and the Feds took over, their emphasis on the vet deaths, Van Zant Inc.'s experiments on humans, orders for disinterment and tissue tests on the suicides already under way. In particular, Pomphrey and his association with Euphrates Ltd., front group for who the FBI really wanted to nail, the crime triad known as Red Sun operating out of Bangkok.

Three more hours, sandwiched around a call to Buckhalter: No mention of Kordell's intervention, but Wil's apology and willingness to cooperate were accepted at face value, something he did not anticipate. Of course there was the discovery of the Art's Bar matchbook in Lannie's drawer. Plus the bartender's recalling a muscular black guy asking for directions earlier that day. At any rate, Buckhalter informed Wil he was no longer a suspect.

As expected, the load fell heavily on the dead: Eric for his role in the clinic's maverick operations; Pomphrey for his Red Sun–sanctioned hits—Ohana particularly interested in him for the Waipio carnage, including the murdered family, the Hawaii homicide detective more than pleased to line out that particular piece of mayhem. Then there was Lannie for best strong-arm in a supporting role, Charles Laird as well as Joe Avenal laid at his door.

No one argued for any of them.

Carmen Marquez didn't even make the cut. Lack of interest.

After Al Vega had finished with Wil, Mo Epstein made good on their postponed dinner at Phillipe's.

"Tell me something," he said, watching Wil bite into lamb French dip. "What makes an outwardly normal type like yourself do this shit?"

Wil looked up. "This is *you* asking?"

"I just thought it might get old being out on a limb all the time."

"It's not *all* the time. Besides, look at what I get for it: iced tea, meat on a roll, thou beside me in a restaurant. And for the record, I resent being called normal."

"Whatever."

"What about the old man?" Wil asked.

"Hell, nobody but you seems to care. We've got no interest, Huntington Beach is wrapping the Avenal killing around Crowell, and the Feebles are doubtless deciding not to bother with him as we chew."

Wil dipped his sandwich, took another bite.

Mo smirked. "Trial of the century, remember? You have any idea what Van Zant would cost to prosecute given *his* dream team? You want justice, wait'll the stock market opens Monday."

"I was thinking about something he said: *Go die alone.*"

"Nah, too strong. And guys like him always die in their sleep."

"Your basic design flaw." Wil drank iced tea, put down the glass. "What about Trina?"

"Have to catch her first. You have any idea where she is?"

"None."

"I sincerely hope not." Mo finished his beer. "So. What do you do for an encore?"

"Go to bed for about a week."

"After that?"

"Maybe head off someplace," Wil said. "Talk to me then."

Mo said, "LAPD found the Lumina you rented and called the outfit. Probably still totaling up that sucker."

"And laughing, I know. Anybody seen my car?"

"Huntington released the Bonneville and sent it to the yard. We can pick it up anytime. You some kind of VIP or something?"

it was nine-thirty when he finally got to La Conchita, saw the note on his door that a neighbor had taken in his mail and newspapers. *Mañana* for that; same for phone messages, same for all of it. Enough just being home. But from the moment he walked in, the house felt odd, neither here nor there somehow, time away the most likely factor. Or maybe it was just him.

Putting his stuff on the kitchen table, he opened the fridge, cracked a mineral water, went out on the deck, collapsed into a chair. The night air was cool on his hands and face. Traffic hummed by on 101 and a waxing moon showed through breaking-up clouds. Its light trembled on the water, like a once-brilliant star attempting a comeback.

He was nodding off when he heard the sound, felt the touch on his shoulder. Jumped about a foot.

"I'm sorry," she said. "I was waiting in the bedroom, but you didn't come in." She stepped in front of him, moonlight framing her. She was wearing his bathrobe; letting it hang open to show she had nothing on under it, her skin like alabaster.

Feelings whipsawed; he took breaths to settle them. "How'd you get in?"

"Saw you stash the key when I was here last. Remember?"

"I'll have to be more careful."

She took it in stride. "I heard about it on the news. About Eric. And Dad."

Wil said nothing.

"I figured you were there."

"Yeah."

She touched his cheek. "They showed pictures of the fire. It looked horrible. Are you all right?"

He nodded.

"Can you tell me about it?"

"I'm tired, Tree. Not much I can really add."

She bit her lip. "I understand you probably hate me. But would it make a difference knowing I regret what's happened? That what started out being one thing isn't that way now?"

"If you mean you're richer, I wouldn't count my chickens quite yet. The coop's about to empty."

"That isn't what I meant. I meant you and me, Wil. What we mean to each other."

"What happened? Did Denny come to his senses?"

She just looked at him.

"He's alive, isn't he?"

Her breath caught slightly, enough for him to be sure.

"Don't take it personally. Talking to your father made me see it: the timing, you showing up at my place all full of resolve after that scene at the restaurant. Not settling for your mom's action anymore, wanting Denny cleared right now. Using that thing about you and him and feeling guilty. Sucked me right in."

"That was true, I swear."

"I didn't say I didn't believe it. Where is he?"

She reached into a pocket, came out with a cigarette and the gold lighter, thumbed it till it flamed, the light bathing her face in warmth and shadow. "There's a little hospital in Baja where I went once to get an abortion." She lit up, blew smoke. "A long time ago when that's what you did after somebody'd made you pregnant."

Rocking, a feeling of capsizing before righting the ship. Determined to stay on course.

"Baja and back," he said. "Explains why you were so beat every time you showed up here. Just in off the road, weren't you? Not even time to get his blood completely off the seat."

She put the hand with the cigarette to her forehead; after a bit she lowered it. "That man shot him, but it was night, and he was able to lose himself in the jungle. His Marine training helped him survive. Somebody he knew flew him here—back to me. But he wasn't safe, we both knew it. Twice on the way to Mexico I thought he'd died. For two weeks he was unconscious."

"And?"

"Today was better, they told me."

"That's good news at least."

"Don't be cynical. Before he went out, he told me about the contract on him, that the man would be coming. What he was like."

"Shame Celeste didn't know," Wil said.

"Don't put that on me."

But it was said without force, and he was already on to other dots, patterns emerging as they connected. "Why bother when there's so much more, right?"

"What do you mean?"

"The takeover. He and Pomphrey worked for the same people. He must have heard about it—maybe even *from* Pomphrey."

"I don't—"

"Den was going to warn your father, wasn't he? And you sat on it."

*"What kind of person do you think I am?"*

"You sure you want to know?"

She just stared at him.

Wil said, "How about a daughter with the same instincts for money as her father? A daughter who figured she could always blackmail her brother if the old man wound up dead."

*"No!"*

"Once you found out who really killed Carmen, it was easy, wasn't it? Just wind up Wil, play to his guilt, and turn him loose. A step ahead of the posse. Just tell me one thing—was Denny ever in on it?"

She smoked a moment, said nothing.

"Come on, Tree. It's called nothing to lose. Very cathartic."

Inhale-exhale. "No," she said. "I tried to get details from him—things I could pass on to you—but he was never part of it. I was going to surprise him. Me and the money—a whole new life together."

"No way he'd have gone along."

"What do you know? It was me he came *back* to."

"Not that it much mattered."

"No, I suppose it didn't," she said, faraway sounding. "By then, the Mexican doctors were sure they were going to lose him. They even had a priest in to give him last rites."

"The call from the motel . . ."

She nodded.

"After we'd made love."

"And loved it, remember? Was that so terrible—wanting you, too?"

"Remind me never to play poker with that face," he said. "Now I understand how you were able to hold out on Pomphrey. *Jesus.*"

She took a long pull on the cigarette, her smoke twisting in the moonlight before dissipating. Hard to think of a time when she'd looked more beautiful. He tossed off the remainder of the Calistoga, stood with effort.

"I'm going to bed, Tree. You know the way out."

"Wil, he's not the same, he's . . . I don't even *know* him anymore. It was all fantasy, thinking I could have what we had again. Thirty years ago, for God's sake. That's why I'm here."

"Right."

"Why do you think I asked you to run away with me? I love you. Being together made me see it." She crushed the cigarette out, slid the robe off her shoulders, let it fall to the deck. Stood there.

"We can still go," she said. "Anywhere you want. Name it."

Despite the fatigue, he felt a tightening in his throat and chest, other parts. Lord, she was something. Maybe everything.

*"Wil, please."*

"Sorry, Tree. I'd always be waiting for the guy with the better offer, the note on the pillow—who knows what? That's really why you burned the house, isn't it? You gave up on me."

"What are you talking about?"

"Arson seemed so out of character—until I got the stakes you were playing for, a million a year from daddy. Thinking he'd shut it down, that he'd won. That's why you went back to him: Denny was dying in Mexico, I was out of my league and damn near in jail thanks to Kordell, and it hurt like poison. You just folded the hand too soon."

She didn't say anything, didn't have to from her expression. He bent down and picked up the robe. "Compliments of the house," he said, handing it to her. "A little something to remember me by."

She just looked at him. "Do you have any idea what you're doing?"

"No more than usual, but I'll live with it."

*Keep telling yourself that, he thought. No point in dredging up more bottom: things that writhed and hissed in the light, flashed rows of pointed teeth.*

"Trina . . . ?" he started to say.

"What is it?"

It passed. "Nothing. Thanks for reminding me to move the key."

He waited out on the deck while she gathered up her things. He heard her boots on the stairs, the sound of her car starting; watched it turn left toward Los Angeles and God knew where. He went inside, turned off the lights and his mind as best he could, lay down without undressing. Her fragrance was still on the pillow—haunting him, like her words: *After somebody'd made you pregnant.*

Staring at the ceiling, he could still see the Jaguar rounding Mussel Shoals.

# 29

**the** rest of the week was uneventful. A check arrived from Kordell that he cashed and one from Trina that he tore up. Lisa and he had a polite conversation about not much after he decided telling her what happened would simply make old wounds bleed. So they talked about the IRS finally deciding on a minimal fine, her client dropping his threat of a suit, Brandon's pitching a no-hitter or some other damn thing at a game she'd been to. Not hearing much past that.

At least the mustard was in bloom on the hills, and patches of poppies—bright plein air brushstrokes, impossible not to smile at. A stone's throw off the beach, dolphins leaped to beats unheard. Pelicans flapped by, their big wings making it look as if they were in slow motion.

One night, he took the telescope up to Camino Cielo and cruised the universe, wondering who might be looking back at him and thinking things might be less fucked up where Wil was. Forget it, he beamed back, but I'm probably not the one to comment. Not right now.

The gym was okay, but made him think of Lannie, and he declared a moratorium. As did the Rincon apparently, nothing happening there; couldn't *buy* a wave at Rights according to his Hollister Ranch friend. Surf magazines on the deck about the best it got.

Still pretty good, he decided one afternoon toward the end of the week, his tan coming back, aches and pains diminished enough to permit a couple of beach runs. He was finishing the morning paper, thinking of asking Claire from the gym over later for marinated shark and a salad, when the mail arrived, and with it a letter.

Ensenada postmark: Monday.

He tore it open, read it. Read it again:

*Mojo,*

*Never was good at apologies. Hope you accept this one, but I'll understand if you don't. When I blow it, I really blow it, right?*

*Maybe it's because where I was, friends were something you couldn't have. Not if you had to tag 'em and bag 'em, wondering why it wasn't you in there. Half wishing it was sometimes.*

*Funny thing about eight years in a Cong prison, you say good-bye to feelings like that. I did, anyway. Try getting stuck in a cage you wouldn't wish on a contortionist, and the pain's so bad you'd do anything for a bullet in the ear.*

*Now try it for months.*

*You reach a point where you'd as soon kill something as look at it. Surprising what that's worth to some people. They blow away ours, we blow away theirs: regular way of life. Just don't look in the mirror.*

*Then one day, it's like a nerve coming back. Hardly noticeable at first. A toothache that keeps getting worse.*

*Three kids under fifteen went with this last deal I nearly did, a family they wanted made an example of. One looked like Trina. That's when I knew it was over, not when old John cut loose on me.*

*That and your face popping up when I'd least expect it.*

*My own personal Casper. Weird, huh?*

*From the window, I can see that devil swell, and when the waves get big, I break into a sweat wanting it so bad. Soon, maybe, if things go the way they are. Hope you'll think of me once in a while. Maybe look me up, though I won't embarrass you by asking. Trina told me what happened, then split. Some family you got mixed up with.*

*Den*

*P.S. About the "remains"? When you can make dim sum in a restaurant window look real, how hard can it be to fool a few bozos? Politicals wanting it wrapped up nice and clean and now.*

*Did I take advantage? Hell yeah—just like the old man would've when that counted for something. Only problem was the cost—wondering who I was, what I was. After that, why. Won't seem like much to you, but it's a start.*

*Friends again? Damn, I hope so. . . .*

Wil let the pages drop to the deck. He closed his eyes and let the sunlight take him. Baja, Trina had said—now Ensenada, Islas de Todos Santos just offshore from there—Todos obviously the big-wave break Den was talking about. Some detective work, he thought; probably wouldn't be too hard finding a fair-skinned gringo recovering from a gunshot wound and looking out his hospital window, either. Let things happen from there. Maybe stop on the way back, thank Kari Thayer in person. Come to think of it, stop on the way down, see if she wanted to see some of Baja with him. Blue water and hot sun, shrimp done any number of ways, all to die for. Maybe meet an old friend.

*Damn, I hope so. . . .*

Putting the shark in the freezer and making coffee for the thermos, packing a bag for the trip, he didn't know whether to laugh or cry, feeling it could go either way.

Let alone both.